If Only You Hurt

IF ONLY SERIES
BOOK THREE

STEFANIE CASTRO

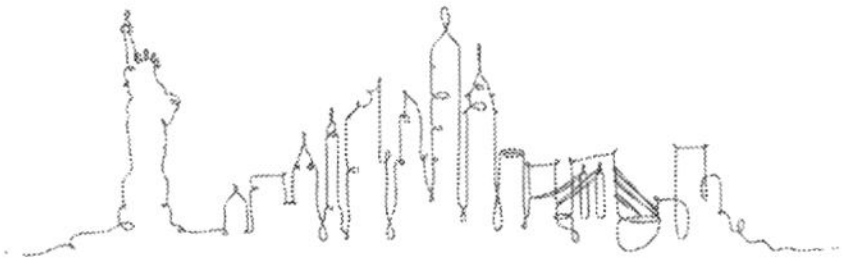

To the survivors of this world. May the light warm your steps into a better tomorrow.

Content Warning

To My Amazing Readers,

Before continuing, it should be said there are content warnings for the story ahead. If you do not want to know what's coming, feel free to turn the page.

This book contains serious topics, which include a school shooting and loss of pregnancy.

Additionally, if you haven't read the previous books in the series, *If Only You Knew* and *If Only You Fell,* I highly encourage you to do so. That being said, each book can be read as a standalone, but I suggest you read them in order to enhance your reading experience.

Enjoy Grant and Laney's love story.

Happy Reading!

Stefanie ❤

Playlist

Please use the QR code below to listen to the playlist or click here. Listen & enjoy!

Laney

19 YEARS OLD - FALL

"Grant, do you have time to talk later?" The phone is resting against my ear, and all I want is Grant here, in front of me, instead of thousands of miles away in a different country. While I wait for his response, I'm dashing across campus to a class I don't want to be late for.

"Yeah, I have something to talk to you about, too. Call me when you're back at your apartment. The only thing I have on the agenda is a photoshoot around sunset. You should see the mountain range here. It's..." He pauses as if he's taking it in right in front of him. He finally finishes with, "... magnificent."

I can hear him rummaging through his things and a smile pulls across my face, knowing he's probably doing too much at once. Forever the multitasker, my Grant.

"Okay, sounds good. Let's do a video chat so I can see your handsome face, along with the mountains." I hear him chuckle, and the sound does something to me.

"Careful, Bean, I'll start to think you're catching feelings for me." His nickname for me has always been something that warms my heart and the smile on my face doubles at his words.

"Imagine!" I scoff, playing it off like I could never imagine such a thing. Little does he realize how much he's my everything, despite me trying to fight this attraction for one another that we've been building for most of our lives.

Regardless of what people might assume of our relationship, Grant Stanley has been my best friend since we were still in diapers, and nothing more. He moved to my small town of Saddle Ridge, Nebraska, from California before he had even turned two, and we've been close ever since. He and I were always together, until he moved to New York City when we were five, and he only came back for visits during school breaks. We were inseparable in those younger years, and even as the miles between us grew, whenever we reconnected, we gravitated toward one another more often than not.

Our mothers are best friends, and so are our older sisters. We grew tight from the beginning, and even though our families have hoped for more between us, we've simply been each other's best friend in the most platonic way possible. Recently those lines have blurred, and now I'm standing here, counting the minutes until I can have a proper conversation with him after class.

"Laney, you still there?" He pulls me out of my thoughts, and I recover as quickly as I can.

"Yes, sorry, I'm here. Got distracted with the changing leaves."

It surprises me how easily my little lie slips from my lips. I hear him laugh on the other end. Luckily, he can't see me right now, because I know he'd read me like a book. He'd see right through my attempt to veer away from what I really want to talk to him about.

"So, I'll wait to hear from you, then?" he asks.

"Yes, I'll call once I'm home. I hope you have a great day until then. Love you."

"Love you, Bean." Hearing him say he loves me is something I've grown used to. It's something we've said to one another for so long, it's automatic. But as the years have passed, my love for him has blossomed into something more, and I'm just not sure he's on the same page as me.

We haven't seen each other in six weeks, and each time he leaves is getting harder. He's been in South America since he left the States, and I know that each day is jam-packed for him as he's trying to get his work out there to eventually become a successful travel photographer. He has to grow his portfolio as he travels, and I can't wait to see the pictures he's taken on this trip. I'm in my second year at Wyoming U, finally back on my usual hectic schedule after being home in Saddle Ridge this past summer. My hometown is quiet and quaint, and even if I love my little hometown, I long for the hustle and bustle of my college life.

Once I hang up with Grant, I see the time and realize I better hurry to get to this class. I'm taking an intro to psychology class to see if it's an area of study I'd be interested in. My sister knew what she wanted to do in life when she was a little girl, but I've always been into too many things to choose.

My mom says I'm more of a free spirit, and I let the wind guide me. I'm more artsy than my family members, and luckily, I grew up in a household that let me follow my own path. Too bad I have no clue what path that is while I inch closer to needing to declare a major.

The leaves are already changing as summer is quickly flowing into fall, and I know I'll soon be bundled up in layers while I make my way through campus. I better soak up these fleeting mornings of warmth before I'll be itching for a hot coffee and mittens.

As I make my way up the stairs, I run into Artie, my closest friend at school. We met last year in the dorms while playing an ice-breaker with the rest of the housing unit. I don't know what it is about our friendship, but after he gave me a panicked look that day, I knew we'd be fast friends.

Right now his smile is from ear to ear, one I assume is thanks to his boyfriend, Eugene. They started dating at the end of last semester and spent every waking second together throughout the summer. I swear each time I meet up with Artie, he's got this goofy smile plastered on his face. But the fact that my dear friend is happy makes me beyond ecstatic for them.

"Hey, Artie. How was the weekend? Did you end up at that Sigma party on Friday?" I ask as he holds open the door to the large building we're entering. We share this morning's class together and I'm relieved I have someone I know in some of my classes this semester. On top of being friends, Artie is much more versed in this psych class than I am so he's been my saving grace.

Luckily, we study together on our free nights and weekends. What starts out as us quizzing one another, always ends with margaritas and laughter.

"Yeah, for about an hour. It was a little lame, so we went back to my place and hung out there." He waggles his eyebrows, and I already know anything beyond that would be too much information for me. I don't need to hear my friend brag about his sex life, while mine is non-existent and might be for the foreseeable future. *Unless Grant feels the same way I do.*

Having a class at this hour must be popular, because it feels like half the student body is walking quickly to their classes. I swear five people have already bumped into my shoulder since we walked inside the corridor. Our school is old; with so much beautiful history… and narrow hallways. I'm kind of wishing I opted for one of those modern, airy colleges with vast hallways where no one ever has to bump into anyone else.

We make our way down another hallway when Artie speaks up, "Eugene is meeting me for lunch over at Hanley's. Wanna join?" I swear my friend is addicted to this little sandwich place on campus. I can't say I blame him; the food is really good and it's a fun spot to lounge between classes.

"Yeah, I think so. I only have this class today, but I can hang out for a little while. I have a call with Grant later, so I don't want to miss my window to video him before he heads out to get the photos he wants when the lighting is right." I pull my bag further up my shoulder before it slides completely off. The moment I look over, I see Artie giving me his mischievous smile.

"Are you going to tell him?" Artie has been on my case to talk to Grant and tell him *everything*.

"I will. I just hate that he has to hear me talk about this over the phone. But even for the few hours I've carried this, it's already driving me mad. I have to tell him and see where things go, you know?"

"Finally, let's see what sexy Grant has to say. I swear that man will hop on the next flight, and hopefully into your bed the moment you spill all your secrets!" I smack him, and he just laughs. I love Artie, but he's a hopeless romantic; while I'm much more practical and afraid of rejection.

He says this whole friendship I've had with Grant is a distraction from something so much better. He's convinced we're headed for a whole *friends-to-lovers* scenario that he can't wait to watch unfold.

The moment I'm about to make a face, that's when I hear it.

Pop! Pop! Pop!

Being in this old hall, the sound echoes off the walls. I can't help the confusion that washes over my face; my brain is having a hard time registering what I just heard. With the way noise bounces around the space, it's hard to tell where the source is. It isn't until I hear the not-so-far-away screams that I realize what's happening. All hell breaks loose as the panic escalates in everyone around us.

My body is pushed in multiple directions as those around me begin running to seek safer, less open, spaces.

I must be stunned in place, because Artie is grabbing me by my forearms and pulling me to follow him. I start to look around, but my brain is firing slowly while I process what's happening.

Artie shoves us, along with a swarm of classmates, into the closest room to our left. Reality starts to set in when I see a girl by my side with tears flowing down her cheeks . I feel my heart racing, fear engulfing me as I watch fellow students moving desks, and anything else that's heavy enough to keep the intruder from entering this classroom, in front of the door.

I can hear my heartbeat in my ears as I take in the random room Artie found for us, and realize I've never stepped foot in here before. Because our school is older, this room hasn't been renovated like others I've had lectures in. There's no auditorium seating in here, instead it's full of desks that can be moved around for various seating arrangements.

I finally look to my side and take in my friend. He has sweat forming on his brow and he's looking around the room in a crouch to see what our next step should be.

"Artie, what do we do?" I can't help the way my voice sounds, the fear evident in my whispered tone. I'm scared, and now we're trapped in this old room.

"Laney, just breathe." Artie moves into my line of sight and sets his hands on my shoulders. I see those focused dark-green eyes aimed at me, while I'm mentally spiralling.

My friend sounds so composed, and I have no idea how he's managing that. Artie lets go of my shoulder and turns around again, surveying what's next to keep us safe. I see students struggling to open windows, the cries from classmates becoming hard to ignore as they realize we're trapped in here. The way the shots are ringing out, it sounds like they're coming from all angles. *Could there be more than one shooter?*

Artie begins dragging me toward a door on the other side of the room. I hear the sound of gunfire getting louder, cluing me in that the person is getting closer to this room. My panic is now at an all-time high. I'm struggling to stay in this moment and not dissociate completely. I owe it to Artie to try to keep it together right now.

We reach a door in the back corner right when I hear banging from the entrance of the classroom. There are students holding the heavy furniture so the door won't open, but whoever is on the other side seems to be stronger than those trying to keep them outside. Right before Artie shoves me through the doorway, I see someone start to make their way into the room, the barrel of a gun leading the way.

Artie, myself, and some fellow students shuffle into a connected classroom and begin to scan our surroundings in hopes of finding another way out. I'm about to tell Artie to go out a door to our right, when we realize someone is trying to come in.

Artie whispers to me, "I'm going to go help. You stay here."

Before I can protest, I'm shoved into the small closet. I try to twist the knob to no avail, hoping to get back out and go with my friend, but I hear him speak to me through the door, where he must be holding the knob.

"Laney, please listen to me. Do not open this door. I'm walking away from this spot so the person doesn't think someone is in here. Stay put until help arrives." If my friend is scared, he doesn't let on.

Artie, the big teddy bear who has the biggest smile and the warmest heart, the person I have known from the moment I started at this school, is protecting me right now. He's always looking out for others, and he's doing all he can to keep me calm when he should be freaking out right now. I hear commotion on the other side, and Artie's words are no longer coming from right beside me, bringing me comfort. This space is small, and Artie must have deduced his large frame wouldn't fit in here.

The closet is so dark that I can't see anything in front of me, but the sounds I'm absorbing from my surroundings are engulfing me in absolute horror. This can't be happening. Today started like a dream and seems to be morphing into a nightmare.

I need to get out and help my friend. I need to protect him. Why did he shove me in here? I've never felt so alone and helpless.

The screams are the worst part right now. With no visual as to what's going on, my imagination is running rampant. Surely it can't be as bad out there as it sounds. It will be over any second. Help is coming.

I crouch down to the floor, trying to take my mind somewhere else that will drown out the sounds from the other side of this door. Soon I hear Artie's voice, not right outside the doors of the closet but close enough that I can make out what he's saying.

"Please. You don't have to do this. I promise you can go. I don't want anything to do with this. Please, just go.

I..." And that's when I hear more shots, and then there's silence.

I cover my mouth; sobs threatening to escape and alert the shooter of my whereabouts. I'm scared of my own voice right now. I think my friend is hurt, and I'm stuck in this fucking closet. I'm about to move toward the door, trying to assess the horror that has occurred on the other side, when I see the shadows of two feet darkening the space between the floor and the door. I stay as still as humanly possible, while my heart feels like it's going to beat out of my chest.

I'm surprised the sound isn't giving away my location. I have never felt such terror engulf my body, knowing each second could be my last. I can sense the moment this monster is about to open the door; his hands are messing with the knob to open it when someone calls over, grabbing their attention away from my safe space. Did a second shooter just save my life?

What I assume is the first shooter begins to turn away, his steps moving further away from where I'm hiding, and soon I hear people screaming in the other direction, where I assume the shooters are making their way to another area of students.

Once the sounds are far enough away that I hope I'm able to emerge from this closet, I begin to inch closer to the door. With shaky hands, I twist the doorknob and slowly let light seep in from the classroom.

It's eerily quiet out here, and I hear some people moaning and moving slowly. I see some crawling toward others who I assume are wounded. I see a trail of blood before I see who it belongs to. The only thought I have is needing to find Artie.

I follow the blood trail as it's going toward my right, leading behind the door as I'm opening it. I look over and see Artie clutching at his chest with one hand while trying to pull his upper body against the wall behind him. He's breathing shallowly, tears running down his cheeks.

All my fears of being discovered are out the door as I rush to Artie's side. I pull my cardigan off my body and press it against his wound, but the blood is coming faster than I can suppress. I press the fabric against him, and Artie's hand engulfs mine, blood staining his skin to the point I can't even tell where it begins or ends.

"Laney, it's okay," Artie says, his voice soft, as if he's trying not to expend too much of his energy. "I love you. Please..." He pauses to take in a shallow breath. "... tell Eugene I love him." He closes his eyes as a pained look takes over his features. When he opens his eyes again, it's evident he's having trouble keeping his eyes focused on me. "I never told him. I wanted to so many times, but I didn't."

I shake my head as my friend is gasping for breath. I can tell he doesn't have much time, but this can't be the end of his story yet. We're not even twenty years old. We have so much time ahead of us. So much life we have to live.

"You can tell him yourself. I'm going to help you." I keep my hand on his chest, my head whipping side to side to see if there is anyone who can help us.

"Lane"—he gives a slight shake of the head—"no one's coming. Promise me you'll stay safe."

I can't form words as he speaks to me, the lump in my throat growing as I see the life of my friend slipping between my fingers. The tears are falling freely from my eyes, my vision is blurred, and I'm unable to grasp the reality in front of me.

I move myself closer to Artie, then slowly position his upper body over my legs. I keep my one hand clutching the fabric against his skin while he has his hand over mine. My free hand moves through his hair. We just keep looking at one another. No words need to be spoken. But soon, I feel his hand lose a little bit of strength.

I look into his eyes. "I love you, Artie. You're one of the best people I know. Please don't leave me."

Right then, he tries to give me a smirk, much like the one I've seen him give a hundred times before. Then I see him take his last breath. The tears are streaming down my face, and I don't know how long I sit there with my friend in my lap, his lifeless body getting colder with each moment that passes.

I keep stroking his hair, waiting for someone to come help him; even though deep down, I know he's gone.

Soon, I feel a hand grasp my shoulder, and I snap my head up, my arm coming up instinctively in fear of attack. It's then I see a police officer with SWAT gear waving toward another officer, yelling something.

The thing is, I see his lips moving, but I can't process any sounds around me. This must be what shock feels like. It feels like I'm in a movie where people are moving in slow motion, and the sound has been muted. Except this is real life, and my friend is dead in my arms.

I see a paramedic in front of me, talking to me, but I still can't seem to process any of the words being said to me. And just as quickly, I snap out of it. I hear the commotion, and I see the officer trying to remove my hand from Artie's body, but that's when I begin to hold on tighter.

"No, don't touch him. He's hurt. Please. You're hurting him!" I'm pleading with them to let Artie go. I don't want him to lose more blood. It's then I see the look of pity cross the officer's face. The paramedic puts her fingers on Artie's exposed wrist, I assume to feel for a pulse, and I see her eyes cast down.

"Sweetie, I'm so sorry," she says to me, and I begin to shake my head; now the sobs are not silent but full of panic.

I start screaming while the paramedic begins to pull me up, away from my closest friend here.

"You're hurt. You're bleeding." I look down and see the puddle of blood under where I was sitting. It's then I realize it's not Artie's blood that I was sitting in.

I start shaking my head even more. No, no, no, no. This can't be happening. Today was going to be a good day.

Not only did the shooter take my friend. He took a future I held close to my heart; the future I had thought was going to hold my everything.

Part One

CHAPTER 1

Grant

4 YEARS OLD - SUMMER

"Mama, she's taking forever." I stomp my foot while I wait for Laney to choose an ice cream flavor.

She does this every single time. She wants to try everything, and she ends up with the same flavor—vanilla bean. I point at her, and my mom follows my gaze.

"Grant, patience, sweetie." I'm four, so I don't know what that word means, but Mama says it all the time to me. It makes me so mad, I stomp my foot again. Mama simply smiles. She always smiles. Her smile is one of my favorites, and I can't help but smile back. I'm not mad anymore.

This right here, me waiting on Laney and her always choosing the same flavor, is why I call my best friend 'Bean.' My sister, Becca, and Laney's sister, Ellie, took us for an ice cream cone at the beginning of summer, and that's when I first got annoyed that Laney can't make up her mind. It's even worse that she always picks the same boring thing. Why can't she pick something fun like cotton candy?

I look over to see Laney thinking hard, her finger tapping her lips, as if she's deciding how to make me even madder. She has to be doing this on purpose. She's always doing things on purpose to make me mad. My mom chuckles, probably thinking she's doing it on purpose too. Mama's reaction makes me even angrier!.

"MO-MMY!" I stomp my foot again, and my mom clears her throat.

"Grant, what did I say about stomping your foot? You use your words, there's no need to be so upset. Now, about Laney—it's okay for her to see what her options are while we're here. You never know, she may one day want to pick a new flavor, and it will become her new favorite."

My mama swipes my hair out of my eyes. I'm all sweaty, and my hair is sticking to my skin. That's not helping me use my words. I don't like being hot. It's been a hot day at the playground, and that's why we are here at Dolly's Ice Parlor to grab something to cool us off.

Mama is just being silly. Laney will never ever like another ice cream flavor. She always eats the same things every day. I know because I eat lunch with her at preschool, and her lunch always has the same snacks in it.

Right when I'm about to argue, Davey Beckett walks in. He has a smile on his face, but it looks mean. I feel my hands ball up in fists. I don't like Davey. He wants Bean to be his best friend, and I won't let him take her away from me.

My mother must see me getting mad and pulls me to her, her voice low for only me to hear.

"Grant, I can see fumes coming out of your ears." Right then, I bring one of my hands up to my ears to feel the heat, but I feel nothing.

She continues, "I better not see you be mean to that child. I remember when the teacher called me at the daycare, saying you pulled his hair when he started talking to Laney. Be nice."

I squint my eyes at him as he passes me, getting behind us in line.

"But, Mama, I'm Bean's best friend. Not Davey. Me!" I try to whisper, but I know I'm loud. Why isn't my mom understanding this? I'm Bean's bestest friend.

There my mom goes, laughing again. She thinks this is cute. I know this because she's telling Bean's mom how cute I am for being all jealous. I'm not cute. And I'm mad, not jealous. I'm really, really mad.

I hear Davey say loudly, "Laney! Hi!"

Laney waves at Davey, then goes back to looking at the flavors in front of her.

I roll my eyes and then feel my mom tug on my ear. I cross my arms over my chest, my irritation something I can't hide now that Davey is here with his dirty germs. He's the worst.

My mom goes back to talking to Laney's mom, and I decide to turn my back to Davey and only look at Laney. She's waiting for what I hope to be her last sample of ice cream, this time mint chip. She tries mint chip every time. Does she think it's going to change after it has been the same *forever*?

"Mmmm, that's a good one," Laney tells Dolly herself.

"Grantie, what you getting?" she asks like that will help her decide. I want to be upset, but I remind myself she could start talking to Davey if I ignore her.

"Maybe chocolate chip or cookies and cream." I shrug my shoulders, not really leaning toward one more than the other.

"How will you choose? I never know." She looks over at me, like she's in shock.

"Bean, how can you say that? You get vanilla every time." I can't help being annoyed when I say this.

"Today might be different." Right then, Miss Dolly

hands her the bubblegum-flavored one, the newest flavor in the store. She licks it and immediately makes a face.

"No thanks. Vanilla bean, please." *No duh!*

We *finally* get our ice cream, and I can't help how calm I feel as soon as we sit down with this sweet treat in front of us.

Laney begins licking her ice cream, melted lines starting to run down her cone. She can't keep up with it, and I just watch as she tries her best. She starts to laugh, and I can't help how my heart feels funny when she does. I can't be sad when she's so happy. Everything feels right when I hear her laugh.

Laney James has hair the color of fire, and her eyes are big and green like the grass in a field. She's so close to me that I can see all her freckles on her nose. She keeps looking at me, and I stare back. She looks like she could be a Disney princess, just like the ones I see in the cartoons we watch.

We sit in silence as we eat our ice cream, a mess all over Laney's face and probably mine too. Our mamas are seated at the little table next to us, this parlor is so small that there aren't any huge tables. At the mess, they both grab napkins and clean our faces. I move my head side-to-side, I hate having my face cleaned. I'm not a baby.

Once we're done, the moms get distracted by someone who walked in and continue their conversation.

Bean stands up a little in her chair, reaches into the pocket of her shorts, and pulls out a paper that's folded in fours. She begins to undo it. Then she puts it on the table, using all her muscles to smooth the creases. I keep my eyes forward for as long as I can, but then curiosity wins out, and I look down to see what the paper has.

It's a picture of a flower, a pink and white flower, one I recognize as some that are outside Dr. Eugene's office. The picture is really pretty. It has hills and green grass in the background. And the flower is by itself and opening up to the sky. I can't help but smile a little bit.

"See, Grantie, I found this picture at the store for you. My mama said it's a postcard that you mail to someone with a message. But I got it because this flower is so pretty, and now it's my favorite, like you. I know your favorite color is green, and I love this flower. Pe-o-nies Mama said it's called."

I look down again. "Thanks, Bean. You promise I'm your favoritest? Like your most favorite?"

Bean is nodding her head really hard, and her smile is big and bright like the sun. When she smiles, I smile back. I love my Bean. My Laney Bean.

Later in the afternoon, once we get back to my house, we play in the backyard while our mamas are sitting at the table talking. I see my sister, Becca, and Bean's sister, Ellie, come by after school. Their boyfriends, Shane and Beau, are with them and are great at playing hide-n-seek with us. We run around the yard until my legs feel like jelly. This is the best day. I hope tomorrow is even better. But as long as my Bean is by my side, my day will shine.

CHAPTER 2

Laney

5 YEARS OLD - FALL

"But I don't want Grantie to go!" I yell and run up the stairs. Grant leaves tomorrow for New York City, and I hate it. I hate New York, and I hate cities. It's not fair. Soon, I'll start school, and now I'll be doing it without my best friend. We are supposed to be in Mrs. Lawler's class together, and we're supposed to be best friends forever. This isn't fair.

I feel my tears falling down my cheeks and sadness in my heart. I run into my room and fall onto my bed. I love my Grantie, and he isn't supposed to go. I asked Mama why we can't keep him, but Grant's mama said we can't do that. Why? I need him with me. She can go with Becca. I want Grantie here.

The tears won't stop now. I can't control them falling down my cheeks. I'm lying face down on my bed, so sad that things will never be the same. I hear the footsteps coming up the stairs, and I know one of my parents is coming down the hall to talk to me.

Knock, knock.

I hear someone's knuckles against my door.

Looking in that direction, I see my bedroom door begin to open slowly, and my sister's head pops in. I guess someone drew straws because Ellie is the unlucky one to deal with me right now. Nothing she says will change how much my heart hurts right now.

"May I sit down?" my sister asks softly.

She's always been so sweet with me. Having her be thirteen years older than me really does make it feel like she's more of a second mom to me than a sister. Not once has she been mean to me. She's always treated me more like she raised me than a little sister. Not counting Grant, Ellie is my best friend, and the way her smile doesn't reach her eyes, I know she's sad too. Grant isn't the only friend leaving; Becca is her best friend, and she's moving away too.

I nod at her because the tears have made talking hard.

"I'm so sorry you're sad." She pushes some strands of my hair away from my face. "I'm sad too. But you know what?" I shake my head in response. "This isn't the end of your friendship with Grant. I know Becca will be visiting, and we can always go to them too. When I go visit, if Mom lets us, I'll have you tag along. Becca's baby will need lots of love." My sister keeps stroking my hair, one of my favorite things she does to make me feel better.

I lean my head against her shoulder. "But what if Grantie makes a new friend and forgets about me?"

I hear my sister let out a breath. "I know what that fear feels like. Have you thought about how Grant feels, though? He might be scared, just like you. You're his best friend too. He might think you'll forget about him."

"I would never! He's my bestest friend, Ellie. I love him like I love my peonies. Having him around is like having all of my favorite flowers in a field."

I hear my sister chuckle. "So, if your friendship is really that strong, it will last, even beyond Saddle Ridge. Does that make sense?"

I nod, but I still feel scared. I don't know life here without my Grantie. I don't know how to play in the yard or the playground without him giggling with me.

"What about this? How about you draw Grant a picture and then have that ready for him before he leaves tomorrow? And after that, you can send him notes and pictures. I bet he'd love to receive some mail while he's starting a new life in New York. How does that sound?"

It's not a solution, but it's something I can do to feel close to him.

"But I don't know how to send anything in the UPSP." I look up at my sister and realize how different we look. She's got dark-blue eyes, blonde hair, and clear skin along her beautiful face. I have red hair with green eyes and freckles along my nose and cheeks.

"That's where I come in, silly." She tickles me, and I can't help the giggle that comes out, even though I'm sad. "And it's USPS. I'll help you address the envelope and put a stamp on the outside. Does that sound like a fun thing to do together?" I feel a smile move across my face, and I feel a little lighter. Maybe everything will be okay.

I stand up and go to my little desk, which has paper and some crayons. I start to draw my picture for Grant, with fields of green and with pink peonies all along the bottom. I draw him and me holding hands, a playground, and a sun shining brightly. Grantie always says I remind him of the warm feeling he gets when he steps outside into the sun. Something about me making everything better when he feels sad. As I keep drawing, I hear Ellie moving around my room, grabbing my clothes from the basket, and putting everything away.

Soon, my eyes feel heavy, and my sister helps me get ready for bed. The sun has set, and I can see the darkness when I look out the window. I see the stars shining bright as I lay my head on my pillow. I feel myself wishing to the stars to keep Grant close to my heart, no matter how far away he is in this world.

CHAPTER 3

Grant

13 YEARS OLD - WINTER

I'm walking home from school and starting my winter break with the biggest smile on my face.

I'm down to mere hours before I see my Bean. We haven't seen each other since last summer when I went to Saddle Ridge to visit for a few weeks. Each time we have an extended break, I get to be with my best friend. As much as our lives look different, she's in our small town back home and I'm in this massive city, we still have so much in common that I never notice how different our lives really are.

I'm close to home when I see someone unloading things from a taxi. It's not until I get much closer that I realize it's Laney's dad who's getting luggage from the car. I take my strides faster until I reach him.

"Hi, Mr. James! I wasn't expecting you for a few more hours. Let me help you." I reach into the trunk and retrieve what looks to be the last bag.

"Thanks, son. And please call me Kirk. I changed your diapers and heated up your bottles. No need to be so formal. We caught an earlier flight in fear the storm would delay us if we waited. The girls are inside, fawning over Olive. She's gotten so big." Mr. James has always been kind. He was very much a father figure for me growing up. We moved to Nebraska after my dad died when I was a little over a year old. But, from what I've heard about him, I think he and Kirk would have been good friends.

"Yeah, she's alright. She likes to bother me when I'm playing video games." Mr. James chuckles as I complain about my niece, even though I adore her to pieces.

We make our way to the elevator, the doorman helping us get everything up in one trip. We get to my floor, and I already hear all my favorite people's voices carry down the hall. In the last few years, so much has changed. Beau and Ellie have been married since the summer I turned six. Recently, my sister met someone and the relationship seems to be pretty serious. His name is Hudson, and he's just starting out as a lawyer at a firm in the city. He's a bit too fancy for me, but my sister seems happy, and he's really great with Olive.

City life suits me and my family, so it hasn't been too bad adjusting after our move from Saddle Ridge. That might be due to the fact that we go back whenever possible, and I spend a good amount of my summer with the James family. Since Ellie moved out, I use her room to stay when I visit. My mom doesn't stay with me anymore, and last summer was the first time I got to fly out on my own. It was a lot of fun to be a little more independent, although my mom cried as if I was never coming back. Something about her baby growing up. Ugh, *moms*. Am I right?

We walk through the door, and I can smell the cookies my mom baked wafting through the apartment. We've moved a few times while living here, and this is the biggest place we've been. My mom met someone last year named

Rick, and he's a cool guy. We moved in with him before the school year started for me, and it's been nice.

Because I never knew my father, it's easy for me to accept my mom's relationship with Rick. He has fit into this family from the moment my mom brought him home. They apparently met at the hospital in the elevator when my mom was meeting up with my sister for lunch in the cafeteria, and Rick was there visiting a friend. My mom is an ICU nurse, they started chatting, and the rest is history. That was last summer, and now Becca is on her way to being a full-fledged doctor. Well, she is technically a doctor, but she's still in the beginning phases of her residency so she still has a long road ahead of her.

I find my mom and sister in the kitchen, getting another batch of cookies out of the oven. I have always loved this time of year, and these cookies are part of the reason. This is a Stanley tradition, and I'm glad some things haven't changed.

I go to grab a cookie, and my sister slaps my hand.

"What the hell, Becca?" I look at her like she cut my hand off. But seriously, what's up with the violence?

"Wait until we get things set up for an afternoon coffee. Leave the cookies alone for a second." She turns around to grab something from the fridge, and I use that opportunity to steal a cookie.

My sister and I have always been close, but our age difference sort of makes her treat me more like I'm Olive's brother, rather than hers. I've seen her go through a lot, and knowing how hard life has been for her I really admire her. She's raising Olive on her own without the person I know she never stopped loving. It can't be easy. I think it would feel like suddenly not having Laney in my life anymore, while trying to navigate some of the hardest challenges I'll ever face.

I make my way into the living room and find the rest of what I call my extended family. Ellie is the first to look up, and she's making her way toward me. Her smile is always full of love and warmth, and I get pulled into a tight hug. I'm finally taller than her, my growth spurt happened a few months back.

"Wow, Grant, you're so tall now! Look, Beau, he's going to catch up to you," Ellie says as she pulls away from me to inspect how much I've changed in a few short months.

I got my height from my father, apparently. My mom and sister are on the shorter side. Becca and I share dark hair and blue-green eyes, along with an olive complexion. The difference is my eyes are a bit more vibrant than my sister's, especially when my tan deepens with the summer sun. We both have dimples, but now I'm starting to realize the power I have with mine when it comes to the female population. Seeing a girl blush after I flash my dimples is addictive. I'm not mad about that.

Beau gets up, gives me a handshake, and pulls me into a side hug. Ellie found one of the good ones, and this guy has been a huge part of my life. I have already gone to him with questions about girls, and he's been nice enough not to make fun of me when I ask a million questions.

It's not until Laney, my Bean, gets up from the floor that I feel my chest constrict. It feels like all the air in the room has been sucked out, and I'm speechless as I see her walk toward me. We write letters and chat on the phone when time allows, but I haven't seen her since this past summer. Obviously, time does change things because Laney looks *grown up*.

We've been friends for nearly the entirety of our lives, and each time we reunite, I notice little changes about her.

It's usually a haircut or something new with her style of clothing. But this time, she's carrying herself differently.

I look her up and down, and that's when I see it. Holy shit! Laney has *boobs*. And *hips*. And her hair is longer than it was this past summer. Is she wearing makeup too? When did this happen?

She comes up to me, her smile beaming like it usually is. That's when I notice her braces are off, something that slipped my mind. Strange, I forgot about it even though she called me screaming about how happy she was to be rid of the wires that had taken over her mouth for two years.

My best friend has always been pretty, but this version of Laney is gorgeous. The moment she reaches me, I pull her in for an embrace. I'm immediately engulfed in the vanilla scent from her shampoo, and just that alone is causing me to have feelings beyond friendship for her. I better pull away before I start to show how excited I am about her being in my arms. Teenage hormones fucking suck. I think even a gust of wind gets me turned on. Now, apparently, my best friend has that effect on me too. This could get awkward very quickly.

"How are you, Grantie?" Laney pulls away and looks up at me. Last time I saw her, I wasn't this tall, but now she has to crane her neck up to look into my eyes.

"I'm good, Bean. How was the flight?" I can't help but pivot from looking into her eyes to her lips. She's breathtaking. I try to recover by bringing my eyes back to hers, but I think she catches me as her cheeks pink up.

I've always loved Laney, but I would never classify that love as something beyond friendship. She's been everything in my life for as long as I can remember. Maybe it's normal to think your best friend is attractive. I'm not blind, but, man, am I fucking screwed. Because whatever this feeling is that's swirling in my chest, it feels like more than just friendship. It's an attraction I can't ignore.

"It was good. I'm so happy to be here for Christmas." She's bouncing on her toes, and it's taking every bit of power not to let my eyes drop lower to her chest. Fuck. This is going to be a long-ass break.

We get called over to the table for some snacks and coffee, a tradition my mom picked up when I did a project on my ancestors. My dad's family is Brazilian, but until I did the family tree I'd never pursued that ancestry. My great-grandparents immigrated to the United States, and throughout the generations, things have gotten lost. When researching my family's past, I found out that having afternoon coffee is a common practice there, and although we have never been to visit, my mom thought it would be a nice thing to start doing when possible. She saves it for days like these when we've got a full house. My mom loves honoring traditions when possible, so it's not surprising that she latched onto this piece of history.

We all sit down, and that's when I notice Ellie and Beau have remained standing. I look over at my sister, and she's got a sneaky smile across her face. What's going on?

"So, now that we're all gathered here, Ellie and I would like to say a few things. We're so happy we could be here to celebrate Christmas with all of you, and we think that this is probably the best time to announce…" I take in everyone at the table and realize most seem as lost as me, aside from Becca. My mom looks over at Laney's mom, Janna, and they exchange a look, which apparently has them smiling even bigger.

Beau continues, "... Ellie and I are expecting!"

Oh, my eardrums. Every woman at this table is screaming, the excitement nearly causing permanent hearing loss.

Everyone is standing, embracing, and here I am, taking it all in.

Once the shock wears off and I have a moment to congratulate them, I hug them and tell them how excited I am for this next step they're taking together. Ellie has tears in her eyes, and Beau couldn't look prouder.

"I knew it! Told you something was up, Mom," Laney says to Janna. "Do you know what you're having?"

"Not yet. We're only twelve weeks along, but now that the first trimester is behind us, we feel comfortable telling everyone." She gives Becca a look, and I can tell my sister already knew her best friend's little secret.

The rest of our afternoon coffee continues; now, the focus is on baby clothes, names, and baby shower plans. Apparently, she's due in the summer, so a late spring or early summer shower is on the horizon. My sister looks like she might burst with excitement.

Once everyone finishes cleaning up in the kitchen, Laney and I decide to hang out a bit in my room. I show her my new Madden game, and she fills me in on everything going on in Saddle Ridge. Laney is the only person I have kept in touch with since I left, but she's still friends with all the kids we used to see at the playground. So, I'm familiar with everyone she mentions in passing. I see most of the kids when I go visit in the summers, but apparently, a few months is a long time in teenage years.

"Yeah, so Davey is still the biggest nuisance. He keeps making fun of me." That gets my attention. Davey has always been the bane of my existence. He makes Laney's life hell. I think he has a crush on her, but I'll never tell her my thoughts. A guy acting like a dick to a girl because he likes her is the dumbest thing ever, and she deserves to be treated like a queen. Plus, Laney is warmth on a cold day, so anything that hurts my friend hurts me.

"What's that dick pickle doing now?" Laney giggles at my nickname for him, and I smile, feeling lighter just hearing her laughter. That's never changed for me.

"He said I'm weird because I've never been kissed." Ugh. Davey *fucking* Beckett. Such a dick, indeed.

"I doubt he's kissed anyone, Bean. I think he's just being a jerk to get a rise out of you." I turn away and put my controller back near the console. She's quiet, and I worry I hurt her feelings or something. I'm still trying to understand girls, so I could have been insensitive, even if I didn't mean to be. My sister always gets on my case that I am too easy-going and that girls like to analyze things from all angles.

When I look back, Laney is looking at the ground and not looking up at me.

"Laney, what is it? Did Davey do something to you beyond saying dumb crap?" I can feel my blood begin to boil. If he laid a hand on her, I swear I'm getting on a fucking plane. I might be pretty chill, but when it comes to Laney, I will stop at nothing to ensure she's safe and happy.

She shakes her head and finally looks up at me. She's being shy all of a sudden, and I have no idea why. We've always been quite open with one another. So, seeing this side of her makes the hairs on the back of my neck stand at attention.

"Then what's going on? Why do you look embarrassed? Oh my gosh. Did you kiss him?" Why am I getting irritated? *Am I jealous?*

"No, absolutely not! Gross. It's Davey freakin' Beckett, Grant!" She makes a show of it like she's gagging. That makes me laugh, and I can't help the relief that courses through my body.

"Then what are you being so shy about?" When I say this, she looks me straight in the eyes, determined to say whatever she's thinking.

"I, um, wanted to, um..." What's going on with her? She's acting so strange.

"What Bean?" I move the hair that has shifted into her eyes. I really love whatever she's done with her long locks.

"Maybe you'd like to be my first kiss?" The moment she says it, I see her eyes go wide as if she's surprised herself with her own question.

I can't help the shock that must cross my face at that moment. I clear my throat.

"Uh, you want to kiss me?" I'm a bit taken aback by her request.

"Well, Grantie, I know you like the back of my hand. And if I have to have a first kiss, I'd rather it be with you. Have you kissed someone before?" I can see the hope that my answer is no move across her features.

I nod slightly. "I kissed Christy Tomlan at the start of school, but that was a dare at a party. It didn't feel like a first kiss the way I had imagined it would. Plus, it was just a peck."

I can see Laney's shoulders sag, not sure if in relief or defeat. Okay, so, what now?

"I wouldn't mind sharing my *real* first kiss with you, Bean." I smile, and I feel my dimples popping out. I know the power they have, but I doubt they'll work on Laney. I'm Laney's best friend. Her confidant. I'll always be by her side.

"You wouldn't?" She beams at me, and I feel like the luckiest guy around to share this moment with her.

I move across my room to check the hallway. I hear the adults chatting downstairs, and Olive is hanging out watching TV; so, I think we're safe from intruders for a little bit. I close my door, hoping no one questions it, as I'm always around Laney when we visit each other, and no one has made a fuss about our friendship before.

I turn around, and that's when the nerves hit.

I'm going to kiss my best friend.

My heart rate has picked up, and I can feel it pumping loudly in my ears. I take a deep breath in and out, hoping to calm myself down.

Laney moves to sit on my bed, and I make my way to sit next to her. We're sitting side by side, and this is the most awkward we've ever been together.

"Nothing will change between us after this kiss, Grant. You'll always be my best friend."

"Of course. We'll just have something extra to add to our friendship as each other's first kiss. That's all." I attempt to smile through the nerves that continue to take over my body.

We look at one another. My eyes are always drawn to Laney's eyes, but my gaze drops to her plump lips—excited about getting to feel them against my own.

We move toward one another, and then we connect. When we kiss, and I feel a little zap of energy between us. The kiss is quick, like a peck on the lips, but nothing like kissing Christy Tomlan. Even this little connection feels like my world shifted. We pull away, and we just stare at each other.

"Um, I'm not sure it's a real kiss if we don't use tongue. Should we try that too?" Laney asks, and I can see she's not as nervous to ask for things between us right now. Like that little kiss gave her the courage to demand more.

"Yeah, we can do that." I'm trying to sound nonchalant, but inside I'm ecstatic about this development.

This time she moves toward me with confidence, and we connect again. Our lips fuse together, then I feel her open her mouth tentatively, her tongue swiping across my bottom lip, almost like permission to open to her. I do the same, and soon we're gliding our tongues into each other's mouths, the kiss deepening. Instinctively, my hand moves up her neck, cupping her cheek. This feels incredible, and I never want it to end. Her lips feel soft against my skin, and I can already tell I'm addicted to this with her.

We finally pull away, and I can see her lips are a little swollen from what we just did together. I doubt mine look any different.

"That was sort of fun," Laney says with a giggle. I can't help the smile that stretches across my face.

We lean into one another, letting our foreheads touch, and I keep my hand on her cheek, my thumb stroking her skin.

"Thanks, Grantie." And just those two words from Laney pull me out of whatever trance I was in. This was something she checked off her list, but it didn't mean something to her in *that* way.

Laney has always been the center of my world, and tonight, I feel like something changed for me. Like she took a piece of my heart with that kiss. I don't know if I'll ever be the same, but I also can't risk our friendship changing and possibly losing her in the process.

"I'm glad we could share that together." I smile at her. Soon, we move from where we were just connected, and she sits on the ground while I stay on the bed. I try to fill in the silence because I have no clue how to move on from here.

Finally, I ask, "Want to see me kick your ass at Madden?" Laney laughs at my question, and all seems right between us. That kiss may have changed my life in some way, but I sure as hell won't let it jeopardize my friendship with my favorite person. I doubt whatever that feeling was will stick, just as much as I doubt she felt anything beyond our friendship as our lips connected.

CHAPTER 4

Laney

17 YEARS OLD - FALL

Today is Grant's last full day here in Saddle Ridge before we both venture off to our senior years of high school. To say I got heart palpitations when my best friend emerged at the arrivals area of the airport is an understatement.

Grant has definitely grown into a man in the last few months. Each time we see one another, it's hard not to notice the changes as we're both maturing into adults. But now, when I look at Grant, I see the hottest guy around.

He's not built in a bulky way. He's lean and muscular, much like he's got the body of a surfer. He's tall, although not as tall as my brother-in-law, and he's got this ease about him as he moves through a crowd.

Things returned to normal after we shared our first kiss a few years ago. We've each dated since then. I can't help but admit that when he tells me of any new girlfriends in New York my heart constricts, and jealousy courses through my body. I'm not sure if it's from a friend's point of view or the fact that he shared something with me. Since that kiss, I haven't found anyone that can replicate that feeling of completion he provided that day. I felt sparks when I kissed Grant when I was just thirteen, while every other guy I've dated hasn't even come close.

I'm downstairs making breakfast, and my parents are out working, while Grant is still sleeping. I didn't realize how late boys sleep in. I'm a morning person, and I haven't deviated from my normal early-riser behavior even as a teenager.

I'm pouring orange juice when I hear Grant walking around upstairs. I look up at the clock and realize it's only nine-thirty in the morning. I take a seat at the table, and in walks Grant as if he hasn't changed the day's dynamic by waking up at least two hours earlier than usual.

"Morning, Bean." He saunters into the kitchen wearing only his basketball shorts. Grant walks around as if he isn't flaunting his muscles for me to ogle, and I can't help but stare at his features. He's beautiful.

I continue gawking, although I've seen him walk around like this quite a bit this summer, and let out a louder sigh than intended.

That gets Grant's attention, and he gives me a full-dimpled smile. Damn him for being not only hot, but cute with those dimples on his face.

"What is it, Laney? You like the view this morning?" His gruff voice pulls me out of my stupor while he runs his fingers through his hair. He knows he's hot, and he's messing with me.

"You wish." I roll my eyes, but I know my blush is overtaking my face now.

"What's on the agenda today? It's my last full day, so I got up early to spend every moment with you. What should we do?" He grabs a few eggs and cracks them into the pan. Next, he gets some bread into the toaster and returns to the eggs. Once done, he puts everything on a plate, and I already know from what he made, he'll be hungry in an hour. That's not enough food to keep Grant satisfied. I've learned a growing boy needs about four times that amount. I've never seen someone demolish so much food and still feel hungry. Where is all this food going, anyway?

"Um, I thought we could hit up the mini golf spot that opened earlier this season, and maybe hang out at the pool? Nothing crazy. Was there something you wanted to do?" I'm looking down at my Facebook account on my phone, scrolling through pictures of my high school friends out and about on vacations with their families.

"Yeah, that sounds good. Can we hit up the mini golf after the sun sets? It's so hot right now." I nod, and we sit in comfortable silence as we eat our breakfasts.

Once done, we begin our day out in town. When Grant comes to visit, it feels like everything is right in the world. He fits into my daily routine seamlessly, and it's hard to ignore how much we meld into one another's lives without much friction.

While Grant's driving us into town to grab some lunch, I decide to finally come out with the question that I've avoided all summer.

"So, Grant, I know you live far away, and it might be a huge ask, but I got my calendar from school, and I wanted to ask you something."

"Sure, Bean. Ask me anything." With that answer, I let out a breath, my nerves taking over. This feels like asking for our first kiss years ago, but on steroids. I just need to come out with it already. I've held onto my question this entire visit, and now I'm down to the last twenty-four hours before he leaves. I just need to put on my big girl panties and ask.

"I wanted to know if you'd go to prom with me in May." I look over tentatively to gauge his reaction.

I see the smile take over his face, and I can tell he likes my question. He looks at me, and that smile nearly floors me. Yep, I'm in love with my best friend, and I have no clue how to cross that line without ruining everything we've built together. Damn my heart for being in love with the one person I could never jeopardize that kind of relationship with.

"Of course, I'll go to prom with you. But only under one condition..." Oh gosh. What is he going to put out there?

"Okay..." I answer, sort of concerned where this conversation is headed.

"Well, I need a prom date, too. So, I'd like you to be mine. I think it's early May. When is yours?"

"The weekend before Memorial Day. And yes, I would love to be your prom date. But what if you have a girlfriend by the time it rolls around?" I know Grant dates girls, and I doubt any of them would like him attending prom with his best friend, who happens to be a girl.

His past girlfriends always found it hard when he would talk to me on the phone. I even heard him, when he thought he'd put himself on mute, tell his last girlfriend that if she couldn't handle our friendship, the relationship between them was over. He's always put us first, and I'm selfish enough not to argue that. I feel the same way.

"Bean, no matter what, I would much rather take you to prom. I'll tell you what: if I have a girlfriend at that time, I'll tell her that we had this prom thing set up already, and I can't back out. That way, she already knows. Does that sound good?" He glances my way, quickly before bringing his gaze forward to the road ahead.

"Yeah, Grant, that sounds good. I'll do the same if I have a boyfriend." I see him clench the steering wheel a bit tighter when I say that last part, but he recovers fairly fast. "Thanks for being the best of the best."

He rewards me by putting his massive hand on my thigh and squeezing it, then returning both hands to the steering wheel. If he only knew that his little gesture shoots what feels like a bolt of lightning right to my belly.

Damn teenage hormones are messing with my head. I feel like I can't think straight this summer with Grant around. I'm constantly going to bed with my mind wandering to the what-ifs between us.

"You still seem a bit nervous, Laney. Are you okay? Was that all you wanted to ask me?" he asks as he keeps his eyes on the road ahead.

"Um, yeah, I actually have one more question." This is the part that has been making me the most nervous, but somehow, the words fly out of my mouth, "You know I'm still a virgin." The car swerves a bit.

"Jesus, Laney. Maybe warn a guy before you start talking about that." I can see Grant gripping the steering wheel tighter, the whites of his knuckles completely evident now.

"Sorry. I just have no clue how to broach the subject with you, and I need to." I need to rip this Band-Aid off! "Are you okay if I continue speaking, or should you pull over?" Grant motions to continue by waving his hand in a way to say *out with it*.

"As I was saying, I'm still a virgin. I sort of wanted to lose my virginity on prom night, and now that you're my date… Even though I've dated and done stuff with guys, I don't want that whole experience to be tainted with someone I don't really love."

I can see the tension in Grant's features, but he nods nonetheless. He seems to be absorbing my words, and I can see he's having a hard time responding. Maybe I took it too far. Maybe I just ruined everything.

"So, you want me to take your virginity?" He sounds

like it's taking everything in him to keep his voice controlled while we venture into this topic.

"Well, yeah, I do. I mean, I tried with Freddie when we were dating, but I just couldn't do it. I didn't love him, and I think I owe it to myself to love the person I do that with, don't you think?" I'm playing with the ring on my right middle finger, a gift from Grant when I turned seventeen a few months back. It has a pink stone, and he said the moment he saw it, it reminded him of my favorite pink peonies, and he had to get it for me.

"You mean the douchesicle? Yeah, I'm glad you didn't love him. He was an ass, Laney. I don't know what you saw in him." Grant always has something to say about the guys I date. He and my dad have a field day making fun of my previous boyfriends. No one passes the James/Stanley test, apparently.

"Okay, so he wasn't my wisest decision. But that's even more reason for you to consider my request. I mean, imagine if I lost my virginity to him?" I see him grip the steering wheel again, this time the whites of his knuckles are definitely cutting off too much of his blood supply to his fingertips.

"No thanks, Laney. I don't want to imagine that, because then I'd have to go kick his ass. Such a dipshit, that one." I roll my eyes. He's so protective. I mean, I can easily say I'm head over heels in love with Grant, but I know what he feels for me is love as a best friend and only that.

"So, what do you say? Can I punch my V-card with you, Grantie?" I use his nickname, which he doesn't seem to love the older we get, but it seems to soften him enough when I really want him to cave.

"Okay, fine, Laney. Just so you know, it will be both of us punching that card." This has my eyes bugging out.

"What? You're still a virgin? I thought you and Darla

may have done the deed after your spring formal." He was dating this very high-maintenance girl named Darla until the start of summer. I was certain he had slept with her, but I guess not.

"No. Um…" He pulls his fingers through his hair, looking slightly uncomfortable. "We just weren't the right fit."

He can say that again. She was super high-strung, and Grant is nothing if not the most laid-back guy I know. They definitely didn't fit together, but I also can't act like a jealous girlfriend when I'm the furthest thing from that role in our dynamic.

Grant continues, "What if you have a boyfriend and want to have sex? I mean, it might make things weird. Going to prom isn't necessarily a deal breaker, but having sex with your date might not work so well." He looks over at me, and I can see so many questions swirling around that brain of his. Grant is an over-thinker, much like his sister. They both have multiple scenarios going through their minds at all times. He might be laid back, but everything Grant does has a purpose and is thought out as much as possible in order to make sure it's the best decision.

"Well, if either of us has a serious relationship by the time May rolls around, you and I will have to talk about it. Does that work?" He nods at my solution, but I can tell he's still on the fence about how this will play out.

I think right now, we can only plan for what we have going on. We'll tackle whatever comes when we have to. I'm living in a small town, and I know everyone, so I doubt I'll have many prospects for dating before prom rolls around.

"Okay, well then, I guess we're doing this." Grant sounds less than enthused about having sex with me. I hope he's just nervous, and he's not thinking I'm a terrible candidate.

The next morning, my heart feels like it's going to plummet to the ground. I hate saying goodbye to Grant. I already miss him, and he's still standing next to me at the departure gate in the airport. Luckily, my parents didn't need to drive us this year, so I get to say my goodbyes and wallow in self-pity alone all the way home. It's a bit of a drive, and I'm looking forward to listening to sad songs and sitting in my little pity-party-for-one that entire time.

"Hey. It's going to be okay. Time will pass super quickly. Plus, we can call and video chat when we need a dose of one another." He tries to make me feel better, but I'm still sulking.

"I know, but I miss you more each time you leave. I hate this." I jut my lower lip out like a toddler, and I have no shame in my behavior.

Grant moves in front of me and gives me a big bear hug. "You know I love you, Bean. Thank you for making my summer brighter." He kisses my cheek, and I can't help but wish I had moved my head so he'd have accidentally kissed my lips.

Yes, I'm mentally crossing that line, because that's the only thing I can do at this point. Technically, we're crossing the ultimate line come May, but there's so much time and water under the bridge until then before we see that happen.

"Please text me when you land." He nods and gives me another hug. I love Grant's embraces. He gives me such a tight squeeze; it's hard to imagine life without this type of love. That's when it dawns on me just how much is on the line if I were to tell Grant my true feelings for him. I can't risk losing this. He's the one person I feel most connected to. Our relationship is based on absolute love, and I can't walk away from that, ever. Ultimately, I'll continue to hide my feelings because losing him just isn't something I can face.

CHAPTER 5

Grant

18 YEARS OLD - SPRING

I'm flying out to Saddle Ridge, and I can't help the nerves that have hit me on this flight. This is it, the moment of truth.

A few weeks back, Laney came out to attend my prom, and my girlfriend—I should say ex-girlfriend—wasn't happy. Shawna knew I was taking Laney. I was very transparent with her about my plans to take my best friend. I'm a man of my word, and going against the pact I made with Laney was not something I felt comfortable doing.

I hate to say it, but Shawna was never someone I saw forever with, so I felt like spending my prom with Laney wasn't a huge decision for me. Yes, I had a girlfriend. But, like I said, this was something I was honest about when we started dating in January. She said she thought I'd change my mind as we got more serious.

I started dating Shawna after we spent some time paired up as partners for a science project. It was right after winter break, and Laney was dating someone at that time, so I felt like I needed to prepare for her to back out of our prom agreement. The thing was, my heart was never in it with

Shawna. As much as I enjoyed hanging out, she and I were complete opposites. So, when she got mad that I hadn't changed my mind about taking Laney to prom, it made me question where she saw us going. I mean, we both graduate soon, and I have plans to travel. I don't plan on being in New York City much longer.

I met a guy through my brother-in-law who works at a travel magazine. He told me about travel photography, and everything he said fit exactly into what I would want to do with my life. Looking into it further, and with the help of this connection through Hudson, I realized this career path is perfect for me.

That being said, I'm off on a new adventure after graduation. I'll visit with Laney before she heads to Wyoming for college, then I'm off to travel the world. My first stop is Canada. I've never been there, and the things I've researched have inspired me to capture the scenery. Plus, it's not too far away from home and has an amazing landscape. Capturing some epic photos there should be a great place to start.

I need to start building my portfolio. My mom gifted me a nice camera for my eighteenth birthday, and I can't wait to put it to use. I've been taking pictures throughout the city, and I think that with proper guidance, I could really perfect this skill. With social media taking off, I'm going to start using that as a platform to showcase my work as well.

Having all these plans, I know a relationship won't survive my schedule and the distance. The only relationship I've managed to hold on to despite the distance is the one with Laney. She's my pillar, my rock, and I can't ignore that my love for her is now growing beyond friendship. I didn't feel even an inkling of that with Shawna, that just shows she wasn't a right fit for me. We almost had sex; I mean, I am a guy after all. But luckily, I saw that it would only complicate things with her. I just broke up with her a week before my prom and to say things are tense when we pass one another down the halls is the biggest understatement.

Last we spoke, Laney said she wasn't with anyone. So, hopefully both of us being unattached will make for a fun prom. Anything is better than what happened at my own. Laney looked beautiful that night, and she was the best companion, especially as someone who doesn't go to school with my classmates. But Shawna was shooting daggers at my best friend all night. Her immaturity was showing that evening, and it confirmed I had made the right decision to break things off with her. Maybe it was a dick move on my part, but I think I would be a bigger asshole if I had kept stringing her along, knowing that I didn't see a future with her.

I can't pretend the proposition Laney put on the table last summer wasn't at the forefront of my thoughts as well. No, I haven't slept with anyone, and for some reason, I really haven't wanted to. I want to save that for Laney just as much as she's been saving that experience for me. Now that I know she's up for it, I want it just as much as she does. Although, my reasons might be centered behind the fact that I love her beyond friendship, and if this is as close as we can get to me showing her that side of my feelings, so be it.

The pilot announces our descent into Nebraska, and my heart accelerates. I'll be seeing my favorite person in mere minutes, and the fact that we're planning on sharing something special together this weekend makes me excited, but also nervous. I know that we've both had relationships with other people since we made this pact in the summer, but it's always different with Laney. I feel like everything with Laney has a deeper meaning. I know she sees this as something to check off a list. But for me? I love her more deeply than our friendship. It's just something I haven't confessed because I have a legitimate fear that I'll lose my favorite person as a result of my honesty.

The moment I feel the wheels touch down, I grab my weekender, which I made sure could house a tux for prom without it wrinkling. Luckily, my stepdad Rick had one that allowed me to lay my suit flat and folded into itself. I make my way through the aisle, and I wish I could push everyone out of the way to get to Laney. I'm itching to see her, and I just saw her a few weeks ago.

The moment I walk through the arrivals section of the airport, I see Laney holding up a sign that says, *Will you go to prom with me?* I can't help the smile that spreads across my face. The minute I get close enough, I throw my bag beside me and pull her into a hug, picking her up in the process. Laney isn't short, about five-nine, but I'm six-three, so I've got some height over her.

"Hi, Bean. I missed you." I give her a kiss on the cheek, put her down, and look at her face. Shit, I love her more than all the peonies in this world. I just wish I had the balls to tell her, but the fear mounts each time I think about it. Having Laney in my life is necessary, much like my next breath. I can't compromise what we've built.

"I missed you too. I'm so happy you're here." She waits for me to pick up my bag and she holds onto the opposite hand, our fingers interlacing. I know anyone looking at us probably assumes we're a couple. Nothing would make me happier, and, in all senses of the word, we are. I show Laney all the best parts of my heart, and I believe she shows me hers.

As we walk to the car, Laney tells me all about who we're sitting with at prom and what the theme is. I can tell she's vibrating with joy about this weekend, and I can't help but share the sentiment. When she left New York after my own prom, I could tell Shawna's behavior bothered her. I tried to reassure her that Shawna's childish attitude was uncalled for, and I really hoped my words sunk in. That reminds me, I have to talk to her about my prom.

"Listen, I wanted to apologize again for Shawna at prom a few weeks back," I begin as we both buckle up in her Jeep. Anytime I'm around Laney, she hands me her keys, and it's assumed I'll drive instead of her. I turn the key and hear the car come to life. "I'm so embarrassed by her behavior."

Laney swings her head in my direction, her eyes wide. "Oh, Grant, her attitude isn't your fault. She's a spoiled brat." She covers her mouth as if she didn't mean to say something bad about my ex. Laney may have her opinions about the girls I've dated, but she's usually pretty quiet about them.

"Did I realize I was dating a selfish princess after what I witnessed at prom? Yes. I'm embarrassed I ever went out with someone like that. I still can't get over how she treated you." I back out of the parking spot and make my way through the parking garage.

Laney's playing with the ends of her hair, the red strands always pulling my attention because she simply immerses me in her movements no matter where we are.

"Yeah, well, I feel bad. I mean, she was pretty upset I was your date. I sort of caused that with the promise we made last summer. And I get it—she liked you, and I was in the way of that." She's biting her bottom lip, worrying about how her request may have fueled this rift between my ex-girlfriend and me.

"Listen, Bean, you know I love you. I'll always choose you over anyone else. That's guaranteed. But Shawna didn't show me her best side that night, and I don't see forever with her. So, prom only solidified my decision to break up with her when I did."

Laney is pensive and nodding, even though I'm not talking anymore. "Okay, well, I'm sorry you experienced all that with her. But I'm not going to pretend I'm not relieved you're not together anymore. She was awful, Grant." She sighs at the end.

Laney hasn't liked any girlfriends of mine that she's met. I guess the feeling is mutual, because her past boyfriends are little shits if you ask me.

"So, does this mean we're still on for everything we promised each other last summer?" Laney's voice is so small, I can't help but laugh at her when she's like this.

"Yes, Laney. I am, if you're still wanting to." I hope I didn't sound too eager when I said that. If it were up to me, I'd pull over and start that part of our pact right now. Although, that would be a dick move.

"Oh, okay, cool. So, like, you haven't, you know, crossed that off your list yet?" She's so shy when it comes to sex or anything relating to it. It's hard not to find this side of Laney cute.

"Um, no, Bean. I have not. My virginity is yours to take." I wink and bring my focus back to the road ahead of me.

"Great. Well, I reserved a room at the hotel where the prom is. I, um, actually got it booked for three p.m. tomorrow, so we can head there early," she says, still wrapping her hair around her finger. I can tell she's still nervous about this conversation.

"I thought we were riding with Jessica and Alan?"

"Yeah, that was the plan, but I thought we could get ready at my house and then leave early. I'm on the prom committee, so it's not weird that I'd need to be at the venue early. My parents just don't need to know I'm going over early for other reasons."

"Laney, are you okay with this? I mean, I don't want you to feel forced to do this with me, just because we planned it months ago."

"WHAT? NO!" I look over at her. She raised her voice a bit there, and she sounded like a seagull trying to get attention. What was that?

"What I mean is: no, I really would like to do this with you. I'm just super nervous. I mean, I've done stuff with other guys, but this feels like such a big deal."

Just the mention of other guys makes me grip the steering wheel even tighter. The fact that another man has touched what I feel is mine makes me feel like a possessive prick, but here we are. Nothing makes sense when it's Laney and me, because we've always set our own rules.

"Okay, well, we can take it slow and see where it takes us." I give her a smile, even though my heart is racing.

This is happening. Laney and I are going to have sex, and I know nothing will ever be the same for me afterward.

I'm waiting for Laney downstairs, my tux feeling like it's cutting off my circulation. We're leaving a little later than planned. Laney's hair appointment got pushed a bit; every teen in this small town is getting ready for prom tonight. We still have time to get our things situated in the room before heading down to the ballroom.

I'm looking down at my watch and see it's four o'clock. The event starts at six p.m., and, with this delay, we may not have time to do anything before the dance. Laney has told her parents we're all sharing a suite together so as not to make things extra awkward between all of us.

I hear her steps coming down the stairs, and I make my way to the foyer, corsage in hand. My hands are sweating because I know that Laney will look beautiful no matter what she's wearing. But I also know that my love for her will grow beyond what it currently is after tonight is behind us. I can feel my heart expanding, and I haven't even touched her romantically.

When she comes into view, I nearly faint. *Fuck*. She looks gorgeous. She's wearing a green satin dress, which clings to her body, while it flows out at her legs. It's got thin straps that tie behind her neck, which are what I've heard my sister refer to as a halter, and her hair is down with large curls framing her face. I can see her makeup is minimal, which I prefer. My Laney looks beautiful without anything covering her natural beauty. Her smile is infectious as she looks at me.

Once she gets all the way down the stairs, she does a little twirl, showing off her exposed back, making me itch to touch her. Shit, her ass looks incredible in that dress too. Every guy is going to be looking at her tonight, and I'm going to have to control myself so I don't lose my temper with any of them. The fact that I'm privileged enough to be by her side tonight is not something I'll take for granted.

"You look spectacular, Lane. The most beautiful person I've ever laid eyes on."

Her smile beams even brighter, and it's hard not to see that I was put on this earth to receive this type of love from her and only her. My heart soars when I'm around her, and I wish the stars aligned for us to be together beyond friendship.

"Thanks, Grantie. You don't look too bad yourself." She walks over to me and places her hands on my lapels as if she's removing lint while she moves her hands across my shoulders. "You're so handsome." She winks at me, and I nearly crumble. I want to kiss her so bad right now, it takes all my might to reign it in.

Instead, I lean down and place a little kiss on her cheek. Then I whisper, "I'm the luckiest guy tonight because you're fucking perfect." I see goosebumps break out down her arm at my words, and I can't help the smile that forms on my features. At least I'm not the only one feeling this pull.

"Okay, you two. Get outside so we can take some photos. There's shade next to the house. I need to get photos to your mom, Grant. Let's go!" Janna calls from the kitchen. The moment she rounds the corner and sees us standing near the front door, she stops in her tracks.

"Oh my goodness. Hold that thought. You two look incredible right where you are. I need to take a photo here first. Grant, put your arm around Laney. Lane, get closer." I hear Laney grumble, but she complies with her mother's request.

Once we take about a thousand pictures inside, we move outside, where each second of putting the corsage and boutonniere on is filmed and photographed. Kirk has been put in charge of filming the entire exchange, and I can't wait to watch the footage later, listening to his little comments about how his wife is micromanaging the simplest task. I hold back laughter when watching Kirk and Janna's exchange. It's taking my mind off my nerves a bit. From the way Laney is smiling brightly, I think it's doing the same for her.

After picture number two thousand, we finally head off to the hotel where the prom will be. We grab our room key and take our belongings up to get things situated. I can feel the pressure mounting as I think about what tonight signifies. Now that we're running on the later side, I know we only have time to leave our things and head back down.

The drive to the hotel takes less than fifteen minutes. The moment we put everything in the room, Laney looks over at me. I fully take her in and continue to count my blessings that the universe brought us together before we ever understood the meaning of our connection.

"I was wondering if you'd be up for something before heading downstairs." She looks up at me, fiddling with the ring I gifted her last year.

"Sure, what were you thinking?" I have no idea if she's going to ask us to pre-party or what. Maybe she's more nervous than I thought, and she needs to find a way to relax.

She walks over to me and grabs my face and pulls me down. Our lips crash, and I feel whole with her in my arms. When we kiss, it feels right in some way I didn't know was possible. I've kissed her before, but now that we're older, it means more. Even though I've kissed other girls since we did this years ago, it has never come close to feeling like it does with Laney.

As we kiss, I begin to walk her toward the bed, the back of her knees meeting the edge. She sits on the bed, pulling me down with her. Soon, she's completely prone below me, and I can't keep my hands off her. I ache to be inside her, and despite lacking experience in this department, I'm certain it will feel right.

I begin to trail kisses down her neck, biting her earlobe while I continue my descent.

"Grant, I want you. I want this. Now."

I pull my face away and look up at her. All I see is love in her eyes. We're friends—best friends. But for me, this will be the most important night of my life. It's my shot to show the woman I love how I feel about her with my body. I know it might hurt for her, but I hope despite that, she feels the love that courses through my body for her with each beat of my heart.

"Before the prom? Are you sure? People will be arriving soon."

"Grant, this was never about prom. This was about us. I want all my special moments to be shared with you."

I can't argue with that. I want the same. I continue to kiss her, our outfits be damned. We already took so many photos, whatever comes after this is just going to have to do.

She begins to move her hands into my jacket, pulling it off. Even over the fabric of my clothes, I can feel her fingers trembling.

I finally shrug my arms out of the sleeves, and she makes quick progress with the buttons of the shirt. I pull at the bowtie, and soon, my chest is exposed. She runs her nails down my skin, and it feels like burn marks are left as she moves her fingers further south. Damn it. I keep my eyes on hers because if I start to look down, I think I'm going to embarrass myself.

Soon, I'm moving my hands down her neck, letting my fingers trail along her collarbone. I move lower and I hesitate as my palm moves toward her breast. Shit, she fits in my palm perfectly. She grabs her bottom lip with her upper teeth, and I can see desire and nerves swimming through her gaze.

"I need this dress off of you," I whisper in her ear.

She gives me a slight nod and sits up halfway to pull on the zipper. I help her, and then she shimmies out of the clothes and is only left with her lacy, green thong. I feel like all the oxygen has been pulled out of my lungs.

"Fuck, Laney, you are perfection."

Her lips are swollen from kissing me, and I can't help but move slowly toward her, hoping my heartbeat isn't loud enough for her to hear. As much as I see her anticipating my next move, I see her breaths quicken as nerves are consuming her just as much.

Once I'm close enough, I bring my lips to hers, softly at first, but then I open to her and I can feel us deepen our connection.

I feel her hands slowly move toward my back and then move down to my ass. The moment she squeezes my backside, I hear her chuckle. I break the kiss and look at her.

"Bean, that's not doing much for my ego."

She beams at me and I know she means no harm with her laughter.

"I'm sorry, Grant. This is all so new to me. Plus, it's you. I mean, you've literally been my best friend since the beginning of time." She tosses her hands in the air and something happens to all the nerves I felt and I'm able to simply relax.

I smile back at her because no matter how you look at this, it's different for us both. I begin to chuckle and that just spears her on to laugh even more. I take a seat next to her and now she's got her unzipped dress halfway covering her chest while I pull my fingers through my hair.

"Lane, we don't have to do this. You know that, right?"

She's looking down and messing with a piece of fabric from the inside seam. She nods, but she doesn't look up at me.

I bring my fingers to her chin and move her gaze over to me. Once her eyes meet mine, all is right in the world again.

"Bean, really, we don't have to do this. I promise, any second I spend with you is the biggest gift."

Right then, I see her smile fade and I don't know if what I said has upset her or not. Soon her hand lets go of the fabric of the dress and she brings her hand up to move the hair away from my eyes.

"It's in moments like these I realize why I love you,

Grant. The things you say, it's exactly what I'd expect my Prince Charming to say to me when I feel the chaos of this world take over."

Before I have time to process what she just said, she's bringing her lips to mine, the connection instantly bringing my hands to cup her cheeks and deepen the kiss.

The bond we share is something so many spend their entire lifetime longing for. I found it without even looking.

She opens to me and whatever hesitation she had before, she lost it as she moves to sit on my lap while my hands cradle her hips. She soon breaks away and whispers, "Grant, this isn't about losing something with you. It's about gaining something more with you. I want this, but most of all, I want it with you."

I move my left hand to sweep hair behind her ear, my gaze locking with hers. "No matter where I am, I will always love you."

Truer words have never been spoken. She may never know the extent of my love for her, because I may just be a best friend to her. But for me, she's got a grip on my heart and I don't think anyone will ever hold it the way she does.

She returns to kissing me and I hold on to her as I stand up and turn around so that I can lay her back on the bed. I gently place her back on the mattress, fumbling slightly as I honestly have no idea what I'm doing right now. That's the thing with Laney though, I don't care if I seem clueless, because she isn't here to judge me.

I bring my hand onto the rest of her dress and look at her for permission before pulling it down. She gives me a slight nod and I begin to remove the fabric for a second time, this time letting it fall to the ground as my best friend lies there, fumbling to bring her hands around her midsection and her chest.

"Don't be embarrassed with me, Lane. Any moment in

my life where I think of beauty, it always comes back to you. Right now is no different."

I bring my shaky hand up to her collar bone and move it down, tentatively gauging how she'll react. She looks down in wonderment and my hand moves along her skin, goose-bumps lining the trail as I allow my fingers to touch the most magnificent person I've ever met.

I bring my lips to her ear and whisper, "Let me love you tonight, Laney. Let me show you how you make me feel."

She breathes out a faint "Yes" and I begin to trail kisses down her neck and across her chest. I try to come off as someone that knows what he's doing, but I'm well aware I don't have the finesse of a person that's done this before.

When I get down to her bellybutton, she giggles a bit and I know I'm tickling her with my breath against her sensitive skin.

I stand up and begin to unbuckle my belt. She takes this as a cue to remove her underwear, shimming the material off while staying on the bed. We quickly get rid of the rest of our clothing and I'm standing there in awe of her, while her eyes are bulging out of their sockets.

"Wow! Um, Grant, there is no way that is fitting. No way!" Her curiosity is now replaced with panic as she looks at me.

"Laney, it'll fit. I don't think it will feel that good this time around though. I mean, that's what I found out when I searched on the internet." Shit. That last part wasn't supposed to slip.

"You looked it up?" She looks like she's on the verge of laughter and bewilderment.

"Well, yeah. I mean, I already knew it wasn't going to be comfortable for you, but I didn't want to come here completely clueless. So, I looked it up online to see if there was anything I could do to make it, you know, better for you." I scratch at the back of my head, this conversation taking a turn from sexy to educational.

"That's sweet of you." Her cheeks pinken in embarrassment.

"Um, do you want to keep going?" Why am I acting so damn awkward?

"Yeah, I'd like that. Come here."

I bring my body toward her, my hands coming up to cage her head and my lower body getting pretty damn close to hers. Shit.

I stand right back up and fumble to find my pants on the ground next to me. I feel the foil wrapper and I pull it out like a prize in a Cracker Jack box.

Laney realizes what I'm doing and smiles wide, while I slowly open the condom and begin to sheath myself. I look over and find her watching me in amazement, yet again.

I move myself back over her, this time my heart is pounding, knowing I'm about to have sex with my best friend. I begin kissing her again and she moves her arms around my neck, bringing my body down on hers.

I pull my head up so I can look at her. Without words, as if she can read my mind, she nods, answering a question I didn't even have to say aloud.

"I'll go slow. I know it won't be comfortable, but I'll try not to hurt you. Okay?" I hate seeing her in pain, so this will gut me. But I hope it won't be the worst feeling for her.

"Sure. Okay."

I slowly start to push myself further, my eyes on Laney's the entire time.

"Breathe, Laney. I got you," I tell her, feeling her tense up.

She nods and starts to take deeper breaths in and out. I continue until I'm fully inside my best friend, and that's right when I hear her intake of breath. My head falls into the crook of her neck, my composure on the brink of destruction.

"Are you okay?" She nods, but I can tell she's trying to stay relaxed.

At this moment, I realize she's utter perfection. I know that no matter what, I'll never feel this type of connection with anyone else. She was made for me.

I start to move slowly, watching how my movements might be hurting her. At first, she's pretty still, allowing me to move, but not moving with me. Then, I feel her tension dissipate, and she starts to move her hips, meeting me thrust for thrust.

Being with her like this feels too good, and I wish I could go on forever, but nothing prepared me for this feeling.

"Shit, Laney. This feeling is unreal," I confess, while trying hard to keep my eyes on hers, knowing this moment will be etched into my mind for all of eternity.

Before long, I have that euphoric feeling creeping up my spine. Shit, I'm chasing a high, and that high is Laney. I feel an explosion of stars behind my eyes, and I'm saying things I know I'll never remember.

I bury my head in the crook of her neck again, both of us panting. My hips slow, and I begin to plant kisses along her neck and on her jaw. I pull my head back and see the smile across her face.

A giggle escapes, but her smile only gets bigger. She brings her head off the mattress and kisses me. I kiss her with all I have and hope she feels my love radiating through our touch.

"That was intense," she admits, peppering kisses along my jaw. "Thank you."

I begin to move my body off her. I get up, knowing I need to get her a washcloth.

"Hold on, let me grab you something to clean up." Laney looks down just then, falling back onto the mattress.

"Ugh, that's so embarrassing!" she complains.

"No, it's not Laney. It's fucking normal. I'm not freaked out by it," I say as I'm soaking a washcloth with warm water from the bathroom sink after disposing of the condom in the wastebasket.

I come back to the bed and hand her the washcloth. I don't quite know what she wants me to do to make her feel less embarrassed. She jumps up and runs to the restroom, closing the door behind her.

I move around the room and start putting my clothes on, seeing that prom is already underway. This is Laney's show, so if we're late, I think she's fine with it. I know I am.

I have my slacks on, along with my shirt, unbuttoned, when Laney walks out. She has no clothes on still, but she wrapped a towel around her. She's back to giving me that shy smile, and I can't have her feeling embarrassed about what we just shared.

"Hey. Look at me." I bring my fingers under her chin and bring her eyes to meet mine. "I love you. What we just did is the most special moment I've ever shared with someone." I kiss her lips and then her nose, a small smile taking over my face. She returns the smile, and all is right in the world. "Also, if you want to do that again later, I wouldn't be mad about that request."

That causes her to laugh, and I feel my own smile widen and take over my face. Her smile and her happiness make my heart grow with love for her.

"Okay, Casanova, I'll keep that in mind." She gives me her radiant smile, grabs her dress and underwear, and saunters back into the bathroom.

Thirty minutes later, we're out the door. Her hair was in a bit of a nest of a situation, so she had to work her magic and redo the curls she had earlier with the curling iron she brought with her. To me, she could have a literal nest in her hair, and I would find her beautiful.

I grab her hand, give her a quick kiss, and we leave the hotel room. Each step toward prom feels like a step in a new direction. The only question that floats over me is, will this change everything, making our bond stronger? Or sever it completely?

CHAPTER 6

Laney

19 YEARS OLD - SUMMER

This summer has been magical. Grant was down here to visit after being overseas in Australia. His photography is getting more popular, especially on posts where he goes shirtless and gets a picture of himself with the view of the beach behind him.

He's taken to surfing while traveling to tropical locations and I can tell he loves it. He seems to gravitate toward the ocean, probably something embedded in him from being born in Southern California before moving to Nebraska as a baby. He has plans to go to South America soon. So, we're making the best of our time while we can before I head back to college.

Tonight, we're hitting the town. I'm visiting New York while Grant is here seeing his family. His sister and Hudson now have three-year-old twins, Mallory and Jackson. They're super cute, and Grant can't get enough of them. Their energy is something to envy. We spent the day with them, taking them to the park and getting them tired while Becca and Hudson worked.

Once the twins were dropped off, we headed over to my

hotel. I decided it would be nice to have some time with Grant one-on-one. Turns out, Grant and I can't keep our hands off each other when we're in the same city. We've sort of made an agreement to be together when we aren't in a relationship with anyone else.

After prom, I won't act like things weren't a bit different between us. I'd catch myself ogling him and I'd find his gaze on me whenever we were in the same room . Finally, one night last summer, we couldn't contain the attraction we had for one another, and we made it a habit of sleeping together whenever the opportunity presents itself. The only thing is, once we got comfortable with that, we never broached the subject of taking our relationship to the next level.

I started school last fall, and he began traveling. We went back to our friendly routine of calling one another, the connection constant. But we also didn't keep from dating and seeing other people. To say I've been a bit confused is an understatement. Then again, much like before, when I didn't want to ruin my friendship with Grant by confessing my love for him, I didn't want to ruin this carefree thing we've got going either.

From what I understand, Grant loves to date, but he doesn't hold on to a relationship because he says traveling makes it hard to keep his partner happy. He tried it a few months back, and he said he had a stage-five clinger. His recap of that relationship had me crying with laughter, even though I also felt the beginnings of jealousy creeping in.

We've been stronger than ever, and our love for each other is only getting deeper. I thought after prom, we'd have a hard time finding a way to be around one another, but all it did was make us inseparable to the point that everyone keeps asking us why we aren't together. Anyone who sees us interact can feel the love we share. But the timing just isn't working in our favor.

I go to school at Wyoming U, while Grant travels the world. I don't want to make him feel obligated to be around me all the time. It feels like we just fell into this friends-with-benefits situation, and it works. He needs to live his life, and he needs to feel that freedom when he's exploring the world. If it were completely up to me, I would confess my undying love for him and see where we land. But I would hate for Grant to feel obligated to be with me. What if he resented my confession and stayed with me for the wrong reasons? That would break me. I want Grant to want to be with me by choice, not because he feels obligated. We're both adults, and we seem to be navigating this thing between us quite well.

The moment my hotel door closes, we start to devour one another. We're diving deeper with each moment we spend together in such an intimate way. But if it isn't hurting us, then why fight it? I mean, in my mind, he's my beginning and my end. That I have no doubt of. I also know that he and I don't have the stars aligning, so I have to bide my time. I have to live my life and let him live his. We'll come together when the time is right.

I've been dating off and on since starting school. I even slept with a guy I was dating during my second semester, but the connection felt forced. It wasn't how it is with Grant. With him, I see stars. I see the sun and the warmth of a summer day. I feel loved and nurtured. And the more I date, the more I think what I have with Grant is unique and not easy to find.

Grant knows all my buttons, and right now, he's caressing my breasts—licking and biting one of my nipples while pinching the other. It feels like it's a direct connection with my core, and I'm desperate for him. We haven't gotten much time alone, because Grant's being pulled in so many directions from friends in the city and his family.

"Grant, enough of the foreplay. I need you inside me," I beg. I need that connection to feel whole again. My shyness has been out the window since we started this with one another. Despite being so quiet and reserved when it came to sex in the past, I've finally found my voice and I demand what I want.

"Shit, Laney. So demanding." I feel his smile against my skin as he trails kisses up my sternum and on my neck. I feel the goosebumps line my flesh, and a rush of adrenaline takes over.

I push him down onto the bed and begin pulling down his boxers. The rest of our clothes have been lost in a trail behind us since we got into the room. Soon, his cock springs out of its confinement from the underwear, and I'm nearly salivating. Grant's dick is perfection. It's long, not too thick, and hits all the right spots inside me. I want to suck it like I did in the shower yesterday, but I'm too desperate to feel us connected right now, so that'll have to wait.

"Bean, if you keep looking at me like that, I'm going to come before this show has even started." He smiles at me with his dimples popping out, and my heart flutters. I love him; beyond friendship. I love him like my soul searches for him in a crowd. I love him like my breath relies on his affection.

I begin to crawl onto the bed, lining myself up over Grant's dick. I start to slide down onto it, and I feel immediately full.

"Fuck, that feels amazing." I move up and then down again, and suddenly, Grant grabs hold of my hips, holding me in place.

"Shit, Laney, I don't have a condom on."

I can't help the whine that comes out of me, like a toddler being deprived of a popsicle.

"It feels so good though." I continue to ride this high because going bare feels incredible. Now that I've felt him with nothing between us, I don't think I can go back. We've never not used a condom, but if there's someone I wouldn't mind taking that step with, it's Grant.

Our gaze connects and it seems to spur us on. The lack of condom seems forgotten, our thoughts only on how this feels right now. He grabs onto my hips and starts to control the pace. I let out a moan, my back arching and my hands resting behind me on his thighs.

I think Grant feels the difference, too, as he moans, "Fuuuccckkk! Laney, this feels unreal."

I begin moving faster, feeling his dick hitting all the right spots, and I'm chasing my release. Grant brings his thumb to my clit, and the moment he touches me there, I detonate. The second I fall off that cliff, he starts to control my movements with his hands still firmly on my hips. He's using his legs to piston into me from below, and fuck does it feel fantastic.

"Yes, Grant, fuck me harder." I can't help the dirty words I'm saying, but he makes me feel feral when we're like this.

"Shit, Laney. Fuck, you're perfect. Your tits bouncing like that. You're fucking unbelievable."

Soon, we're both moaning and screaming, me chasing another orgasm while Grant feels me tighten around him. I see the strain in his neck, holding back his urge to release. Right as I'm coming off my high, he moves me so that my back is on the bed and he's now hovering over me. He pulls out, grabbing his cock, stroking himself until he finally lets go. I feel the warmth of his cum coat my stomach. I can't keep from thinking how dirty and hot this is all in one.

He lets his head drop back and we're both catching our breath, forgetting about the mess we've made.

"Mmmm, that was incredible. I loved doing that without anything between us." I wipe my hair off my face, feeling my heart race within my chest.

"That was fantastic. It felt incredible. Each time we have sex, it feels better than the last. How is that even possible? It's never like that with anyone else."

Many might feel a sting at the mention of sex with another person, but for some reason, it doesn't feel that way to me. Maybe it stems from the fact that we continue to be best friends. The first time we started to date after prom, we felt a little hesitation in divulging that information to each other. But once we came out with it, it felt like a weight was lifted. I never saw myself in this situation, having sex with my best friend, yet completely comfortable with sharing the same honesty we've always had. We've found that no matter what, truthfulness is at the forefront of what we have together.

We share everything with each other… except for the tiny, little, insignificant secret that I love him and want to call him mine. That doesn't count, though. I feel the confession at the tip of my tongue, but then something deep within me stops the words from falling out. I just can't fathom my confession doing anything but ruining what we've got going on. So, we're a bit unconventional, but that seems to work for us.

"I can't argue with that. It's always incredible with you." I lift my head and rest my chin on his chest. "Oh my gosh! You know what we should do tomorrow before we head back to our realities? Get tattoos!"

"What? You said you're not into getting a tattoo, Bean." He had asked me after prom if we should go get matching tattoos before heading off into the real world, and I wasn't into the idea of a needle pricking my skin for the sole purpose of artwork on my body. But my friend Artie has a cool one on his ribs, and it piqued my curiosity.

"Well, now I do. And I want to get one with you there. You don't have to get one." I honestly just want him to hold my hand. He doesn't need to commit to anything permanent like that.

"Okay. My buddy goes to someone in the city who's really good. Do you know what you want?"

I nod, knowing my vision might be a tough one to put onto my skin, but one that I think would look really cool if done right.

"Alright. Let me reach out to Sam and see if he can make you an appointment." Grant winks at me, and I feel my insides tingle. I lay my head back down, savoring these little moments that fill my heart with joy.

I'm sitting in a chair while the tattoo artist preps his station. I came in with Grant about an hour ago, and within a few minutes, he was drawing my thoughts onto paper. His design is flawless. I came up with intertwined peonies that will sit on the right side of my ribcage. Grant said it's perfect for me. He brought a chair right next to me, and he's telling me all about his trip to Chile, which is coming up soon. I leave for college tomorrow, and shortly after I get settled, Grant will be on his next adventure. The fact that he's taking this time to let me hold his hand, as I pretty much use my skin as a canvas, means the world to me.

My smile feels cemented on my face, until I feel the first pinch from the needle. The artist asked me if I was ready, but I guess it hurts more than I expected. I squeeze Grant's hand like it's going to take away the pain, but the more that needle glides against my skin, the more I want to pull away and forget about this plan. But I know he's not even close to done. So, I have to bear the pain for the outcome I want.

Once finished, after what felt like a lifetime of me sitting there and breathing through my nose to steady my breaths, I'm told I'm all done. It's not a huge tattoo, but it's large enough that anyone looking at it will see what it's supposed to be, my favorite flower. I'm looking in the mirror, moving my body from one side to the other to see the beautiful work of art from all angles.

That's when I see Grant in the reflection of the mirror; he stands up and removes his shirt behind me. I'm gawking at his torso, too focused on how incredibly delectable Grant is, when it dawns on me he's taking a seat on the bed I just got tortured on. I swing my body around, my mouth opening, but no words coming out.

I finally speak, "What are you doing?" My best friend is lying there with a sexy smirk across his face.

"What does it look like, Bean? I'm getting a tattoo." The artist seems to be in on this little secret, and he's wiping down his station, sanitizing it for Grant to be his next victim.

My eyes widen. "What tattoo are you getting?" Grant doesn't even answer aside from pointing at my tattoo. I look down at my ribcage, covered with a plastic bandage they use to reduce infection, then look back at him.

"You're getting a matching tattoo?" I say, my voice a bit pitchy from surprise.

"Well, we've shared all our firsts together, why not one more?" The moment he says it, the tattoo artist, Jared, looks up at him and arches a brow. Grant has the audacity to nod and then throws a wink my way. I feel my cheeks flame from embarrassment. Jared gives Grant a smile, like he knows exactly what *all our firsts* means.

"I didn't invite you here to make you feel obligated to get a tattoo, Grant." Jared is cleaning Grant's skin on the same part of his body where my tattoo is on mine. Grant's version is a little larger than mine; however, the artwork itself is an exact replica of mine.

I take a seat next to him in the chair, the same seat Grant was just sitting in supporting me, and grab his hand. Once he's ready, Jared begins, and I see the moment the needle makes contact with Grant's skin, he squeezes my hand. I bring his hand to my lips and lightly kiss his knuckles.

I try to distract Grant with stories of how Artie is dating someone new, Eugene. This summer has been one of *finding love,* Artie's words, not mine. I also talk about declaring a major and how nervous I am to make such a big decision at the end of this school year.

Once done, Grant stands and looks at his reflection in the mirror. He's pensive at first, and I worry he regrets what he's done. He can't go back now, but I also don't want him to hate looking at it.

"Laney, this is my most treasured possession." He looks at the tattoo a little more, then turns to Jared. "Great job, man. It's perfect, just like my Laney here."

We finish up at the tattoo parlor and make our way to dinner. We were getting our tattoos for the majority of the day, and now we're both starving. I can't help but put this moment in my heart next to all the treasured memories I've stored in my years with my best friend.

CHAPTER 7

Grant

19 YEARS OLD - FALL

"So, I'll wait to hear from you, then?" I ask Laney as she's rushing to class.

"Yes, I'll call once I'm home. I hope you have a great day until then. Love you."

"Love you, Bean." I miss her, and I've only been away from her for about six weeks. I can't keep doing this. That's why when she calls me later, I'm going to confess that I love her beyond our friendship. I can't continue to act like what we have is just friends with benefits between us. I think I'm ready to lay all my feelings out there and hope she feels the same. I already loved Laney as more than a friend back when we crossed that line at prom, but now it's snowballed into something larger.

I hang up with her and start to get my things unpacked. I got here late last night but then slept in this morning. I was exhausted. Once Laney left for school weeks ago, I stayed in New York to soak up some time with my friends and family. Many of the friends I made while living in New York are no longer in the city. They've all dispersed to schools across the country. But most were back this summer, so we got to catch up. It was nice to hang out and relax before starting a new leg of travel around the world for me. Next up is Brazil. That's a place I've been itching to step foot in, but haven't had the means until now.

I have a friend who is studying abroad in Rio, and he comes from a pretty well-off family. He saw my work on my social media platforms and asked me to come visit, even offering a place for me to stay, free of charge. I couldn't pass it up, and while there, he said he has a paid gig for me to do. He's made friends with some locals, and they're looking for someone to capture some images of their gear being worn by surfers in the area. Because I know how to surf, and I love pictures taken with the ocean element mixed in, my friend threw my name out there.

It's surreal to know I'll be going back to a country my ancestors emigrated from decades ago. I feel privileged that they took that leap into a new life somewhere completely different for a better future. If that hadn't happened, it's hard to say if I would even exist.

Once I'm done pulling everything out of my suitcase, I make my way out onto the streets of the little city I'm staying in. Chile has some incredible views, and once the sun starts to set, I think the shots I can capture will be quite incredible. Too bad I still struggle with my Spanish-speaking abilities. So, for right now, simple terms are all I have to lean on. I took French in high school, thinking it would come in handy; however, I haven't spoken a word of it since I graduated. Figures.

I walk around, taking in the scenery and the people around me, and the smells of the little cafetería I pass start to pull me in different directions.

I find what looks like a hole-in-the-wall restaurant that serves every type of empanada possible. Once I figure out which ones I want, I put in my order and make my way to find a seat. A lot of travel involves embedding oneself in the culture, and so much of that happens with the food. There's a story behind every meal, and I've learned to embrace that wherever I go.

I sit at the makeshift bar they have set up, looking up at a soccer game, I mean *futebol* match, when breaking news comes up. I can't understand much of what's being written in the bottom scroll, but I can tell something happened in the United States. The violence seems to be constant in my home country.

I look outside, distracted by the locals walking around the streets. My internal clock is off from traveling, so I'm just getting these empanadas, then I'll find a spot to park my ass to take in the surroundings. Hopefully, Laney will call while I'm out, and I can show her the views. Plus, what's more romantic than confessing your feelings to the love of your life while sitting outside with a Chilean sunset as the backdrop?

Once my food is ready, I take it to go and dig in the moment I find a grassy area to sit. I take in the green grass surrounding me, thinking of my favorite green eyes. For as long as I can remember, her gaze has pulled me into a trance. I rub the area where I share the same tattoo as her, feeling a pull toward my Bean. I hope she made it to class on time.

Speaking of which, I realize I should have heard from Laney by now. Her class ended a while ago. I look down at my phone, but I have no missed calls. She only has *Intro to Psych* today and should be done with it by now, but maybe she got caught up with friends.

I let that go and just take in the views. I capture a few pictures, but decide to walk back to the hotel to grab a different lens for my camera, that I forgot thanks to the jet lag. I'm fighting sleep as I get closer to my hotel, but I've found the more I push through when I travel to other time zones, the quicker I adapt.

The moment I get in my room, I feel my cell buzzing in my pocket. I place my camera bag on the bed and reach into my pocket. My mom's name flashes across the screen. For a moment, I think about calling her back, as I really want to get back out and get the photos for the magazine that hired me. But something causes me to push that aside and answer. She's normally good about simply texting and only calls if something's up.

"Hey, Mom, how—"

I'm interrupted by my mother, "Grant! Oh my God! Thank goodness you answered!"

"Mom? What's wrong? Is Becca okay? Are the kids okay?" I hear the panic in my own voice. My mom is sniffling on the other end.

"Grant, everyone here in New York is fine. It's not them, it's Laney. Oh my God, Grant. There was a mass shooting at her school."

I don't hear anything more. I drop my phone, and I feel my knees give out. I fall to the ground, and I'm struggling to breathe. No, not my Laney. I just talked to her. She has to be okay. *She has to be okay.*

I have no idea how long I sit, trying to get oxygen into my lungs. I hear my mom screaming on the phone, probably panicked that I went silent. Somehow, I find the strength to pull the phone up to my ear again.

"She has to be okay. Please tell me she's okay." I'm crying now. Sobbing, actually. I can feel my heart shattering as I wait to hear how Laney is doing.

"She wasn't shot. But she was there. She saw it, Grant. All I know is that she's in shock. Her parents are driving to her now. She's at the hospital, more for observation than anything. At least that's all we were told."

The moment my mom says Laney is alive, I take in a breath. My mom keeps speaking, telling me what hospital she's at while I'm packing my belongings. Once I hang up with my mom, my movements are a blur.

I email my friend and let him know an emergency back home calls for me to fly back to the States. Then I look at flights and find one with more connections than any flight I've taken across the world, but I book it because I need to get to her. She needs me. I need to hold her. I need to see she's okay with my own eyes. Unfortunately, I don't consider that her life, as we all know it, is forever altered. And this is just the beginning of a new path.

Twenty-three hours later, I'm sitting beside Laney while she sleeps. Janna and Kirk sit opposite me, and Janna still has tears falling down her cheeks. I'm emotionally exhausted. I had no idea what state I would find Laney in when I got here. I keep looking up at her monitors, feeling a sense of relief each time from seeing her heart rate flashing with the EKG monitor.

I hold her hand while she rests. Even her expression looks stressed. Her brows are furrowed, and she's restless as she tries to sleep. I've slept by Laney's side enough to say she's never had a night terror. She's never so much as laughed in her sleep. She usually has no issues finding comfort when dozing off, but in this short span of time where I've watched her take a nap in this bed, she has twitched, thrashed a bit, and whimpered. I even saw a tear fall down her cheek. My girl is hurting, and all I want to do is wipe away the events that destroyed her life yesterday.

Soon she starts to stir, and she slowly opens her eyes. The moment her mind must catch up with the reality of what she just experienced in the last thirty hours, her face is panic-stricken. She looks to her left to find her parents. She doesn't smile at them like she usually would. Her face is vacant; lost is the woman I left behind just a month and a half ago. In her place is someone who saw things no one should ever witness.

When I got here, Kirk told me what he knew about the incident. There were two shooters—two students who felt wronged by the university and apparently took it out on innocent lives. Fucking cowards; using guns to show their strength instead of simply talking about their issues and seeking help.

They chose the large auditorium near Laney's classroom where the professor they were after usually taught. But the class had moved locations for that one day, so they began their rampage throughout the rest of the campus, splitting up and taking out whoever crossed their path. Unfortunately, the classroom in which Laney was hiding happened to be directly above their intended target.

After speaking to the police, we've gathered that Laney's friend, Artie, shoved her in a closet. One survivor saw what he did to save Laney's life, but his actions exposed him. Kirk explained that Laney was found with her friend in her lap, refusing to let anyone take him. She wasn't harmed by the shooters; however, events she witnessed, combined with Artie's death, put her in a state of shock, and she hasn't really said much since she was admitted.

Laney's gaze moves from her parents over to me. *Empty*. That's all I can say about her eyes. She looks lost, or maybe she simply lost too much too quickly yesterday. It's hard to tell. But what I do know is that somewhere, my Laney was left behind, and this shell of her is in her place right now.

"Hey, Bean." I squeeze her hand and move my palm to cup her cheek. She looks down at my hand intertwined with hers. I pull her hand to my lips and kiss her knuckles. She barely reacts to the motion. She just looks at me and then moves her gaze back to her parents.

After about another minute of this back-and-forth motion, she puts her head back on her pillow and turns toward me, in a fetal position, and closes her eyes. It's like she needs to protect herself from this world, and I don't blame her.

Laney stays in the hospital one more night. While the nurse is getting discharge instructions in place, I'm in the hall with her parents, figuring out the next steps for her. Laney hasn't spoken since I arrived, and her parents said she hasn't spoken to them either. We'll come up with a plan and then tell her to see if she approves. We have to let her lead, and we'll follow.

We decide that going back to Nebraska might be what's best, but we have to get her apartment here figured out. If she wants to return to school, she'll have to tell us, although a decision now isn't necessary. The school is locked down at the moment until the investigation is over.

Right as we're about to go back into the room, a young man around my age is walking toward the room. He looks distraught, and I'm immediately on alert. I have no idea who this person is, and now everyone is a suspect to me. I move in front of the door, waiting for this person to introduce himself.

"Hi. I'm Eugene. My, um, boyfriend was, uh…" He begins to cry, using his sleeve to wipe away the tears. "… my boyfriend was Artie. He passed away."

The connection is immediate for me. I only met Artie through video chats with Laney in the past, and I have never met his boyfriend, but I remember Laney mentioning Eugene in passing this past summer. I pull him into an embrace, and I feel his shoulders shake.

I whisper, "I'm so incredibly sorry for your loss. From everything we've been told, Artie is a hero. He saved my Laney." That's all I can say before I, too, feel the tears well up in my eyes. This could have turned out so differently, like it did for Eugene and so many others, but right now, Artie is a hero to us all in this hallway.

"May I go in and see her? I wanted to come by earlier, but I've been trying to wrap my head around everything." I nod, unable to remove the frog from my throat.

I step aside, and Eugene opens the door to Laney's hospital room. The moment she sees him, she gasps and starts crying, opening her arms to him, and he runs toward her. I see them sobbing in one another's arms while the door to the room slowly shuts, and I feel even further from my girl in that moment than I ever have in our lifetime.

CHAPTER 8

Laney

19 YEARS OLD - WINTER

My parents are sitting up front while I take in my hometown from the backseat. The holidays are usually one of my favorite times of the year; however, I feel absolutely nothing for the festivities that just passed. In all honesty, I feel so lost in general. My sister, Beau, Becca, my parents, and Grant have all tried to get me out of this darkness I feel, but it just seems to pull me deeper each time I open my eyes.

The night terrors are intense, Artie's gaze haunting me at every corner. Loud noises still make me freeze, and I feel utterly terrified in crowded places. My parents took me to the winter bizarre in Saddle Ridge, a tradition I've loved participating in for as long as I can remember, but this year, I felt like the crowds were caving in on me. I was uncomfortable and wanted to leave within minutes of arriving.

At this point, I think everyone feels clueless about what to do for me. I get it; I'm not myself. But I'm not sure I ever will be again. And forcing me into habits I used to love in hopes that the old me will return seems useless at this point. I feel empty. Things that brought me joy nearly shatter me now. That day, the shooters didn't just take lives, they took our innocence. And I think mine is buried somewhere in my past. I feel like I may not ever recover it in order to feel like myself again.

"What do you think, Laney? Want to head to your sister's for dinner tonight to start 2013 off on a positive foot?" The hopefulness in my mom's voice is evident. I can tell, just from the tone of her voice, that she's walking on eggshells when she speaks to me, much like she and everyone else have been doing since the day they met me at the hospital in Wyoming.

Today is New Year's Day, and my family is doing anything and everything to make me feel comfortable. The fact I have such incredible support really means the world to me; but, I just feel a little lost right now. My ability to give more than this shell of myself feels foreign.

"Yeah, sure." I see my mom let out a breath. She may not notice it, but she's been doing that since I got discharged from the hospital. This quiet demeanor is very much not a common trait of mine. I have always been vocal and spirited, and here I am now, feeling void of many emotions aside from fear and sadness.

Leaving the hospital was overwhelming for me. I didn't know how I'd react to leaving a place I felt safe in. However, I felt safe on campus, and that turned into a nightmare. Anywhere I go the shooting causes a lot of anxiety for me. Nowhere feels safe. Eugene's visit felt like the only time I was connected to someone else that understood the pain that pierced my heart that day.

I don't know if this connection stemmed from the fact that I was able to tell him Artie's final words, or if it was telling him that his boyfriend saved my life. I explained how he sacrificed himself to ensure my safety. And a part of me is dealing with survivor's guilt, because it's hard to come to terms with the fact that I was saved and someone as good as Artie had to die. Eugene listened, and we both cried. There's no good to come of such a disaster, but having him there brought me comfort.

It turns out twenty-five people were injured, and sixteen lost their lives. The shooters were killed by police, and every day, it seems another piece to their plan comes out. Of course, their need for vengeance stemmed from their perception of being ostracized and unsupported by the university. They felt wronged but somehow thought their actions were right? That question seems to be on repeat in my mind every hour of the day.

I feel tears pricking my eyes, and I try to keep myself from spiraling while sitting in the car with my parents. I've been able to at least keep myself from crying uncontrollably for a few days now. It's my longest stretch yet! *Four whole days.*

Grant was here for a few weeks after the incident but had to head out to a project a while back. I begged him to go, and it took everything in him to pack his things and travel. I could see the pain in his eyes from what I went through, however, I needed space to process the events from that fall day without feeling like every move I made was being watched. It's the first time I ever wanted Grant to give me space. Normally, I would have begged for him to stay.

We arrive home, and I head straight to my room. I see sadness each time I look over at my parents, and I tend to flee from their gazes. I can't stand the version of myself that I can't seem to step away from right now. I need a change, but I have no idea how to accomplish that.

Hours later, I'm lying on my bed, and I hear my phone vibrating. I have a feeling it's Grant, so I'm surprised when I flip my phone over and see Becca calling me. Picking up, I can't help the panic that enters my thoughts, thinking something is wrong with someone I love.

"Hey, Laney! Happy New Year!" Becca might be the only person who hasn't coddled me throughout this entire experience. She has given me space to process and feel the necessary emotions, but she doesn't treat me like a fragile puppy who's about to break at any moment.

"Hi, Becca. Happy New Year to you and the family. How was your evening? Do anything fun last night?" This earns me a little laugh on the other end.

"If by fun you mean hanging out with nearly four-year-olds and a teen while my lawyer husband worked all night, then yes, it was loads of fun." That makes me smile, which has been a rare occurrence here.

"I'm actually calling with a proposition for you. I know you're dealing with so much. I heard from Ellie you're not planning on returning to Wyoming to finish out school. I hope you don't mind her telling me that, she's just trying to process the best way she knows how. You know her, she's always so full of sunshine and she doesn't want to overwhelm you with that, so she's talking my ear off instead."

"Yeah, I just can't fathom going back on campus. It's too painful." Add in my panic attacks, and it just won't work.

"Well, I spoke to Hudson and the kids, and we'd like to offer for you to stay with us. We have an extra room, and we'll give you the privacy you need. But I thought maybe a change to a busy, noisy city might be just what the doctor ordered. You know that my mom decided to move us to Saddle Ridge after my dad died, and it really did help. New scenery, new memories. I know New York is crowded, but it is just what you might need to get your mind focused on something else. There's just one catch." I knew there was something Becca would add to her proposition. She's picking up on her lawyer husband's negotiating skills.

"Um, before I agree, what is the last part of this offer?" I love the idea of leaving Nebraska and starting anew. A crowded city seems like the opposite of what I'd run toward, but I also find the idea thrilling to be somewhere completely different than Saddle Ridge, Nebraska. Also, nothing about New York City reminds me of Wyoming.

"I have a friend who's a therapist, and I'd like you to connect with her. I think it will help you digest what happened to you."

I saw a therapist in Wyoming while I was in the hospital, and it felt like a waste of time. I just sat there, unable to form words or put my feelings out there for a complete stranger to digest and analyze. Then, when we made it back to Nebraska, I felt like I was being examined by everyone in my small town, and my skin was crawling when I saw Dr. Newsick.

I grew up with his daughter, and it felt weird confiding in someone I knew on a personal level. I mean, I knew his daughter peed in the community pool when we were seven. That thought made me chuckle when I sat in his office one morning, and it was the first time I had even smiled since the shooting. That then catapulted me into grief because I was laughing after my friend had just died in my arms. The cycle caused me to fall into a deeper darkness, and I haven't returned to therapy since then.

I stay quiet for a bit longer than Becca might find comforting, so she speaks up again.

"Laney, listen, I'm not trying to fix you. I'm here to support you. I know you're home and near your family, but I want to find a way to—"

"I'm in. I'll do it," I tell her with as much enthusiasm as I can muster. "How soon can I come?" I think this might be what I need to find myself, or at least a new version of myself, which I'm desperate for.

"That's great, Lane. You can come whenever you're up for it. You take some time to think it over and just let me know when you're coming?" I can hear the relief in her tone, and knowing I'll be around Becca feels right.

"Let me get some things handled here, and maybe this coming weekend? I can do that. I just need to figure out the drive and see if someone will go with me." I don't have much to bring with me.

Grant had packed my apartment off campus when I left Wyoming, and I have no plans to use the items again. I need a fresh start. I don't want to look at my things and remember where I had them last. That apartment is a part of me that signifies the old Laney, and I'm not trying to go back to that exact version of myself. However, I think finding a purpose after what I lived through is what I need the most for my mental recovery.

"Well, I hope you don't mind, but I sort of let your sister know my plans. I didn't want her to be blindsided by you moving. She's on board to drive out here to get you settled. If that's something that interests you, you can talk to her." I know how close Becca is with my sister, and it doesn't surprise me, nor does it bother me that she spoke to Ellie.

My sister has been worried, and I think Becca didn't want to step on anyone's toes with this offer. Now I just need to speak to my parents. I know that they're worried about me, and I'll have to be patient as they wrap their heads around me leaving. As much as that day changed the trajectory of my life, it brought to the forefront of my parents' minds that the world wasn't what we thought it was. Our safety is never guaranteed, and the shooting really highlighted that, for not only me but for everyone around me.

"That's no problem. I'm going to Ellie's later, so I'll chat with her then. I guess I'll see you soon." A small smile takes over my face, and it might be the first time I've had a genuine smile since that morning I was chatting with Artie.

"Great. I'm so happy to have you. I think you'll really love immersing yourself in the city. It's got something for everyone." She takes a moment to take a breath, and I know she's got more to say. I can't help the uptick in my heart rate. "Also, Laney, do you mind reaching out to Grant? He's missing you, and I noticed when he was here over the holidays that he's driving himself crazy with worry over not hearing from you as much as he used to."

I've been distant with everyone, but most of all with Grant. The morning of the shooting had started on such a high for me. I had something exciting to tell him, and now I'm empty inside. I don't know how to tackle this side of me, and it feels like an out-of-body experience in many ways. Am I broken? That's something I ask myself constantly. I feel like I'm missing a piece of myself, yet I have no idea how to fix that feeling.

"Yeah. I've been a little quiet, which is new for us. I'll reach out and talk to him." I just hope I can muster the strength to call him and actually have more than a two-minute conversation.

"Okay, great. Don't shut him out, Laney. I know you're going through something none of us can relate to, but just know that all of us, especially Grant, come from a place of love. We're here to support you in whatever way we can." I can hear the relief in Becca's voice when she speaks.

We finish our call, and I feel the tear fall down my cheek. I feel lost, either in myself or in this world. I haven't figured out which yet. I wish I could say I hung up with Becca and called Grant, but I just can't deal with connecting with the one person who holds a piece of me in his heart. I feel myself cocooning into myself, and I have no clue how to pull away from the fear I'm feeling and reach for the things I once thought were easily attainable. I think I need to figure out who I'll be from this point on in life. But a part of me will hold the weight of what could have been on my shoulders as I walk this earth for the rest of my life.

CHAPTER 9

Grant

19 YEARS OLD - WINTER

My sister comes down the stairs, and I'm in the kitchen coloring with her kids. My heart is racing in anticipation of hearing what Laney had to say about the offer to move to New York. I can feel the uptick in my pulse, and I just want to know if I can expect to see Laney here at some point in the near future, or not. I miss my best friend. I miss seeing her smile. Most of all, I miss seeing life in her eyes.

The last time I was with her, she seemed empty. She barely spoke and simply sat quietly by my side. Oddly enough, it wasn't that the interaction was uncomfortable, but the fact that she looked lost. The worst realization is that the version of Laney I have known all of my life seems to be a memory, and this person in her place will now have to conform to a new lifestyle.

I feel like she's never going to be the same, but that doesn't mean she'll never shine the way she used to. Even with so much of her light dimmed, my love for her remains. Actually, I feel even more love for her, because the appreciation I feel that she's still living in this world overwhelms me with gratitude.

I hear my sister's footsteps as she enters the kitchen, and I put the crayon down and wait for her. The moment she looks over at me, the smile on her face tells me that Laney agreed to her proposition. I let out a breath, and tremendous relief washes over me.

I move the chair back, the noise causing the twins to cover their ears, and I walk over to Becca, my strides eating the distance between us quickly, and hug her. Without saying a word, I know that this is a step in a different direction and, hopefully, one that will pull my Laney back to the surface. But that's the thing about love: no matter what version I get of her, I just want to see *her* again.

I want to feel her warmth in my hands. I want to feel her heart beating when I lay my head down on her chest. I can't fathom a moment on this earth without her soul with me. She gives me life in a way that's hard to describe. My next breath is dependent on her being here, and I'll do everything in my power to show her that she is loved beyond all the pain the world tries to throw at her.

Eight days. That's how long it takes to see Laney. She drove into the city with her sister. They made their way across a handful of states, and she's finally here. I'm upstairs in the hallway, looking out the window of my sister's brownstone, and I decide to wait in the room Laney will be staying in.

I hear my sister, Ellie, and Laney downstairs and I take a seat on the bed in Laney's new room. What was once a reunion with laughter and screams is now muted, much like the new version of Laney.

I hear my sister tell Laney that her room is upstairs and down the hall. Next, I hear soft footsteps moving up the stairs, I imagine Laney is slowly taking in her new home.

The door opens slowly to reveal my beautiful girl. It's at that moment I realize that this is not a sprint but a marathon, slow and steady, to show Laney that I'm here to stay. I can't fathom loving another human being the way I love her. But I think I have to take my time to get her to the point where she'll accept my love in that way.

"Hi," she says, almost in a whisper. I can't describe her demeanor as shy exactly. It's almost as if she's hesitant to enjoy this moment because she now knows how fragile life is after experiencing something so tragic.

"Hey, Bean. I missed you." I stand, rubbing my hands down my jeans, then slowly move closer to her.

I haven't spoken to her since Christmas day. I texted her on New Year's, but I only got a heart emoji as a response. That's how it's been between us since that day months ago, me putting everything on the line and her taking what she can handle. I get it, she's hurting. It's not my job to push, but rather to nurture, and that's exactly what I'll do for as long as she'll let me.

I get as close as I know she's comfortable with, and then open my arms out to her. I watch as she slowly moves toward me and rests her cheek against my chest. I started seeing a therapist after the shooting, trying to wrap my head around how I can best support the woman I love. In therapy, I learned to allow Laney the ability to make decisions about how she wants to move forward, not making her feel trapped or smothered. Therapy has also helped me process my own grief and anxiety that have stemmed from the shooting. I'm grieving the Laney that I've always known, and coming to terms with the fact that she may never be that version of herself again. I have also been getting very anxious any time I don't know where she is. I think having her living with Becca may help with that a little.

The moment she rests her cheek against my chest, I envelop her in my arms and feel the warmth radiating off her body. Touching her, feeling life coursing through her body, is a feeling I will never get sick of. The fear I held while traveling back to the States after hearing of the shooting nearly broke me. I didn't know what state I would find Laney in, and when I saw she was in one piece, I was grateful. I promised myself that no matter what, as long as she was okay, I could deal with the rest. I didn't account for the fact that inside, she would be broken. But I'm willing to put in the effort to help her navigate this new normal she's now living in.

Soon, I feel her body shake, and I know she's crying. I feel her tears wet my shirt, and I know that she's overwhelmed. Something else I learned in my few sessions of therapy is that each day, each moment, holds a new piece of sorrow for her. That each happy moment will come with a million moments of regret for feeling even a second of joy.

The fact that Laney survived means that she also carries the pain of that day in all her movements. Each joyous moment will be tainted in a way, and I have to be aware that there will be guilt walking side-by-side with beauty for her. It's not my job to cover up what happened but to allow her the space to process each experience. And a huge thing to remember is not to encourage any shame she might feel. Her feelings are warranted and valid. So, in each step forward, as much as it pains me to see her like this, I have to accept that she needs time and safety to allow herself to come out of this shell she has put herself in.

Once she pulls away, she looks up at me, and I could swear I see a little more life coming through in her eyes. I think this move is exactly what she needed. I hope she embraces everything this city has to offer. I know living here brought me immense joy, feeling like I belonged in the hustle and bustle of New York life.

"So, you drew the short straw and have to help me unpack?" She looks up at me, and I know she's putting in some effort, trying to tell a joke.

"I guess so. My sister promised pizza, and that's the only reason why I'm here." I wink at her, and it feels nice that we can at least have these simple moments of normalcy in the middle of the chaos that I know she's living with in her mind.

We make our way downstairs and each grab a box. I tried to tell her I would carry everything while she unpacks, but she insisted she wanted to stay busy for as much of the day as possible. Ellie and Becca stay downstairs, keeping the kids occupied. Ellie brought Colton, her son, to visit as well, so I know everyone is pretty busy downstairs.

Laney and I work in tandem, we aren't talking much but still setting up the room easily, as if we do this all the time. I'm familiar with how Laney likes her room; so I set up her bookshelf, and hang some new artwork above her desk.

"I think I'm going to call it a day," Laney says as I'm placing the last handful of books on the shelf. I look over, and I can see the exhaustion in her eyes.

"Okay. Maybe a shower to freshen up? It might feel good after traveling so much." I smile, hoping she knows I'm here to help her through it.

"Yeah, I think I'll do that." She grabs some clothes and walks into the adjoining bathroom. I finish up a few little things around the room, then sit at the end of her bed, waiting for her to come out. I know Laney feels lost, but if she feels supported by me and those in this home, I think she will start to use that strength that I know she has to begin taking steps in the right direction.

Soon, I hear the water shut off and movement on the other side of the door to the ensuite. I sit here, my hands all of a sudden damp with sweat. My nerves are shot as I try to shift this friendship that is now taking strides down a new path.

We've busied ourselves since she arrived, and now we're here without much to keep us occupied. Something that came naturally to us in the past feels slightly foreign as we navigate this time together. But the moment she opens that door, all my fears are put to rest.

Laney stands there with her red hair damp, dripping water onto her bare skin, the towel wrapped around her body. Her eyes are puffy, and I assume she cried while she sat under that stream of water. I sit here, waiting to see her next move.

In what I can only describe as a flash of the old Laney, she walks over, each step determined to wash away the pain, and she sits in my lap. I instinctively wrap my arms around her. She puts her face in the crook of my neck, and I simply hold her. My sweet Bean, full of life but unsure how to live it now.

I put my hand on her head and whisper, "I've got you, Laney. I'll step through fire to make sure you are safe. I love you." And I kiss her exposed shoulder. She hugs me tighter, and right then, I know that we'll be okay.

As long as we have each other, we'll be okay.

Part Two

CHAPTER 10

Laney

30 YEARS OLD - SUMMER

"So, you think it's a good idea for me to go on this trip, across the country with Grant, after everything I've told you?" I can't help the frustration seeping from my voice. I turn my head to the side to look at my therapist's face.

Dr. Evelyn McNeal has been seeing me for a little over ten years now. She knows everything about my life, and, believe me, I've been candid with her. She knows about my childhood, about the life I left behind after that tragic day in Wyoming, and she knows how I've dealt with the pain since then.

"Why do you feel it wouldn't be a good idea?" She always answers a question with a question, and I'm realizing that's the foundation of psychology. Slightly ironic, I was toying with the idea of going into this profession.

"Ugh. Why do I have to answer that?" I get irritated that she won't just tell me flat-out how to react to something. But I guess that's part of the path to growth.

"Listen, Laney, it's been over ten years. Your friendship with Grant seems to be on solid ground now after years of what felt like unknown territory for the two of you. Why are you hesitant to do something with him when you know being around him brings you joy?" She has a point, but now I'm being stubborn. I know deep down why I'm reluctant.

"I can see by your expression that you know why. Tell me. Say it out loud so we can talk through it," she continues, and I let out an exasperated breath, knowing that I dug this hole and I'm the only one who can see myself out of it.

"The last time I felt this good about us, everything went to shit. Life is ugly, and I was a witness to that. Not just a witness but a survivor of that. I feel like I'm finally standing on my own two feet without feeling like a gust of wind is going to knock me down. But if I open this door, I feel like I may not be able to close it." So much has happened in the last ten years, yet, in some ways, not much has changed at all.

Grant and I took time to heal. He thinks I was healing from the incident as a whole, but he doesn't realize what we lost that day was what I was really having a hard time coming to terms with. I felt like the detour my life took me on had a lot more to do with the what-ifs in the scenario, versus the trauma that day brought into my life.

Survivor's guilt is something I have learned to deal with since starting therapy. It doesn't mean that I don't feel an ache each time I get to accomplish something, knowing that Artie and many others who lost their lives that day will never have a chance to do the same.

Eugene has been a part of my recovery throughout the last decade. I did a twelve-step program of sorts that involved forgiveness toward myself. I needed to feel that Eugene felt no anger or resentment toward me for surviving while his boyfriend was taken.

I still have a connection to Artie's past love. Eugene met a lovely man about seven years after the incident in Wyoming. I was at his wedding last year, and it was beautiful to see him smile. He lives in Oregon with his husband and their golden retriever. He and his little family are thriving.

With that part of my heart mended in some way, I feel like I've been able to put more of a focus on Grant recently. Since everything happened at my school, Grant and I haven't been intimate. It's like that part of our relationship never rekindled, but not from a lack of desire on my part; Grant Stanley has only gotten more handsome with age. But each time I felt a tug toward reconnecting on that level, I found something inside stopping me from taking that happiness back.

He continues to travel the world, his photography really took off not long after I settled here in New York. His glimpse of life through a lens is something to envy. He's currently in Japan, and the photos he sends me are extraordinary. His smile still manages to warm my heart in a way no one else has ever accomplished.

We've kept our relationship fully in the friendship zone. We haven't crossed the line, and a part of me is craving him more in that way each time I see him. But another part of me fears how I'll react if we start things up again. My mind wanders back to that morning and how naive I was to think life could simply exist with no difficulties or ugliness creeping up. I fear that if I let myself get as happy as I was the morning of the attack, something will erupt and cause things to go backward again. I'm letting fear derail the possibility of us being together.

I know he hasn't been a saint, he's not waiting around alone for me to initiate things again. Nor have I. Let's be honest: a girl has needs. And I meet them, but without any emotion attached. I date someone for a little while, but then I just don't find a deeper connection. In reality, I can't find what I have with Grant anywhere but in him. So, I'm just avoiding what I know is right in front of me.

Evelyn pulls me from my thoughts. "I think the key word is you're a *survivor*. Laney, what I'm about to tell you is something you're going to try to push back on, but I'm going to say it, and I want you to listen. You are not *just now* standing on solid ground. You have always been steady, but your mind just wanted to protect you. You've been strong from the moment you walked onto that campus until this moment in time here with me. You haven't lost strength. If anything, you've gained it. But I know that it's hard to see life with that outlook because life has shown you its nasty side. I know you feel this divide between the Laney before the shooting and the one that's in front of me now, but please remember you're a survivor, and you're still you."

I hear everything she's saying, and it takes everything in me not to fight her on each point she made just now. Absorbing her words, I know I'm a strong person. I think I'm coming to terms with that more this year than in years past. It doesn't mean I'm not hesitant. I'm scared.

"I feel like things are finally right with us, and I don't want to mess that up. It mimics how hesitant I was before the shooting; telling him how I felt was something I kept avoiding for fear of ruining what we already had together." That's really the center of why I'm pushing this—really him—away from having me the way I wanted before the incident.

"I get it, Laney. I really do. I understand the fear; it's natural, but I think if Grant has done anything, it has been to show you that he's not going anywhere. He sees you for all you are. The cracks, the strength, the unknown, he's been there. He's not asking anything of you except for your unconditional love. Can you give him that?" I can see the care in Evelyn's eyes. She's seen me at my worst, when I felt like a shell of myself, and looking at where I am now, I can sense the warmth she has for my well-being.

"I guess there's only one way to find out." That makes her smile, and I know that it's my time to stop here. I think the fact I've admitted that trying is an option means I should take that, and try to step toward something that I walked away from many years ago and have avoided ever since.

When I leave Evelyn's office, I'm quickly reminded of the hustle and bustle of the city. People are walking all over, everyone has a place to go. Maybe that was what I needed when I got here ten years ago. I felt lost, and in a city like this, you don't have a choice but to commit to a path. Feeling lost wasn't really an option once I decided to engulf myself in this life. I took a step forward, even if it felt scary and unknown.

I lucked out in getting connected with Evelyn early on in my relocation to New York. Becca was serious about me starting therapy on a more regular basis after I moved out here. Evelyn and Becca met when they attended NYU together. There, they became fast friends. Throughout the years, many of Becca's patients have been referred to Evelyn, and I can see why. Evelyn McNeal doesn't feel like a doctor who's psychoanalyzing my thoughts. She feels like a confidant who's helping me lay a strong foundation for my world that once felt like it was up in flames.

While working with Evelyn through my recovery, I took up yoga per her suggestion. I fell in love with the movements. The clarity my mind found when on my mat was something I had never experienced, and it opened up a part of me that had felt closed off from the world for a long time. From there, I got certified as an instructor, and now I teach at a little studio not far from the brownstone I live in with my sister and her kids.

Life is really quick to remind us that each day is fragile. My brother-in-law, Beau, passed away five years ago after a battle with cancer. Much like I moved to New York to get a change of scenery after the attack, Ellie relocated her family here following his passing, and we've been living together ever since. We work well together, molding our lives into what works for all of us. Being near my nieces and nephew is a gift I never expected, but that it came at the expense of losing the love of her life leaves my heart aching for her.

I take a step out of Evelyn's office and I'm immediately assaulted by the sounds of the city. As I make my way through the streets, the warmth of the summer envelops me. I decide to pull out my phone and tell Grant my news. If I don't do this now, I may not find the courage later.

He picks up after one ring, his voice groggy with sleep. "Hello, Bean."

Shoot, I forgot about the time difference, especially as he's about to get on a plane and begin his long travels in the days to come. His next assignment is in Europe.

"I'm so sorry. I didn't mean to wake you. I forgot to calculate the time difference." I feel awful. I know that of anyone who calls, he picks up whenever I reach out, no matter the time.

"Don't apologize, Lane. I was wiped after the day I had. I must have fallen asleep early." Grant tries to reassure me. I know how hard it's going to be for him to fall back asleep now. His clock is all off with the recent back-to-back travel he's done.

"Well, I just finished up with Evelyn, and I thought I'd call. I have good news." I can't contain my excitement. Now that I've made up my mind to go to California with Grant, it's like I'm bursting at the seams to tell him.

"Oh, yeah? Well, now I'm really happy you called. What's the news?" I can imagine his smile spreading across his face, probably showcasing those dimples that make my heart melt. Every piece of Grant has been the balm to my broken heart throughout the years.

"I'm going to California with you in October. Is that offer still on the table?" It's then my heart rate accelerates. I didn't factor in the possibility that he may have invited someone else. Oh crap. What if he invited someone else? Shit. I should have started this conversation with questions first. But my excitement took over, and I blurted it out and assumed I was still the only one on his list of invitees. I feel like I'm asking him to prom all over again.

He still hasn't spoken, and I have no idea how to read the silence. Then, to my relief, he speaks up.

"Fuck yeah, Laney! Shit. I wasn't sure you'd come. Let me get on my computer and make sure your name is added to the list. I'm pumped we get to do this together."

Grant is referring to the yoga retreat he invited me to in Joshua Tree. Of everyone, he's the most aware of my discomfort in crowds. Little by little, he's been taking me places, mostly here in New York and surrounding states, where I can start to feel more comfortable in a larger crowd. That being said, he's getting me to California, where the list of yogis attending is nothing like a large crowd I get nervous in. It's a place where I can become vulnerable with my feelings and what have become some of my insecurities.

I was never one to shy away from going out and having fun with my friends. But once everything happened years ago, I sheltered myself. I saw too much danger when out in a crowd, and I started to revert to simple things. This past year, with the help of Evelyn, those around me have tried to help me get more comfortable in other settings. Grant has taken this task to another level. Top that off with everyone around me going to therapy to see how they can be the most helpful, it seems every person I love has a hand in my recovery.

It's been over ten years, and I feel like my progress has been slow. But I'm constantly reminded in my sessions that each person has their own journey. Sometimes, taking a few steps forward causes me to fall back more than expected. I've tried to be kind and give myself grace when I'm really trying to live a more fulfilling life. I know I'll never be the same exact person I once was, but I see slivers of myself coming through in my movements, and that's what I get most excited about. And with each stride forward, Grant is usually the one by my side to witness it. That spurs me on to keep trying, and I can't wait to take this leap.

"I hope I'm able to pull myself out of my shell a little more on this trip. I looked at the website, and it looks like an incredible experience. I'm happy to be doing this with you," I tell Grant. I'm hoping the happiness in my tone is carrying through the phone and that he feels this jolt of excitement from my words alone.

"Each moment I spend with you is a gift, Laney. I'll take all the moments you'll give me." I feel his genuine words hit me in the chest. "Let me get through the next few weeks, then I'll head to New York, and we'll take a flight from there together to California. Does that work for you? Can you get a few extra days off so we can fly into Los Angeles and drive up the coast for a few days?" He sounds so hopeful, and he's always been great about giving me options when it comes to making plans.

"I have no doubt Loni will accommodate my travels. She was one of the first to tell me to go on this trip with you." Now, I can't stop smiling. This is finally happening.

We go through a few more details, and once we hang up, the plan is in place to fly across the country for a week together. I have just about six weeks to get myself ready, physically and emotionally.

We've been working hard to get our friendship moving forward instead of being stagnant and stuck on that terrible day. I have my reasons for being closed off. But I hope that with time, I can face the pain I've carried with me since that day and let Grant in. He doesn't understand the hurt I experienced that day, but that's mostly due to the fact that I didn't allow him to see all of me after I was released from the hospital.

We've been quite reserved; in reality, I have been, with all the pain I've carried with me throughout the years. Letting Grant see the wound that I feel has never healed is something that might cause us to completely separate. So, I've kept it close to the chest. And if possible, I'd like to finally open my heart to him and find him waiting on the other end of that with open arms. I still want more with him, and now I'm finally able to own up to that desire.

Maybe this trip can be that first step.

CHAPTER 11

Grant

30 YEARS OLD - FALL

I'm driving up the coast with Laney beside me and I feel complete. She's got her hair down, her beautiful red locks flying as we feel the fresh breeze on our faces. We made our way up the Pacific Coast Highway into Malibu to enjoy one night near the water. Tomorrow, we begin our drive to Joshua Tree, and I know this will be a great time to unwind and soak up some necessary self-connection.

Since Laney took up yoga, I started to practice as well. I found it soothing to move my body in a way that was slower than my usual pace. I still surf where possible, but yoga has been incorporated into my daily routine. I'm not as bendy as Laney is by any means, but I can get myself moving enough to keep up.

I peek over at her again, her eyes closed, and I can see her shedding layers of her previous pain as we move along the road. Our hotel is close by, and we'll have a nice view of the ocean while we're here. I splurged a bit on tonight's accommodations because I feel like this trip is one we'll carry with us for a lifetime. Plus, I barely have expenses as I haven't really settled down and have saved quite a bit over the years. My work has taken off, and it's been nice to travel the world and soak in the cultures of different countries.

I've kept my promise to take my time with Laney as she finds her path to recovery. I've learned a lot about trauma and recovery. I've also learned a lot about myself. This entire process has been a learning experience for both of us. While Laney is working on discovering who she is since the attack, I've realized what love really looks like between two people.

I have to keep reminding myself that the goal isn't to bring the old Laney back but to find ways to show this new version of her that life has beauty. Life shouldn't be lived with the expectation that something is hiding in a dark corner, waiting for the ugliness to appear. It's about thriving despite the darker days trying to loom over us.

The last ten years have been painful for me. When Laney first moved to the city, I put too much emphasis on expecting that the change in location would cure her. I was hellbent on getting my old girl back. I was fighting demons that just couldn't be taken down.

I was constantly frustrated when I'd leave on an assignment. Then I'd channel my anger into mornings on the water or hours at the gym. I was impatient, and the more I attended therapy, either remotely or in person, the more I started to learn that my role was to be supportive, not overbearing. I knew that was how I started this process, but when you're seeing someone you love fall into a deeper Hell, it's hard to keep a clear mind.

I had to come to terms with the fact that if I kept up with the way I was approaching Laney and her recovery, trying to find someone who no longer existed, I would lose her for good. I decided to take a step back and restructure my game plan. I think our love for one another has grown in the process, and I finally see a light at the end of the tunnel. This trip is part of that light.

With time came clarity, and I started to navigate this road with her with more openness. That helped us build a more solid ground on which we could walk together. Our friendship was never compromised as far as I'm concerned, but it felt like the fragility of her experience was at the forefront of our minds constantly. Once we found a way to move through our lives with that, instead of finding a way to push it into the past, it felt like a weight was lifted.

We're almost at the hotel, but I spot an ice cream shop to my right. I put my blinker on and merge over until I'm in the parking lot. When I shut off the engine, Laney looks over at me.

"Why did we stop?" Laney turns her head to take in our surroundings. "We shouldn't be far from the hotel. Everything ok?"

I can't help the smile that spreads across my face. "No problem at all, Bean. I thought it would be fun to grab some ice cream and make our way over to the beach for a bit."

She looks over at me, taking me in an extra beat before answering.

Finally she inhales and lets her smile take over her face. "I like that plan."

We make our way into the small ice cream shop, the comforting smell of sugar from what I assume are the waffle cones, takes over my senses.

I don't know if it's my hopeful side, but Laney beams when she looks into the glass enclosure that houses the variety of flavors they stock.

"There are so many options," she says, bringing her finger to her lips and tapping them.

She acts like she's deep in thought, and maybe she is, but I know some things haven't changed in all the years I've known her. Her gaze will always land on vanilla bean, as if her heart is pulled toward it.

I stand back, not at all focused on the flavors, but looking at this woman that stole my heart so long ago. In all honesty, she stole it the moment she looked at me. I just didn't realize it then.

"What can I get you?" An older gentleman makes his way over from the back of the shop.

Laney looks up. "It all looks so good. What do you recommend?"

"Salted caramel is a fan favorite. Want to sample it?"

Laney nods, still looking down at the flavors.

He hands her the miniature spoon and the moment the sample touches her lips, I see the slight disappointment take over her features. She's quick to correct herself without offending the man behind the counter, but I always know the truth in her expressions.

I let her keep playing this mental game she's in, savoring every second together.

Unlike the younger version of me that felt irritated when she'd ask to sample flavors of ice cream that she'd never pick, I soak moments like these up now. I know how precious our time is, it's something I've learned far too well in the past decade.

Finally, as if the epiphany hits her, she looks up and says, "I'll take a scoop of your vanilla bean on a cone, please."

It's hard to hold back my laughter. When I let a chuckle escape, she turns to me, trying to look irritated.

"Sorry, Bean. I can't help it! Every time I watch you concentrate like that and end up with the same flavor it makes me laugh."

"Well, Grant, I like what I like. Deal with it." She

makes a grand gesture of throwing her hair over her shoulder and sticking her nose up in the air.

We grab our treats and make our way across the street, toward the beauty of the Pacific Ocean.

There aren't many people out right now, except for the few playing in the ocean.

We find a spot to settle down and sit.

"There's something so relaxing about staring at the ocean. I could get used to it here." Laney licks her ice cream, her gaze fixed on the waves.

I keep my eyes on her while I answer, "I agree. This view is breathtaking."

She peers over at me and I see a slight blush creep over her cheeks.

This is what I've missed with her; these stolen moments where it's just us, the troubles and horrors of the past not taking priority. I feel like she peels back the ugly layer from that morning where so much innocence was lost and I simply sit with her. She's free and so much like the version of herself I know still lives deep inside her.

I pull my phone out, hoping she doesn't notice, and start taking pictures of her staring out at the water. I get away with only a few before she catches me.

"Grant, I'm not your subject today." She rolls her eyes, but sounds more shy than annoyed.

"Laney, if I could simply photograph you for the rest of my life, I'd be the happiest man alive." I continue snapping shots.

"Wow, such a smoothtalker." I see the side of her mouth quirk up, a hint of a smile pulling through.

"Just speaking the truth." I shrug my shoulders, but continue to focus my phone to get the best angle at this hour.

"Is that the line you use on all the girls you find when

you're on location?" She tries to sound indifferent, but something about her tone makes me think she's trying to pull information from me.

I let my smile glide across my face, knowing she's fishing for information from me.

"You think what I say to you would ever be a line? I guess I have to do a better job of showing you how much of my heart you hold in your hands."

She turns to give me all her attention. "Really, Grant? I hold that much power, huh?"

I nod, feeling the smile grow across my face. "Oh, Bean. If you only knew, my heart has always been yours."

She keeps inspecting me, as if she senses there might be humor behind my words. When I don't take back my statement, she simply goes back to her view.

"Do you ever think about it?" Laney draws a line in the sand with her finger.

"About what?" I ask, confused what she means.

"If we could have been more had we continued hooking up like we were before the–" She swallows, hesitation coating her words. I start to think she won't finish the thought, when she finally says, "Before the shooting?"

Laney isn't one to bring up much about that day, so this question catches me by surprise. I have no problem talking about what we were before our lives changed, but I still take my time to answer.

After a few beats, I keep my gaze on the water and respond, "Yeah, I do. All the time." I could lie to her, but I think the truth goes a lot further. It's okay to let the feelings out and see where they lead us. At least that's what my therapist tells me.

Telling Laney how I really feel is still a line I'm teetering over. I don't want to mess things up between us, but I know we could be more if we both just took that plunge together.

I think the fear of the unknown holds me back, and maybe that's exactly what she's feeling too.

But since we started our adventure to this retreat, I've dropped some hints that I'm interested in more. I know she's finding the clues I'm leaving along the way, hoping she wants to move past friendship with me again.

So far she's laughed most of them off, probably thinking I'm joking around with her. But there's nothing funny when it comes to my feelings. I want more with this woman and I'm sick of being subtle about it. I'm not scared about taking that leap; I'm more fearful of letting this go unexplored.

She nods, as if my answer is one she needs to process. But then her next question really throws me. "Why didn't you ever try anything with me once I started to get better? Is it because I'm not the same person anymore?"

When her eyes meet mine, I can't help but feel gutted. Is that what she really thinks? Does she not understand the way my day starts and ends with her on my mind? Can't she see the way she carries my heart in her hands?

I open my mouth to answer when she jumps in again. "I know I'm not the same as I was. I'm not stupid. I feel different, but I've wondered lately if I'm not someone you're attracted to anymore because of what I experienced."

Her words crush me. I feel like a part of my heart is breaking again, knowing that she's been doubting my feelings for her.

I keep staring at her, apparently unable to form words. She's thrown me for a loop with her thoughts and I can't seem to find my voice.

"It's fine, Grant. You don't have to answer. I just thought I'd ask. Throw it out in the universe." She shrugs her shoulders and looks back at the water in the distance.

I'm about to say something, but she stands up and brushes the sand off her butt.

"Maybe we should head out. I'm ready to relax and not sit in the car anymore." She smiles at me, but I can tell my silence has ruined the mood between us.

We finish our ice cream as we walk back to the car. The silence feels like a vice around my neck and it's suffocating. But her questions are swarming through my mind, trying to find the right words to convey how immensely my feelings for her have grown. The fact that she could think that I'm no longer attracted to her after what she went through is mind-boggling to me.

Buckling in, I look over at her and see her hair is a mess from the ocean breeze.

I can't stop myself; I run my fingers through her hair, taming it and brushing strands away from her face. Her eyes simply watch the movement, and I see her breathing accelerate.

A part of me hopes she can feel my love through this simple touch, but I know she needs an answer instead of my silence. Gestures like these won't ever truly express how I feel for her.

Without saying anything, I bring my hand to her shoulder and squeeze, before starting the car.

There isn't much left of our drive and soon I'm pulling onto the road leading to the hotel. The moment we get closer to the valet, Laney looks over at me.

"Um, Grant, where are we? I thought you said you booked a simple little spot for us to settle for the night. I've seen this place on Instagram," she gushes and I simply chuckle. At that, she realizes I've got a little plan so she continues, "It's too nice. I can't let you do this. Is this how you always travel now? What happened to hostels?"

"No, Bean, this isn't how I usually travel, but I don't

stay in hostels often anymore. This is special; what's the point of traveling the world and seeing my career take off, if I can't enjoy these moments with my favorite person? Come on. Let's go check it out." I'm just as excited to see this place as she is.

The moment we step out of the rental car, and take in our surroundings, I smile. I can hear the ocean perfectly from here. The waves are crashing against the rocks below and all the beauty life has to offer is right at our fingertips. I grab Laney's hand and walk through the lobby, beaming from ear to ear. *I've wanted to do something like this with my girl for so long.*

Once we're checked in and make it to our room, Laney runs toward the balcony attached to our suite. The view is absolutely breathtaking. But the most beautiful part of this trip is the gorgeous redhead in front of me, with eyes that remind me of an endless field of grass. She chose to wear a huge sun hat, and she looks like she stepped out of the pages of a travel magazine. She looks the part here, and I can't help but feel the warmth of my love for her take over all my senses.

"Grant, this is amazing. Thank you for doing this. You didn't have to go through all this trouble, but seeing this, it's just… wow!" She turns toward me, and her smile is enough to knock me on my knees. I see everything I want in life in her gaze. I just hope that she'll see that in me at some point.

My life is only full with Laney by my side. She brings purpose to my days. She never stopped giving me the love I needed to walk toward tomorrow, even in her toughest and darkest moments.

She looks back out to the ocean, then proceeds to close her eyes and take a big breath of the ocean air. When she exhales, she opens her beautiful eyes, and she just stands there. I imagine she's reflecting on everything that led to this moment. I know how survivors of trauma live with a lot of guilt. Hopefully, in this moment, she can feel the joy of living and not the sorrow for lives that were cut short.

As I stand here, taking in the beauty in front of me, I hear a knock at the door. Laney stays put, knowing it's likely the bellhop. Once I retrieve our belongings, I start to put her bags and mine near our prospective beds. It took everything in me not to book a single bed, but I'm trying to be mindful of where she's at. I can't push her, but damn if I didn't think about being "forced" to be near her in that intimate way again.

I've been with women since my last time with Laney. I wish I could say I haven't, but I can't. After everything that happened, I was trying to forget about the pain and anger I was harboring. For a period of time, when I traveled, I coped in the best way I knew how. I drank, I met women, and I moved on from each one. No connection felt right, and each time, I went back to my girl, hoping things would be better. But when I started to climb out of that hole I dug for myself; I felt like she needed me to be strong.

Much like my mother always said about her life with my father when he was still alive, a relationship is about being the support when your partner feels the weight of life on their shoulders. I never saw Laney as weak, but she needed comfort, and she needed to feel like she could lean on us when she was early in her recovery.

Once Laney's done looking at the ocean, she turns around to find me sitting on the edge of the bed.

"Daily," I finally confess while looking down at my hands.

When I look over at her, she's staring at me, confusion marring her features.

"I think about you and what we could have been daily. When my mom called me with the news of what happened to you, I…" I move my hands through my hair. "… I thought everything I was feeling for you was lost forever. I thought I had lost *you* forever. But then I got to you and there was this calm that washed over me the moment I got to hold your hand again."

I swallow past the lump that has formed in my throat and realize Laney is holding back unshed tears. Seeing her sad is the last thing I want, but I have to get this off my chest.

"That calm came crashing down when you opened your eyes in that hospital bed, and I knew you were lost somewhere far away from me and everyone else that loves you. I knew it would take time to get you back to where we were. Hell, I even came to terms with the fact that we might never get back to that place together. I kept chasing the version of us that *could have been,* until I finally understood that no matter how much I ran toward the possibility of it, it might not be what you want anymore. So, to answer your question; I've thought about it. Every. Day. Not a moment goes by where I don't let my mind wander to building a life where we're happy together. Laney, you're…" I sit up straighter."… you're my everything. You're the perfect sunset I seek wherever I go."

A weight is lifted as I let the words pour out of me and I keep my eyes on the floor in front of me; too scared to see what might be reflecting in her gaze.

I hear a rustle by my side, then her frame stands in front of me. I look up to find Laney staring back at me, a little more confidence in her than I've seen in over a decade. Standing between my legs, she moves closer to me and I spread my knees for her to walk closer to me. She's hesitant at first when I notice her hands move up, her fingers brushing through my hair. I can't help the moan I let out at her touch.

I angle my head back, her contact causing me to close my eyes. I haven't had Laney's touch in this way in so long that I've forgotten what it felt like. The electricity I remember coursing along my skin is still there, maybe even more intense than it had been in the past. I open my eyes, and I see her looking at me much like she used to when we were barely adults.

My hands are along the outside of her thighs, and I let them travel up, gauging her reaction to my touch. Her eyes are hooded, and she leans even further into me. My palms move up her back, underneath the shirt she's wearing.

As I glide my hands across her skin, I can't help but feel the connection go beyond our touch. Everything I love about her goes further than what I see in front of me. I love her down to her soul. I feel her pain in my heart. I feel her accomplishments deep inside, which always fuels me to move in a better direction.

Before I have time to think past my hands on her, she bends down and captures my mouth. This connection, feeling her lips on mine, feels like seeing the stars after years of only being engulfed in a haze. I open for her, and soon, she's pushing me backward to lay my upper body down on the bed.

At first, I'm stunned. I'm in utter shock this is happening. Of course, whenever I spend time with Laney, I hope she'll open up to me again. I've wished to have this back with her more times than I can count, but I can't say I've been expecting it. Once upon a time I was confident we were headed toward more together, but that was a long time ago.

Soon enough, we become frantic as we both seem scared to break our connection. There's fear that we'll snap out of this, and seeing her push me away is the last thing I want. I need her like my next breath; my life depends on feeling her by my side.

I feel her pull away, and panic sets in, thinking she's regretting this between us. I quickly realize that she just wants to remove my shirt, so I help her. Soon, I'm completely exposed from the waist up. She begins to plant kisses along my neck and down my clavicle. Then, she's moving further down my torso, but I notice she suddenly stills. I look down and see her inspecting the side of my body.

I know what she's taking in. She hasn't seen me without my shirt on in a long time. But now, she sees what's on my body, and I don't know if she's going to kiss me harder or run for the hills.

She glides her fingers across my skin, the ink below feeling like it's on fire.

"Grant, when did you do this?" She's not referring to the tattoo that matches hers, but to the part I added not long ago.

"I did it last year. Do you like it? Are you mad?" I can hear the nerves in my voice. I feel like everything moving forward depends on how she responds to what I've done.

"It's beautiful. Whose is it?" She's still running her fingers across my chest, and I can't help covering her hand with mine.

I pull her hand off my body and kiss the inside of her palm, before returning it to the tattoo she's staring at.

"It's yours. I wanted your heart beating next to mine," I say to her, still tentative, as I let this secret out into the open for her to absorb.

I kept the tattoo we got together intact, but I added something to it. The artist did a seamless job of incorporating a heartbeat, an EKG strip, of Laney's heartbeat. I had snapped a photo when she was sleeping in the hospital back in Wyoming years ago. I don't know what made me do it.

For years, I stared at the photo, reminding myself that she was alive and that her heart still beat—even when I was across the world and couldn't feel her warmth for myself. But then I had the idea to put the waves of her heartbeat onto my skin. As my sister likes to correct me, it's the beating of the chambers of the heart. My sister, *ever the romantic*, ladies and gentlemen.

Laney's heartbeat took my breath away years ago while she lay in that hospital bed; full of life yet a shell of who she had been the day before. I needed a constant, permanent reminder that she was okay. While she lives, I live. That's what I told myself each time I had to walk away from her.

I wish I could read her thoughts; I can't tell if this is pushing her further from me or if she's feeling more connected to me. This discovery could either pull us together or wreck us. I should have thought this through. I'm about to say something, when she finally speaks.

"I love you, Grant. I never stopped loving you." Then she kisses me again, this time softly against my lips. I bring my hands to cup her face, my fingers in her hair, deepening the connection between us.

I move her onto her back and start to unbutton her shirt, slowly revealing the best gift I've ever been granted access to. The moment her skin is exposed on her chest, I kiss her directly over her heart, and I can see the goose-bumps erupt along her skin. I move toward her breasts, giving each one the attention it craves. I pull down her bra and expose her left breast, nibbling the skin and sucking on her nipple. She arches her back, her reaction spurring me on.

I continue my descent and unbutton her jean shorts. I look up at her, and our gazes lock in that moment in time.

She seems to read my thoughts and gives me a little nod. I shimmy her shorts down, bringing her panties along with them. I throw the garments behind me and look at the beauty that is Laney James. She's perfection. I don't know what I've done in this life, or maybe in past ones, to deserve to have this perfect creature in my life.

This is love. This is completion. She is everything I've looked for in life. I've traveled to the ends of the earth, and I've never found another woman like her. She's my beginning and my end. She's my past, my present, and my future.

I kiss along the inside of her knee, moving up her inner thigh, my brain focused on one spot and one spot only. She's so wet for me, and I greedily take what's right in front of me.

I swipe my tongue along her folds, and she moans while I feel her fingers move through my hair. The sound is music to my ears, and the slight sting to my scalp has me losing a bit of control; combined, they give me the confidence to keep going.

I let my tongue continue, stimulating that little nub. I move one of my hands up her leg, and I insert one finger, followed by another. I continue to fuck her with my mouth while I let my fingers reach into that secret spot where I know I'll have her screaming my name. Soon, I feel her constrict against my fingers, and the satisfaction at having done this to her spurs me on to see her explode. She's riding my face while saying my name, and my dick is about to combust.

She finally lets go, and she rides her climax until she comes off her high. A satisfied smile crosses her features, and she's panting from that ride.

I move up her body until I'm hovering over her, my clothes still completely intact below my waist. She seems to notice this and begins to unbuckle my belt, and then I feel her tug until my clothes are falling to the floor. I help her out and remove my boxers while she fully removes her open shirt and unbuckled bra.

We're now completely naked, and she seems to be taking me in. I know that I've added some muscle since the last time she saw me like this. I'm still lean, but I've added more definition to my physique. It's nice to know she's noticed. From the look she's giving me, I can tell she likes the view.

"Hey now, Bean. If you keep looking at me like that, I may not get much further without making a fool of myself." I smirk.

She laughs, and it continues to be one of my favorite sounds.

"We can't have any of that, Grantie." She winks back, and fuck if that's not a turn-on.

I move over her, my dick at attention and begging for some contact. It's when I look down that I notice I didn't grab a condom. I'm about to move away when I feel her legs wrap around me and tighten.

"No, don't go. I've been tested." It's the first time I realize she's scared of losing this connection. That's the last fucking thing I want. *It scares the shit out of me, too.*

I let my head fall forward and take a deep breath. "You sure? I've been tested since my last partner."

She nods and uses her legs to pull my hips closer to her. When my dick feels the slickness in her folds, I nearly come on the spot. Fuck, I forgot how perfect she is. I haven't even slid inside her, and I already know I'll never be able to walk away from her, from our connection, again. I can't fuck this up.

I slowly begin to inch forward until my head is inside the one place I've been dying for it to be. I'm taking deep breaths in and out through my nose. I have to stay composed.

She moves her hands down and grabs my ass, urging me to move further into her. Soon, I'm fully seated, and fuck if this isn't nirvana. The fullness makes her moan, and she arches her back. I pull out and slowly glide back in. Her moans only get louder, and I feel like all the little moments of my past have led me back to her.

I'm pumping in and out, our moans and our skin slapping are the only sounds in the room. Seeing her gaze on me fuels me to keep going. She keeps telling me what she wants, and I'm quick to obey. I put my thumb against her clit, and she detonates around me. I feel her strangling my cock, and it's taking everything in me not to fall right off that cliff with her. But I don't want this to end. I don't want to leave this perfect moment and possibly face the repercussions of our actions if she regrets it.

Unfortunately, my dick has other ideas. The moment Laney orgasms, I only move faster, chasing my own desire as I piston in and out of her.

"Fuck, Laney. This feels euphoric. Fuck, fuck, fuck." And I'm falling right off, my cum shooting into her, and it feels like a never-ending orgasm. I can't stop moving my hips, letting her tight pussy milk me until I'm spent.

I lay right on her, my breathing labored, while I try to catch my breath. I feel her fingers in my hair again, and I just want to close my eyes and fall asleep in the arms of the woman I crave forever with.

I pull back onto my forearms and push her hair away from her face. Both our bodies are covered in sweat, and there is nowhere else I'd rather be. I look down at her, and I can't help but lean forward and kiss her lightly on the lips. It's then I say what has been eating me alive for all these years.

"You're my home, Laney. No matter where I go, you're who I come back to. I love you. I've always loved you."

It's then I see a tear fall down the side of her face. I go to wipe it, but another falls. That's when I realize that I'm the one who's crying. She brings one of her hands from my hair to my face and cups my cheek. Fuck, I need to be strong for us, and here I am crying after we just had sex. *Shit*. I fucked this up.

I go to pull away, but she holds me there, her legs once again moving around my waist and locking me in place.

"You're my everything, Grant. I'm always looking for you because you're my forever."

She brings her head up, and we kiss, this time deeper. Love is what we never lacked. Life had its ways of fucking everything up. But here we are, hoping that love will win the battle this time around.

We lay together for some time, kissing, embracing, and holding onto this moment for as long as possible. We may not have everything figured out once we walk out that door, but we know that we have love to carry us part of the way. Let's just hope life doesn't have other plans once again.

CHAPTER 12

Laney

ONE MONTH LATER

We're heading into one of my favorite times of the year, Thanksgiving. I have always loved the kick off to the holiday season when everyone comes together. It's been a few weeks since we got back from Joshua Tree, and I'm still on a high from that trip. Being loved by Grant has never been hard. Feeling his love, even from across the continents, is something my heart has always been able to do. Even in my darkest days, I could feel his love for me, I just wasn't in a place to do anything about it. When I started to come out from under the haze of my despair, I knew he loved me, but I wasn't sure he was still attracted to me. Our week together felt like a recalibration of sorts between us.

We didn't leave the hotel room after we had sex. We continued to connect in that way throughout the rest of the evening and into the early morning hours. His kisses along my skin felt like an electromagnetic shock across my body. He and I are connected in a way I have never experienced with another person.

Our adventure continued on the yoga retreat. We met

some incredible people who I hope we stay connected with as we move forward in our lives. Cleo was our instructor, and she was full of rejuvenating practices, messages of hope, and a zest for life. Not everything she said was eye-opening, but I was in a place of receiving at that time. So, it found a connection deep within me, and I've carried it ever since.

Grant has been practicing yoga for some time. His movements were proof of that. His ability to bend in certain ways was impressive, and I couldn't keep my eyes off him. The warmth of the sun was perfect for outdoor yoga, and we were able to spend some time in the yurt, which was something I'd never done. Grant has traveled to so many places and has embraced so many new experiences along the way. But he said that doing those things with me made it feel like a first for him.

We came together beyond the physical sense. We were finally vulnerable and embraced each other's truths. I didn't let everything out, though. I still harbor a secret I haven't told anyone before, not even my sister. The only person I've ever told was Artie, and he took my secret with him when he died.

During my recovery, my feelings were mine, and only mine; at least, that's how I interpreted them. I didn't feel like sharing my personal tragedies was something that someone else could make me do. It was the only thing I felt I could control at the time, and I didn't think they needed to be shared. The longer I hold on to this, the more I know it will bring many unhealed wounds to the surface, not just for me, but for the man that holds every aspect of my heart in his hands.

That's the hard part about all this; I want everything with Grant. And from the little hints he's been leaving me over the past decade—his simple touches, even moments where he opened up to me—I can feel he wants the same. I think we're finally on the same page, aside from the fact that I might cause things to implode between us if I tell the whole truth about what happened in the hours after the events on my college campus. I can't have a life with Grant until he knows my whole truth.

I just hope he can understand the hurt and the pain that I've taken on since that day years ago. I hope that my confession can relay all the pain I harbored throughout the years. It goes beyond the lives I saw lost that day. It's a loss so personal that it sometimes takes over my soul in a way that I feel deeper in my bones than anything else I've experienced.

Since returning from California, I feel a little lighter. Sometimes I feel completely open to trying things with Grant, but then I feel clarity seeping in and concern takes over. In those moments, I feel myself retreating from throwing myself into his arms and into a future together.

I've kept busy with my sister and her family, along with teaching at the studio. Connecting with students has been a nice change of pace for me and makes me feel like I'm finding comfort in some areas of life that once brought anxiety for me.

I'm making my way upstairs after seeing my sister and her kids off to school. I was having trouble sleeping last night, so I am hoping a cup of tea will do the trick and help me lie down for a few more hours. I got a message from Grant that he would be flying back for Thanksgiving, so my excitement for the holiday has increased tenfold.

Maybe I'll be ready to tell him my whole story by then.

"Well, how do you feel about just opening up to Grant and letting him decide how he wants to move forward?" Evelyn once again throws a question in my direction and I feel like that particular one gives me the most anxiety.

"I feel anxious about it. Hence my inability to open up to him," I give her an exasperated look through the camera on my tablet.

Sometimes our visits need to be remote because she's got a packed schedule. Today it's my fault, I opted for a virtual visit versus an in-person one. I teach in a few hours and needed to get a session in.

The more I sit around with my thoughts, the more uncomfortable I am with how to move forward. Now that Grant's arrival is hours away, instead of weeks like I initially had, I feel like my secret is getting heavier on my shoulders.

"Listen, I know it's hard. You know holding onto things like this is bad for your emotional well-being, on top of that it will hurt more the moment you confess it to him. You owe it to him, but also to yourself, to get this off your chest. It won't be easy, but I don't think you can really focus on what you and Grant could build without resolving what's behind you."

She's said this to me before. All this isn't news to me, but each time I get a morsel of courage to come clean with Grant, something holds me back. I've done this so many times with Evelyn and she's always so patient with me as I work through my thoughts.

"Losing Grant is my biggest fear. Before the shooting, and all the loss, our relationship wasn't threatened by anything but our own fear of ruining our friendship. But, now, this feels like something he'll never be able to see past with me. I can almost see his expression of pain and sadness when I say it out loud to him. I'll break him, Evelyn. I just know I will." I sigh and feel the tears pooling in my eyes. I know my fears are warranted, but the way I'm procrastinating telling him is making this whole thing so much worse.

"Laney, that's definitely a possibility. He could be angry. He could choose to walk away. We've talked about that scenario and I know how heartbreaking that would be for you and for him. But let's play out another possible scenario: what if he doesn't leave you behind? What if he finds it in him to understand your point of view? I think you need to give him this opportunity to shine for you. You're not only holding onto this big piece of the puzzle, but you've decided how he's going to react without allowing him the chance to prove you wrong. You're not giving him the opportunity for your love for one another to shine. That's not fair."

"You're right. Everything you're saying makes sense. I just feel a bit fragile letting this out after so long. I can't guarantee I'll say anything before the holidays. I'm going to try though." I sit up taller, determination in my posture.

"You'll figure out when the right time is. Just know you aren't alone. And even if Grant is angry, you have to let him live in that feeling and give him time to figure this out for himself too. Don't disregard him if he needs space afterwards. He might very well need some time to grieve. You've had your time to process, remember that he's allowed to do the same," she says and I nod in agreement.

We finish the call, and I know what I need to do. The problem remains: when is the right time to possibly ruin everything with the man you love?

CHAPTER 13
Laney

"Take a collective breath in, then open your mouth and let it all go. Let go of your worries, your frustrations, your pain, and simply feel the strength you possess on your mat right now. Nothing else will serve you while you're in this room. Feel free to continue in Savasana for as long as you'd like. I will be at the front desk when you're ready to make your way out."

As class comes to an end, I make my way through the bodies lying on their mats, each student on a personal journey while in this sacred room. There's something transformative about yoga in general, but now that I've started teaching the new hot classes Loni began offering, I feel a radical shift in myself teaching this area of yoga. The heat just really brings out the ability for the body to be pushed to new limits and shows people how resilient they truly are.

I feel a wave of nausea take over, and I concentrate on my breathing, calming the discomfort as I get closer to the door and into an area of fresh air. I grab my phone, the music playing softly through the studio speakers, and I walk out into the lobby. I let the coolness of the air conditioning flowing through the hallway wash over me. Soon, the nausea subsides, and it's like nothing was ever wrong. I brush it aside, hoping whatever it was passes quickly. I'm always catching germs from my sister's kids, and this is probably a last-minute Thanksgiving treat the kids have brought home.

Loni isn't in today, so I'll be locking up after this class. I'm looking at the computer, making sure everything is ready for the weekend, when a few from my class start to filter out into the lobby. They're giving me well wishes for a happy Thanksgiving holiday and the gratitude I feel as I see everyone is washing over me. I took next week off to spend with family and to visit with my parents and Becca's oldest, Olive, while she's in town.

With Thanksgiving less than a week away, I'm feeling my excitement build in anticipation of seeing everyone. My parents, who still live in Saddle Ridge, will be in town. They aren't home much these days, using this time to travel and usually making frequent stops here in New York to visit all of us now that their whole family is here. The worry my parents have for me is constant, but seeing them let go a bit and travel gives me hope that they're seeing me thrive more than suffer.

Tonight, I'm kicking off the weekend by going out with Becca and my sister. Ellie has been struggling with a difficult parent of one of her students, and she needs a night out. I really didn't want to join—if I'm being honest, crowds in confined places are still a source of stress and anxiety for me. But I could see the excitement on my sister's face when she proposed a girls' night, so it's in the works for a few hours from now. Grant has permission to crash, and I hope he does so early on, because his presence soothes my nerves.

I'm typing something into the computer when I hear a

throat clear in front of me. I look up and find one of my regular students standing there, nerves evident on his face.

"Great class, Laney. Thanks so much. It's always wonderful watching you teach." *Watching me teach?* Yeah, he's nervous and uncomfortable. He's been in my class many times in the last year since he joined the studio. By now, I'd expect him to feel a little more at ease around me, but he's still bashful and awkward most of the time.

"Thanks, Tad. I appreciate your dedication to your practice. Your tree pose is really coming along. I remember when you had issues balancing, and now you're swaying your arms with minimal movement of your standing leg. That's amazing." He smiles as I say this.

I move out from behind the desk, saying my goodbyes to more students while Tad stays planted where he has been. He seems a little more tense than usual. As I wave to one of the students walking out the door, I turn my attention back to Tad.

"Um, so Laney, I was wondering if, um—" He coughs, clearly having issues getting his thoughts together. He closes his eyes, takes a deep breath, and I swear I hear him say under his breath, *get it together*. "Yeah, so I was wondering if you have plans this weekend?"

I'm shocked, to say the least. I'm not usually one to date a student, especially one from a studio I don't see myself leaving anytime soon. The awkwardness this would pose if things didn't work out would really throw off my chakras. Plus, with my whole Grant situation, it's a hard pass.

I'm about to answer when I hear a voice I didn't expect.

"Sorry, man, she has plans with me all weekend." Grant's imposing frame stands next to me, his arm draping over my shoulder.

I look up at him, my brows furrowing with his alpha-male personality shining through. Grant is usually so easy-going that it's rare to find him acting like this. I can handle myself, and I can't help the irritation that bubbles up from Grant pushing himself into this conversation.

"Oh, sorry. Um, I didn't know you had a boyfriend." Tad is looking at me, discomfort etched all over his features. Shit, this is exactly why I try to avoid situations like these.

"Now you know," Grant says, his smirk coming out in full force.

Tad says a few quick goodbyes and nearly sprints out of the studio. I watch him leave, amazed he didn't leave a puff of smoke in his trail like Wile E. Coyote.

The moment Tad is out of sight, I swing my gaze to Grant, who is full-blown smiling, dimples popping and all. He's about to have a rude awakening that I'm not amused by his little show.

"What the hell, Grant?! I think you made him wet his pants!" I move out from under his arm.

Grant doesn't seem phased by his behavior and rests his tall frame against the front desk.

"Well, Laney, last I checked, we have some unresolved things to discuss. I think it's safe to say you and I are more a thing than you and your student would be. Also"—he looks me right in the eyes—"let's stop running from this."

Well, shit. That's not what I was expecting him to say. So, after all these years, this is finally coming to the surface? Here at the yoga studio where I'm currently standing in my sweaty gear and looking like a drowned rat? Gross.

Shit, the nausea is coming back. I'm about to say something, but instead, I make my way through the studio to the back, where I throw the bathroom door open and rush to the toilet. I feel that nasty taste overpower my salivary glands, but then the feeling subsides.

I walk to the sink and throw some cold water on my

face. I look up and find Grant behind me, his easy, charming smile gone, now replaced with concern. His eyebrows furrow as he looks at me. I see my reflection in the mirror in front of me. I've gone pale.

"The kids probably brought something home from school. I think I've been fighting it all week, now that I think about it. I went to bed early last night, and I think I'm just getting it out of my system. Best keep your distance, 'boyfriend.'" I use air quotes for the term that Tad used, noting Grant didn't correct him. Although, neither did I.

This doesn't seem to appease Grant, as he watches me walk out of the bathroom and move through the studio, cleaning up the yoga room and then shutting everything off. I get my coat on, along with my puffy boots, and wait for Grant to walk out with me. He's been quiet since I had my little episode in the restroom. I know he's taking everything in. I'm going to let him do that. I have an evening out to prepare for.

We start to walk toward the house when he finally speaks, "You think it's a good idea to go out tonight?" His words are laced with concern.

I roll my eyes. "Grant, it's fine. It was probably the sandwich I ate yesterday. It did sit funny after I finished it. Maybe the deli meat went bad. I'll be fine. Like I said, I went to bed early, and even with the crazy dreams thrown in there, I got enough hours to get through a night out. I'm fine." I feel like I'm not just saying this to him, but to myself. I can't get sick right before everyone comes over this coming week. That would make for an awful Thanksgiving celebration. Usually, I'm the first to bail on going out somewhere, but now that Grant is back, I'm excited to try something new tonight with all of us hanging out.

"Well, I can cancel with Timothy tonight if you want. I

can just go with you girls to the bar instead of meeting you there later." I know he's worried, but this is a bit much.

"No, Grant. Go out with him. I know you've been meaning to see him the last few times you've been in town, and you haven't had the opportunity. Go, have fun, then meet us when you're done. I think my sister needs some girl time, so this will work perfectly."

We reach the stairs leading to the brownstone. Grant seems to be dressed to head out to see his friend, so he doesn't need more time to get ready. Of course, he feels my forehead to ensure I don't have a fever before turning to look for his Uber. I think he forgets his sister is the one with the medical degree, not him.

I roll my eyes but follow it up with a smile, and he gives me a small smirk in return. He gives me a quick peck on the cheek, but as he turns to walk away, I grab his hand and give him a proper kiss goodbye. He doesn't hesitate and returns the kiss, my body feeling like jelly as I feel myself melt into him. Then, as quickly as we started this connection, he pulls away, and I watch him walk toward the awaiting car.

I can't help but consider how easy life would be if we simply molded into the couple we could be together. For a split second I forget how quickly that might come crashing down when I finally I open up to him completely.

I make my way into the house to get myself ready to hang out with two of my favorite women. However, even after telling Grant how much better I feel, I realize I'm going to need some coffee or something. I can already feel my eyelids drooping.

The music is pumping, and I feel a little lighter tonight. My sister and Becca are beside me, and we're all letting go. Becca recently reconnected with her old high school boyfriend, and I can say this is the happiest she's ever been. She looks free in a way I didn't realize she wasn't before. I guess there's something about love that simply transforms a person. I hope I can open myself up in the way I've seen her do these last few months with Shane.

The number of people that were here when we arrived was not too overwhelming, but then the crowd started to multiply and I see more people are getting on the dance floor. Even with me working hard to merge into this part of my life again, it's hard to feel confident in a small space with a lot of people.

That day in Wyoming, I wasn't in the crowded hall for long. But the claustrophobia I now experience rises from the fact that I don't want to feel trapped. I think that feeling of being unable to get out simply overwhelms me to my core.

My eyes are dashing left and right, and I feel my pulse accelerating. Right then, I feel a set of hands move around my hips. The moment I'm about to react to being touched without permission, I look up to find Grant gazing down at me. As soon as I register his presence, I feel my whole body relax. He's a balm to my nerves, a source of calm in the storm.

"It's okay, Bean. I've got you. I won't let anything happen. Just close your eyes and feel the music." I feel him move behind me, swaying his hips, my body flowing to the same rhythm. All I feel is love where, a moment ago, I felt hesitation.

I hear Becca pull Grant's attention for a moment, and I can't help but chuckle at her scolding of Grant for not greeting her. It's pretty funny to see her all worked up, but the moment he gives her his puppy eyes, she caves every single time.

They share the same eye color, but something about the way Grant uses his charm pulls everyone into his orbit when he wants their praise. He's magnetic and vibrant in a way that no one else has been for me.

As the Stanley siblings have their little squabble, I feel eyes on me. The hairs on the back of my neck stand and I can't help swinging my gaze from left to right, unable to shake the feeling I'm being watched. I look all around me, but the people are filtering onto the dance floor quickly as the music picks up. Just then, I feel my hand being pulled and I focus on the man in front of me.

Grant pulls me from my thoughts and that unease washes away. Grant's attention is purely on me again, and I feel us moving further into the crowd. I know what he's doing, trying to get me more comfortable surrounded by the bodies moving on this dance floor. I'm lost in his touch, forgetting the panic that was coursing through my system moments before he arrived.

We sway, moving to the beat of the music and caressing one another with our hands everywhere, except in the places I need him most. This dance is like our foreplay, and for some reason, that's the only place my mind has gone. I crave him in a way I haven't really leaned into for so long. But since our trip out west, I feel like I've opened Pandora's box, and I need to feel us together in an intimate way again.

After what feels like hours later, although it most likely wasn't that long, I feel my eyes get heavy. I'm wiped in a way I haven't felt in a long time. Whatever I was fighting earlier, it's still making its way out of my system. The nausea has subsided at least and from what I can tell, no one in my sister's house has caught it yet.

I look up at Grant, and he can see from my expression

that I've exceeded my limit of being around so many people. My battery drains faster when I'm surrounded by an excessive number of people in a public place. I focus so much to get through a scenario that the moment I succeed, my body succumbs to the anxiety and stress and needs rest.

We make our way across the dance floor, finding Becca and Ellie still moving to the beat of this nineties music they grew up with. I say my goodbyes, Grant promising to get me home safely.

I know that Grant will spend the night. My sister knows he either stays at her house or crashes on the couch at his sister's place. Tonight, I think he'll be sharing a bed with me, because I long for his comfort.

Grabbing my coat from the booth we were sitting at earlier, placing it on my back, and interlacing his fingers through mine, we make our way through the exit. The cold of the evening hits me like a slap to the face.

We aren't far from the house, so we use this time to walk through the neighborhood, enjoying that some of the houses are decorated for the holidays already. I've always loved this time of year, and it's taken me time to finally feel like I can embrace this season the way I did once. Slowly, I'm picking up pieces of myself that were a normal part of my personality before the shooting. That one day truly catapulted my life in a completely different direction, and I feel like I'm seeing myself rise from those ashes bit by bit.

My strides have been great but also slow as I maneuver life since the attack. I think that's what has been the most surprising. The nightmares afterward were expected, but years later, I find myself frustrated that I can still wake up in a cold sweat. People talk so much about how an event like a mass shooting is devastating, protesting gun control and fighting for change, but soon the news outlets move on, a new tragedy hitting us from another direction. The survivors are left to deal with the aftermath, and the desertion is felt in a way I can't explain.

What I experienced has become too common. Now, when another shooting occurs, it's almost like we expect it. That realization was devastating for me. I'm here, struggling to put one foot in front of the other while the world carries on.

The post-traumatic stress I suffered then and continue to walk through life holding will never leave. I can learn to cope, but it's now a chronic issue for me. Like a disease that I'll never find a cure for. For everyone who watches the news and simply pleads with the universe to never let that happen to them, countless others and I are struggling to navigate a lifetime ahead.

I might be living my life now, finding ways to thrive, but people forget my efforts are still an uphill battle. I keep what little control I can within my world so I'm comfortable. On nights like tonight, I'm reminded I can push my limits, but the exhaustion I experience afterward is extensive.

"Laney, you okay? You're far away with your thoughts." Grant moves my hair back off my shoulder.

I look over at him and smile. "Yeah, just thinking about things. Thanks for coming tonight. I was about to have a little panic attack with all the people entering the dance floor, but you helped me fight it. Thank you." I give him the biggest smile I can muster while I'm freezing my butt off.

I wore pants and a cute top, along with a huge puffy jacket, but it feels like I'm outside with a towel wrapped around me. The cold is going right through the fabric tonight.

"I'll always be here for you, Laney," he tells me, and I believe him.

"Yeah. But you're not always going to physically be

here, Grant. You work. You travel. That's literally your job." I'm not complaining, just stating the obvious. From the moment I left Wyoming, I noticed I could fall into a pattern of reliance on Grant if I wasn't careful. I felt safe around him, and the moment he'd leave to work, I felt the anxiety creep in. I've made it a part of my recovery to find ways to live my life independently, so I didn't pull him back to the point where he was stuck.

"I'd give it all up for you. Laney, you're my purpose. I'd do anything to ensure your safety." He puts his arms around me and hugs me closer to him.

"I appreciate that. But let's stick to what we know to be true. I can't rely on you while you're away. I have to find a way to navigate life on my own." This conversation has gotten heavy pretty quickly.

Grant stops, grabs me by the shoulders, and turns me so we're facing each other. I see him close his eyes, probably figuring out what he wants to say without letting his frustration show.

I can read him like a book, and I know he's upset about what I'm saying, but my truth is exactly that. This is our reality. As much as I want a full life with Grant, his life isn't stationary. It's full of movement. It's full of adventure. I don't see my life in that way. I like to stay put, I like order, and I like control where I can achieve it.

"Laney, please stop talking to me like I don't know how I live my life. I get it. I travel. I move around the world like a free spirit. I embrace change. I walk into situations where I have no idea how they'll turn out. But never, not for one second, believe that you aren't my home. You're my compass, and I'm constantly making sure the direction of my arrow points back to you. I'm sick of fighting this. I'm tired of walking away, wondering if you'll let me in. I want in. I want you. I want forever. Please. Life is full of unknowns, but nothing about what I feel for you is questionable. It's fact."

I feel a single tear fall down my cheek. Our love for one another has never been questioned. It's his ability to love me unconditionally that I question. It's whether he'll still want my heart when he knows everything that I worry about.

How can he say all the right things, all the words that make my heart soar, yet I know the minute I say what I've held on to for so long, he might take it all back? The unknown that lies between us keeps me from saying anything in return. It's at the tip of my tongue to confess, but I simply nod. The lump in my throat is consuming me, and I can't get words out.

This appeases him enough, and without another confession from either of us, we continue walking until we get home.

At some point in the night, I wake from my sleep, gasping. I had a night terror. I relived that dreadful day, but instead of Artie, I was holding Grant. I'm pulling as much air into my lungs as I can. I haven't had a nightmare in a few months. They come and go, seeming to increase when I go out into a crowd, much like I did tonight.

I look to my side and see Grant's side of the bed empty. I must have crashed right when we got back. I was wiped. I brushed my teeth, feeling my body deplete the longer I stayed awake. Grant was still getting ready for bed when I laid my head on my pillow and fell into a blissful sleep. Too bad I didn't stay that way.

I get up to use the restroom, and when I come out, Grant is making his way through the room.

"Sorry, did I wake you when I got up?" He looks over at me, in his boxers and no shirt. Gosh, he's gorgeous.

I shake my head. "No. Nightmare woke me."

I see the sadness cross his features, and I know that as much as I hate the trauma that I live with, it guts him almost as much that this is my life.

We both make our way back to bed, and once lying back down, he stretches his arm out, my head resting in the crook of his armpit. My upper hand immediately moves to rest over his tattoo, and I run my fingers along his skin, loving how soft he feels under my touch.

He moves his fingers through my hair, each movement pulling me into a state of calm.

"I'm sorry you woke up in a panic. I hate that you experience that fear when your body should be in a state of rest." He kisses the top of my head, and I can easily say I've never felt so loved by another human.

He lulls me to sleep with his movements in my hair, and soon, I fall into a state of slumber, and luckily, my dreams don't take me back to darkness. They never seem to when he's next to me. Too bad he won't be here once he learns the truth.

When I wake the next morning, I try to broach the subject of things that happened years ago. The week is much the same, me trying to figure out when I should ruin his Thanksgiving break. But after building up the nerve to talk to him with my therapist's help, I ultimately chicken out. I make the mental promise to talk to him next time he's in town. I have to, or we don't stand a chance of having a future together.

CHAPTER 14

Grant

SIX WEEKS LATER

Laney is sitting next to me with what I would say is a look of awe on her face. Since moving to New York, she has never had the confidence to try going to a Broadway show. I knew it would be a leap for her, but I think if we have a goal for this new year, it's to try some new things. I think it's time to start living life to the fullest.

For Christmas, I took a chance and got us tickets for the Broadway show *Aladdin*. I know how much she loves the movie, I had to watch it on repeat with her growing up, and I can easily say those are memories I now cherish. It may have taken a decade to get her into a crowded theater like this one, but now I get to see the smile spread across her face. *It's been so worth the wait.*

I reach over to grab her hand and she looks over at me, her eyes shining with unshed tears. I know how hard this was for her. The moment we walked in and took our seats, I felt the rigidity of her shoulders. I could feel the tension radiating off her, and my heart sank. I started to regret my purchase, but then the show started and I saw her come to life. She hasn't looked away from the performers in front of us for longer than a second, and my regret dissipates the longer we sit here. I'm in awe of her strength.

That's all Laney does: surprise me with her incredible heart and ability to try, even if at first she feels hesitant. I've learned that as long as Laney trusts the person or people surrounding her, she'll take a leap. But I also know that pushing her too hard will only set us back. I've taken incredibly small steps forward throughout the years, and now I see that it's paying off.

She squeezes my hand as the show is coming to an end. There are loud sounds and unexpected movements, but thankfully, it hasn't startled her in the way I feared. It helps that there have been no sudden movements from the crowd, and the sounds are only coming from the stage.

Laney doesn't react well to loud sounds that come out of nowhere. She's had moments of pure terror from a simple car backfiring or screaming in a crowded place. Moments like those seem to paralyze her from the inside, and when she first started her recovery process, seeing her pull back and withdraw into herself gutted me.

Once the show is over, I stay with her in our seats as people make their way around us. I know she likes to wait, not standing in the aisle where she feels trapped and confined to the movements of others. As I sit there, I hear Laney humming the music we just finished listening to. I take her in, all her mannerisms and movements next to me; she doesn't realize how she defines mine.

"Did you enjoy it, Bean?" I move my hand down her arm, needing to feel her skin against mine.

I wish I could say that after sleeping together in California, we were able to find a rhythm together, but it's still a work in progress. I made my feelings clear to her that night leaving the bar a few months back, but we haven't really taken the time to go back to that conversation.

I thought we were moving in the direction of finally being together, especially after I pretty much laid my heart out that cold November night. But that hasn't quite been the case. She loves me as much as I love her, but she's hesitant. When we're together, everything feels right, but when I go out on a job and return, it feels like I have to take so many steps forward to get us back to where we were.

Whatever's holding her back, I have yet to figure it out. I'm giving her space, not pushing her in a way that would make her feel forced to be with me. I want to be her choice, not her expectation. In many ways, I feel like I'm transported to thirteen years ago at prom when I wanted to profess my love for her but was scared of ruining what we had.

"Grant… it was… *magical.*" I had no idea her smile could get any bigger, but I was wrong. She's radiant right now, and I wish I could bottle up these moments for when I'm miles away and missing her warmth.

I kiss her cheek and I hear her take a breath in, maybe more affected by my touch than I gave her credit for. She turns her head then and allows her lips to meet mine. The kiss is quick, but enough to spark all my synapses to attention.

We move from our seats once the auditorium is easier to exit from and make our way through. Laney is rushing more than I expected, and she starts to speed walk toward the restrooms. Although she loved the performance, she got up multiple times to use the bathroom. She blamed the excessive amounts of water after doing yoga this morning. I have no idea how much she drank, but it must have been a wheelbarrowful with the number of times I saw her get up.

As she's rushing in front of me, she yells, "I'll be right out. I'll meet you out here in a second!"

Red hair is flying behind her, and she's gone in an

instant. I pull my phone out and order a ride. I then pocket the phone, and look up to check my surroundings.

I look to my left, scanning the sea of people, and I swear I feel eyes on me. I keep moving my gaze from left to right, trying to bury my unease, but I can't shake it. I'm still processing it when I feel a hand wrap around my bicep.

"Hey. Sorry. I think the older I get, the smaller my bladder is. Ready to go? I'm wiped." We make our way through and out the doors into the cold January chill.

Laney has been a little off recently. She's been feeling under the weather on and off for the last few weeks. I think she's overdoing it with her teaching schedule, especially now that she's started teaching hot yoga a few times a week.

I've told her to call her doctor and get checked, as whatever she has is consuming her days and not really letting up. She keeps fighting me, saying she doesn't need to see anyone and that her body is simply tired from the extra hours in the studio. I know her real hesitation is the idea of possibly having to go into a hospital. Since the shooting, she hates them.

Once we get outside, it's a hassle to figure out which car is ours, but we finally find the correct one and make our way back to the house. The drive home is easy, even with the tourists roaming the streets of this city that always seems to be awake.

We find Ellie and my sister in the kitchen, laughing their heads off. The moment we walk in, I can tell there's something to their chatter. It takes a bit to get Ellie to confess, but she finally admits to having started seeing someone. But the most shocking part about it is the fact that she's not just dating anyone; she's with *Xander Christianson*. I nearly pass out when she says his name.

I'm a lover of all sports, but when Xander was playing hockey, I really paid attention. He made gliding around on the ice look effortless in so many ways. It was obvious his life revolved around the sport.

Of course, I want to press Ellie to introduce us, but it seems, much like her sister, she's not putting a label on whatever this is with them. I guess time will tell.

We say our goodnights and head upstairs.

The moment we close the door behind us, Laney jumps into my arms. On instinct, I wrap my arms around her, her legs automatically come around my hips and lock behind me. She pulls her hands through my hair and kisses me with so much passion that I'm having trouble thinking straight.

I turn us around and lean her against the door, devouring her mouth while I feel her moving her hands down toward my shoulders. I bring one of my hands up her ribs and cup her breast in my hand. I pinch her nipple, and I swallow her moan as I continue to kiss her.

I'm fumbling to get us to the bed, my cock eager for whatever is about to happen. I've longed for her touch so much that I feel greedy with need. I've let her set the speed for whatever this is between us, and all I feel is relief knowing she feels this desire to connect with me the same way I long for it with her.

I lay her on the bed and slowly start to peel her clothes off her. Once I get to her bra and panties, I nearly tear them off her. She starts pulling at my belt buckle, unbuttoning my pants, and pulling them off, my boxers following. I unbuttoned my shirt and slipped it off while she was removing the bottom half of my clothing. I pull at the back of my neck and hike my undershirt over my head.

I stand there, both of us panting, and I admire the beautiful creature in front of me. Her fair skin in contrast to my olive tones. Her lips are swollen from our connection earlier, her red hair wild from us trying to devour one another.

Now, I simply take her in. I see the desire swimming in her gaze. I bite my bottom lip, thinking about what part of her I want first.

I lick my lips, and I can see her writhe under me, only getting more turned on.

Like a lion on the prowl, I begin to approach her, my hands resting on the bed, my eyes taking her in as she leans back. Once she's fully prone on the bed, I kiss her neck and begin to trail kisses down toward her breasts. They seem fuller than they used to; I'm all for it. I suck a nipple in my mouth, and she arches her back, moaning a bit too loudly while there are others in this house.

I pop right off and look up at her.

"Shhhhh, baby. We don't need everyone in the house knowing what we're doing right now."

I go right back, this time giving attention to the opposite breast. She can't keep still. She's even more turned on than usual, with my attention on her chest.

Soon, she's begging for more, and I'm not dumb enough to deny her. Without warning, I line myself up and slam into her.

I let myself get used to her tightness, feeling like I'm finally home. I look down and see Laney's hands gripping the comforter. I know she wants me to move, but I need a moment. I just need to savor this because I know it will be over too quickly.

I begin to move, painfully slowly, feeling my cock sliding in and out of her wet pussy. Fuck, this is heaven. Each time we're together, it feels like the puzzle pieces align. Nothing feels right, unless it's with Laney.

The more I pump, the more I chase my release. But I have to take care of my girl.

I pull out and flip her onto her hands and knees. I give her ass a light slap, and she yelps.

"Fuck, Laney—your ass, your pussy, were made for me. You're gorgeous, my sweet girl."

I bite her ass cheek then slide back in and begin pumping. In and out, I watch my dick move, and I'm even more turned on in this position. I see her pussy take me, and it urges me to keep moving. I feel her start to tighten around me, and she moves her hand to her clit.

Something about that causes me to grab onto her hips and piston into her faster. She's spurring me on, but I can't jump off that cliff before her.

"Laney, fuck baby, I need you to come. Come for me. Let go."

I feel her orgasm around my cock, and I fall off right behind her. It's euphoric being with her in this way. My orgasm feels like it goes on forever, ropes of my cum shooting into her. She constricts my dick in a way that feels like her release is lasting just as long.

We fall to the mattress, both of us panting and sweaty messes. We're lying on our sides, her back to my front, and I let my fingers glide along the side of her body. My touch leaves trails of goosebumps behind.

I bury my nose in her hair, taking in that vanilla scent I love so much. I close my eyes, contentment filling me. I feel like my life is complete. I bask in this until Laney tells me she has to get up and use the restroom.

The moment she's gone, I feel her absence like I'm lacking oxygen. Our connection is so intense I forget how I live without her when I'm away.

It's so great to feel *alive* again.

The next day, we go out to lunch. We head into a little place not far from Laney's house, my mouth watering the moment we enter the restaurant. This New York winter cold runs deep, and I rub my hands together in hopes of getting my fingers warmed up as we follow the hostess to our table.

Laney looks at the menu, biting her lower lip with her teeth, heavy concentration lacing her features. I can't help but picture that mouth around my dick, much like it was this morning while we got ready in her shower.

Last night, it felt like we had some unspoken agreement about our relationship moving forward. I always do this, falling into the mindset that things will change and we'll finally put a label on what we're doing. I can't be with anyone else. She's it for me. Enough of this back-and-forth behavior. We've lived a life where we tried to be without one another, keeping our friendship front and center.

Being around her and seeing parts of her shine as we move through life together brings me so much joy, and the moment her mouth was on mine last night, it felt like home. I can't walk away from her, from this, without putting everything out there. I want this just as much as I wanted it years ago and had to table that discussion after the shooting.

Now, I feel like Laney can handle what I have to say. I think we're ready for this to be a natural progression for us. After everything in California, I told her I wasn't with anyone else. She assured me she wouldn't be dating while I was away for work. But I can't ignore the distance she puts between us when I return from working abroad. I want a future with her, in all senses of the word. She is my tomorrow, no matter how many bumps we find in the path ahead.

Laney finally looks up from the menu, a smile crossing her features.

"I think I'm going to get the spinach omelet. I'm craving something light, but also something that will keep me full."

Right then, one of the servers walks by, a big plate of what I can see is eggs in her hand and the smell carries over. The moment she passes, it's almost like Laney's face turns green, and her smile disappears.

"On second thought, that smell is not going to work for me. Maybe I'll have pancakes."

I can't help but look at her for an extra beat. My mind travels back to last night, all her symptoms not adding up. She's hot and cold with her health. Her body can't seem to decide what side of the fence she's on, and she's teetering a fine line. I'm about to comment that she should see a doctor, but we're interrupted by our server.

We put in our orders; I opted out of anything that was primarily eggs and got a BLT, while Laney stuck to her pancake order for lunch. This restaurant is known for serving breakfast all day, and Laney has been on a mission since we left the house to have breakfast food no matter what.

After we eat, we decide to walk a bit, despite the cold weather. The sun has made its way out, and we decide to soak in some sunshine before the clouds move in. A storm is said to be headed in late tonight, so we want to enjoy this little bit of sunshine while nature gives us a break.

While we walk, I grab Laney's hand, and she accepts the gesture.

"So, Bean, I wanted to talk to you about something."

At my words, she stiffens slightly, but tries to cover it up with her response, "Okay, what's up?"

"I'm thinking of taking a break from my photography abroad and focusing on some local work instead. My last trip was draining, and I want to be closer to home for a little bit. After this next assignment, I have a break and I think I'm going to stay in the city and see how it feels."

She isn't looking at me, her eyes fixed on the ground in front of her, but she nods, waiting for me to continue.

"With that, I wanted to give *us* a go. Take what we have together and see where it goes. I know we've skirted around this topic, but I really want to be *all in*—I'm committed to staying close by to make it happen."

This has her stopping to look up at me. She pulls her hand out of mine.

"Um, so you want to be *together* together? Aren't you afraid we'll ruin a good thing?"

Her words throw me off balance. Ruin a good thing? Who said making things official will ruin anything? Would being with me romantically be so bad? We're already sleeping together, and not dating other people. My confusion is evident as I furrow my brows at her.

"Laney, I think we've crossed that line already. This seems like the next logical step, one I've been wanting to take with you for so long. Plus, why would anything be ruined? It could be better than we both imagined." My voice is tight, finding it hard to hide how hurtful her assumptions about us are when I'm trying to put my heart on the line for her.

"Grant"—she pinches the bridge of her nose, probably barely getting a good grip through her thick gloves, and closes her eyes, seemingly annoyed by this conversation—"I think it will complicate things to take what we have a step further."

I can't help the stab of pain from her words.

"Laney, we deserve to be happy. You can't keep pushing something this good away. We work together on so many levels. Why is that so bad?"

"You don't get it, Grant. You don't know what it's like.

If only you hurt the way I do, then you'd understand that my trepidation comes from somewhere deeper. I can't risk losing you, losing us. It's the only thing that keeps me feeling like myself. It's the only tie I have to the person I was before everything went to shit."

We're completely idle, standing on the empty sidewalk, having a very deep conversation in the middle of winter. However, the cold of the winter is forgotten as I feel my blood boil from the fact that she won't even consider being with me beyond this friends-with-benefits situation I've once again started up with her.

"Laney, maybe I haven't hurt like you have throughout the years, but I have felt pain watching you suffer. Why do you think I haven't said anything about my feelings? I want this, but I've never wanted to push you."

I see the determination in those emerald eyes of hers. She's straightening her spine, ready to ground her feet into the pavement to prove the point that she can't fathom a life with me beyond our friendship.

"Yeah, well, there's more to it. There's more to the pain I've dealt with all these years. You won't understand, you don't get it. I've carried it for both of us so you wouldn't live life hurting the way I have."

"What else do I need to get, Laney? If it's so complicated, make it less complicated for me. Make me understand." I throw my arms up, my voice raised in frustration.

I hate the shock that crosses her features as I try to calm myself down. I never raise my voice with her. I take a deep breath, and when I exhale, I feel myself calm just enough to continue speaking to her.

"I get it. You lost your friend that day in the most horrific way. You lost a lot of trust in the world. I get that, and I want to stand with you. But I feel like, as a friend, that's not the only way I can show my support. I love you, Lane. I love you beyond anything I've felt for another person. You're it, Laney. You're the person I want forever with. Stop fighting this."

I feel the tears pool in my eyes. My emotions are coming to the surface, and unlike the last eleven years, I'm not going to push them aside. I deserve happiness too.

"You don't get it, Grant!" Now, her voice is raised, her frustration evident in her tone. "I didn't just lose Artie that day! I lost a piece of myself. I lost a part of me I'll never get back."

She storms off, apparently done with this conversation, but I'm not having it. I deserve answers. I deserve more than her pushing me away. The shooting is the main reason for keeping my personal feelings aside; if there's more to that day than she's told me, I need to know. But now I feel determined because if I don't have this conversation now, I'll live my life with regret, and I don't need more of that sitting on my shoulders.

I have, since that phone call before she entered that hell on campus, regretted the fact that I just didn't confess my feelings to her right then. Since that dreadful day, I've held my truth close to my chest because I never wanted to confront my feelings.

I move toward her, my steps eating the distance between us physically. But emotionally, I know she's much further than I'd like.

"Laney, what the hell do you want from me? I've given you time. I've given you my best, and you're just tossing me aside? For what? What are you waiting for? Something better? Because let me tell you something: I have searched all over and no one holds a drop of wax, much less a candle, to you! Don't you get that?" I go to grab her hand to pull her attention back onto me.

She turns and pulls her hand away, acting like my touch hurts her. That act alone hurts me to my core.

"Grant! Fuck! I lost myself that day. Literally lost myself in a way that scares me. You don't get it, because I never told you."

Tears are falling down her cheeks, and I'm stunned by her words.

"You didn't tell me…what?" I can't help the confusion lacing my words. What could she be referring to? We tell each other everything.

She looks up toward the heavens, closing her eyes and letting the tears fall into her hair. She then rights herself, her gaze firmly on mine.

"That day, I didn't just lose a friend. I didn't just lose my innocence. I lost us, Grant. I was pregnant and I lost the baby."

CHAPTER 15

Laney

19 YEARS OLD - FALL

Morning of the shooting

I'm standing in my little bathroom, the early morning already showing me what a beautiful fall day we'll have ahead. I stare as the timer on my phone counts down the seconds until I can see the results, willing it to move faster.

I'm late. I've never been late before. My period has been like clockwork since I first got it. The thing is, I completely lost track of time coming back to campus and getting back into my college routine. Now I'm sitting here wondering if my life is about to change. My heart races as I think about how cataclysmic this will be if it turns out to have two little lines on the test.

Last night, I was out with Artie and Eugene, grabbing some food down the street. I felt nauseous from the smell wafting out from the kitchen, and it was then Artie's eyes widened, and a scream pulled from him that could have shattered glass.

He put this crazy idea in my head that I could be pregnant, and of course, I couldn't let it go. I barely slept last night, thinking of what this test could say.

Somehow, I waited until this morning to take it. I read online that the morning urine sample is the most concentrated, and I want to know for sure at this point. Plus, these damn tests are expensive. I don't need a false negative and then have to buy a ton more to test every other day. What college student can afford such things? Not me, that's for sure.

If I'm pregnant, I won't be far along. But one thing is for certain: Grant is the father.

A smile spreads across my face just thinking of that scenario. We're young, but something about imagining Grant holding our baby, loving on our baby, makes my heart flutter. Becca was still able to go on to be a doctor after having Olive; I know both our families would support us so we can follow our dreams and raise a baby that is so loved by everyone around.

The timer startles me out of my thoughts, and I quickly stop it from chiming. With shaky fingers, I grab the test and drag it closer to me, keeping it face down the entire time.

My gaze looks up, praying to whomever watches over me to please support me in whatever direction this test takes me.

Taking a deep breath, I bring my gaze back down to the little white stick and flip it over.

The moment I allow my brain to register what it's seeing, my other hand flies to my mouth, and the tears that form are instant.

Holy. Fuck. I'm fucking pregnant!

I can't believe it. Even though I tossed and turned, knowing this could be the case, seeing those two lines makes a hell of a difference. I'm filled with emotions that don't even belong together—happiness, fear, concern, anticipation. I'm overwhelmed by the way my heart has grasped onto these two lines.

I feel love for this little being that can't be more than a little pinprick in size. The way my heart is growing within seconds answers all my questions about how I feel about this.

This is a piece of Grant and me. I'd like to think it's the best parts of us coming together to bring us a child. I feel empowered knowing that I'm growing life, not just anyone's, but a child with Grant. Something about that makes me feel like I can soar.

I stare at the test for a few more minutes, snapping a photo to send to Artie.

The moment I text it to him, I immediately feel the vibration of my cell in my hands. I didn't think he'd be up.

"Hello?" I act completely chill even though I feel my nerves getting the best of me as I pick up this call.

"Don't 'Hello' me, missy! You send me a text like that and think it's chit-chat I'm looking for at this hour? No way, no how!" I hear him yawn even though he's awake enough to chew me out in true Artie fashion.

I start to laugh. "Well, I can't tell Grant through a text, so you're my first one to lean on."

"From the photos you showed me of this Grant and the brief video call I've seen of him, you're lucky to be carrying his child. He's a chiseled god from what I saw."

I hear some rustling, and someone, I assume Eugene, whisper-yells, *"I thought I was your chiseled god, Art."*

Then, I hear Artie respond with, *"You know it."* I roll my eyes and smile because I love them together.

"Yeah, well, he's in South America, and I have to find a way to tell him. If I wait until he returns for the holidays, I'll be a little obvious with the protruding belly." I smile, just envisioning this baby growing inside me in the months to come.

"So, when are you going to tell him?" Artie's energy is palpable, even through the phone.

"I think I'll talk to him later today. We have never kept secrets from one another, and he can sniff one out of me pretty quickly. So, it's best I let this one out of the bag, even though it's pretty early on. I think Becca said the first trimester is the riskiest in miscarriages. But the father of the baby should be told." I straighten my back, determination coursing through my veins.

I wonder how Grant will react. What will he say? Will he be mad?

That last question makes me shake my head even though no one can see me.

Grant won't be mad. Something about this entire situation feels serendipitous. We belong together. We've been playing this little game, sleeping together any chance we're in the same vicinity. The attraction is there, the friendship is there, and the love is never changing; we're meant to be together, and this baby is a symbol of that.

I continue to chat with Artie, making sure he's going to make it to class today. We hang up, and I continue to stare at the test. Then, my gaze moves up to the reflection in the mirror. I'm still standing in my bathroom, apparently frozen in this spot, taking in the events of the last hour and trying to absorb as much of this feeling as I can. I'm excited, and I really can't wait to tell Grant why.

I decide sleep is lost to me now; the few extra hours I'd get if I tried to return to bed are not enough to warrant going back under the covers. I get everything in order and decide to take a stroll outside. The weather is a bit chilly at this early hour, so once I find a light jacket, I go outside and begin to walk around the neighborhood.

I take in the trees and leaves that are starting to change. The fall weather is just right this time of year, before the intense cold chills us to the bone. I bet Grant is enjoying the weather in Chile right now. He's been anticipating this trip for some time, and it seems he'll get to see things during their spring, so the pictures will most definitely be spectacular.

I walk around until I find a bench, watching the sky change colors to welcome a new day with the sun. I take in how beautifully blue the sky looks, a bluebird day, as I used to say as a little girl.

My hand instinctively goes to my flat belly, and I wonder who this little human that's growing inside me will be. Who will they look like? Will this be a little girl to capture Grant's heart and make him succumb to everything she desires? Or will this be a little boy with Grant's cute dimples and a mix of both our eyes? Something about this what-if scenario makes it even more exciting.

I know my parents will love this child with all their hearts. I know Grace, Grant's mom, will be filled with love for this child, much like she was when Olive graced our lives. We have love, and we have support from those around us. That's something I don't take for granted, and I know that this child will never feel unloved.

I look down at my watch and realize I should head home and change before my morning class, the only one I have today. Hopefully, Grant can chat a bit before I get to class, but I know I'll have to video chat with him later to tell him the news. I don't want to feel rushed, and I want him to be able to have the freedom to stay on the phone with me for as long as he wants.

I can feel it; this day is going to be one I'll never forget. I'll hold on to this memory for as long as I'm on this earth, and I know my best friend will be by my side throughout it all.

CHAPTER 16

Laney

PRESENT DAY

For all the years I've held onto that secret, this isn't how I envisioned telling Grant.

That day lives on repeat in my mind, not just the shooting, but the moment I realized I had lost a baby I never really got to celebrate. The fact that I lost a piece of our love cemented it as a horrific day in my heart, coupled with the fact that it was the most traumatizing day of my life. I can still feel the heartbreak that coursed through me when the paramedic noticed the blood on the floor.

At first, I wasn't able to understand what was happening. I was so lost in grief with Artie passing away in my arms that I wasn't registering the magnitude of my own personal loss. When I got to the hospital, it was confirmed that I had lost the baby. Before my family arrived from Nebraska, I was seen by staff at the local hospital near campus. I let the staff know this baby wasn't something I had announced to anyone yet.

My family thought I was there for observation from the shock of what I had endured and witnessed. In reality, the staff wanted to make sure I wasn't heavily bleeding after the miscarriage. They didn't put me on the maternity floor since everyone on that floor was welcoming life while I was mourning it.

In addition to my personal loss of the baby, I was mourning the loss of my dear friend, Artie. My friend who sacrificed his own safety to save me, knowing I was pregnant with Grant's baby. I couldn't handle the depth of my sadness at that point. I retreated into myself and had no idea how to verbalize my emotions.

The only other person who knew about my miscarriage was Evelyn once I moved to the city. My therapy sessions were filled with tears from not only watching my friend die in my arms but the reality that my baby would never take a breath. That took many sessions to process, and it was draining, to say the least.

Much like she was doing months ago during our virtual session, Evelyn has been urging me to tell Grant about the loss. But I honestly never found a good time. When I started to pull myself out of my stupor, I wanted to focus on my future, not my past. I wanted to find meaning in what my life looked like now, not how the impact of that day catapulted me into a different dimension of the life I had envisioned.

Plus, the better I did, the more weight I saw come off Grant's shoulders. My recovery reflected in Grant's demeanor, even if he didn't mean for that to happen. The longer I went without telling him, the more I convinced myself it was better for him to live without this pain I've carried for both of us.

For so long, I tried to find love somewhere else, in someone else's arms, but it never felt right. Then, when Grant and I reconnected intimately in Malibu, I couldn't fight the attraction any longer.

Maybe I was wrong in keeping this to myself, but I

didn't see what Grant would gain from knowing. It's selfish; I know that now. By the look on his face, I can almost say with absolute certainty that I had judged this entire thing incorrectly.

"I'm sorry… what?" he asks, his voice no more than a whisper.

I look down. I can't look at him. I feel the guilt mounting in my chest from how horribly I misjudged this entire situation. I saw everything as my pain and mine alone to bear.

"I was pregnant that day I called you. The day of the shooting." Tears are falling down my cheeks, and I feel like my entire body is going to crumble.

There is a very likely chance we won't recover from this. Forgiveness might not be possible for him and I don't know how I'll cope with that loss on top of everything else my heart has endured.

He's got a look of utter devastation on his face. The weight of the silence between us is consuming me, so I repeat myself in case the words aren't registering for him.

"The day of the shooting, that's why I said I had to talk to you."

He's nodding, absorbing my words, until he finally speaks, "Yeah, I heard that part already. I missed the part about why you didn't tell me this when it happened?" He's calm, but I can feel the tension radiating off his body.

There's barely anyone out right now. The cold streets are quiet, but even if there was a crowd moving along this path we're standing on, I think nothing could take my focus away from the look of utter heartbreak I see on Grant's face.

It feels like we are the only two human beings here, standing in New York, our hearts being ripped out in ways I never thought possible. I thought I had already lived through my hardest day, but it seems this one is a close second, and it's one I could have avoided had I just taken Evelyn's advice and been honest.

"I just didn't know how to handle everything. It's weighed on me this entire time, but I didn't know how to tell you. Each time I opened my mouth to confess, I just felt like the happiness you were feeling at that moment would be tarnished. The more I held off, the longer I was worried you'd be upset with me."

He keeps looking at me, those vibrant aqua eyes dimmed slightly, taking in everything, but also looking at me like he doesn't recognize me at all. He's taking in my demeanor, the way I'm fiddling with my hands, much like my sister Ellie does when she's uncomfortable, yet he doesn't say a word.

The discomfort is growing in me. I don't know what Grant looks like when he's disappointed in me. I've never been the one to hold that type of reaction from him.

He takes another long breath in, letting it out, the tension remaining in his shoulders.

"Let me get this straight: the day you wanted to tell me ended up being the most tragic day you've lived through? A day you lost your friend and our child. *My* child. A child I didn't know about, let alone a child I never got to mourn."

He's speaking, not giving me any room to interject or confirm. At this point, they're statements, as if he's making a mental list of all these pivotal points in my life that intersect with his. Most of all, listing all the ways I've broken his heart with my confession today.

"Add to that, you've been around me for years, in reality, over a decade, not uttering a word. You simply carried this with you and didn't think I deserved to know?" He comes to some sort of realization, and then his face is stone.

"If I hadn't pushed you right now, would you have ever

told me? If I didn't come begging to start a relationship with you, would you have wanted me to know? Did you not think I deserved to know?"

Each question feels like a dagger to the heart.

The problem is, I can't answer that with complete honesty. I don't know why. I was so used to this loss being a part of my past that I never thought sharing it mattered as time kept passing.

My silence is confirmation enough for him. Without words, he moves around me and starts walking in the direction of Ellie's house.

I follow, not uttering a word. Once we reach my sister's place, he takes the steps up two at a time, waiting at the top and using his own key to get into the brownstone.

He hurries upstairs, and I can't help but follow him. We get to my room, and he immediately starts grabbing clothes and shoving them into his bag.

"Grant, what are you doing? Why are you leaving? We need to talk about this."

"So, now you want to talk?" His words echo off the walls. Grant has never directed this tone toward me before, but I can see he's shaking with anger.

I can't help the tears that are falling down my face again, watching someone I love hurt and knowing that I'm the cause of that.

"Laney, I have lived each and every second that I can remember for the two of us. Without knowing, I paved my life to include you. You've always been my center and my light, but right now, I feel like you're my storm. Right now, you are throwing me into a hell I didn't know I belonged in.

"I get it; my reaction feels foreign to you. But please take a moment and realize the weight you just dropped on me. You've gotten ten-plus years to live with this reality. I've had a few minutes. I need to wrap my head around this.

I need to find some space for myself to think this through. I need to process what you've said. I need to understand the reality you just painted for me."

My shoulders fall. I feel defeated. I did what I thought was best for me without really caring about how this might impact him. I made a decision to keep that loss my own, not including him in something he made with me.

I know what he's saying. I've hurt him, and I've never been the one to hold that title. I have always been his biggest cheerleader, and he is mine. But today, I was the bearer of bad news. I allowed my pain to simply be that—mine.

I didn't allow this to be *our* pain, and I get that now. I chose so much of that pain to be seen as only something that affected me and not both of us. In many ways, the effects of the shooting were mine to harbor, but this could have been something we shared together. I could have let him in instead of pushing him out. Maybe if I'd done that from the start we wouldn't have lost so much time together. I see that now.

I nod, unable to form words. It's at that moment I realize my life is nothing without Grant by my side. He wanted to start something more with me less than an hour ago, and what I did may have wrecked that in a way I can never mend. He wanted tomorrow, and I never gave him yesterday.

He pauses his packing and looks up at me. It's hard to see the utter devastation on his face.

His shoulders sag and he starts to speak, "You're my compass, Laney. You're the direction I'm always running toward. Don't you get that? In your little secret, not only do I realize that I was not a priority for you to tell, but I'm someone you *chose* to keep in the dark. You should've *wanted* to share this with me. I would've held your pain with mine.

I would have nurtured the seed of healing. Instead, you kept it all to yourself."

He returns to shoving things into his duffle bag, and something about it feels so final.

"I love you," that's all I can get out before I feel a sob break free.

He looks up at me, once again pausing his packing.

"I love you, too. I think you need to figure out if my love is enough for you. I know yours has always been enough for me. You've always been enough for me—even when you, yourself, didn't feel whole."

He waits an extra moment, then he moves past me and walks out of my room.

He needs to grieve. Not only that, he has to find a way to see me and know that I want to walk alongside him in this lifetime. He's my everything, but with my actions, I have shown him the opposite.

After everything I've been through in this life, you'd think the pain of watching my best friend leave wouldn't hurt as much as the loss of life. But it guts me. Because I know it's *my* actions that have caused this divide tonight. The pain of that day nearly crippled me eleven years ago, but I had Grant there to help build me back up. A slow, tortuous build that he took on, and he had the patience to do so. But I didn't give him the chance to know the details of why I felt so broken inside.

For so long, I took on the narrative that he had no idea what this kind of hurt felt like. But I didn't take a moment to reflect on the fact that I didn't give him the opportunity to feel this pain.

CHAPTER 17
Grant

Walking out of Laney's room, I pull out my phone and order a ride. I don't go through the house and say my good-byes. I have a feeling I'm shit company right now, and I honestly feel so blindsided that I just need to get away. The moment I step through that front door, I'm met with the frigid winter cold. Each step away from her feels like the ice is seeping deeper into my heart.

I didn't want to walk away, but I also couldn't take a full breath while I was standing so close to her. The one person who gave my body life turned out to be the one to pull the life out of me with one confession.

I knew Laney was holding onto something; I knew there was something in her that needed to be let out. I never imagined this was what she had to tell me, though. I never thought this was the crater that had lodged itself between us, keeping the two of us from taking the next step. I was completely thrown by her confession, and I need time to break down what all this means. I have never felt this way toward the person I called my closest friend.

Laney has held my heart since the moment I could form

memories. I'm not mad that she had to process the miscarriage. I'm not upset she had to come to terms with what she witnessed that day, watching her friend die in her arms.

What guts me is all the time since then. She could have said something. I can't even say I knew there was something this big in her heart. How could I have known how she was going to cope with a fucking mass shooting? I thought she was still processing the attack all that time. My therapist always said that each victim who survives such a trauma deals with it differently. It was my job to give her space, to let her decide the pace at which she wanted to take each step forward.

I'd like to think I did that for her. I gave her so much fucking breathing room, and she couldn't even, not once, give me a morsel of the reality she was living with. It wasn't just a piece of her that was lost that day. It was a piece of me, too. That's the part that hurts most. I felt like I was an outsider looking in, trying to understand my best friend as she absorbed the shock of what occurred to her in that school. Top that with the fact that my love for her runs deep, and I made it my mission to help her through the trauma.

I saw her pain as mine, but not literally. I didn't even think for one second that she was pregnant. All I remember from my call with her that morning was the fact that I wanted to tell her I wanted forever with her beyond our friends-with-benefits relationship that was going on at that time. I wanted to explore being together as a couple. My thoughts were singular. I never thought what she might want to talk to me about was a pregnancy.

I look over toward my sister's place, knowing all I would have to do is walk over there and tell her everything. Becca could sit me down and give me her two cents on what she thinks of all this. I could figure my shit out and hopefully go straight back to Laney, and we could move forward.

But that's the thing: I don't want to go back that quickly. She needed eleven years to process how to tell me, I can take a fucking minute.

Does this change my love for Laney? No, I still love her. I love her to the point I'd lay myself on the line to see her happiness shine. Loving her was a balm to my heart, but right now loving her feels like a vice *around* my heart. It feels like it's suffocating me because I'm so fucking pissed yet so damn hung up on her, that I feel conflicted on how to move from this precipice I'm currently at.

The thing that stings lies in the fact that she disregarded my feelings in favor of her own. She put her own thoughts first. She didn't put my needs, my emotional well-being, anywhere in her grief. I didn't need her to put me first, especially during one of the hardest times of her life. But it feels like I was literally last. I fucking gave her all the emotional breathing room possible, and she couldn't give me just a bit of this pain she carried?

People don't put enough weight on the need to feel pain when that discomfort is warranted. I was raised by a mother that taught me that pain is part of life. It's something we have no control over, yet it's something that allows for growth and perspective.

Losing a child, even if she lost that baby at an early stage of pregnancy, still is a loss. Maybe, even knowing about that child, wouldn't change where Laney and I are today, but it would have allowed me time for reflection and growth. Laney made a choice for both of us and for that, I'm resentful. I can't help feeling this way and I'm allowing myself this space to feel everything that's bubbling up with this news.

Making my way to the train, I'm lost in thought. My

emotions are everywhere and what this will look like moving forward with Laney. Once I get settled in my seat, I close my eyes, and I see those emerald eyes staring back at me. The problem is, my emotions carry me in completely opposite directions: I feel my heart ache to hold her again, yet I feel a twinge of pain as I think about this huge weight she's carried while I lived life unaware.

She needed time, I get that. She needed to process, understandably so. But so many questions hit me at once: Why not share the loss of *our* child with me? Why act as if this was her burden, her pain, to carry alone? When did I ever give her the impression that I wasn't part of her team?

Those questions are the foundation of why I had to leave. How do I move forward with trust being at our center when she couldn't even trust me with such a huge piece of her grief?

For all these years, I've grieved the life Laney could have had if she hadn't been at that school at that time. In the beginning, I constantly went through the what-ifs of Laney's pain, but at the core of that pain, I imagined her loss was that of her friend.

Now, I'm grasping to process the fact that the shooting signified more than just loss of life for those students. It signified more than the loss of future happiness for those who lived through it and grieved their friends and loved ones. I'm now having to come to terms with the fact that I not only lost a part of Laney that day, I lost a part of *us*.

So many different feelings pass through my mind, and they're on constant replay. I continue to lay my head back on the headrest and keep my eyes closed. This drive will give me the time to sit with this information and figure out how I move forward.

The moment I feel the train slow down, I open my eyes and realize I had, indeed, fallen asleep. The news Laney shared drained me, and I must have needed that time to rest my mind.

Upon arriving in town, I make my way to the person I find comfort with. I look up to see my mom's door open, and her head pops out. I see a smile spread across her face, and it feels a lot like Becca's welcoming expression. They look a lot alike, and it feels like coming home no matter what age I am.

I make my way up the pathway to her door, and the moment I reach her, I throw my bag down and pull my mother into my arms. When I embrace her, my mom must sense I'm in pain and holds me in her arms, even though I tower over her.

We pull apart, and as soon as she sees my expression, I think a part of her breaks a bit. Without asking anything, she turns and opens the door a little more, welcoming me in without asking any questions or requesting clarification.

The house is quiet, and, as if she can read my mind, my mother says, "Rick and Olive went to grab some food from the store. I think Shane is on his way too, trying to outrun the storm that's headed this way."

I nod, the frog lodged in my throat making it hard to form words right now.

I place my bag in the foyer and follow my mom into the kitchen. Even though I didn't grow up in this house, no matter where my mom goes, I feel like I belong there. She has this presence, this welcoming heart, that wraps me up when I feel like I'm plummeting.

"Why don't I make us some tea, and then we can sit down, and you can tell me what's bothering you." It's not a question, but a statement. I nod again, my words still not at the forefront of my lips.

My mom busies herself, and soon she's at the small kitchen table, looking at me, and it feels like all my secrets are safe with this woman. Being raised solely by her, I feel a bond with my mother that is exponentially different from Becca's experience, yet not in any way better. We just formed a different relationship.

Becca allowed my mother to lean on her while she mourned the death of our father, while I got to be a kid my entire life without feeling the weight of my father's loss. Sure, he wasn't around, but he also wasn't someone I ever got to know. Because of that, he wasn't ever someone that I missed. His absence was felt by my mother and sister, but for me, life carried on and never felt like it was lacking anything. And that's thanks to my mom. She was always a pillar of strength in a way that helped me throughout all stages of my life. So, I only see her as a stable force and, right now, I need to lean on her more than ever.

I see the worry lines etched across my mom's face, but, much like me, she gives me the space to figure out my thoughts before I say them. I've never been a reactionary person. I pride myself in the ability to hold in my initial reaction and allow myself the room to process what's happening around me. Earlier, I wanted to explode and tell Laney how selfish she was at that moment, but I held back. I kept my hurtful words to myself and thought through what I should say. I've found that by keeping my reactions minimal, I can keep from causing more pain. I learned that from my mom.

"Laney, um, she, she—" I pinch the bridge of my nose, the headache I felt in the back of my head when the confession first came out starting to rear its ugly head. I take a calming breath in, and when I let it out, I word-vomit everything, "She was pregnant that day of the shooting. She was pregnant with my child… our child. And she didn't tell me. She didn't ever mention she was pregnant prior, nor did she tell me she lost the baby that day the shooting occurred."

It feels just as painful saying it as it did hearing it from Laney hours ago. I feel my chest tighten, and the tears pool in my eyes. I don't even try to hide it, and I allow the tears to fall. I'm heartbroken. Sure, the pain stems from the life lost, but most of all, the pain resides deep inside because I realize I wasn't a priority for Laney, even once she'd started to heal.

I put her first; I made sure she felt seen and heard, but her actions proved in an instant that my feelings came last. Not even that they came second, but that I was not at all at the forefront of her mind as over a decade passed from the moment she found out about the life we made to the moment she told me that precious life was lost.

"I feel betrayed by the only person I've ever fully loved. Laney is my everything, and, in an instant, she showed me I'm nothing. That's how this feels, at least. It truly feels like a betrayal.

"And it's hard for me to accept that I've been over here, trying to mend this bridge for her, a bridge I thought I had nothing to do with. Except I come to find out that it has a big something to do with me. Like I was in an uphill battle that I didn't realize I would never climb over."

I'm playing with a part of the wood on the table that seems to have a bit of an indent, avoiding my mother's gaze. I finally look up to see my mother's expression mimics mine. It's pained, but she's also crying with me.

She continues to sit with me, our tears the only expression between us, until she finally says something in return, "I have gone a long time in my life knowing what loss feels like. A loss of a spouse. A loss of a child."

With that last confession, my mouth drops. This is news to me.

At my shocked expression, my mom pats my hand and continues, "I know. It's not something I've ever confessed to you or your sister."

She takes a sip of her tea and sets it down, as if she's choosing her words carefully. "I remember the look of devastation when I told your father. As if I could feel his heart break at the news that we were no longer expecting. Your father was many things, but he was not great at coping with difficult things like that. The moment the words were out of my mouth, I felt like I was caring for his needs and his emotions, instead of comforting myself. He wasn't selfish, but he also felt lost in many ways and all I wanted to do was assure him we would be okay. I wanted him to know that I would be alright afterwards.

"I can only imagine how this felt for Laney. A lost pregnancy is already devastating. Add to that, a catastrophic shooting, in which one of her friends dies in her arms—it's a lot on a person's heart." She brings her eyes to meet mine. "I've known Laney almost the entirety of her life and the person she has grown to be is a lover and protector. She dealt with that day the best way she could and she most likely wanted to shield herself from having to care for your needs on top of her own.

"I have no doubt Laney wanted to tell you about the pregnancy. But I bet time awarded her some strength to start finding a way to live this life for herself in a way she could control, after a tragedy that took a lot of power from her."

"But to wait all this time and then tell me? It feels like I was shielded from something so impactful. I could have helped her. I could have been there for her more." I run my fingers through my hair, frustration coating my words.

My mom chuckles, but there's no humor in it. "Aside from going back in time and stopping that awful day from happening, there was nothing you could do to right this wrong that occurred. And don't forget, Grant, loss, no matter when you hear about it, is still loss. Laney went through something horrific. No matter how you slice it, she's experienced something most of us hope to never witness. She sat in that room, knowing her classmates were being killed, knowing one of those was her friend, who chose to save her instead of himself. She found a way to move forward the best way she knew how. Add in the fact that she had life growing inside her, something she had just discovered, only to have that ripped away from her. I just... my heart hurts for her."

I nod, because I agree. The loss Laney experienced was too great for anyone to bear.

"I don't say that to diminish your pain. I really don't, sweetie. But it's hard for me to look at this one-sidedly. I see both of your pains, and I feel them in such different ways. I can't imagine the shock you felt at her confession. I bet it was a slap to the face in many ways, especially coming from someone as close as Laney." My mother takes a breath to gather her thoughts before continuing.

"But then my heart hurts knowing that she felt so alone with the pain only a mother can feel. The hormones had been coursing through her body, and she felt like her only way to cope with it was to carry that with her, alone, without confiding even in the one person she loves most—you."

That's the thing, it's not that I'm angry to the point I won't speak to her again. A part of me automatically forgave Laney the moment she let out this secret she held so close to her chest for so long. That stems from the fact that I truly love her, and my whole being hurt knowing she was in pain. But the other part is hung up on the fact that she hasn't felt comfortable telling me about this huge part of herself and of us. And I wonder if she ever would have said anything had I not broached the subject of wanting more with her.

My mom sits with me, allowing me space and freedom to feel my emotions without judgment. She simply lets us feel, which is more than I can ask for. In a world full of so much stimulation, sometimes sitting with our emotions is the most important thing we can do to process how we feel.

"I don't know how to look at her and not think that she didn't see me as someone she could trust enough to tell. She didn't feel like I was a safe place for her when that's all she is for me."

My mind is going in circles, constantly going back to that thought: while I did what I could to show her where she stood in my life, I feel like I wasn't thought about at all in her decisions or her processing of the miscarriage.

"Have you considered that maybe you were her only focus when it came to the baby and the loss it brought to her life, and ultimately yours?" my mom throws that question out there, and I'm immediately confused.

"How so?" I ask because my mind is exhausted trying to figure out the intricacies of the human brain.

"Grant, you start, and Laney ends. You've always been that way, even when you two were too tiny to fully form sentences. You molded into this unit, and I never saw a more perfect soulmate for someone. Even Shane's bond with your sister, whose relationship sometimes feels Heaven-sent, doesn't compare." My mother rolls her eyes because she was never a huge fan of my sister's ex-husband, Hudson. The day they got divorced, it was like I saw my mother take a full breath of air again. "You and Laney fit together effortlessly. You were never careless with one another. Each decision always led to making the other happy.

"Never did I see you treat her recklessly, even with all the girlfriends you had. In return, she never made you feel less than when she was in different relationships throughout the years. No matter what the two of you have been through, never has there been animosity or bickering. It's always been a level of respect for the friendship and, ultimately, the relationship you two have worked so hard to maintain." The way my mother is speaking, it feels like all those times I thought we were hiding our feelings, my mother saw right through it.

"Grant, have you pondered the idea that her omission wasn't a sign of disrespect but one to hopefully help you feel like life continued beautifully? Laney's life changed that day years ago, but have you ever considered she didn't want it to mute yours? She sacrificed her own pain in order for you to feel like life didn't rob you of something special as it had hers.

"She did something that may seem selfish in your eyes, or maybe feels like she lacked love in doing so toward you, but in reality, I think Laney came from a place of conservation for you. She made this unilateral decision to rid you of the possibility of hating that day more than you already did. Add to it, she had to put her needs first, as hard as that might be to hear."

My mom gives me a minute to process her words then continues,"I won't sit here and act like I know Laney better than you, but I will say I know her well. I saw the way she looked at you. I saw the love she held in her gaze whenever her eyes darted in your direction. She's never lacked love for you. And I can't picture her doing this without putting love first. The only thing is, her love is being expressed differently than you would have done it. Which is understandably hurtful for you. But it doesn't make it ultimately wrong. Does that make any sense?"

I take in everything she's said and try to see this from a different point of view. My thoughts start to spin with these new possibilities.

"Also, Grant, I know you and Laney thought you were all discreet, but pretty much everyone knew what you two were up to."

My mom pats my hand that's clenching the mug in front of me. My mouth drops open, and I almost get a word out when she continues.

"Oh, sweetheart, you and your sister think I'm not observant, but I am. I knew you were more than friends with Laney quite some time ago. I just kept my mouth shut because I didn't want to freak you out. I know what love looks like. I saw it every day in the eyes of your father until the day he died. I saw it in Shane when he was young, and I see it today when he looks at your sister.

"I'm lucky enough to get to see it directed at me from Rick now. I see love, Grant. A lack of love isn't the problem between you and Laney. She has always loved you. Her love is what kept her from divulging this secret. She loves you so much that she didn't want you to hurt even more."

"But her actions are currently hurting me now." I leave it at that, feeling more like a child than the thirty-year-old man I am.

"Yeah, I know. It stings. It will sting. And maybe every time you think back on that day, a part of your heart will be permanently hurt, knowing that more was lost than you were ever given the privilege of knowing back then. But with pain comes growth.

"You know this. I've said this to you before when talking about how I coped with your father's death. I'm not disregarding your feelings or the gravity of this lost life. I promise I've seen more death in my career as a nurse than I would ever wish upon anyone. I do have clarity with the pain, though. Love shines through during the darkest of times."

"Yes, but I put so many of my needs aside to make sure she was okay. She ignored my needs. She made a huge assumption about what was best for me, and it feels like she chose this because it was easier for her."

My mom looks around her kitchen, biting into her lower lip, pensive as always.

"Grant, I hate to say this and sound insensitive, but I'm going to anyway: miscarriage is such a personal thing. Usually, it's not about what other people need. It's just about what the person who literally lost the child is feeling. It's perceived as selfish, but in all honesty, it's self-preserving in so many ways. Laney needed to have some control in her life when everything else was chaos."

I take in what my mom just said, and I'm starting to understand things a little more clearly when she puts it that way.

"When Laney was in that hospital in Wyoming, you brought to her life a touch of beauty when things were ugly everywhere else. She needed love. She needed comfort. She needed care. And you didn't hesitate. Any chance you got, you were there for her. Even if you couldn't physically be there, you made sure she had what she needed to put one foot in front of the other. That's love, Grant. But what she did to you is love, too. It's painful, but love is agonizing sometimes. That's the other side of love, sweetie."

It's so true. Love is messy, something the Hollywood movies don't always depict. In the era of social media, we're constantly fed this version of love that's flawless. But love is raw, and it's full of fissures. Small cracks that can lead to a split if you're not careful. It's full of moments where you're standing at a crossroads, and the only person that can navigate the path is you.

Laney was standing at that crossroads, and I see now that she was making the best decision she could to ensure she would make it out of that pit of darkness whole again.

My eyes feel heavy and I'm tired of crying.

"I appreciate you listening to me. I can always count on you to hear problems with love. I appreciate you never holding judgment." I take a breath, then add, "And I'm sorry you went through that. I'm sorry you felt you couldn't share that with us."

My mom smiles, standing from her seat and wrapping her arms around me she whispers, "I appreciate that. I really do, but a few years later, I was given this beautiful gift of a boy, who shines bright each time he smiles at me."

I give a slight nod, that lump in my throat getting bigger with her confession.

"Also, Grant, my role isn't to judge. It's to serve as your guidance. My job is to be the person to introduce you to love in the purest form; that's a mother. I'm not your judge and jury. I will always be your mother. One that cares deeply for both my kids in a way that takes over my mind daily."

She moves to cup my cheeks, her love a warmth I feel deep into my soul.

"One day, Grant, you'll be gifted a child. One day, you'll get to hold that child in your arms, and you, too, will be at a crossroads. You'll be standing, wondering how to move left or right. And all you have to help decide which way to go are your instincts. There's never going to be a right path versus the wrong one. It's about the best path for that situation.

"Remember that when you feel yourself leaning toward resentment and anger with Laney. She was at that fork in the road, and she chose what she felt was best for her and, ultimately, what was best for you in her mind. It doesn't feel that way right now, but it's what the love she felt for you pushed her to do. She did it for you both, even if it feels like it was a self-centered decision. You were always on her mind. That I can guarantee."

She wipes the lone tear that escapes my eye, and I lean into her hand. I kiss the inside of her palm. I smile up at her, and it feels like things are starting to slot into place. I I think I might be ready to start moving things in the right direction.

I hear a commotion at the front door, and the door opens. Life is breathed into the house once again, with Olive, Rick, and Shane walking inside. My mom quickly wipes under her eyes and winks at me. I know that everything we discussed, my mom will keep to herself. She's a vault when she needs to be, and I feel like a heavy part of what I carried on my back has been let go.

"Grace, we stocked up for the storm of the century. Got all the essentials—hot chocolate, marshmallows, Nutella, bread, eggs, flour, and anything else that we can use to whip up something on a whim."

My mom chuckles. Rick has the biggest sweet tooth, so it's no surprise he went for all the high-carbohydrate snacks to keep him entertained during this upcoming storm.

"Hey, Nana. Thanks for letting me stay here while I wait this storm out. It's sort of scary to be in that apartment with the power flickering. Last time, I slept with a bat next to my bed."

"Olive, I've seen you try to hit a ball that one time we played softball with the twins. I wouldn't say that a bat would have helped you in an emergency." That's Shane, and I hear my niece gasp at her father's words.

"Excuse me, I'm very good under pressure, I'll have you know." She's huffing away into the kitchen and startles when she sees me sitting at the table upon her entrance.

"Hey, Liv. How are you?" I stand up and take Olive into my arms.

My niece is seven years younger than me, and we have more of a sibling relationship than an uncle and niece dynamic. I mean, she's closer in age to me than my own sister is, so there's that.

"Hey, Uncle G. I wasn't expecting you." She isn't as short as her mother, but she's still smaller than me. She stands up on her tippy-toes and kisses my cheek. I pull the bags of groceries out of her arms and bring them to the counter. Rick walks in with a few more bags, Shane trailing behind him with more.

"Geez, did you buy the entire store?" I chuckle. I've been traveling so much that I haven't been home on the East Coast for some time to weather a storm in recent years.

"Well, you know I like to be prepared." Rick pats his belly, and I see my mom rolling her eyes behind him. This man is all love. He has embraced all of us as his own.

"I think you may have overdone it with the random snacks, but I think with an extra mouth to feed, we'll need some more food anyway. Grant, grab a bag, let's get this stuff put away."

I move toward Shane and give him a hug. I will admit the moment I heard my sister mention his name, a warm welcome was the furthest thing I was planning for him. But Shane, Olive's dad, was wronged in a way I know he will never recover from.

He did break up with my sister before he ever knew she was pregnant and went twenty-five years before discovering he had a daughter with Becca. I can see each time he looks over at my niece, a part of him hurts knowing he lost all those years with her. Although, I'll give him credit, he's showing up now, and I know he's here to stay.

Once we get everything put away, we all head upstairs to get ourselves comfortable before we play our first round of Rummikub. This game can get vicious, especially if Becca's involved. Luckily, the group that's here tonight won't be screaming nastiness from across the table. My sister isn't competitive in most things, except for this game. She's full of comebacks and loves to push everyone's buttons. A tame game of Rummikub works fine for me after the long-ass day I've had.

Once I'm showered, and in some comfortable flannel pants and a warm long-sleeved pajama top, I pull out my phone, turning it on after I shut it off when I started the drive up to my mom's earlier today.

Multiple messages appear, some from Ellie, some from Becca, and one from Laney. I click on Laney's first before filtering the others.

BEAN

I'm sorry for only thinking of my own feelings years ago. I promise it didn't come from a place of malice. I really didn't want to hurt you more, and I needed to feel some sense of control with everything that had happened. I love you, Grant. Please forgive me.

My mom was right. I think I still need some time to process it, but I know that my heart still belongs to her.

I look over the rest of the texts, making sure nothing urgent is happening.

BECCA

Is everything okay with you and Laney? She's been extra quiet this afternoon in her room. Ellie reached out earlier, asking if I knew what had happened. Are you okay?

Then, I find a text from Ellie expressing similar sentiments.

ELLIE

Is everything alright, Grant? You seem to have left suddenly, and Laney has been distant all afternoon. Please let me know if something happened so I can make sure she's okay.

I decide to respond solely to Laney.

I love you, Laney. I just need some space. I came up to my mom's and will weather the storm here. I'll be in touch. Also, my sister and yours are worried about you. Maybe let them know you're okay? I don't want to overstep and tell them something you're not ready to. Please be safe in this weather. I think the city is going to get hit hard too.

Laney loved the comment, but I don't see the three dots that mean she's typing on the screen. I wait an extra moment to see if something pops up, but nothing comes through.

I take the time to respond similarly to both my sister and Ellie, explaining that I needed some space and to ask Laney what's going on. I feel like it's cryptic, but also, I really don't want to tell them something Laney's not ready to divulge. It's then I really take in how private this is.

I allow my mother's words to wash over me again, and focus on the fact that Laney's actions came from a place of love. I'm starting to accept that, but I still can't help the sting that overcomes me when I think about how long Laney took to divulge this important piece of information.

CHAPTER 18

Laney

I open my eyes, and it feels like they're lined with sandpaper. The moment Grant left my room yesterday, I felt a part of me leave with him. I just sat here, replaying our conversation—my revelation really—unable to move. I kept staring at the door he walked through, hoping he would change his mind and walk back to me, embracing me and holding me like he's done so many times before. But the longer I waited, the more my heart fell into the pit of my stomach.

I barely slept last night. My mind wouldn't shut off, and I felt like my entire world shattered in a matter of minutes. I saw the pain I had caused in Grant's expression, and I've never seen him so hurt before. The worst part was I was at the helm of that pain.

I wanted to run after him, but I know that he needs to process the information I shared. I realize my omission is seen as selfish through his eyes. No matter the trauma I suffered, there was nothing to gain by not telling Grant sooner. He was right to be mad. If the tables were turned, I know I would be livid with him.

I walk into my bathroom and brush my teeth. I inspect myself in my reflection, realizing my face is etched with exhaustion. I feel defeated. I haven't felt like this in some time, and I can't help but feel my anxiety grow, wondering where we'll go from here.

My emotions are everywhere, and feel overwhelmed with the thought that nothing will ever be the same between us. I hope I didn't destroy years of friendship, the most important relationship with a non-relative that I have ever had; the possibility of never coming back from this makes my stomach roil.

I feel the tears falling down my cheeks again as I walk out of the bathroom. The fact that Grant needs space isn't surprising, but knowing it's space from me feels crippling. He's the person who centers me, and without us being in a good place, I feel lost.

I pull myself together in the best way I can and head downstairs. The storm hit the city in the middle of the night, but it has veered a bit, and it wasn't as bad as it was expected to be when it was first announced. Upstate New York got hit a little more harshly, so I hope everyone at Grace's house was prepared to lose power this morning and they have enough snacks. I have nowhere to be today, so I'll likely be indoors and away from the snow that's falling outside.

The house is quiet with everyone back to their routines. Hopefully, the weather wasn't too bad getting out the door this morning. Ellie is always excited for the new year with her students. The way she embraces her career is admirable. I don't know how she juggles all that energy the kindergarteners have to run around her room all day, just to continue the workload with her own kids here at home.

I pour myself a cup of coffee, the smell wafting up my nose and causing my stomach to roll. I leave my mug behind, the craving for the caffeinated beverage taking a backseat now, and head to the fridge instead. I see some extra cut-up fruit Ellie likely made for the kids' lunches, and I scoop some of that into a bowl.

Making my way to the couch, where I hope to drown my aching heart in some documentary, I sit down and let myself rest. My body is exhausted after the long night of tossing and turning, along with this emotional rollercoaster I've been riding since confessing everything to Grant yesterday.

Although I'm relieved he now knows, I feel uneasy about where we left things. I reach for my phone, but the moment I stare at his number, I toss the phone to the side. I need to give him what he asked for—space. I need him to process what happened, and hopefully, we can connect soon and figure out how to move forward from this heartbreak.

I flip through the different options on the streaming services, finding nothing to grab my attention. So I decide to grab my e-reader and read one of my steamy books. I find it in the foyer, in my purse that's hanging by the door, and make my way back to the couch. I look outside, where the snow looks like a holiday movie.

Usually, I'd find days like today soothing and relaxing. Unfortunately, I'm on edge with everything that's happened, so I can't concentrate on the book I'm trying to read. I feel the vibration of my phone for an incoming text and nearly leap to get it, hoping it's from Grant. I'm soon disappointed.

ELLIE

Hey, Laney. I hope you're ok. You didn't come down for dinner last night, and I barely saw you at all. I'm here if you need me.

Thanks, El. I'll chat with you tonight. Still home and attempting to read. I have no classes to teach today. Love you. XOXO

ELLIE

I'll see you after school today. Love you. XO

I toss the phone aside again and try to get into the book in front of me, with no luck. The words are meshing together, and the exhaustion is catching up to me from lack of sleep. I feel my eyes droop, and soon, I succumb to the sleep my body needs.

Hours later, I'm in the kitchen, trying to figure out what I can make with whatever's in the fridge. My sister is always cooking; maybe I can jumpstart things to make her evening a little lighter. I have to keep my mind busy while I'm fighting the urge to call Grant as he continues to stay silent on his end. The text he sent last night was the last one, and I was hoping by now he'd have sent something else.

I'm pulling veggies out of the fridge when I hear the front door open and close, the rowdy voices of my nieces coming through. Their excitement is palpable after being out all day.

Once their stuff is deposited on the hooks, they make their way over to me, both giving hugs and telling me how great their days were.

Mia, Ellie's youngest, tells me all about the book she chose at the library for independent reading. She's going into detail about this alien that attacks Earth, only to find out he's not alone.

"So then, Auntie Lane, he goes to the barn, and what does he find?" Her eyes get big, waiting for me to guess.

"No clue. What?" I act as if I'm at the edge of my seat.

"There are aliens coming out of the hay bales. Can you believe that?" Her hands go up into the air, like she's just as dumbfounded about it now as she was when she first read the book.

Mia is a bookworm. She loves to collect information from any source possible. She's also very much into medicine and could sit with Becca for hours listening to stories from the hospital. Not sure what direction this girl will go in the future, but I'm excited to see her flourish no matter where she ends up.

Hannah comes in soon after the alien discussion has ended, taking me in. She's the little nurturer, and she doesn't say anything, embracing me with enough love in her arms. For that brief moment, I feel like all my problems will go away as long as I have their love surrounding me.

"Hi, Auntie Lane. How was your day? Did you have class?" Already at the age of nine, she's full of compassion for others. She's always asking about everyone's day, even inquiring about things like she's an adult coming home from work. It's cute to see in a kid.

"No class today, so I just read a little of my book."

"Ooohhh, what book, Auntie Lane?" Mia asks. Unfortunately, the books I read aren't appropriate for her eyes, hence the e-reader.

"Umm, not the type of books that have me on the edge of my seat like the aliens you're reading about. Where's your mom?" I look up, trying to change the subject because I don't need a seven-year-old to come snooping into my reading preferences.

"Yeah, I pick good books," Mia says proudly. She's moving toward the pantry, probably in hopes of finding a snack before dinner.

"Mom is taking off all her layers of clothes." Hannah

chuckles. My sister is not a fan of the cold, and she must have donned a ton of layers to get through today's weather.

Soon enough, Ellie is walking into the kitchen, her smile growing when she sees me standing here.

"Hey. I thought I'd help with dinner." My sister takes me in as I try to look the part of someone who hasn't felt heartbroken for the last twenty-four hours.

My sister looks around, noting all the vegetables lying across the counter.

"Hey girls, why don't you go and wash up now and then come down to set the table?"

"Okay, Mom," the girls say together, then yell out, "Jinx! You owe me a Coke!" Once again, saying it in tandem. They both laugh and head upstairs.

Once they're out of earshot, my sister turns her attention to me again, and I can feel the intensity of her glare.

"What happened, Laney? You had me worried sick," she scolds, the mom side of her taking full charge right now.

I let out a breath, exhausted by this already, and I haven't even said anything. "Grant and I got into a bit of a disagreement, and I'm just processing it."

"That's not like you two. What happened? Does he have a new girlfriend or something?"

Just the thought of Grant with someone else feels like a knife to the chest. I guess I want this relationship to move forward more than I realized. Nothing like losing someone to make you appreciate what you had. I feel like I need him with me in every way now that I've told him about the miscarriage.

"No, not a girlfriend thing. Honestly, I'm not ready to talk about it just yet. Is that okay? I don't want to leave you in the dark, but I do want to talk to Grant first. Then, once I'm comfortable, I'll sit you down and explain. Is that alright?"

My sister worries her lip, likely wanting to push me a bit more.

"As long as you're okay, that's all that matters. I'm here if you need to talk, alright? You're not alone in whatever you're going through."

That's the thing about the people who surround me; I feel their love constantly. Even with the trauma I suffered, I never felt alone. Did I feel like I had no control over my life? Definitely. But alone was never something I felt in all the moments following the shooting. I wanted space, and my loved ones kept their distance to a degree, but they ultimately made it known that no matter what, I wasn't facing a future by myself. They nurtured me and loved me through all the hardships, and I never took it for granted.

Suffering through an event like I had, I was never alone when everything settled down. It dawned on me early on that I am blessed by the people I have surrounding me. I'm well aware that many who've witnessed what I did lacked the same love I received. Not everyone felt themselves surrounded by care and support after what happened that day at the university.

I heard that many moved toward an outlet that didn't provide love, and it pushed them over the edge. I know some can turn to unhealthy habits to ease the darkness. Sadly, it just pushes them further into the depths of depression.

My sister, my parents, and my extended family in Becca and Grant have all given me the space, but are only ever a phone call away, so I never saw myself spiraling. We all got counseling, myself, for the pain I witnessed, but for them, to figure out how to help me handle my trauma.

I smile at my sister, feeling her love in this moment yet again.

"Of course, I'll come to you. And nothing I'm dealing

with feels overwhelming to the point where I can't handle it. I promise if that changes, you'll be my first call."

"You mean, your first call after Grant?" She winks. There's no malice in her words. It's true, Grant is the first person I call for anything. I just hope that in light of recent events, he'll still pick up.

CHAPTER 19

Laney

I can easily say today has been the best I've felt since Grant left the city. He may have taken my heart with him, but today is the first time I can say I feel like myself again. Last night, I crashed on my bed when I got home. The lack of sleep finally caught up to me.

My days have been long since Grant left. I'm used to him being away from me for extended periods; however, we're never on this type of break from one another. We always talk every day in some form no matter where he is. I feel lost without him, and I have no clue what comes next for us.

I knew when he found out about the baby that he'd be mad, but the extent of it was always what I wasn't sure about. I knew deep down that the damage was getting worse the longer I waited to tell him.

That fear is something that kept me from telling him as each day, each month, and then each year passed by. That might be why I always hesitated to tell him before. I guess my concern was warranted. I don't blame him for being upset, even disappointed, but I don't know if I really comprehended how difficult his cold shoulder would feel directed toward me.

I'm in the kitchen getting ready for the day when my sister and the kids come rushing in. The two younger ones are trying to reach the bagels on the top shelf of the pantry while Colton is trying to find every snack possible to carry him through basketball practice.

"Hey. You look so much better." My sister is forever assessing my health, so I'm glad I pass the Ellie test.

She's looking well herself now that she seems to have found a man to keep her busy. My sister has been through so much that I'm glad she finally has someone that makes her smile again.

It's slightly ironic that just when she and Becca have finally found their footing, I'm feeling more out of control with my personal life. I've always felt like no matter what I've been through, I had Grant to hold me up. Now I feel like I'm trying to pull my head above water while he's been away and upset at me.

Ellie pulls me out of my thoughts as I continuously stir my tea, looking out the kitchen window at the sun trying to win the battle over the clouds.

"Any word from Grant?" My sister still doesn't know the details, but I did confide in her that we got in a fight regarding some things I kept from him years ago, and he was taking some time to himself.

I shake my head. "He hasn't called, nor do I know when he'll be back. We've texted a bit, but it just feels strained when we do."

I can't help but hold pain in my voice when describing how I'm feeling about the entire situation. I take a sip of tea and feel the warmth pass through me like a warm hug.

"Give it time, Lane. He loves you. He'll be back," my

sister says this, but little does she comprehend how deep my love for Grant goes.

I've loved Grant for as long as I can remember. Now that he knows about the pregnancy, I feel like he's seeing me, all of me, for the first time since the shooting, and he's disappointed in who stands in front of him.

I nod toward my sister, and she's quickly pulled from this moment and begins getting things in order to get the kids ready and out the door.

Mornings in this house are hectic, much like my mornings were when I was living with Becca. I watch as Ellie and the kids move quickly through the kitchen, making breakfast and grabbing lunches in order to get themselves to school.

Colton stays back a few minutes, even though he's getting a ride from his mom to avoid the cold weather. Ellie and the girls are running up and down the stairs, claiming they left things upstairs.

"Auntie Lane, everything okay?" my nephew inquires as I continue to stand in the kitchen, my movements minimal as the rest of them are scurrying about.

Colton has always been a little more attentive than a usual teen. He's constantly checking in on me, and it doesn't feel like it comes from a place of pity. He simply cares, which is rare for a teenager. I can't help but think of his dad when this side of him comes out.

Beau was a lot like this, always looking out for those around him. There isn't a moment I don't miss my brother-in-law, but it's in moments like these I feel like he's still with us when his son shows this nurturing side of himself.

"Yeah, just some stuff going on with Grant and me. Nothing to worry about." I rub my hand on Colton's bicep, hoping he can sense how grateful I am to him for caring.

"Whatever it is, it can't be so bad that he won't go back

to talking to you again." He smiles at me, and I hold on to his words in hopes that the universe hears this and grants me this wish.

"Thanks, Colt. I hope so." I feel the emotion creeping in again, and I can't continue with more because I'm afraid the tears will start.

Soon enough, they're all running out the door, yelling to me to have a good day, and before I can even grasp it, the house is silent. I usually lean into the comfort of the quietness of the house, but today, it feels deafening.

Before I have much time to sit with my own discomfort, there's a knock on my door. I place my tea on the kitchen counter and make my way to the front. I can't help the hope that blossoms in my chest that Grant has decided to come back to the city and work things out with me.

My hopes are quickly shattered when I find Becca on the other side of the door, holding up some pastries, with Betty by her side.

The moment the sweet pup sees me, she rushes toward me, tail wagging, full of love to offer. Becca follows her dog into the house, I greet her with a hug, and we make our way to the kitchen.

"Hey. What brings you by, Becca?"

I can't help but wonder why she's here. I have no problem hanging out with her on my own, but it's not as common now that my sister moved to the city. We usually hang out the three of us together, rarely finding time for it to just be the two of us.

"I got a text from your sister before she headed out to school saying you were up, so I thought I'd swing by with some snacks and your favorite fur baby." She looks down at Betty, and I see her feign disappointment when she sees her dog looking at me like I hung the moon.

I can't help but smile. Betty has taken to me in a way I

never expected. She seems to sense I need a little tenderness compared to others and is not shy about showing her love for me each time we're around one another.

"I appreciate that. Thanks for coming by and for bringing my favorite girl over." I bend down and scratch behind Betty's ear. She leans into my touch, and my heart melts a little more for this canine buddy of mine.

"Let's go sit. I'm going to grab some tea too. Just walking a few doors down made my muscles freeze." She shivers, and I can't help the smile that consumes my features.

"I'll make you the tea, you sit down. Thanks for the pastries!" I open the bag and take a big whiff of the blueberry muffins she brought by. For some reason, this smells even better than it usually does. I can't help the big inhale I take of the sugary goodness in the pastry bag.

"No problem. Hudson picked up the kids this morning, and I have a little while before I have to head over to the hospital. I have a patient in labor, but she's not anywhere near delivering, so I've got some time." She removes her jacket and sets it down.

Once she's comfortable, she takes a seat. Betty has long been let off her leash and has taken a seat in a corner nearby. My sister keeps a bed for Betty in the kitchen because Becca claims the dog can't be away from her. I think Becca's love for this dog goes beyond what some feel toward humans. It's quite cute to see.

I get another mug of tea ready for Becca, bring my drink along with hers to the table, and sit across from her. She's inspecting me; I'm not sure what she's hoping to find.

"So, no word from Grant yet about when he's coming back to the city?" Becca asks me.

Usually, I know Grant's plans and whereabouts better than anyone, even his sister. Not lately, though. She probably knows more about his plans than I do, which feels incredibly uncomfortable for me.

I shake my head, unable to elaborate further.

"Just to let you know, he didn't tell me what's going on with you two, but he did say he needed to get away. Anything I need to be concerned about with him?" she asks, genuinely worried about her younger brother.

"I don't think so. He's taking a break from me, not from anything or anyone else. I kept something from him, and he has every reason to be upset now that he knows. Sorry, I'm not saying more. I just need to get things figured out with Grant before I dive into the why with others. I hope you don't mind."

Becca shakes her head in return. "Of course not, Laney. I understand. We all need our space and our own time to move through the motions of life. Please know I'm here for you, much like I have always been. I know Grant is my brother, but you're my family too. I know that whatever you guys are going through, whatever you failed to tell him, you had your reasons. Grant will see that eventually." She winks, probably trying to make me feel better.

"I hope so. He's everything to me. I've just gone about showing him that the wrong way." I'm being incredibly cagey with my words, but I have no idea how to navigate this new territory with Grant. I'm frustrated by how much unknown lies between us.

"I get that. You look a lot better this morning, though. You get some more sleep last night?" She takes a sip of tea, but keeps her eyes on me, looking me over like she's trying to decode my emotions using sight alone.

"Yeah. I was wiped yesterday, and I think the lack of sleep finally caught up to me." I smile at her and hope it's enough to shift this conversation toward something not centered around Grant and how his absence is constantly felt in this city full of people.

Luckily, Becca must sense my need to move along and she changes the subject.

"It seems like our Ellie has been hiding a little secret of her own. What do you think is going on with her and that hockey guy she's sneaking around with? Think it's serious?"

I laugh because Becca is all about my sister finding love again. I know how hard Beau's loss was on everyone, but what people neglect to talk about is the emptiness the spouse feels after a loss. There's a period of sadness and mourning, but then people go about their business. The family is left to continue life on their own and maneuver through the grief the best they can. I only got a sense of this because I live with them. I'm immersed in their grief and see the sadness reflected in my sister's eyes.

My sister has been a pillar of strength for her family. She has put all her energy into her kids and ensuring they thrive. Somewhere in the mix, she lost a bit of that love for herself, and it seems she's finally coming up from the sorrow she has held. Or at least I hope she is.

Becca stays for about an hour, and then she heads off. She has to force Betty to get up from the comfort of her bed, and I can see the irritation in the dog's expression. I laugh as Becca rolls her eyes.

Once they're out the door, I make my way upstairs to get ready for a few classes I'm teaching at the yoga studio today.

"Lift your left leg up into a three-legged dog. Now, bring that leg through into a left-sided pigeon." I'm taking large breaths in and out as I coach my students using verbal prompts. Tad keeps looking up at me from his position, and I wonder if he senses that I'm struggling. Although he always seems to watch me a bit more than most students do. I wonder if he does it to all the instructors, or just me?

I started to teach the hot classes in recent months, and they are taking everything out of me lately. My body is exhausted as I move through class this morning.

Top it off with the stress of not seeing or hearing from Grant in a week, and my mind is just as tired. We've texted, but our communication is short and to the point. He's checking in on me, and I do the same back. We've never been this way with one another, and each day is adding to my anxiety.

It seems he's spending time with his mom and niece while he's in-between jobs. He flies out to Fiji in ten days, photographing some beach resorts for a local travel magazine. He said he'd find a moment to come back into the city before flying out from here. I just wish I knew more details instead of this cryptic messaging back and forth.

We're usually so involved in one another's lives that this feels superficial. I hate how surface-level our conversations have become, and I hope we can find our normal interactions together again. I know he's hurt, but I just need to know we'll be okay.

Now that I've let go of this secret I carried for so long, I see things more clearly. Each day he's been away, the clarity that I want to be with him, *completely with him,* is becoming more evident. I want all the memories in the future to be with him by my side. I just couldn't focus on us creating anything moving forward while I was holding on to old wounds. I couldn't move forward without letting go of this big piece of the past.

As I finish out class, the students are moving through the poses, and I'm trying to keep myself upright. The moment everyone is in Savasana, I excuse myself, stating I will meet everyone outside once they're ready to head out.

The moment I exit the hot room, I'm hit with that cool air, and I'm gasping for breath, my body attempting to adjust to the change in temperature and humidity. As much as I started the day feeling refreshed, I began to feel awful the moment I entered that hot room today. Maybe with the days I took off after the holidays, my body needs to reacclimate to the hotter room again. The fluctuation of temperature from the over one-hundred-degree hot room to the winter wonderland that's outside might be contributing to how I'm feeling right now.

I move toward the desk, fanning my face, black spots clouding my vision, as I notice a few students starting to shuffle out.

"Great class today, Laney," I hear some students call out.

Then I feel someone touch my shoulder. "Hey, are you okay?" I recognize my student Kendra's voice, but I feel my vision go, and soon, I'm fully engulfed in black.

CHAPTER 20

Grant

THE NIGHT BEFORE

I'm flipping through the channels, trying to occupy my mind, as I'm truly feeling an emptiness without seeing or talking to Laney the way we usually do. I hear someone shuffling around in the kitchen. I'm expecting to see my mom or Rick walk through, but Shane emerges.

"Hey, man, can I join you?" He has a plate of hummus and carrots. I want to roll my eyes. Doesn't he know the proper moping food is something greasy like pizza or wings?

"Don't look at me like that. I have to recover after your sister and I had a movie marathon over the holidays. I ate so much junk food that I feel like I was preparing for hibernation. Add to the fact that Rick made so many sweets during that storm, I need to balance them out with some vegetables. I think I might be at risk of scurvy at this point," he says as he sits on the opposite side of the couch. He brings the plate out in a gesture of sharing with me, and I shake my head.

"Nah, man. I'm good, thanks. I need something more like Becca's snacking tendencies versus this healthy stuff you think is acceptable for winter eating." I smile at him, feeling like I have a brother now that Shane's back.

"I need to keep up this beautiful figure, Grant. I can't snack on that stuff all the time."

"Don't you spend hours at the gym?" I know from what Becca has told me, this guy works out any free second he has.

"Hey, I'm old. I need to work twice as hard as you young people to have any kind of muscles. Plus, it's a great way to let off some steam. It might help you right now, too. You doing okay?"

I contemplate how to answer and decide if there is anyone who'll feel remotely similar to how I felt blindsided by Laney's pregnancy announcement and loss, it's Shane.

"Hey, let me ask you something. I'm sorry to dig deep here. I know Becca is my sister and all, but why don't you hate her for not trying harder to get you back and tell you about Olive?" I can see the surprise pass through his features. I doubt he sat here expecting to have this deep of a conversation with me at ten o'clock at night.

"Um, wow." He places his plate of veggies on the coffee table in front of us, bringing his hands through his hair. "In all honesty, the moment I realized what Becs had experienced, I never once blamed her or felt anger toward her. I don't know that I would have really sat with anger for long, even if she had kept me in the dark. I guess that's just what love is. It's blinding, taking away resentment in many ways."

I don't answer, hoping he'll elaborate on the why behind his statements.

"I guess when I first saw Olive, I felt really confused. I will admit I was upset, seeing a grown child of mine standing before me. Initially, I wanted to turn to your sister and explain that her actions were horrible and unforgivable. Of course, I'm the one who walked away and there was way more to the story. Obviously, she tried to tell me, and she went decades believing I didn't want her or our child together. So, I understand where your sister was coming from. Feeling rejected is something hard to pull yourself out of. And what my mom did, writing that letter under the guise it was me, solidified her choice to keep Olive to herself. I mean, I would've probably done the same had I felt that rejection the way she did with that letter."

He's scratching at the scruff on his chin, lost in thought. His mom is the worst if you ask me. She didn't want Shane to feel weighed down by my sister and the pregnancy, so the woman wrote a nasty letter and passed it off as Shane's words. Many years were lost, and now Shane is left to deal with the repercussions of her selfishness. Last I heard, he still hasn't spoken to his mother since he confronted her after Thanksgiving.

I look at him, still unsure how I'm going to move past this pain I feel inside for what Laney kept from me all these years.

"Laney was pregnant." At my words, Shane drops his hands and looks over at me, shock written across his features.

"I assume you know Laney was at school during that shooting at her university. She was literally in the hall where the shooting started. She lost a good friend that day in her arms. Shane, I was so fucking scared I had lost her when I heard about the whole thing. Then, when I got to her, the relief that washed over me, seeing she wasn't hurt physically, made me feel like the bulldozer that was sitting on my chest was lifted.

"I knew we would have a ton of work ahead of us as we navigated life with this immense pain as a part of her fabric, but I understood that and walked with her. Much like I always did. Turns out she was physically hurting that day too. She was pregnant. With my child. And she lost the baby during the shooting."

I can see the shock on Shane's face as I explain. He's the only person aside from my mother that I've told since Laney confessed everything to me nearly a week ago. Shane swallows, his eyes looking down at his hands, his fingers fumbling with a piece of thread sticking out of the couch cushion.

He looks up at me again, sadness taking over his expression. "I'm so sorry, Grant. I mean, really, I'm so incredibly sorry about the loss of your child. I don't know what to say aside from that."

"I appreciate it. The thing is, I just found out. Like, days ago." I feel the lump building in my throat, the pain of this loss feeling like it was yesterday versus over a decade prior. I feel so much pain, and it's fresh for me, unlike how it feels for Laney.

"I assume this is what caused you to come up here instead of staying in the city before your next work assignment?" Shane asks, no pity evident in his tone.

"Um, well, yeah. I didn't take the news very well. I was upset. I didn't want to say something I would later regret, especially because she confessed it when I was pushing her to start something more with me. Before the shooting, we were moving toward being together in that way. And the moment the shooting happened, it was like that page of our story was removed, and we went back to simply having a platonic relationship. Until a few months back, when I couldn't fight it any longer, and we crossed that line once again.

"I pushed for more recently, and that's when her confession flew out. I was stunned. And hurt. And, if I'm being completely honest, I felt disappointment in her for the first time in my life."

I close my eyes, upset that I felt such a thing toward the one person who has owned my heart. Even more because she has experienced so much loss and tragedy, and I'm sitting here stuck in my own feelings of deceit when I know that's not where her actions are coming from.

"Yeah, I get that," Shane says, although I can tell he has more to add to this thought. "But I think it's important to remember that her miscarriage wasn't just that. It was a loss so profound it spans beyond the actual loss of a child. That day is etched in her memory as a day she lost a lot of who she thought she was. Add to that the fact she thought she was going to be a mother.

"She didn't just lose something personally, something you both made together, but she lost a life she'll never regain. That shooting took more than a child from her. It took, in many ways, the innocence and the beauty that this life can bring to many people's lives. She has never looked at her days the same way, I can promise you that."

I nod, knowing what he's saying is right, but still circling back to that feeling of personal loss for me.

"I guess, for me, it spans further than the loss of that child. It just feels like despite everything I've done to show her she's not alone, that I'm here for her, to live this life with her, she still didn't feel compelled to tell me. I feel like she only told me when she did because I was pushing for more between us. But what if I hadn't done that? What if I simply carried on? Found someone else? Married someone else? She wouldn't have ever told me? That's what I'm stuck on." I feel the tears pool in my eyes. I'm not one to feel ashamed for expressing myself with emotion. But I feel like I'm late to this mourning journey while Laney has processed it for so long. She's come to terms with the loss, while it feels so fresh for me.

"Believe me, I understand that deviation in life. I mean, the woman I saw everything with did move on. She had children with another man. She let someone else love her the way I was supposed to love her. Even with all those moments between Becs and Hudson, she still loved me. She still thought of me. That sucks for Hudson, I can't even pretend to ignore how fucked up that is. But at the same time, I realize that her finding a way to love her life in a new way, with a new path, doesn't take away from the love she felt for me.

"And I think that's how Laney views things as well. She loves you so much she felt like she would spare you the pain. She felt like she could hold on to the pain for the two of you instead of letting you feel like the pain needed to be shared. I bet if given the choice, she would have spared all of you the pain she felt after that shooting as well. She would have shielded you and the rest of those around her, but she couldn't. It was out in the open, something everyone knew about. This loss, this baby she made with you, was the one thing she could keep to herself. She could hold on to the grief and feel like it was sort of in her control at that point. I think it goes beyond the miscarriage, Grant. I think for her, it's something that has a different meaning."

I look at him, and he continues, "She needed to feel like she had a choice in her life after the shooting. That tragic event was not something she was ever shown how to navigate. The way everyone reacted toward her after that day is something she couldn't feel steady about either. But the way she chose to grieve the loss of the baby is something she finally felt like she could hold in her own heart and cope with in the best way possible. Having control is very empowering, Grant. It's something that, for some, it's all they have. And for her, she lost a baby, but that wasn't the only loss she had to deal with.

"I think you need to start looking at it with a new perspective. Realize that her keeping it from you has so many layers, so many facets necessary to understand her intentions, that it has nothing to do with her wanting to hurt you or her wanting to keep you in the dark. I think it comes from a place of love, although it is hard to see that side of it right now. It's still fresh for you. But hopefully, with some time, you'll start to see her intentions weren't coming from a bad place of purposely alienating you. There was a reason behind it, even if it seems selfish and hard to comprehend."

I nod but can't form words after that. Hearing what he said, especially as it lines up with what my mother was saying when I first arrived, seems to make the impression it needed for me to see things a little more clearly. I needed to hear this again from someone who has felt a pain that isn't at all the same but revolves around a life he was robbed of.

I know Shane has been through a lot, especially recently, finding out he is a father and missed an entire life of milestones with a daughter he had no knowledge of. Even though my sister tried to get a hold of Shane and went most of her adult life believing he had rejected her and their unborn baby, it turns out that wasn't at all the case.

He and I turn our attention to the television, turning the volume up the moment we find a movie that catches our attention: *Die Hard*. I still remember when I snuck into the room and begged my sister to let me watch this movie with her. Olive was just a baby, and my sister was too tired from parenting and being a full-time student to argue one night when my mom had a shift at the hospital, and my love for the series of movies was born.

I sit back, my eyes trained on Nakatomi Plaza, but my

mind is far away, thinking of my girl with the fire-red hair and bright-green eyes.

I miss her, and I can't help the question that comes out of my mouth next, "Hey, any chance you'd like to head back to the city tomorrow?"

Shane was mid-bite of a carrot and stopped, turning toward me and smiling. "Took you long enough." I laugh at his response, and my smile is now spreading across my features, because I know I'll soon have Laney in my arms. I'll keep this to myself and surprise her when I get back to the city. We have a lot to figure out together.

CHAPTER 21

Laney

I wake up surrounded by students, and I can hear the faint sounds of the ambulance in the distance. What happened to me? And why am I on the floor?

Kendra is hovering over me. "Laney, you fainted. Don't make any sudden movements."

I turn to my side, and the moment I do, I feel a wave of nausea pass over me. I put my hand over my mouth, and another person grabs the wastebasket from the front desk and shoves it in front of me right as I vomit all the water I was downing throughout class.

I sit back, embarrassed but unable to focus on that, as I see a few paramedics come through the lobby doors. I'm now surrounded by EMTs while the students make room. I can see the worry etched on the faces of those that were just on their mats, here to relax, and I'm creating the exact opposite of a calm environment.

"Ma'am, I heard you fainted. Did you hurt anything when you fell?" I move my upper body up, leaning against the front of the reception desk in the lobby. I'm still catching up to what happened, unable to recall anything after I fainted. Luckily, Kendra chimes in.

"Laney fainted in front of me when I went to talk to her. She was pale, and it looked like she couldn't focus on me. Then her eyes rolled back, and her knees gave out. Tad was there to break her fall."

I look over to my left and find him standing in the distance, a look of concern etched across his face. I give him a small smile that I hope depicts my gratitude. Thank goodness he was there to help me, or I could have really injured myself by bumping my head.

Tad missed a few classes while traveling back home for the holidays, and this was his first class back. What a way to ring in his first yoga class of the year. I internally roll my eyes at my body's inability to do a simple hot class.

"Thanks for the information, Miss..." The paramedic is looking at Kendra.

"Kendra." She bats her eyelashes at him.

"Well, thank you *Miss Kendra*."

Is she fucking flirting right now? What on earth is wrong with her?

I look over at the guy wrapping a blood pressure cuff around my arm while another has a clipboard where he's writing down everything Kendra and the other students are recalling.

The cuff squeezes while another device is connected to my opposite finger to calculate the oxygenation in my blood. I remember all this from when I was rushed to the hospital in Wyoming. It doesn't bring back memories I'd like to relive right about now.

"Dan, her BP is eighty-five over fifty. Miss? I think we should take you back to the hospital and get you checked out. They'll want to monitor you to see if this was related to something more serious."

Right then, I see Loni rush through the doors. She looks panicked, something I rarely see. She's usually what people would expect of a yogi—fully immersed in her chakras and feeling connected to her own spirituality. In other words, calm.

"I'm the studio owner. Laney is one of the teachers here. What happened?" She looks over at me, giving me a once-over.

I hold up my hand. "It's okay, Loni. I think my body didn't adapt well to the change from hot to cold when I came out of the room, and I fainted. I'm okay. Really."

The paramedic wants to say more, but he states, "We have to take her to the hospital."

Loni nods, grabbing my hand, most likely trying to pass some spiritual essences my way to heal me without the need for Western medicine. I assume this because each time I've had a cold or a headache, she gives me some really interesting homeopathic remedies.

"That's no problem. Laney, I'll take over the rest of your classes, and you let me know how you're doing, yes?"

I nod toward her, the exhaustion hitting me again. Luckily, the nausea seems to have subsided.

"Oh, you might want to toss that trash bag." I point over to the waste bin next to me.

"Don't you worry about it. Nothing I haven't seen." She winks at me, her calm nature starting to return. She's pushing my hair back from my face, and the comfort it makes me smile.

The paramedics put me on a gurney, and the embarrassment is causing me to turn beet red. I hope I can laugh about this later. Because, right now, I want to crawl under a rock.

We make the quick trip to the hospital that I know is

the same one Becca works at. I don't know if she's already here for her shift today, but I'd better text her.

The moment the ambulance doors open, I realize my plan to text her is out the window. She's standing there, stricken by the sight of me on a gurney.

"I'm okay," I tell her when they bring the stretcher down and start moving me toward the emergency room entrance. "I fainted after my hot class. I think my body is just not acclimating well to the changes in temperature. This is all a bit more dramatic than it has to be. How did you find out?"

Becca's in doctor mode, taking in what I'm telling her and giving orders even though she works maternity and not emergency.

"I must still be your emergency contact at the studio because Loni called me immediately after the paramedics left. I'm waiting for my patient to fully dilate, so I thought I'd come check on you."

Once we're in the room, Becca continues her bossiness, not caring that I'm telling her I feel fine now.

"Also, Lynn, add a pregnancy panel to the blood work," she says to the nurse who's in the room taking my vitals and clicking things on the monitor in front of her.

I start laughing. "Very funny, Becca. Pregnancy panel. You're crazy." I continue to laugh, thinking she's going to join me.

When I look over, Becca is looking at me, no laughter or even a smile crossing her face.

"You can't be serious?" I ask her.

"Let's list off all your symptoms, shall we? Nausea, vomiting, fainting, peeing like you're on diuretics, napping almost every day, eating random things… need I go on?" She looks at me, my expression probably morphing from this being a ridiculous joke to a possibility I hadn't thought of prior. She continues, "Yeah, I think you've got a classic case of being knocked up and ignoring all the signs until you end up here."

I sit in silence, then realize once again what a preposterous idea this is. "*Oh please,* I just had sex not that long ago. I've had these symptoms for months, right around the time I started to teach these hot-as-hell classes. I'm drinking double the amount of water due to the hot room, along with feeling exhausted and needing more food to keep up. My body's just not used to it yet. That's all," I tell her, convinced I know my body better than anyone.

"Oh no? You didn't have sex a few months back? Maybe when you, I don't know, went to California?" She looks at me, now sporting a sly little smirk.

My mouth drops. "Grant fucking told you? What the hell, Becca? You guys talk about that? Gross!"

She makes a face, like she sucked on a lemon. "No, disgusting. I couldn't give two shits about what my brother does." Then she gives me a little wink. "Or who—but I did see how chipper you two were after that little getaway, so I made assumptions. Plus, you've had every symptom like a fucking textbook, and I made an educated guess. You know I studied this, and I see it daily, right?"

Yeah, she knows her stuff, but there's no way. I have that IUD that can stay in for ten years. I'm not due to replace it yet.

I keep thinking about it, and Becca sits and watches me as I calculate everything in my head. As it clicks in my mind, I see Becca puff out her chest like she's fucking Einstein. Doctors are so damn cocky.

"Is it all coming together now?" she asks, standing on her Goddamn pedestal while I can feel all the color in my face drain out.

"It's happening again," I whisper, feeling too much familiarity with what happened years ago.

"What do you mean?" She looks at me while tears pool in my eyes.

"This has happened to me already. I've been pregnant, and I miscarried."

I look down, the tears falling from my eyes and directly on the hospital blanket in my lap. I'm still in my sweaty clothes, and the energy to change is not even close to being in my body right now.

"Oh, Laney. When? I'm so sorry you went through that. Your sister never mentioned anything." She brings her arm around and squeezes me while I let her take me into her arms.

"I lost the baby the day of the shooting. I found out I was pregnant that morning before everything happened." I feel like I'm reliving a nightmare. Although, this time, I have no idea where I stand with Grant. At least that day, when I saw those two lines, I felt confident he'd be excited. I felt like it was a new chapter for us.

But right now, I feel lost in whatever phase we're going through. I feel like we're both wandering aimlessly without one another to lean on. The fact I'm possibly pregnant for a second time, with Grant's baby *again,* I feel like the parallels are absolutely crippling me right now.

Becca caresses my head, and I lean into her grasp even more.

"I had no idea. All those times I came home and complained of exhaustion after a tough delivery or even shared my story of a loss on my shift, I did it so carelessly in front of you while we lived together. Your sister never told me."

I shake my head. "I never told anyone. I only told my therapist when I moved here."

I pull away, ashamed of my previous behavior about not leaning into the love that those around me showered me with to help me cope.

Becca sits down next to me, the chair scraping against the hospital floor. She grasps my hand and crouches down so we can be at eye level with one another.

"You're not alone this time, Lane. Grant isn't going to abandon you. He loves you. Whatever this rough patch you're going through is, he'll let it go the minute he finds out."

"I'm not so certain. I really hurt him." I close my eyes, knowing this confession will hurt Becca. She's Grant's sister. There's no way this won't break her heart, not just for the life that was lost but for the pain I caused her own brother.

"I doubt that," she scoffs. She has no idea what I'm about to say.

"Grant was the father," I say a little above a whisper.

"Yeah, Laney, I deduced as much after that trip a few months back," she dismisses my comment, not realizing what tense I used. "Hold on. What do you mean 'was the father?'" *Guess she caught it after all.*

Her hand flies to her mouth the moment she connects the dots, and tears pool in her eyes.

"Oh no. No, no, no, no, no. Please, Laney, tell me I'm misunderstanding. Grant? Grant was the father of the baby you lost." The last thing she said wasn't a question but a statement.

I keep my gaze down, shame taking over my face as I feel her eyes on me.

We sit there a bit, taking in what I just said and letting it sink in. I tell her about how I just revealed all this to Grant days ago instead of years ago, like I should have. But in true Becca form, she stands up, brushes off her scrubs, and then straightens herself, standing tall with her doctor's coat as her shield.

"Okay, Laney. There's no time to dwell on this. I can't judge you for something you did during one of the hardest moments in your life. I have no idea how I would have handled all that. But I do know my daughter came into this world, and I had a decision to either be upset that her father left us behind, or I could forge on and make her life the best possible. I love you, Laney. What you just told me doesn't change that, you understand me?"

I look up, my face covered in tears, my pain evident in my expression.

"I'm so sorry. I'm so sorry I didn't say anything earlier. I just didn't know how to tell him. I didn't want to make him more sad. I saw how hard he took the shooting and seeing me in pain. I couldn't add this to his heart. I just couldn't."

Now, I'm sobbing, hiccuping as I speak, having difficulty letting everything out to the person who played such a huge role in my recovery. She welcomed me with open arms into her home, and I couldn't even tell her I lost a baby with the only man my heart has ever belonged to. And he's *her brother* of all people. The baby was her family, too.

"Shhh," Becca comforts me as I continue to soak her white coat, feeling like I'm not just letting out the pain of my past but the pain I've recently caused to Grant's life. I feel like I'm shedding a part of me while Becca holds me in her arms.

Eventually, my sobs slow, and I feel myself able to take in a full breath without feeling like the tears are going to threaten to take over again.

The nurse walks in, little empty tubes in her hand, ready to get me some answers. Though it feels a little redundant at this point. I don't know how I didn't see it before.

Once the labs are sent off, Becca sits with me,

explaining that she won't tell anyone what I just confessed. She also reassured me that whatever the results were, she wouldn't tell a soul. She wants me to know I'm supported in whatever means I need.

She did, however, confess that she texted Grant right when she heard I was transported to the hospital by ambulance. He responded immediately, stating he was on his way. It's going to take him a few hours to get here, so I should know what's going on by the time I see him in person.

It turns out that if I got pregnant when I went out to California, that would mean I'm nearly out of my first trimester. The thought that I could be that far along is mind-boggling. I don't feel pregnant; however, with this IUD, I have some strange spotting sometimes. I've had irregular periods since I got this thing placed, and I've gotten used to it. The problem is, the last time I bled could have simply been implantation bleeding and not my actual period. Add to the fact that I don't even look pregnant, my belly just as flat now as it was before my trip to the West Coast.

Becca did say with me possibly being this far along, I could just do an ultrasound, but she felt that it should be something she did with Grant here if that's the case. The only other factor is the IUD itself. She needs to do an ultrasound to see where the IUD is.

Depending on the placement, she will remove the IUD once an ultrasound is done. There is a risk of miscarriage when removed, but she said some rest will be required and that she'll monitor me if my tests show I am, indeed, pregnant. Grant and I were both robbed of a positive experience last time, and all I want is to feel just a piece of happiness if this turns out to be our second chance as parents.

CHAPTER 22

Grant

The drive is going smoothly this morning. My mom hugged me so tight, I wasn't sure she was going to let me get on the road. Rick had to pull her arms off the car as she was plastered there while Shane's driver started pulling away, prolonging our goodbye. I think it's moments like these when she realizes how great it is having her family all in the same state. I know that my traveling is something she has never gotten used to, but after this next assignment, I'm going to start settling down. I just need to talk to Laney about it first. I think we have stuff to get off our chests, and I'll start by telling her how much my life needs her in it, in whatever capacity she'll give me.

I want to be with Laney as my partner, but I need her to want the same. I won't have this relationship be one-sided, nor will I let her think that I'm going to hold this secret against her. If after everything she told me, she feels moving forward as my best friend is all she truly wants from us, then I have to allow that to be the case. But if these last few days have proven anything, it's that I need her in my life in whatever way I can have her. I want to make the assumption that she wants me romantically, but who knows if my behavior has made her think twice about being with me.

We're only an hour out of the city at this point, and I'm itching to see Laney again. This time away from one another is so different from the countless times I've traveled for work. I've never felt so far away from my girl as I have these last few days. I've only been a car ride away from her, and I've felt like we were oceans apart instead of miles.

Today is all blue skies, and it's hard to believe we were all staying indoors because of a storm a few days ago. I'm looking out the window when Shane pulls my attention with questions about what I'm going to do when I get into the city.

"So, you ready to do this?" he asks while he types nonstop on his phone.

He's most likely texting Janine, one of the women who works with him and keeps him in line. I had to chat with her once when Shane couldn't pick up the phone a few weeks back, and she was feisty. I had a good chat with her, but I can't imagine having that person ordering me around all day. I guess it works for Shane, though. To be fair, Becca has always ruled his life too, so he must like it.

"I think so?" I turn to him, wondering if I should have planned this out a little better.

"Remember what I said—keep an open mind and remember that her actions didn't come from a place of anger. Listen to what she has to say. Nothing she says is an excuse. It truly was a way for her to cope with everything that happened that day."

Shane is heavily working through his own emotional turmoil after finding out about Olive, so I bet he's reiterating some advice he got from his own therapy sessions. I nod at what he's saying to me, knowing that I need to stay open to whatever Laney tells me. I'll never understand everything she experienced that day, nor can I change the outcome.

I fly out in a few days, so I have to get things sorted out with Laney before I leave for this next trip. I'll be gone for about three weeks, taking photographs for a big magazine that's starting to finally see a boost in sales now that travel is resuming after the pandemic brought the world to a standstill for so long.

I'm scrolling social media, and I can't help clicking on Laney's story at the top of my account. She posted a story this morning. It seems from the timestamp that it was a few hours ago, and it's of the beautiful trees lining Ellie and Becca's street. She posted a pretty passage from a book she's apparently reading at the moment, and I immediately "like" the content. I can't help the smile that spreads on my face, but then it hits me. Was she teaching a class today, and I forgot?

I quickly open my browser and search for the teaching schedule on her yoga studio's site. Sure enough, her name is listed for the last class that ended about forty-five minutes ago. I know when she has a long break between teaching classes, she'll head back home, so the timing of my arrival will work out great.

I put my phone down and take in the drive. I've slept like shit since leaving the city, and I can one hundred percent say it's from being in this state of uncertainty with Laney. I know the moment I see her, all these feelings of unpredictability will fall to the wayside, and we can find a way to navigate the path forward.

Shane and I begin talking about watching the upcoming NBA game tonight. Hudson has the twins tonight, so Shane always tries to plan his nights with my sister if she isn't at the hospital. I don't see how these two are going to keep this up much longer, because I know all these years apart are probably leaving them antsy to get things moving forward.

"When are you going to move in with my sister, Shane?" I blurt out, curiosity winning over right now.

"Well, that came out of nowhere." He chuckles. "Believe me, I wanted to move in the moment I knocked on Becs' door, but I need to slow things down because of the kids. She wants them to get used to me being around, along with allowing Hudson some time as well."

I roll my eyes. My sister's ex-husband is a douche if you ask me. This hold he has over what happens between Shane and my sister makes me even more irritated with him. I don't know how, but Hudson won Olive over, but I never saw the appeal. All I can really say is I was unsurprised by the fact that he was caught cheating on Becca with his secretary. The guy is a living, breathing cliche if I've ever met one.

"Don't roll your eyes. I have to keep things civil with the guy." I didn't realize I did that when Hudson's name was brought up. "He can make this whole transition a living hell for me and your sister, so we've come to a comfortable point where we can at least be civil with one another. Hopefully, that continues, and he'll stop staring at my Becs like they're going to reconnect at some point," he huffs out.

"Believe me, the guy will never redeem himself for being a major dick to my sister. I promise she didn't choose wisely with him. But she got two great kids out of the whole thing, so there's that."

"Can't argue there. The kids have been great. There is some hesitance from Jackson to accept me right now. I think he's seen himself as the man of the house for a while, so I'll have to put some added effort in with him. Maybe a basketball game or something like that in the near future will help my cause."

"I think you're onto something there. Jackson is pretty chill for the most part. Last year, though, he was quite a handful for his parents. Middle school is tough, it always has been. I mean, I remember having some technology, but nothing like what we have today. I don't know how parents do it now." I don't know how Ellie and Becca have done it so far. It's a lot to juggle.

"Sheesh, Grant. You sound like an old man complaining about the younger generation. You're really not that far out of high school yourself compared to *some of us*." That earns a chuckle from me, he's not wrong. When did I start acting like a real adult who's too old to understand teenagers?

We continue chatting, deciding on possibly grabbing dinner to bring home to Laney and my sister, perhaps getting Ellie to join if she's up for it, when my phone chimes in my hand. I look down, and the moment my sister's words register I feel my heart quicken.

"Shit, Laney's in the hospital. Fuck. I'm not with her... again." I text back, firing off questions without giving my sister time to respond. Soon, impatience wins, and I press the phone icon and bring the phone to my ear, hoping my sister picks up. Once she does, I can already deduce she's in the hospital where the service is choppy.

"Becca, what's going on? What happened to her? We're on our way." I can hear the panic in my voice, but I can't help the fear that's creeping up my spine. "Was she in an accident? Did someone hurt her?"

"Grant, I don't—" The line goes dead. Fucking hell. Damn hospitals and their spotty service. I'm so agitated, and it's only after I take a few breaths that I hear Shane trying to call Becca on his phone to no avail.

I feel his hand on my shoulder. "Hey, Grant, try not to let your mind wander to all the different scenarios. The driver is going straight to the hospital, so we'll be there before you know it. I get it; you need to see her, but I think Becs would have elaborated if it was urgent." He's saying everything to me, but nothing is truly sinking in.

My mind is going to the worst scenario, because that's all I know when it comes to Laney. She's lived through tragedy before, and I can't help the fear that is consuming me in this moment.

My head is bowed down, and I see the teardrops pooling on the cotton of my clothes. I didn't even realize I was crying until this second. I wipe my eyes, trying to cover up the concern I'm feeling for the person who has held my heart since I was old enough to understand the concept of soulmates. That's who Laney is to me, and the only place that feels right is by her side.

CHAPTER 23

Laney

I sit in the emergency room until the blood work comes back. She gave me the option to wait and see that portion of the results with Grant, but I couldn't sit here and not know. Becca had already seen the results, and I just couldn't handle the anticipation. It's best I know what I'm dealing with here.

After she came in to talk to me, she left me to wait, knowing Grant was on his way. I tried reading my book on my phone, but I couldn't stay focused.

I hear a commotion near the nurses' station, and I already know it's Grant. He must have flown here if he's already back. There's no way he drove here that quickly.

He rushes to the entryway of my room, and he's panting, sweat on his forehead despite the weather outside.

"Grant, what the hell? Did you speed on the highway to get here?" Becca puts her hands on her hips, tapping her foot, scolding him like the mother figure she is. It's hard to keep a straight face with their interaction.

Grant shakes his head, unable to form words when he's still catching his breath.

"No. I—" He coughs, resting his hands on the tops of his thighs, bending over, and trying to slow down his breathing. "I was actually driving into the city when you texted me. I was already more than halfway here. I was worried, so I may have asked the driver to get here a little faster."

I can't help but smile. Even though he's upset, he rushed here to make sure I was okay.

He looks up toward me, and the moment we lock eyes, my heart flutters.

I reach my hand out to him, hoping that he'll come and grasp it. He walks into the room and immediately comes toward me, pulling me into his arms, completely disregarding my outstretched hand.

"I'm so fucking sorry, Bean. I'm sorry I wasn't here, and I'm so incredibly sorry I went away for days without giving you the attention you deserve after everything you told me. I was stuck in my own head, in my own grief, forgetting that I did to you exactly what I was accusing you of—disregarding your feelings. I love you," he whispers this, at first in my ear, then moving to cup my cheeks, finishing off with a kiss to my lips.

The contact alone awakens something inside me, and I can't help the smile that spreads across my face. This man was put into my life before I understood anything about love and compassion. And through the years, my heart has become rooted within his soul. We're intertwined in a way that I assumed was part of friendship. He's so much more, though. He's a part of me that I feel deep in my bones.

I shake my head, having a hard time letting words come through as the lump in my throat is just sitting there. I take a few breaths, ready to spill everything, and let him know my heart is his.

"No, Grant, you needed space, and it's the least I could do. I'm sorry it took me so long to let you in."

A deep sigh pulls us out of our little bubble, only to realize we've had an audience of one this entire time. Becca has fresh tears streaming down her cheeks, her hand over her heart, looking at us like we're actors in her favorite romcom.

"Um, Becca, any chance you could give us a minute?" Grant says, and I can tell he's annoyed his sister is still hovering over us while we're having this moment together.

"No, not really." She has a smile on her face, one which clearly says she's got a secret that her brother isn't privy to.

"Becca can't go. She needs to do one more thing before she heads upstairs," I tell Grant.

His head swivels toward me, and he has a look of confusion across his face.

"What do you mean?" His head swings back to his sister. "I thought you said she's okay?"

"I did. She will be."

His voice rises with his next question. "What do you mean *she will be*?" He looks over at me. "What is it, Laney? Tell me, just tell me. Are you hurt? Oh my gosh, are you sick?"

I can see the fear etched in his features.

I smile because I don't want him hurting.

"No, not at all. I'm going to be fine. *We're* going to be fine." I put my hand on my belly and let the moment register for him.

His eyes bounce from my face to my belly, back and forth, putting everything together.

"Oh my God! No way!"

Right when he realizes, his sister exclaims, "Fucking finally!"

Grant looks over at her, annoyed she's still spectating this entire thing.

"Oh, don't look at me like that. I can't believe it took you this long to figure it out. I thought you would have known by now. I mean, she's been sick, peeing constantly, exhausted; come on!"

Grant isn't amused. His gaze comes back to me.

"You knew you were pregnant?" I can see the hurt in his expression, probably feeling like I left this out of my confession the other day on purpose.

"Nope. Had no clue. Becca was playing her own version of Pregnancy Clue all alone. I just found out before you got to the hospital and wanted to wait until you got here to tell you. I wanted to see the look on your face in person."

I wait, watching him, seeing him process the information he's been given.

I see a tear fall from his eye, and then he crumbles. He pulls me into a hug, kissing me all over my face, telling me he loves me, giving me all the words to soothe my soul now that he's back with me.

"Are you happy? Are we going to be okay?" I can't help the insecurity that comes out of me just then. I'm so worried my actions, or omissions really, may have damaged what we had.

He grabs my face again. "Of course, I'm happy. The one girl I love, who I've loved my entire life, is bringing a life we made into this world. Not only that, a piece of us together to walk beyond us is something I'll never take for granted." He kisses me again, this time not so PG in nature. I can't help but fall deeper in love with him.

"Um, excuse me, you still have me in the room." Becca's words cause Grant's lips to break our kiss, his gaze shifting back to his sister.

"Why are you still here?" he says, and I can tell he's over her presence right now.

"You're going to want me here, little bro. I have the ability to give you photos. Also, we need to chat about some risks."

I can see the alarm on Grant's face immediately. His shoulders tense, and I wish I could wash away his fears, but right now, I'm also nervous.

Before Grant can word vomit his questions that I know he's tabulating in his head, Becca puts her hand up and continues, "The bloodwork showed really good HCG levels. That's the pregnancy hormone we test for, and if Laney's calculations are correct, then she's probably close to the end of her first trimester." Becca's gaze passes between me and her brother. I give a small nod for her to continue.

"That being said, Laney has an IUD, and that can complicate things a bit. Getting pregnant with that in place can increase the possibility of miscarriage. We'll do an ultrasound and see how things are going and also remove the IUD if the placement allows. Do you have any questions for me?"

Becca is in full doctor mode again, and I can see why she's so good at her job. She's not condescending in her explanation and makes us feel seen. I've been around plenty of doctors to know some can really make someone feel like they're taking up too much time. I know we're family to her, but I have a feeling she's simply this good with everyone. She caters to her patient's emotions and not just their physical necessities. That's something I've always loved about her demeanor in her profession.

"No, I don't have any questions. Lane?" Grant looks over to me, his excitement replaced with concern.

I shake my head, then grab his hand and squeeze it. "No

matter what, we can do this together, Grant. I know we can."

A soft smile appears on his face, and he leans in and softly kisses my lips.

Right then, the ultrasound machine is pushed into the room by the nurse from earlier. She gets everything set up, probably not used to the doctor staying for this part of the exam. Becca informs her that she can handle it from there and will let the nurse assist in removing the IUD when that time comes. The nurse leaves the room to grab supplies while Becca gets the ultrasound plugged in.

"The ER really doesn't like handling pregnant patients and usually sends them up to my floor, but since it's early days, you can stay here while I do all this. We're completely full upstairs, so the staff here have no option but to allow me to do my thing. This nurse of yours is probably ecstatic not to be fully caring for you. I don't know what it is about emergency rooms and pregnant people, but the two just don't mix. I always find it funny how flustered the staff is when a pregnant person walks through the door." She chuckles to herself as she makes sure the machine has all the things she needs.

I lie back, ready to pull my yoga pants off, when Becca stops me with her hand over mine.

"I don't think that'll be necessary just yet. I have a feeling you're far enough along that I can start with an abdominal ultrasound until the nurse returns." She gives me her reassuring smile, and I lie back, exposing my belly. "I'll use a transvaginal Doppler ultrasound shortly to check your cervix and see what's going on with the IUD. But for now, let's start with checking everything out from your belly."

Becca drapes a small towel onto the front of my pants, tucking it into the fabric to keep them from getting the ultrasound jelly on them. Then she squirts the gelatinous fluid on me, the cold making me squeak.

"Sorry, these machines don't have the bottle warmers like the ones in my office. Now, I'm going to use the wand to look around. Give me a second, then I'll explain everything after I look at it. Grant, sit back down. Your pacing is making me nervous."

I don't even think he realized he was moving around the room until his sister called him out.

He complies with her demands, and soon, I see the black and white image on the screen. At first, it's just a lot of random blobs, most of which look nothing like anything I can make out. But then Becca swipes across a little lower on my abdomen, and I see a black space with something inside it. That's when I see that little something move in there, like a jelly bean with a head and limbs bouncing around. I bring my hand to my mouth, a sob breaking through as I look at what I know is our baby.

"There you go. There they are." Becca smiles brightly when she points to the screen.

The baby is fully formed. I expected a little speck, but our baby has arms and legs, a fully formed head, and is moving around in there quite a bit.

"How far along am I? I mean, this looks like a fully-formed human. Oh my gosh. I haven't been taking vitamins, Becca!" I start to feel my heart race, and Grant is quick to grab my hand and kiss my knuckles.

"It's okay. I've seen the vitamins you take. They're for women of childbearing age. They have folic acid, but you'll have to switch over to prenatal vitamins starting now. Just make sure that you take the vitamins with food in your stomach. You have obviously had a longer bout of morning sickness, so you'll probably get a little upset stomach if you don't have food in your system. And to answer your other question, you're about fourteen weeks if these calculations are accurate."

She's clicking things on the screen, doing what looks like measurements with the buttons at her disposal. I watch in awe as she keeps taking photos, and I see the paper spitting out the images.

Becca tells me all this, but she can't take her eyes off the screen either. I have to remember that she's not just my doctor right now, she's this baby's aunt. I think she's enraptured by what's in front of her. When she looks over, her eyes are filled with emotion.

She moves the screen for us to have a better view and then points at the baby in front of us. "So, that's the head, the arms, the legs right there. You've got an active one in there. You might start feeling little flutters in the weeks to come, but don't worry if it takes a while. Some people are super sensitive to the feeling, while others may not feel anything until well into their second trimester. It might feel like the tail of a fish swimming in your belly at first. At least that's what it felt like for me." Her smile is warm, and her excitement is palpable.

"Okay, now I need you to strip down, removing your yoga pants and underwear. I'll leave the room so you can do that. Grant, just poke your head out when she's ready."

"Becca, stop." She's cleaning off the wand and looks up in confusion when I speak.

"You don't need to leave the room. If you're going to be delivering this baby, you're going to have to get used to seeing me, all of me, at some point. May as well start now. I mean, you changed my diapers, for crying out loud." I laugh, and Becca sits back down, in shock from whatever I just said.

"You want me to deliver your baby?" She looks between

me and Grant, and I can't help the confusion that crosses my face.

"Well, who the hell else would deliver our baby, Becca?" Grant speaks this time, apparently on the same page as me.

"I just assumed I was too close for comfort on this one. I'm honored you want me to deliver the baby. Thank you." She tosses the ultrasound wand and gives me a huge hug, then pulls away and moves around the bed to give her brother an embrace. Becca is so short she gets lost in his hug.

I notice her pinch his side, and he lets go. "You're such an ass! I hate when you hug me that tight and then won't let go. I can't breathe, and then when I try, I smell your gross armpit stink."

I roll my eyes. I guess they'll always be siblings, even in a moment as special as this.

"Excuse me, but I smell amazing. I showered this morning." Grant stands a little taller, smugness dripping off him as he defends himself.

Becca rolls her eyes and then straightens herself out, mostly getting back into her doctor character before resuming the ultrasound.

Once I'm disrobed from the waist down, I lie back down and follow Becca's instructions to bring my feet together, then let my knees fall to the side. The nurse comes in with a few items in her hand.

I see her grab the transvaginal wand, and memories of that day return to me. I try to keep my breathing calm, but I can't help the tears that prick at the edges of my eyes.

"Hey, I'm here. You're not going through any of this alone, Bean. I'm here for you. I love you." He kisses my temple, catching the tear before it escapes down my face.

I nod and smile at him. I squeeze his hand tighter as Becca guides the wand in, and I watch the screen.

She's looking, clicking buttons much like before, inspecting everything. "I'm sorry for any discomfort. I just want to make sure I look everywhere and also get a good picture of your cervix to measure the length. That's important too."

She seems to be getting more pictures of the inside of my vagina than I thought possible. The baby is still bouncing around, and it's surreal that there's a living human inside me, growing away while I had no idea of its existence until the last hour.

"Look at what we made, Laney. You're amazing." Grant threads his fingers through my hair, pure love in his gaze at the screen. He kisses my knuckles again, and I truly hope life will give us this child after all we've lost.

"There it is," Becca says, pointing at the monitor. "See this little thing right there?"

I nod, still not completely sure what I'm looking at.

"That's your IUD. It's just floating in your cervix. How did you not feel it, Laney? Also, it would have made sex uncomfortable for you or even both of you if it was hanging this low."

"I don't remember anything out of the ordinary that was uncomfortable for me," Grant says, his cheeks turning a bright shade of pink, realizing he has to have this conversation with his sister.

"Yes, this is an awkward topic, so we'll leave it at that." She looks over her shoulder, and the nurse has the speculum ready for Becca to grab. Becca continues to explain, "If it's just floating in there, it shouldn't be an issue to remove and hopefully won't interfere with the pregnancy in any way. Are you okay for me to attempt a removal?" I nod my consent and she proceeds with the procedure.

Once the IUD is removed, which I didn't even feel her doing, she inspects the area where the speculum is, removes it, and stands up. She's got a smile on her face as she walks toward the trash to toss her gloves, then washes her hands before leaving the room.

Becca comes back in while the nurse leaves to finish charting.

"So, that IUD failed, and I can't really explain why aside from it simply fell out. And, obviously, here we are." She gestures at my belly, then continues, "Now, the IUD was just sitting there, not at all implanted where it was supposed to be. I want you to take it easy for the rest of the week due to the fact that there was an IUD in there, coupled with the fact that you fainted teaching your class."

"You fainted?!" Grant exclaims.

Shit. I forgot to explain what happened. I guess we got too caught up in the fact that I was pregnant to fill him in on why I was brought here in the first place.

"Um, yes? And technically, I fainted *after* class…" I had to clear that up, at least. I'm embarrassed by the fact that I was out there, living life with no idea of this baby growing inside me. The last thing I need people thinking is that I fainted in the middle of the yoga studio mid-pose.

"Oh my gosh, Laney. I told you something was off. You kept brushing it off. No more classes for you," he says, immediately causing me to go on the defensive.

"Excuse me? What do you mean 'no more classes?'"

"Yeah, Grant, what do you mean she can't teach classes anymore?" His sister is shooting daggers at her little brother. Becca is not one for the whole alpha-male type, and she is quick to stand up for me.

"Oh, come on… she fainted while teaching today. Am I the only one concerned here?" He stands up from the chair he was sitting in by my side. Did he not hear me? It was *after* class. *Get it right.*

"Listen, Grant, I'm Laney's doctor and one of her

closest friends. I'm your sister. This is my niece or nephew in there. So, I will say this as nicely as I know how. Laney's pregnant. She's not sick. She's not unable to be herself. She can still do all the things she did before, after this week of rest." She looks over at me to make her point. "I'd maybe stay out of the hot room if you weren't acclimating well to begin with. Aside from that, you can do yoga." I beam at her and she turns her attention to Grant. "Do you understand me, little brother?"

She's got her defensive mama-bear look going, hands on hips and all. I can't help the chuckle that escapes as this little woman stands tall against her brother, who towers over her.

"Yes, ma'am," Grant says, looking defeated by his sister.

"Good. Now, Laney, I will repeat what I said. This next week I want you to rest. You're not on bed rest; but no heavy lifting, no excessive bending. Got it?"

I nod. "Yes, I understand. I'll be a good patient."

"At least there's that. *You're* a shit patient, Becca," Grant says, and I swear his sister looks like she could murder him with her glare.

"You better watch it," Becca says with a fake smile that spreads across her face, her teeth clenched as she speaks, "or I'm telling mom that you and your high school friends are responsible for the hole in the wall and not the vacuum cleaner handle!"

"You wouldn't dare!" The look of horror on his face is priceless.

"You best believe it!" Becca is far too proud of herself right now.

Returning her gaze to me, Becca continues, "Also, you better come up with a plan to tell Ellie and eventually the parents. I'll also warn you that our mom"—she looks at her brother then swings her gaze back at me—"and yours,

Laney, have been planning your wedding since you were two. So, be prepared for a lot of screaming and excitement upon your announcement. Oh and don't be surprised if they don't let you have a say in any of the details of the ceremony. They've had way too long to think about it." She returns to tidying the room after removing the ultrasound machine.

"Oh gosh. I didn't even think of that whole aspect of our relationship." I bury my face in my hands, knowing that my mother and Grace are going to drive me nuts with their questions and planning.

I hear Grant chuckle, apparently undisturbed by the prospect of the moms taking over and hounding us.

I decide to drop the next bomb, "Hey, don't stand there all proud. You're going to have to face my dad, and he's going to be pissed you got his little girl pregnant." I smile like I won this little game we're playing. The moment my words are out, Grant's face loses all color, and I laugh. Becca can't help but enjoy this too.

Becca basks in this uncomfortable moment for her brother a minute longer, and then her expression changes, and I can tell the maternal side of her is about to say something.

"You've been through a lot, Lane. I hope you know how proud I am of you. You'll be an incredible mother. You love with your whole heart, and I know this baby already feels it."

She then moves her gaze over to her brother and begins to round the bed and stand right in front of him. "Grant, you have no idea the beauty your heart holds. I see so much of Dad in you, and I know you're going to fill this baby's life with so much love and joy, this child will lack nothing."

At that, she picks up the printed images she had grabbed off the machine and hands them to us. We both stare, shocked that life has given us the chance to love again. Our baby, here to bring us an extra level of love that we are both going to embrace.

Becca moves toward the door. Then she turns back and blows us kisses, and I mouth a silent *thank you* to her on her way out. She gives me a little nod of acknowledgment, and then she's off to work on her floor of the hospital.

We lay there, looking at this little being and simply awestruck that we created a life together. Our love carried over, beyond all the sadness, to this moment.

Grant looks up at me, tears falling freely, and says, "Now it looks like I have a new Little Bean to love." His lips softly cover mine, and I try to remember this feeling of completion that wraps me like a warm blanket on a cold day.

CHAPTER 24
Grant

Walking out of the hospital, my hand intertwined with Laney's, I take a deep breath. It feels like days have passed since I got to the hospital, even though it's been just hours since I arrived.

I look to my left and see Laney's eyes twinkling, and I can't help but fall deeper in love with this woman. I feel the smile grow on my face and my hand automatically goes for her belly, even though there is nothing evident from the outside to signify that she's pregnant. I'm looking down, and I see her hand over mine, and I move my gaze up to her face. She's perfect, and I can't wait to see who this little person is growing inside her.

Before I got into the city, I already had a plan of what I wanted for us moving forward, but now I feel compelled to bring it up immediately, making my feelings known.

I slow my steps until I come to a complete stop. I turn toward her and grab her face, my forehead on hers, my lips lightly kissing her, taking her in.

"I'm sorry I left the way I did." She's about to interject, but I stop her with my words.

"Let me get this out. I've had days to think of what I want to say to you, and I feel like if I don't say this now, it will eat at me. I was mad that day. I couldn't grasp why you would live with this secret for you to digest and process alone, especially when it was *our* baby you were mourning. I felt like I was left out of something we could have gone through together. I'll admit, I was so hurt. I made it about me when no matter how we look at this, it's about *us*. I don't know how I would have reacted had I been in your shoes, experiencing the events of that day the way you did. It doesn't take away the feelings I've had to process over our child that we lost, but I do understand your side. I get why you did what you did, even if I don't agree with it."

She closes her eyes, tears escaping, but instead of pushing herself away, she brings her arms around me and squeezes my midsection. Her head rests on my chest, and my heart feels like it's growing in size for this woman.

I pull her away from me so I can look into her eyes. "Laney, I want forever with you. When I started my drive back this morning, I had so many things I was going to say. I wanted to give you a choice to be with me, to start something more with me, but now I can't think of you moving through life without me by your side. I don't want us just to be friends and share a child together. I want more. I need more. I want *everything*. Please tell me I'm not alone in this." I can hear the vulnerability in my tone, and I don't even care anymore.

I want her to understand I'm in this one hundred percent. It's the three of us now, and I'll stop at nothing to ensure she and the baby are safe in this world. Tears stream down her cheeks, and I automatically use my thumbs to wipe them away.

"I want forever with you, too, Grant. I want this, and I want you. I was pushing you away before because I was scared. I wasn't sure if you'd hate me for what I did, and I was petrified I'd lose you. I'm so sorry." She looks down, and I bring my finger to her chin to bring her eyes back onto me.

"You don't have to apologize. I don't completely know how you felt that day, but I can only imagine it was a lot of fear, hesitation, and shock. I don't blame you for keeping it from me, and I'm sorry I was too self-centered to realize sooner that you were simply doing the best you could with the cards you were dealt."

She nods, but doesn't speak. She grabs onto my jacket and pulls me toward her to get my lips on hers. I kiss her, gliding my tongue along her lips, feeling like I've been brought back to life after this week away from her.

Once we pull away, I smile and grab her hand again. We begin to walk and hopefully catch a cab. The hospital was a madhouse, so we thought going down the block would help get us a ride and avoid the chaos.

While we wait the few minutes it takes for the car to get to us, I look around, feeling eyes on me yet again. I feel the same eeriness from when I was waiting for Laney at the theater. I scan our surroundings, finding nothing to signal something is wrong, yet that feeling persists.

Our ride arrives, and we get in and start the process of defrosting before having to exit the car once again and freeze our butts off.

We make it to Ellie's house quickly from the hospital and start to remove our many layers, hanging our jackets and scarves on the hooks. Soon enough, we are walking toward the kitchen, starving after hours at the hospital.

"Want to tell me what happened at the yoga studio? I think you skipped over that part earlier today." I point to the stool for Laney to sit down and begin this week of rest. I know she'll be a handful this whole time.

"It was exactly that. I fainted. What can I say? My body reacted to everything, I guess. I don't think it was just the teaching aspect. It was the exhaustion from not sleeping much while you were gone, coupled with the fact that I'm pregnant and the room was really hot. I think it was just too much for my body to adjust to, so I fainted," she says this casually, as if it's a completely normal reaction by the body.

"Well, just so you know, I'll be watching you like a hawk." I hand the tea to her and walk to the fridge to grab her a snack.

"Until you leave in a few days. Then I guess you'll just have to leave me with someone to make sure I follow directions like a good patient." She chuckles to herself, but I don't follow along.

"Yeah, about that. I'm not going on my work trip. I can get out of it. You need me here."

My back is to her, but I know she's probably not smiling anymore, and I bet she's glaring at me in shock.

"No, Grant. No, you're not staying here while you have a job to do. I won't let you stay back and have your career fall to the side. You've worked too hard for this." She crosses her arms over her chest, apparently believing this is an intimidating gesture on her.

"Yeah, it wasn't a question. I'm staying. That's it." My sister might not like the alpha-male thing, but this is the woman I love and our unborn baby. I'm staying back and making sure she's safe and healthy.

"I appreciate what you're doing, Grant, but I'm vetoing this decision. You're going. I'll be fine. Honestly, I think we can tell our families, and I bet my mom will come stay with me while you're gone. No big deal." She shrugs her shoulders and acts as if that should suffice.

"I don't think it's really up to you if I go or not. I've gone years with minimal expenses, traveling and getting jobs all over the world. I don't need the money right now. This was a great opportunity with the travel magazine, but I bet letting this one job go won't make or break anything for me."

I turn my attention back to the fridge and start rummaging through the contents of the shelves. Colton is a growing kid, and I know he's got some great snacks in here to consume after basketball practice.

"Okay, let's meet in the middle. Why don't we table the work discussion for a moment and discuss telling our families? Once we have that in order, we can come back to your job plans and see if we can find a way to make it work? I mean, really, Grant, I was pregnant this entire time, and we didn't know. What's a few more weeks of you getting work done? I don't think it's a problem."

My patience is wearing thin right now, but I also think she has a point. Until a few hours ago, we had no idea there was a baby involved. Had she not fainted, I wonder how long it would have taken for her to figure out she had our child growing inside her.

"Alright. Full disclosure, I did reach out to Rush to see what my options are. So, we *will* be discussing this later, once I have all my options laid out for this trip."

I hired Rush as an assistant to work remotely for me. We've actually only met in person once, but he's great at multitasking and filters through all my DMs, along with my emails. He books assignments for me that fit with my plan and has a great way of talking to executives at big magazines and outside organizations. He's been a great addition to my inner circle professionally these last few years.

"I can accept your terms, Mr. Stanley." Something about the way she's talking to me is getting my full attention. I can't help that I'm insanely attracted to her, but now is not the time.

"Please don't say things like that. I'm trying to focus on taking care of you when all I want to do is strip you down and kiss you all over, Laney. Besides, I don't think that will lead to anything doctor-approved during your week of rest."

I see her cheeks flush, and I know she's now thinking the same thing as me. I know anything like that will have to wait at least the week my sister insisted Laney rest because of the IUD being fully removed. Even though it seems that thing was just hanging around in there and not really doing much else.

I fix her a plate of the most random assortment of snacks imaginable. I'm going to blame the pregnancy cravings because the chocolate-covered pretzels, along with the butter pickles and cheese squares I found, all sound horrific together, yet she's making these gross little pretzel sandwiches with all of them mixed together. I want to gag, but I just smile and let her do her thing.

"So, let's figure out the family situation. How should we go about announcing this to everyone? I mean, I live with my sister, and I think it will be hard to keep from her." She makes a big show of eating the next bite of her snack, and I can't even lie, it's hard to concentrate while she's eating this nasty assortment.

I swallow and try to focus on anything but what she's eating right now. "Yeah, I guess we should start with Ellie. I think we could get away with not telling our parents, but I also think it's not fair to keep them in the dark. Would you hate me suggesting asking them to come into town? Maybe we could have either Becca or Ellie suggest they come visit? I assume we'll tell Ellie before our parents find out?"

Laney's nodding, and from the look of happiness spreading across her face, I can't tell if it's from my plan or the last bite she took of this gross concoction she's orchestrated.

"I think that's a great idea. Let's tell Ellie tonight, because she's going to be hounding me to tell her what happened that caused me to rush to the hospital. She'll also know something is up if I'm resting most of the week, even if I'm not going to be bedridden."

"Like hell, you're not. You're not lifting a finger. I'm going to help you with everything. I'll even offer my services to help you bathe. That's the part I'm really excited about." I smirk, and she narrows her eyes at me, but the smile she's giving me shows she's loving the idea just as much as I am.

We chat a little more about the details of our big reveal, and I start to itch with excitement to tell my mom she's going to be a grandma for a fourth time. I know she's been secretly wanting this for me for so long, but has never made me feel pressured to settle down.

I have a feeling that's all about to change.

Ellie has some sort of "*S*pidey" sense because the moment she gets home and finds us on the couch, she begins to question us.

"What's going on, you two?" she starts without even greeting us.

Laney decides to prolong her sister's torture and acts clueless. "What do you mean? We're watching TV. Wanna join?"

"Don't give me that, young lady. You two weren't speaking for well over a week, and now you're all *cozy* on the couch. Not to mention, you're completely glossing over the fact that *you*"—she points at Laney—"were in the *hospital* less than five hours ago. Out with it!"

Ellie gets feisty when it comes to her family, and this is a complete reminder of that fact.

She won't let up until we spill, so we do just that.

Laney's looking down at her nails, acting as if today is just like any other day. I can't help the pull on the side of my lips, the beginnings of a smile I'm having a hard time hiding.

"Looks like you better gear up, Auntie Ellie!" Laney says, and before I can even think straight, Ellie is pulling her sister to stand and embracing her. I can see their shoulders shake and I assume they're sobbing into one another as they hold each other close.

Then, somewhere in the mix, my sister is called, and she ends up showing up after her shift. They're all screaming in excitement, and I realize my sister was really holding back her happiness earlier at the hospital. I guess she really does have to keep her composure emotionally when she's with patients.

Rubbing my ears in hopes that no permanent damage was inflicted by the volume of hysterics I've just lived through, I look up to find Shane in the doorway. He's looking at my sister and the James sisters embracing while they're yelling about what to do in the upcoming months to prepare for the baby.

Before Shane turns to me, I can't help but notice a bit of sadness passing over his features. I know he comes from a place of happiness for Laney and me, but I think a part of him wishes he could turn back the hands of time and be there with my sister when Olive was born. I know he'll always want that lost time.

The moment he sees me looking at him, he smiles,

genuinely and full of love. He walks over and extends his hand, pulling me into a hug.

"I'm so happy for you, Grant. You're going to make an amazing father. I can't wait to see you in action."

I feel my smile pull so wide, I might never stop. I realize now that this is everything I've ever wanted.

"Thanks, man. Uncle Shane sounds pretty good to me." I wink at him, and he puffs his chest out in pride.

"You're right, it does." I give him another hug, then turn my attention back to the three women making plans for my growing child and its beautiful mother.

Ellie announces a celebratory dinner must be ordered, then rushes upstairs to shower and change into something more comfortable.

Once dinner is ordered and served, the kids join us, and we all celebrate this miracle Laney and I have made together, expanding this amazing group of people I love into an even bigger circle.

CHAPTER 25

Laney

It's been three days since I found out I was pregnant. Grant and I will be parents, and I can't seem to wrap my mind around it all. I guess we have been parents to our baby that never made it onto this earth for over a decade now. This little one growing inside me is our miracle rainbow baby. They've already bypassed an IUD to get here, and I know they're going to take the world by storm.

After letting the thought seep into my mind, I finally called my parents, asking them to meet us in the city this weekend. I wanted to tell them, but I felt strongly that they needed to hear the news in person. Grant did the same, and now I'm sitting here, pulling the clear polish off my nails, nervous about seeing both my parents along with Grace and Rick.

I don't see why I've got a knot in my belly about this, but I feel like nothing in life has gone as planned. I didn't see myself starting a journey into motherhood right now, and yet, it feels right. But, no matter what age you are, telling your parents you're expecting feels strange. Especially because Grant and I have never been a couple as far as they know.

I'm in the middle of my spiral when the doorbell rings, and Grant walks from the kitchen to the front door while I slowly get up off the couch.

Smoothing out my jeans, which in no way need smoothing, I walk toward the foyer to see Grace walking through the threshold with Rick behind her. She's got the same smile as Becca, welcoming and kind, and I feel at peace seeing the happiness radiating off her.

The way she looks at Grant, I can see the love she holds for her "baby." To think I'll soon have my own child and look at them in such a way really is something I look forward to. She finishes hugging Grant, then spots me and moves toward me with her arms outstretched.

"Oh, Laney. You look amazing. You're radiant. Winter seems to agree with you, while I'm feeling like my hands are drier than snakes, and my old lady muscles are more sore by the hour." She chuckles, and I smile at her comments.

Much like Becca, Grace Stanley is someone who has taken life's hardships and made the best of them. They are both fun to be around and extremely nurturing. I give Grace a lot of credit for how Becca brought me under her wing. I know that the way Grace cared for Becca impacted the way she, in turn, cared for those around her when they needed it most.

I pull away, and the smile on my face grows.

"I guess it does. My parents aren't here yet. How was the train ride?"

"Oh, easy. I started a new book, and it felt like no time passed, and we were already in the city." Grant's mom and Rick went to Becca's place to see the twins really quickly, dropping off their bags.

She begins to pull off her scarf while Rick makes his way inside and greets me with a quick hug.

"Why don't we grab a quick snack while we wait for Laney's parents? They should be here shortly, right Lane?" Grant asks.

"Yeah. Mom said their car was close by when she last texted," I add.

"Wonderful. I spoke to your mom earlier, and she assured me you're both okay, so my curiosity is piqued as to why we were summoned," Grace says as she grabs some coffee from the machine.

"You weren't summoned, Mom. We simply wanted everyone together. It's been a while." Grant is horrible at lying, and this is a true example of that.

"Right, because the few weeks since the holidays feel like a lifetime ago. Plus, that week you just spent at my house really wasn't a lot of bonding time, right, Son?" Grace deadpans, knowing her son is full of crap.

Rick laughs, knowing we're up to something, yet I doubt a pregnancy is on their radars.

We sit at the kitchen table, the house quiet as Ellie and the kids are out—Colton's with his girlfriend and her girls are at a birthday party. Ellie will be back shortly after she drops them off. Hopefully, by the time she returns, we'll have filled the parents in on everything we recently found out.

Chatting about Grant's next work trip, which he will be leaving for in a few days, despite him trying to back out of it. He tells us about all the photographs he's planning to take on his next adventure. Pulling out his phone, he's sharing photos of the resort where he's staying, explaining where he'll be and how far he'll be from the locations he needs to photograph.

Grant was able to postpone his departure date, but I didn't let him fully back out of his commitment to this project. He's been waiting forever to work with this company and showcase his work for them, so it's an opportunity I couldn't allow him to step away from. Luckily, after I explained I was fine here with my sister and his, he finally relented and will go for the required days to get his work done.

Grant's in a discussion about the cuisine he heard about at a local restaurant he'll be near when the front door opens, and my mother calls out for us.

I head to the front and find both my parents removing their layers of clothing and putting their bags by the door. Their trip here will be for a few days, then they're heading out to Florida to see some friends who moved there recently. My mom said she's ready for some warm weather, because the Nebraska winter has been harsh this year.

"My Laney, sweetie, how are you?" My mom hugs me and gives me a quick kiss on the cheek. The moment I feel her arms around me, I close my eyes and soak in her love. Something about my mother's embrace is like a balm to my nerves.

"Hey, quit hogging my daughter. I need to say hi, too." My dad practically pushes his way through, this being a part of their regular banter when they see either of their daughters.

"Oh, hush, Kirk. You'll get time with her. Let me say my hellos, and then you can have your time with her." She smiles; my parents have never lost that playful side with each other.

Once my dad gives me a huge hug, lifting me off the ground like he did when I was still a little girl, we make our way into the kitchen. The moment everyone greets one another, it dawns on me that the time has come to tell them our big news.

Grant must sense my anxiety and comes over to pull a chair out for me to sit. He sits next to me and puts his palm on my thigh, a quick squeeze indicating he's here for me and we'll be okay. At least, that's how I'm interpreting his physical touch at the moment.

Grant clears his throat, taking the lead for me as I feel like I've lost my voice all of a sudden.

"Thanks for coming over on such short notice, everyone. Laney and I appreciate it."

At those words, my mom takes a huge intake of breath and looks over at Grace, both of their smiles sneaking across their faces.

I hear one of them whisper, "It's happening!" and they grab onto one another's hands over the table, then bring their gazes back to us.

I internally roll my eyes. Since we were in diapers, these two have been waiting for this day. I guess we'll be giving them more than us dating—a lot more.

I hear Grant chuckle, probably having the same train of thought. "As I was saying, we appreciate you being here. Laney and I have some news." He pauses, and I can feel the crimson wave of color splashing across my cheeks.

"I'M PREGNANT!" I yell.

I can see Grant's head whip in my direction. Yeah, I sort of went off-script just now. The nerves got the best of me. I look over at him apologetically; I know we hadn't planned for it to come out that way, but I couldn't take the way everyone was holding their breath. We had planned on easing them into the news, first sharing that we were dating and then moving toward the pregnancy announcement. I was the one who insisted on slowly dropping the news, yet I caved so quickly.

The moment the words are out, I hear the scrape of chairs across the wood flooring, and both mothers are jumping up and down, screaming. I hear a lot of "OH MY GOD! ARE YOU SERIOUS?! A BABY?!" being thrown out and echoing off the kitchen walls.

My father, the carefree, lovable guy I'm used to seeing, is looking at Grant with an expression I can't read. Oh no, he's mad. That's all I can think of.

"Kirk, sweetie, we're going to be grandparents again! Isn't that amazing?" My mother can't contain her excitement.

"It's definitely something, Janna, that's for sure." His gaze is more like a glare at Grant right now, and I'm not sure how to react. I'm thirty years old, and I think I can make my own decisions and take my life in whatever direction I please. This can't be that surprising.

Both mothers are making their way over toward us, each one embracing us and saying how excited they are. Tears are flowing down their cheeks, and it's hard not to have the same reaction. My hormones have been all over the place, and it's difficult to suppress the emotions I'm having now.

Finally, the mothers settle down and Rick makes his way over, shaking Grant's hand in congratulations. He gives me a hug that takes only a little of the edge off, with my father still not giving us much of a reaction.

Once everyone calms down, all focus goes to my father, who is sitting and looking at us, mostly staring at Grant with an expression I can't quite get a feel for.

He finally stands and walks over toward us. I stand quietly, waiting to see what he says.

"My baby is having a baby?" he says, unshed tears in his eyes.

I feel the lump in my throat and can't seem to get past it,

so I nod, a smile gracing my features because I can't help but feel so much love for this little being inside me right now.

He's holding my shoulders and looking at me in the eyes, really taking in my emotions. We look at one another, matching eyes soaking in this moment. "Are you happy, Laney?"

He almost whispers this to me, and I nod, finally finding my voice, and respond, "Very much so. Yes."

"Your happiness has always been my priority since you were little, but especially since that day many years ago. All I want is to see you happy. If Grant is that piece of happiness, then that's all I can ask for."

I feel a tear escape and fall down my left cheek as my father's words make their way into my heart. I don't need his permission, but I think as his youngest child, I feel like I need to know he's happy for me.

He pulls me in for a hug, and it feels like a blanket surrounding me. I give him an extra squeeze, then he pulls away, his focus on Grant this time.

"You've always felt like a son to me, Grant. I hope you know that I've been rooting for your success as much as I do for my own children. You're going to be an amazing father, and I feel blessed to stand by and watch you grow into that role."

I know my father's words are ones that Grant holds close to his heart. He's grown up with no father of his own, and having my father's blessing feels like an immense win.

Grant wipes away a tear and then pulls my father into a hug. My dad doesn't hesitate to embrace him with all his might, knowing this is something Grant needs as well.

"Thank you, sir. It means a lot to hear that," Grant finally speaks, and my dad chuckles.

"Grant, I've seen you run through the yard naked. I

think calling me 'Sir' after all this time is senseless, no? Call me Kirk like I've asked you to before." My dad smiles then asks, his voice a little more stern, "You love my daughter?"

Grant nods his head, "Very much, si—Kirk. I do, very much. For most of my life, I have," Grant says, no hesitation in his voice.

"That's all I can ask for from the person who will be by her side. Now"—my dad claps his hands together—"what's the plan moving forward?"

"Dad, if you're asking about marriage, that's not something we have discussed yet. We just found out about the baby, and we wanted to make sure everything was okay before saying anything to you guys."

"Nope, not asking about that, although that is something that is on my mind. But, from the glare your mother is giving me, I suppose I can't ask about it further." He moves across the kitchen to grab a coffee. "What I mean is, what's Grant's plan for his job? He's gone more than he's around, and I think it's a fair question."

"Dad, she won't be alone." I hadn't even heard my sister come through the door, but there she is, coming in like the supportive person she has been in my life. She makes her way around the room, giving everyone a hug and giving them her big, happy smile.

Once she reaches our father, she hugs him and continues, "What am I? Chopped liver? I have raised a few kids of my own, you know. I can help where Laney needs it." She looks over and gives me a quick wink.

"Um, if I can chime in?" Grant begins. "Laney and I still have a lot to discuss when it comes to how things will look moving forward, but after this next assignment, I'll be taking a break. That was always the plan, even before we found out about the baby. I think Laney and I need to sit down and see how things will fall into place. I appreciate the support, Ellie, but I also think we need to figure out our lives together. We promise to keep everyone in the loop so that you know what our plan is. Does that sound reasonable?"

For most of our lives, our parents have played a key role in ensuring we're all cared for. I know it comes from a good place, but Grant's right; we need to discuss this first. I know with my income alone I can't afford my current lifestyle in the city. This is something we'll need to figure out together to ensure we're making the best decision for our little family.

I smile at Grant, and he grabs my hand and gives it a squeeze. On autopilot, I lean in and give him a kiss, a small peck on the lips, but it still is the most affection our parents have ever seen us show in front of them.

I immediately hear my mother sigh, and I know she's probably got hearts in her eyes.

My sister is keeping busy, something she does when she's nervous or anxious; however, I don't see what this situation is doing to provoke that reaction. She keeps looking at her phone, and I wonder what it is she's checking on.

As much as she's been a single parent for a handful of years now, she never hovers over her phone in this manner, even when her kids are out, and my senses tell me there's more to her little life than she's letting on right now. I bet it has something to do with a certain retired hockey player.

Grant breaks the silence and stares from both our mothers by bringing the focus back to the baby.

"Would anyone like to see pictures?" The moment he asks this, everyone starts jumping up and yelling their excitement. I can't help but sit back in my chair and embrace this moment of change that's happening in our lives. This is a joyous time, the sounds not setting off any moments of fear or post-traumatic stress for me. The loud voices and hollers from our families are an indication that something magical is happening, and it's almost like all the pieces that felt so far from fitting have finally found a place in my future.

CHAPTER 26

Grant

"I don't ever want to leave you, Little Bean." I kiss Laney's belly while she giggles from the stubble along my jaw that's tickling her skin. I'm soaking up the last few hours we have together, before I have to fly out to my last international job for the foreseeable future. Afterward, I'll return to the city and figure out our next steps together.

"Just remember my voice, little one. I promise I'll be back. Don't give your mama too much trouble." I continue to drop kisses all over her abdomen while Laney threads her fingers through my hair. The movement is so simple, yet it makes me feel like I could doze off again, sleeping in her arms for an eternity.

This is what I've always wanted. Yet, for so long, I was too scared to push for us to be more than friends. I let myself believe that what we had together was enough, and now I see how wrong I was. My heart feels like it's beating at a new rhythm, and the beauty of my world has shifted immensely.

Since that scare in the emergency room, Laney has been

taking it easy, although making a terrible patient, much like my sister was when she had to spend the last few weeks of her pregnancy with the twins on bed rest. But this time, knowing my child is inside there, growing, and I have to miss the next few weeks is agony for me. I know I have to finish off strong with my work, but it doesn't make it easier. I'm already counting down my days away, and I haven't even stepped foot on international soil yet. This is going to be a damn long trip.

I kiss my way up her torso, spending a little extra time on her nipples, because she's already told me they're even more sensitive than usual.

"Grant, don't start something you can't finish. It's agony for me that we can't have sex." She pulls my face to hers so I can kiss her. I relent, because denying Laney means denying myself, and all I want to do is devour her now that we're finally together in all the ways I've ever dreamed of.

"As long as you get the all clear, once I get back, I promise I'll make it up to you. *All the orgasms* when I make love to you."

"Ugh. No. Not that. Don't call it making love, Grant. No thanks." She starts to laugh again, and I can't help but smile. I've always known Laney hated that term, but I love to ruffle her feathers, and now is no different. As long as she's smiling, that feels like winning the lottery.

"What is it with you and the phrase 'making love?'" I rest my head on my right hand while my left continues to caress her belly, imagining her as she grows with the passing months. To feel my son or daughter kick me will be the most beautiful experience.

"Don't you remember my mom took me to her gynecologist, Dr. Wilmer, when I was seventeen? I think the woman was around back in the eighteen hundreds. Well, she did the exam on me and then kept asking me if I was 'making love' instead of bluntly asking if I was having sex. It was so awkward. I think I blushed so hard, I was the color of a tomato. I was so embarrassed. Well, she ruined the term for me. It creeps me out! Now, when I hear the phrase, I think of that old lady doc all up in my business." She's getting worked up, and I'm now covering my face, my body shaking with laughter as I remember her telling me this story when we were teens.

"Of course, I remember. I just wanted to hear you tell the story again because of the disgusted facial expression you make when retelling it. It's absolutely classic!" I legit have tears coming out of my eyes.

The moment I stop my hysterics, I look over to see Laney scowling at me, but I see that little uptick of her lips, indicating she's holding back a laugh of her own.

"Too far, Grant! Stop laughing." Even though she wants me to stop, now she's chuckling, too. Soon, she's laughing so hard, she's crying. Seeing her like this pulls me back in time when we would laugh at absolutely anything. It feels like, although this pregnancy came with a scare, it has brought back a piece of the girl I fell in love with so long ago. I just hope with each step forward, she finds her bearings in a way she hasn't been able to before.

I bring her lips to mine, and I can feel the dampness of her tears on my skin. Laney has never been emotional when I go away for work, but this time feels different for both of us. She was finally allowed to leave the house after Becca swung by and did an in-home assessment on her.

We're standing amongst the crowd of people at the

airport, and all I want to do is call a ride and drive back to the brownstone. I don't want to leave. Not this time. I feel like my entire heart will stay behind and Laney will have it in her hands.

I open my eyes to see those beautiful greens staring back at me, and I feel my heart constrict. I love this woman beyond anything I've ever felt, and I can't wait to hold her again.

"I promise to call you if it's not too late when I arrive." I kiss the top of her head, and she buries her face into my chest, hugging me tighter around my torso. I want to bottle up her smell and take it with me everywhere I go, but I know I'll miss my flight if I don't start going through security now.

"Not *if*. Call me no matter the time. I want to hear your voice. Please?" She rests her chin on my sternum and looks up at me, and I wish she fully comprehended how far I'd go to see her happy.

"Okay, I'll call no matter what." I give her another kiss, this time deepening it. The moment I stop kissing her, I let my forehead rest on hers.

"I love you beyond myself, Laney Marie. Know that you are my everything. Take care of our baby. I know they're in good hands." I kiss the tip of her nose and wink at her.

Somehow, I pull away from her, and I can see the tears falling down her cheeks freely this time. I move through the security line, and I can still see her standing there, her attention on me the entire time. The moment I go through, I know I'll lose sight of her, so I wave and blow one more kiss. I see her turn around and walk toward the exit of the departures terminal, and I can't take my eyes off her.

I turn around to undo my laces and place my shoes on the X-ray scanner, but the moment I stand back up, I feel eyes on me. And it doesn't feel like they're Laney's. It feels similar to the times I've felt this way before, making the hairs on the back of my neck stand up.

I quickly look back to where Laney was, but she's no longer there. I scan the area to see if I can spot anyone I recognize, but no one stands out. I shake my head at the ridiculousness of my actions. I think the nerves of travel are finally getting to me.

Reluctantly, I turn around when the TSA guy gets my attention to go through the full body scanner. Once through the device, I grab my items and make my way to a coffee shop located near the gate I'm flying out of.

The moment I have my coffee and a snack for the plane, I sit down and pull out my phone. Before I left Ellie's house today, I took pictures of the ultrasound photo and put them under my favorites. I scroll through all the black and whites of this little being we made, and I'm still in awe. I think about how, in a few months, our lives will look totally different, but a difference I've longed for without even knowing it. I feel like everything in our lives is starting to make sense after years of fighting against the ugliness that day brought all of us, especially Laney.

Nothing we do will take away the pain she experienced. With each new moment, though, I hope we can see that no path is perfect. We each live a life full of imperfections, but it's how we handle those difficulties that truly defines who we are as human beings.

I get lost in thought for some time, and before I know it, my flight is being called, and I'm boarding the plane. I make sure to take that step forward onto the plane with my right foot, something my mom instilled in me as a superstition from my dad's side of the family. I can't help the smile that seems to be plastered onto my face, because nothing will take away the joy I'm feeling about the future I get to live.

I wake up and take in the views of the ocean and sand in the distance. Fiji hasn't disappointed, and I've only been here for twelve hours. I got in late last night and called Laney. Luckily, it was nearly six in the morning for Laney, and she had fallen asleep early enough that I didn't disrupt her sleep by too much.

The moment I heard her groggy voice, my heart settled. It's hard being here and feeling I'm only complete in her arms. I know that I have left the most important part of my life in New York, and I can't wait to get back. But looking at this view, I can't help but imagine Laney and our baby by my side as we take in this beautiful spot of the world together one day in the future.

I snap a photo with my phone and send it off to her. She's probably in a yoga class and won't see it right now, but I can't help but include her in any way I can. She's back to doing a few sporadic classes and she said it feels good to move her body again.

I've got too much energy, so I decide to start my morning with a run, maybe capture some photos along the beach before I have to meet the company I'm working with on this part of my trip. I know that they have some ideas of what they'd like me to photograph, and I'll be meeting them at a location about thirty minutes away from my hotel.

I've been going non-stop for two weeks while in Fiji. We had a weather delay halfway through the shoot, but we got back on track and finished the photos they requested. I've been itching to get back to Laney, so the weather has been souring my mood. My flight is tomorrow, and I can't get home soon enough.

"Hey, Grant. Want to grab a few beers at the bar before we call it a night?" Antonio calls out to me as I'm about to walk into my hotel room. Going out will help pass the time, so I decide to do just that.

"Sure, man. Let me take a shower and get my suitcase together, and then I'll meet you down at the bar in an hour?" He nods and walks off toward the elevator.

Antonio is one of the crew members from the shoot I'm doing with the magazine. He's probably the most laid-back guy I've met while working in this industry.

I let myself in the room and take a moment to grab my phone and call Laney. It goes straight to voicemail, and I know that she's most likely doing something at the yoga studio. I take a moment to type out a quick text and put my phone aside while I gather my belongings to get myself ready for my early morning flight.

"When I heard you scream, I thought I was going to piss myself."

Actual tears are falling down my face as Antonio and Corey are retelling one of the many times the jungle made itself known during our travels here.

Today, a snake came out of nowhere, and Corey was standing next to a plant that hid the slithering beast until it was right next to his foot. We all started running, but the screams Corey let out were something out of a horror film. Now that we are away from danger, it's hard not to fuck around with him.

I glance up at the screen and see something flash about the United States. I feel the uptick in my heart rate in fear something has happened, which is common since Laney's shooting. But this time, it seems that it's a segment summarizing the violence we see in my home country. Something eases inside me when I realize it isn't a live segment but a compilation of news coverage from over the years outlining the escalating violence in the United States.

I'm about to turn away, but then I see something—no, someone—who looks awfully familiar on the screen. I'm trying to make sense of what I'm seeing on television; however, my mind is firing at a million miles a minute.

The person on the screen looks about ten years younger, in distress and consoling someone who's in his arms. The overall stature of the person is different, but it's him, I know it.

I stand up abruptly, causing my chair to slide along the floor and fall to the ground behind me. I ignore it and start gathering my things. Nothing around me is registering; my focus is only on this image on the television. The moment the broadcast goes to a commercial, I'm rushing out the door.

"Grant, what's up, man? You okay?" I hear the guys calling after me, but I wave them off, and I start toward the elevator, pulling my phone out of my back pocket.

My fingers are trembling because the fear that has taken over my body feels like it might overcome all my muscles.

I pull my phone to my ear, and it rings endlessly, and I feel like my concern is turning into panic. Laney is in trouble or she will be if I don't get ahold of her. Something inside is screaming at me that my instinct isn't an overreaction.

"Hi, you've reached Laney. Just leave me a message, and I'll get back to you as soon as I can. Have a blessed day!" The sound of her voice recording doesn't bring any relief, and all I feel is extreme nervousness. I need to get near her, to hold her, to know that she's safe inside my arms.

Once I get to the elevator, I press the button, turning into one of those people who finds the mere notion that the elevator doesn't open the second I walk up an inconvenience, and I continue to press the button. I feel the bile rising in my throat at the likelihood that something is wrong; I just know it is. Seeing him on that screen, even if it was years before, isn't just a coincidence. There's something about him being somehow connected to Laney that causes me to nearly fall to my knees in fear.

The elevator finally opens, and I rush in and press the button for my floor. I don't care that my flight isn't for hours, I'm going to the airport now and I'll try to get on a flight home sooner than my scheduled one.

As my elevator ascends the floors, I start to text Laney, but her phone is off. I know it because she does that when she teaches or does a class. I know she just started teaching classes again, none in a hot room, though. She got back to the studio right after I left for Fiji, and she said it's been going well.

The pace is a lot slower, she's able to move with the students easily as she teaches the class, and hasn't felt light-headed at all. It was a relief a few days ago to hear how happy she is to be back teaching. But now? Now, I'm in utter fear that she's in danger. If not at this moment, she will be soon.

I'm jumping to conclusions, but something about connecting these dots is leaving me uneasy and on edge. I just need to know she's okay and that she's not in harm's way. Once I can be assured of that, I'll talk this through with her and see her thoughts on the matter.

I get to my floor and decide to call my sister. Ellie is teaching and will most likely not have her phone available to her, but my sister might actually pick up the damn phone.

It rings twice, and the stars must align because she picks up.

"Hey, Grant. You miss me?" my sister says in a playful tone only a big sister can possess.

"Listen to me, Becca. Something's wrong and I think someone wants to hurt Laney..."

CHAPTER 27

Laney

Strolling along the neighborhood this morning, it's hard to ignore how beautiful everything looks, even though we're still in the dead of winter. The trees are bare and lack their regular beauty that comes along with spring, but something about the promise of the warmer climate in the months to come brings with it a sense of a new beginning. I know for Grant and me, it brings a new start to our lives together.

I touch my belly, an automatic thing I've found myself doing for comfort since Grant left, and I feel the smile on my face grow. I can't wait to feel those little flutters that will then escalate to kicks, something I know we are both excited for as we move through the pregnancy.

Each time I speak to Grant, he's quick to ask how *we* are doing, not just me. Even though I knew he would welcome this change, it still catches me by surprise sometimes. For so long, I pushed this away, the possibility of more, because I was hurting from the pain of my past.

I lived life without really dreaming bigger. Because surviving each day felt like the biggest hurdle. I love the life I have built for myself since moving to the city. Finding the strength to get up each new day and try to do better than the last was no easy feat. I know that with this new chapter beginning, I'll feel like I've been given another chance at part of a life I'd previously lost.

I'm well aware that I'll never be that exact same Laney from nearly twelve years ago. I know that I walked away from that trauma a different person, but I've worked so hard to keep putting my best foot forward. I may have kept myself at a distance from many people and experiences, but I didn't fully shut down. Many classmates I had kept in touch with in the very beginning turned to unhealthy ways to release their stress and found themselves completely different versions of who they could have been.

I don't blame them. I understand the pull toward something that numbs the pain. It crossed my mind multiple times. I suffered. I imagined what it would be like to pick up something, anything, to simply take me away from my thoughts. If it weren't for my family getting me the help that truly saved my life, I would have fallen down into the pits of despair. Therapy, guidance, and good support kept me from seeking something that may have pulled me down a hole that would have left me in more darkness than I was already in.

I reach the yoga studio and find a few students walking out of the hot class that just finished. I watch them, their smiles infectious, as they try to bundle themselves up after being in a hot room for the past hour. I will say if there's one thing I already miss, it is the movements in those hot rooms. There's something cleansing about that heat and the way your muscles move a little more easily that really helped me focus in my practice.

I reach the door, and as I'm about to pull it open, I see a hand reach ahead of me and grab the handle. I look back to see Tad standing behind me, his smile present but not reaching his eyes.

"Hey, Tad. It's good to see you." I smile at him. I will always be grateful for his help that day I fainted. I know that seeing someone faint can be too much for some, but from what I was told by those students who were there, many took the lead and helped bring me aid, Tad being one of them.

"Hi, Laney. You feeling okay?" I haven't seen him since the day I fainted, although I haven't been back to the studio much since the incident. Loni is slowly easing me back into teaching.

"Yeah, much better. Seems I'll just have to lay off the hot classes for a few more months, then I'll be in the clear."

I walk toward the back of the studio, pulling out my lock to put my things in a locker. I have back-to-back Yin classes today, and I'm so incredibly excited for them. If I can't be in a hot class, Yin is my next favorite practice. I added new classes to the schedule as I'm limited in my movements still, per Becca.

Tad hasn't said anything, and it has me looking back to see if he's still trailing behind me. I find him following me, his gaze down, his eyebrows drawn together.

"What do you mean you're laying off the hot classes?" He looks completely confused, and I realize maybe word hasn't gotten around about my pregnancy.

Each time I get to tell someone that I'm expecting, I find myself smiling to the point that my face hurts. Right now is no different.

"Oh, um, I'm pregnant!" My voice always raises a bit at the end when I tell people. I sound like a kid letting this personal secret out.

The moment I tell Tad my news, I see his shoulders

stiffen, and the hard look on his face is almost immediate. But then, as fast as his reaction came on, it disappears.

"Wow. Congrats." His words don't match his tone. He sounds less than thrilled, and I honestly don't have the time to dwell on it. Many don't know about my past in Wyoming, so they don't realize how much I have gone through in my short life already. But his reaction lacks any depth and that's off-putting.

What I've experienced is unimaginable to most people, and I try to keep my personal life outside of the studio. The only problem is you can't quite hide a pregnancy bump with yoga pants and tight tops. It's better I let the cat, or baby in this instance, out of the bag now. Plus, with each day that passes, Becca feels more confident that the IUD didn't hinder me from continuing this pregnancy.

I try to show Grant that I'm fine, but inside I feel so scared of doing too much and harming this baby. She keeps telling me that I've lived too much of my life walking on eggshells. I've leaned on my sister and Becca a lot in the last few weeks. Becca wants me to embrace this new step forward with as much love and excitement as possible.

"Thanks, Tad." I smile again and turn away to finish putting my personal belongings in the locker. I place my phone on airplane mode and get my playlist ready for me to cue the music once I get into class.

"Is it his?" Tad's voice is low, but it startles me nonetheless.

"I'm sorry?" I never have super personal conversations with any of my students, so this feels out of my comfort zone.

"Is that guy from a few months back the dad? The tall one with the bright eyes?" He saw Grant for an instant, and he remembers his features down to the eye color? It leaves me unsettled, but I try to brush it aside.

"Yes. Grant is the father." I push through the doors into the yoga room to make sure everything is in order for the next class. Some students are already setting up, and I make sure I'm mindful of their space as they sometimes arrive early to meditate.

I can feel Tad's presence behind me, but luckily, I don't hear any more questions from him as I move around the room, plugging in my phone and distributing yoga blocks and bolsters.

I make my way out the door, grab a water bottle, and speak to Serena, who just finished teaching the last hot class. She's finishing up cleaning the floors of the studio.

"Hey. You teaching another one after this, or are you done for the day?" Our schedules got moved around now with the holidays behind us, and some shifts have been rotated. Yoga studios aren't open at all hours of the day, and there's usually an extended gap after lunch where no teachers are here, and the studio is closed. We open back up when we know more people are coming from work or after school for a class.

"No. This was my last one for the day. Tyson will be teaching one at three p.m., and then I think Nora will be here for some classes later tonight. Are you good to teach your classes then close up?" She's mopping the floor right at the entrance to the hot yoga room and I'm at the front desk, scanning the schedule.

"Don't worry about it. My Yin classes are so chill. I'll finish them, and then I'll head home. I'll be done for the day after that and lock up."

"Okay. Sounds good. I have about another ten minutes here, and I may wash up and then head out. I have a date tonight, so I have to get ready." She winks at me, and I smile back. Serena is newer here, but in the short time she's worked with us, I've really grown to enjoy her company.

She's always telling me about her weird dates with guys from whatever latest dating app is the new craze. I bet she and Olive could exchange some strange stories. Last I heard, Liv was on the verge of giving up on men because the last few dates were that bad.

I wave goodbye to Serena, wishing her luck on her date, and head back into the studio. The moment I start the music, I feel my body instantly relax, and my mind is completely set on the task in front of me. Ensuring my students get the most out of this hour of practice is my biggest wish.

"Laney, that was just what I needed." I'm at the front desk, ensuring all who were in my classes are accounted for on my roster. The timing of this session makes it very difficult to get a full class, but I had a good number of students in both. Tad, along with two others, stayed for the entire two hours, which I've had happen when some students need to get a longer break from the outside world.

I'm focused on the screen in front of me until the last student walks out the door. I lock the front door before I head back to the room, ready to clean up. I notice all the mats have been pulled and placed back, so I go ahead and grab some towels to begin cleaning up. As I enter the room again, the door closes behind me.

I jump, startled to find a student left behind when I thought it was just me in the studio. My heart is already racing when I notice Tad standing in my way, making it impossible for me to pass.

"You scared me, Tad. I thought everyone had left." I bring my hand to my chest, hoping to calm the racing beat beneath my palm.

"Yeah, that's the thing. I'm nearly always dismissed by those around me." He stands there, that unobtrusive student I was so used to now replaced by someone completely different.

His posture is contradictory to the shy person I've grown accustomed to. His features are stone cold as his eyes narrow, taking me in. This isn't the Tad I have gotten to know since he started frequenting the studio.

"What do you mean?" I feel completely lost by his comment. I'm used to him being timid, maybe a little uncomfortable in crowds when we'd have packed classes. I never felt drawn to him, but I will say that his aversion to crowded places was the one thing I thought we had in common. Although I tried to show myself as confident when I was in class, I was never fully comfortable if we had a class that was so packed, that students were mat to mat.

"Tsk, tsk, Laney. Come on. Let's be honest. You never saw me. You just saw some weak guy that came to your classes." He's still standing at the door, blocking my exit, and I feel the panic set in because I know that whatever he's trying to accomplish here isn't a situation I want to be stuck in.

He continues, "You never saw me each time I watched you from afar. At that club, grinding yourself against *him*. Or outside of the hospital. Or at the damn theater! I saw how distraught you were at the airport, saying goodbye like it was the end of the world."

Realization dawns on me that he's been following me outside of the studio and I can't help the unease that rolls through me.

"Listen, Tad. You've always been super kind. That's what I saw each time I had you in my classes." I'm trying to keep my voice calm and even, but I can sense the unease in my words.

"Don't placate me, Laney. You think I'm stupid too?!" he yells the last part at me. I can tell my kindness is being taken as a form of offense to him, and it's not making the situation better. It's only feeding the anger he has within him.

"Tad. I'm so confused. Please, tell me what's going on. Is this because I didn't agree to go out on a date with you?" The moment I say it, I regret it. The look on his face proves that my question was a step in the wrong direction.

A creepy chuckle escapes his mouth, and it causes the hairs on my arm to stand at attention. "You think that your rejection is what's upsetting me right now? No, your inability to see what's best for you is what's infuriating me right now. You think I don't know the kind of guy Grant is for you? And now you're having *his baby*." He's shaking his head in disgust, and I'm feeling even more clueless now than I did when he first trapped me in here.

"Seriously, Tad. What is it? Did I do or say something to hurt your feelings?" He starts to laugh harder now, and it only pulls me further into a pit of fear. I feel like I'm on the outside looking in.

"Laney, listen. You're someone I saw a future with. I saw something special in you, but now I see you're no different than the rest of them. You just brushed me aside like the rest always have. I mean, look, we lived through the same experiences, like our lives are parallels of each other, and you still don't see how special we could have been together."

Now I'm getting mad. He keeps talking around whatever fucked up notion he has conjured up, and I really need to understand what it is that he's referring to. Parallel lives? What the hell is he talking about?

The thing is, Tad is bigger than me. He isn't as tall as Grant by any means, but he's stockier. On top of that, I'm pregnant. I won't jeopardize my baby by physically struggling with him so I can get free. I have to be smart about my next move.

My phone is too far from me to call for help. It's still connected to the audio system in this room and in airplane mode. My one hope on that front is that someone will find that my absence at home is worrisome and come looking for me at some point.

I have something bigger than myself to live for, and I won't live a life of fear when it comes to this man in front of me. I've faced the ugliest of demons, and I won't cower anymore. That's what my therapist has always told me. No matter how much I might run from the darkness, it always finds a way back in when we least expect it.

For years, I had prepared for the nightmares. For so long, I expected to be swept down into the depths of depression. But never in all my time did I expect myself to be trapped with some crazy person that keeps talking in code, never getting to the fucking point.

I pinch the area between my eyes, the headache already starting because my anxiety is through the roof. "Tad, I'm begging you. Please tell me what you're talking about. Nothing you're saying makes sense."

"Of course, it doesn't make sense. I'm the only one who was seeing what we could have been with clear eyes. You've been ignoring this thing between us, and now here we are and you're carrying another man's baby." He begins to pace in front of the door. I can't run out without him grabbing me. "You've ruined everything!" he yells, and throws his arms up toward the ceiling.

His tone is escalating, and I am still frozen in the spot I was when he first got my attention. With his rising anger, I feel the first tear fall down my left cheek. I keep my eyes on him, hoping that if I remain quiet, he'll continue to explain his behavior, maybe moving a bit to his right and giving me an opportunity to run out of this room.

"Laney, you and I are meant for one another. I thought that's what I had with Nori, but with you, it's stronger. Nori didn't know any better. She leaned on me when she needed to use me, and then she left me behind. She and I lived through the worst day together, then she used me to feel better. When she was done she tossed me aside. But you and I? We're meant to be together. We both lived through the unthinkable, and we're here, crossing paths. It's meant to be."

The moment he says we've lived through the unthinkable, I feel like I'm going to be sick. Was he there?

"Were you at my school that day, Tad?" I whisper. It's hard for me to bring up the shooting, and my voice always gets lost beneath the trauma I have left within me from that day.

"No, Laney. I wasn't there with you. But, two years later, I lived the same day you did. Except I was left behind, never finding my way back into this life. That is until I found you. You and I belong together. I know our paths didn't just cross out of coincidence. We lived through horribly similar events, and I'm just supposed to ignore that?"

His voice raises the more he talks. I can feel his anger, it's palpable.

"I'm really sorry you went through—"

"Don't treat me like a victim, Laney. You sound like everyone else. No one understands what it's like going through something like that and trying to piece together the life we're left behind with. That day caused me to completely change everything about myself. I walked on this earth, completely shattered, until I met you."

"Tad, we've both lived through something horrific,

you're right. And I think it's incredible you're standing here with me. We've both been able to give life another chance." I speak as calmly as I can, hoping not to anger him further.

"You sound like a fucking shrink!" I probably do because it's something I was told very early on when I first survived the shooting. But saying it in this instance, I feel it to my core now that I have perspective from that event. Had I given up years ago on myself, I wouldn't be able to have what's about to happen next: a life with Grant and our child.

"The last thing I want you to think is that I'm psychoanalyzing you. I'm being honest. It took me many years, but each moment I get to live, I now see what a gift it is. It's not a burden."

"Speak for yourself. It's been a burden for me. But then I entered this yoga studio and took your class. You greeted me and gave me that big smile. I was told to try a class to see if it would help. And sure enough, of all people to teach the class, it was none other than a survivor herself.

"Of course, I didn't know that at the time. It was simply an attraction that first moment we met. I went home and googled your name, learning more about your yoga journey. It took some time, but I found your name buried in web postings of the shooting in Wyoming, and my heart nearly burst, it was beating so hard. Don't you get it? We're meant to be together."

I remember my therapist telling me that becoming obsessive could be a coping mechanism after surviving a trauma like I had. I started to show signs of it when I first started practicing yoga. I would practice multiple times a day, diving into it to the point that I ate, drank, slept, and breathed yoga. It wasn't until she saw my behavior sway toward becoming obsessive that she asked me to start weaving in some different activities to keep my mind occupied. That's when I picked up romance books, and from there, I've branched out to walking, going outside to spend time with my family, and doing other activities to keep my mind occupied in a more healthy manner.

"Tad, I'm so sorry if I gave you the wrong impression. You're so incredibly sweet, but—"

Tad slams his hand against the wall, startling me. I can't help the tear that escapes, and I feel my hands begin to tremble.

"Stop, Laney. You're not understanding me. *We* are together. Not you and Grant. That's not how this is supposed to go. I saw everything so clearly the moment I realized we shared so much in common. You're supposed to be with *me*. You're *mine*. Not his. He'll never love you the way I can love you. There's not a part of me that wouldn't sacrifice myself to ensure your happiness. That's what our love would be. It would be divine. You'd forget all about Grant the moment I showed you how I could love you properly."

I hear how much he believes his words, completely ignoring the fact that this idea is ludicrous. I bow my head in defeat because no matter what I say, he won't let me out until I start to play into this little game he's conjured up in his mind.

We stand there, me trying to absorb the situation I'm in while he's seeing me as his only salvation.

I feel the lump only growing bigger in my throat. What I'm about to say is so far from the truth, but it might be my only way out of this situation. I need to get myself and our baby to safety. The only way that's going to happen is if I get out of this studio.

"You're right, Tad. Grant can't give me the life you can give me. I was hiding my feelings from you because I felt trapped with Grant—like I owed him."

At first I think he's not buying my words. But then he begins to nod, liking how I'm uplifting him, while taking Grant down with my confession.

I continue, "If I ever saw my future with anyone, it's with someone like you. We can get out of here, you can raise this baby as your own, and we can begin anew."

I speak softly, hoping somewhere deep inside, he'll understand that my safety is key right now to ensure the wellbeing of my child first and foremost.

"Exactly, Laney. That's what I've been trying to say. I'm so glad you see it clearly now. Grant is no good. I hate that he got you pregnant, but I can raise that baby as my own. We can do this together. Nothing in life needs to be as difficult for our child as it was for us. We can make sure of it."

I'm nodding, unable to formulate words as it feels like bile is making its way up my throat. I feel disgusted with myself for what I just said. But I need to keep focused on getting out of here, hoping that once we get outside, someone will be walking by, and I can catch their attention and get away from Tad and his crazy idea of a future together.

I begin to walk toward him slowly to ensure he won't see through my lies, moving my hand out for him to grab. The moment he grasps my palm, I want to vomit. I feel disgusted by this man because he's claiming he loves me, but instilling fear in me while doing it.

I understand he's in a fragile state, something I can relate to more than I'd like, but at the same time, it's hard to see past the hurt he's causing me. Worst of all, the potential damage he could be posing to me and my baby.

He pushes the door open, and we begin to walk, me leading him toward the door while he's got my hand in his. I'm a few steps away from the front entrance of the studio when I feel him tug on my arm, pulling my body back. I turn my attention back to him, even though all I want to do is get outside on the busy street.

"Wait, wait, wait. You're playing me, aren't you? You really think I'm that dense?"

Right when this realization dawns on me that my plan may go to shit, I hear a firm banging on the window of the glass door. I swing my gaze back toward the front of the studio and see Becca and Shane at the door. The panic when they see me standing inside with Tad and the doors locked seems to increase their need to get inside.

"Laney, open the door!" Shane yells, his gaze jumping from my eyes to Tad's.

I look back at Tad, trying to have the same even tone I had in the yoga room, but failing as fear begins to creep up with each second that passes.

"They're going to break the door down. I need to let them in." I look up at him right then and see the defeat in his gaze, but he doesn't let go of my hand.

"No, Laney. I'm sorry. But I finally have the ability to have peace and love in my life. I'm not giving that up." He grabs my upper arm and begins dragging me toward the back door. I can hear Becca screaming while I'm trying to resist him.

He turns his body toward me, trying to get a better grasp on me, and that's when I find the opportunity to knee him in the balls.

With a curse, Tad falls to the ground, grabbing his groin, his face turning red.

I rush toward the front door, my fingers shaking as I turn the latch to lock it.

The moment I feel the cold air of the New York winter upon my face, I feel the relief wash over me. Shane bypasses me and goes straight to Tad, bringing his hands behind his back and putting all his weight on Tad's back to ensure he can't move. Normally, Tad would probably have struggled, but the pain he's still feeling from my fight is keeping him from getting out of Shane's grasp. It helps that Shane is ex-military and this likely isn't the first person he's put to the ground.

Becca engulfs me in a hug, and I begin to cry. The fear I have rushing through my veins feels like it's going to consume me. I've never been more grateful for the self-defense classes I took with my sister and Becca than I am right now. The moment the three of us were in the same city, we took classes because we didn't feel comfortable living on our own without some way to protect ourselves.

I hear Becca shushing me as my body shakes from the sobs breaking free.

"You're okay now, Lane. You're okay, sweetie. I've got you. He won't hurt you."

I grasp onto her coat and allow myself to let go. All the emotions from the last thirty minutes pour out of me.

I'm sitting in the police station after giving my statement. The warm cup in my hand is providing me with all the comfort I need while I wait for Becca and Shane to finish talking to the authorities. The police took Tad into custody, and I'm still baffled by what transpired this afternoon.

I hear footsteps, and I look up to find a flustered Ellie searching the precinct for me. The moment her blue eyes find mine, she rushes toward me.

"Oh my gosh, Lane. I'm so sorry." She pushes my hair aside, searching my face for any of the pain she's once seen in my gaze. "Are you okay?"

I nod, the emotion creeping back up and threatening to spill again. I finally find my voice to explain more.

"Yes. The paramedics checked me out before I made it over here. They cleared me, probably because Becca said she'd be taking me back to her office to do a proper assessment. But I don't feel hurt, and he didn't do more than tug on my arm really hard."

The moment I say this, my sister takes the blanket that's wrapped around my shoulders off to inspect for any injuries. There are red marks on my upper arm, but nothing that won't heal with time. The emotional damage is always way deeper anyway.

"I'm so glad you're okay." She pulls me into another embrace, and I can feel that it's more for her comfort than mine. I know how much I've put my loved ones through with all the *experiences* I've had, so I let her have this moment to ensure I'm okay. Soon enough, though, her phone is vibrating, and I can almost bet money it's our parents.

She keeps an arm wrapped around me while grabbing her phone to answer the call.

"Yes, she's fine.... I promise, Mom.... No, Dad, the guy isn't here.... No, I won't give him a message...." A second passes, and then she sounds like she's trying to get through one of those automated calls to reach an operator. "No.... Yes.... Yes.... No.... I don't know.... Yes.... No...." She steals a glance over at me and winks, knowing that our parents aren't going to allow her to get off the phone until all their questions are answered.

"I promise, if there is anything to report, I'll keep you informed.... Yes, I'll start a group chat with Laney... I know, you're right, we should've had one going before now....Uh-huh.... Yep.... Nope.... Okay.... Got it.... Yes.... No need.... Okay...."

She finally hangs up but doesn't complain. I think now that she's a parent herself, she doesn't find their behavior as overprotective or overbearing. They care, and that's where this is stemming from.

"You know you'll have the Spanish Inquisition waiting for you when we get back home. They're home with my girls. Colton is none the wiser. He has a game, and I didn't fill him in beforehand. I hope you don't mind. The kid has enough to worry about."

I give her the best smile I can muster and nod. My parents are just in town for a day between trips.

"I know Mom and Dad come from a place of concern. I won't judge them for making sure I'm okay. I've been through enough to know they need to see me to believe I'm okay."

We take each other in. As much as I'm dealing with my own traumatic event right now, I can't help but notice my sister looks different. Now that her concern for me has dissipated, seeing I'm overall going to be okay, she looks relaxed in a way. I wonder what that's about. I know I can steal her away at some point and have some sisterly time with her to get the scoop. I know I'll need it after the day I've had. And I'm well aware I can point all this back to a certain grumpy man who has been spending time with her, and it seems to have relaxed her in a way I wasn't expecting.

That's when it dawns on me, I haven't updated Grant. Shit. He probably called on the way to bed, and my phone is still in the yoga studio.

"Can I use your phone? I need to message Grant." I bring my palm out for her to hand me her phone.

"Sure, but just so you know, he's a step ahead of you. He's probably in the air right now. He pieced things together and called his sister. That's why Becca was at the studio when you were arguing with Tad."

I'm about to open my mouth to ask more questions, but she stops me before I do, as if reading my mind.

"I don't know how Grant figured it out. I don't know if Becca really knows. He called her and quickly started telling her that you could be in danger and asked her to go to the yoga studio to check on you. He told her he was headed to the airport to try to catch an earlier flight. I'm not sure if he was able to do so, but I'm assuming he did. He's quite persistent when he wants to be."

I type a quick message to Grant, hoping that the moment he can see it, it will prove to him that I'm okay.

Right then, one of the office doors opens, and Becca comes out. Shane follows right after her, shaking the officer's hand behind him. Once they reach me, I can feel my emotions getting the best of me again. The tears begin to pool in my eyes when I look up at everyone surrounding me.

"Thank you both for being there when you were. I don't know what would have happened. I lied to Tad and told him I would go with him, with the plan being to get outside and run or scream… or I don't know what. But he figured it out, and that's when you caught us. He was trying to go out the back, and luckily, that self-defense move got me out of a bad situation."

The mere thought of him touching me makes my skin crawl. I rub my arms with the memory of his forceful hands on my body. It's hard not to let my mind wander toward what could have been had I not escaped.

"Miss James, Mr. Lameley will be held, and bail will be set in the morning. Here's my card if you need anything. I'll reach out once I know more." The officer hands his business card to me, my fingers still shaking as I grasp the small paper.

I nod my head, trying to get a full understanding of

what transpired today. Everything started out so well, and it's hard not to feel the polarity of the shift from giddiness when my day started to how it ended, much like that day in Wyoming years ago.

Becca is the first to speak once Officer Sedder leaves the area, "Listen, Laney, I know you're scared, but we're all here for you." She embraces me, and I feel completely at ease knowing they've got my back.

"But the baby," I croak out with little volume to my voice.

"Are you feeling any cramping, or have you bled?" Becca asks. I shake my head, and I see my sister's shoulders visibly relax with my answer. I think they're all on edge, concerned about what another loss might look like for me emotionally. I understand their concern all too well, because it's passed through my head multiple times since this whole thing started with Tad this afternoon.

"I'll do a full assessment after this at the office, and I can even get the little one on the monitor for you again so you can see them with your own eyes. But your body is stronger than you think, and remember that you're keeping that baby safe, much like you were even before you knew you were pregnant." Becca's reassuring voice carries over me like a soothing hug.

"How did you know to come to me?" Now I'm finally able to sort out my thoughts, and my mind is racing with questions as to how she knew, or I guess Grant knew, that something was wrong.

"Grant called me in a panic. He saw something that made him want to ensure your safety, and he begged me to drop everything and make sure you were okay. He didn't elaborate. When I tried calling him once I knew you were safe, it went to voicemail. Then one of the associates on the trip sent me a quick text explaining Grant was able to get on a red-eye home and gave me the flight details."

"Could someone grab my phone from the yoga studio? I left it in the room where I taught my last class." I worry my lip with my upper teeth, wondering how I'll feel stepping back into a sacred place like that again without thinking of Tad.

Shane is the first to speak up, "I'll make sure to swing by and grab it for you. I'll meet you all at Becca's practice before heading to my friend Neil's place."

"Okay, well, that's settled. Now, let me get you to the office so I can check on my niece or nephew," Becca says, showing no sign of fear or restraint when referring to the baby being okay.

I can only hope that she isn't wrong.

CHAPTER 28

Grant

It feels like I've been transported back in time eleven years as I'm running through the airport to get to Laney. Luckily, the stars aligned when I got to baggage claim. My suitcase is one of the first to come out, and I'm off to find the car I ordered when we were getting hooked up to the gate.

From the various texts that came through on my multiple layovers I saw that Becca offered to pick me up, but the last flight got into LaGuardia at an ungodly hour, and I thought it was best that I find a way home without disrupting her sleep.

While I was hopping from plane to plane, I was able to communicate with Laney via text. Just brief check-ins to ensure she's okay. I don't know how much of my concerns were warranted, but I also haven't had a chance to properly talk to anyone aside from updates on my flights and making sure Laney and the baby are okay.

The moment I pull up to Ellie's brownstone, I try to keep my movements quiet. I unlock the front door and move through the house, making sure I don't drop anything or make too many sounds that might scare anyone who's sleeping in the house.

The moment I'm upstairs, I can feel my pulse quicken. I've needed to have Laney in my arms for days now, feeling like this distance has taken years off my life.

The moment I open her door, I see her lying with her back facing me, her breathing even. I toe off my shoes and remove my clothing, leaving me in only my boxers. I need to get in bed with her and feel her warmth against me.

I pull up the covers, and I see her stir. By the time I slide in next to her in bed, she turns her body toward me, her eyes only slits as she takes me in.

"I missed you," she says it in a whisper, and the moment I bring her into my embrace, I feel like everything has fallen into place. But while I'm feeling relief, I feel her shoulders shake.

"Laney, what's wrong? Are you okay? Is the baby okay?" I feel the panic creep back in, when, moments ago, I felt instant relief being by her side once again.

With her face against my chest, her voice is muffled, "Yes, we're okay. But things weren't okay yesterday, and all I wanted was you near me."

I stiffen with her confession and feel the anxiety I felt in that bar start to slither its way up my spine, much like it did when I called my sister with dread in the pit of my stomach.

"Tell me what happened, Lane." I bring my index finger under her chin, and her gaze connects with mine. Her lashes are wet from her tears, and I know that she's hurting, and all I can think about is making it right.

"It was Tad." At the mention of his name, I know whatever she's going to say to me might leave me seeing red. I rub her back, hoping that movement alone will motivate her to continue, and she does.

"He held me against my will at the yoga studio because

he wanted us to be together. He seemed to be upset with the news of the baby and that I was with you. I was terrified, Grant. I was so scared something was going to happen to our baby. I'm so sorry that happened."

"You're sorry? Why are you sorry, babe?" I take in her beautiful face, the moonlight seeping in and giving me just enough light to take in her beauty in this natural setting.

"I just put myself in harm's way again. Why am I always in the wrong place at the wrong time? I've had bad things happen before, and then I lost the baby. I was so scared that it would happen again."

Now, the tears are flowing down her cheeks, and all I feel is a need to make the pain go away. She's here, though, looking as if she's okay from what I'm seeing.

"You're okay, Laney. It's okay. I'm home now. I won't let anything happen to you." I hold her as she lets the emotions seep out, slowly calming down, and her breaths become even.

"Sleep now. The baby's okay?" She nods, and I feel a part of me relax, even if it's a very small part. I want to continue this conversation, but I also know Laney needs her rest. I can see her fighting sleep, which I assume comes from a long twenty-four hours of whatever happened.

Laney falls asleep with her head on my chest, but I'm wide awake. I know my restlessness comes from all the possibilities going through my head of what Tad may have done to her. Fucking Tad. If he ever comes near my girl again, he's a dead man.

The next morning, Laney wakes up as I'm getting out of the shower in her bathroom. She slowly moves around the cramped space, not leaving much room for me to maneuver without touching her body here and there. Each time I touch her, I can see desire in her gaze. I know what she wants, but we need to talk about what happened while I was gone. The lack of sleep is a testament to the fact that it's taking over my thoughts. Too bad my dick doesn't have the same mindset.

I harden as I move around her, and she must feel it because she pushes her ass out to mess with me a little more. I give her a light tap and then kiss her cheek.

"Good morning, beautiful. Want some tea?" I can tell she's disappointed right now that her advances didn't work on me, but hopefully, we can resume this seductive dance later. She nods at me in response to my question, so I dry myself off and start to get some clothes on to make my way downstairs. She puts some toothpaste on her toothbrush and starts to ready herself.

"I want to talk to you about everything that happened. But I also know you can be a beast in the morning if I don't feed you and the little one, so I'll meet you in the kitchen." I kiss her head, and she smiles around her toothbrush while simultaneously rolling her eyes at my beast comment.

I head downstairs. The house is quiet with everyone else at school. I reach the kitchen and start a cup of coffee for myself while heating up water in the kettle. I look in the fridge and find some eggs to scramble and some bread to toast to get Laney some energy to start the day.

Soon enough, I hear her footsteps coming down the stairs. The moment I turn, I see her beautiful face brighten with a smile. I can't help the smile I throw back in return. How I kept myself from expressing my feelings for her sooner will always be a mystery to me. Because, right now, all I want to do is stare at her and tell her how whole she makes me feel.

I hand her the tea and then begin plating the eggs and

toast. The moment I'm about to give her a scoop of scrambled eggs, she says, "No, thank you!" scrunching her nose in disgust. When I left, she was all about eggs again, but it seems she's back to feeling sick at the thought of them.

This is new, and I think the shock on my face urges her to explain. "Since you've been gone, some food aversions have returned. I now don't like eggs… again. The thought alone makes me want to gag." She makes a disapproving gesture and reaches for the plate with the toast.

Once we both have food, we sit at the table, and I make sure to keep my plate on the other side of me so the eggs don't bother her too much.

"Grant, you could be sitting across the street, and I could probably smell them. Don't worry about it. I'll breathe through my mouth for now." She winks as if it's no big deal. "I should have told you before you came downstairs."

I chuckle and start to eat, still trying to keep the scrambled mess away from her line of sight, even though it's probably a pointless feat.

"So, do you want to tell me what happened?" I start because I can't truly express to her how anxious I am to hear what she has to say about the last twenty-four hours.

"I feel like you have just as much to explain on your end. How did you know something was up? I know you told Becca to rush to the yoga studio," she fires back, curiosity painting her features.

"It was a total coincidence, I guess. I was sitting at the bar with some of the guys from the crew, and the TV just happened to be on a documentary of sorts talking about violence in our country. Of course, the segment focused on mass shootings, something that's not as common outside of the U.S. I didn't think much of it at first once I realized it wasn't a breaking story. But then something on the screen caught my attention. Had I not really been looking at that time, I would have missed it." I take a sip of my coffee, still in shock from the timing of it all.

I continue my retelling, "When one of the news segments captured some students from one of the school shootings here a few years back, one of the spectators looked familiar. At first, it didn't hit me, but then I realized who it was. I thought it was maybe Chad, but then the more I said it, the more it didn't sound right in my head. It dawned on me that it was Tad, and he was the guy I got the creeps from at the yoga studio."

I run my hand through my hair, exhaustion forgotten as I recount how I was feeling before calling my sister. "I knew something was off about the guy. But I never thought it was something like this. I honestly just put two-and-two together that you had never mentioned Tad having a commonality with the school shootings, which would have been something you would have told me about as it's an unusual coincidence. So, I literally ran with it, calling you, then proceeding to call my sister for help."

When I'm done telling Laney everything, the look of shock is evident on her face. She takes a moment, most likely processing everything I just said.

She clears her throat and begins, "Well, to say your timing is impeccable is an understatement. I hadn't seen Tad since I fainted at the studio. When I got there yesterday to teach my yin class, he was there. He asked how I was feeling, and I told him I was fine, but just have to avoid the hot yoga for a while. That led to me telling him that I'm pregnant. I could tell the news agitated him, but I honestly let it go. I barely know the guy. Turns out I should have listened to my instincts because he turned on me at the drop of a dime. The moment the studio cleared out, he hid from view until I was most vulnerable. He closed the door of the class I was cleaning up and didn't let me pass. He went on and on about how you were wrong for me and he and I were meant to be together."

I see a flicker of remorse across her features, and I know there's more to the story she's not telling me. I grab her hand, allowing my fingers to rub against her knuckles in hopes that she continues speaking.

After a deep exhale, she continues, "I had to say some things to try and get him to let me out of the locked room. I lied my way out that door, and I feel awful, Grant."

"It's okay, babe. I know you were in an unimaginable situation." I hope my expression is full of compassion because right now, I know whatever she's feeling guilty over isn't fair to put on her.

"I had to tell him that you and I weren't a good match and that he would be a better choice. I lied in the most awful way in order to get him to side with me. I was hoping it would save me and the baby. It got me out of the room, but he still caught on to what I was doing. That's when a struggle ensued. I fought him off of me. Luckily, nothing more happened, and he didn't hurt me or the baby."

"I promise, Laney. Nothing you said to him is being held against you. Where is Tad now?" I'm trying to keep my anger at bay, but the fact he laid a hand on someone I love, in this case, the mother of my child, is something that is making me see red.

"He's out on bail. I'm not sure what comes next. The officer told us he'd keep us updated. That's all I know."

I nod, knowing we're all in a bit of limbo as we wait to see what comes of Tad's future. The fact that he likely has PTSD that is untreated and unmonitored makes me think that he began to live in a fantasy versus the reality of his life after the shooting. It makes sense, as everyone copes differently.

"I feel for him, too. That's what's so strange about this whole thing, Grant." She's fiddling with her fingers, a habit I've seen her sister do a lot of the time when she's anxious. Laney has only done it a few times when she's under extreme stress.

I engulf her hands within mine, squeezing them so that her gaze meets mine again.

"You care because you're compassionate. Something I love about you. I see why you'd feel a part of you leaning toward that side, but you have to remember that you had the same devastation as him, and you didn't go off and do such things to others. You may have had a hard time coping, but you never put someone in harm's way. That's what I need you to focus on. What he did could have impacted you and the baby."

She's nodding along while I speak to her, and I know she's aware of all this, but a part of her really is feeling bad that his life mimicked hers in a huge way, and then his mental health deteriorated.

"No one is ever the same after trauma. People are forever altered. It can shift our lives in a way that is unexplainable, so that's the part of me that hurts for him. I know that what he did was wrong. And I just know that this whole thing will only make things harder for him, especially if he doesn't get the help he needs. It will only worsen everything for him."

"I think we've both had endless talks about how the mental health system here is subpar at best. I think with all that has deviated in the safety of places we once considered the best ones to go to in a crisis has really had lasting effects on all of us. And it keeps worsening. So, I will agree that he may not get the help he needs. I think what we need to do is make sure we stay on top of the investigation. We need to ensure that he doesn't fall through the cracks, no matter what way this all goes."

I know for me, I will not sit still until I know this man is no longer a threat to Laney or our family. I see this as a wake-up call that we need to be mindful of our surroundings, and Tad is an added factor that we must keep vigilant about.

We finish up our breakfast and decide to head back to bed. I don't argue, as I barely slept. We have a few more hours before we are meeting at my sister's house to have an early dinner with my niece and nephew. Ellie's kids will be with us as she's got plans tonight. It seems this casual fling is growing into something more, although Laney said Ellie is fighting it. *It must run in the family.*

As we're walking up the stairs, Laney says, "I got to see the baby after we left the police station." She has the biggest smile on her face, and I realize that it's moments like these I live for. Of course, I'm going to have to bug her about this because I missed out on seeing our baby.

"Oh really?" I tickle her around her ribs when we get to the top of the staircase, and she starts to squirm. "You kept that little factoid to yourself for quite some time. That's pretty sneaky, Bean."

Her laughter carries down the hall, and I pull her into my arms and kiss her. Once we get to her room, things turn fairly quickly from a simple kiss to something more urgent, my exhaustion from the lack of sleep long-forgotten.

She's clawing at me, vibrating with need as we move closer to her bed. I melt into her touch, longing for her hands to touch me all over.

I finally pull myself out of this haze she has me in and realize we might not be in a position to do this yet. "Baby, can we do this? Did you get the all-clear?"

A small smile takes over her features. "It *may* have been

something I asked about when I got that ultrasound yesterday. You should have seen Becca's face twist at the thought. It was *hilarious*."

I can't help it, and my head goes back as a thunderous laugh comes out. It feels good to let go a bit and enjoy these little moments together.

"Well then, on that note, less talking about my sister and more of us getting these clothes off."

We've been apart too long at this point, and we both need this right now. I start to bring her sleep pants down, and that's when I realize she has nothing else underneath.

My gaze shoots up to hers, and I can't help the appreciation when I say, "Looks like you came prepared."

"I'm prepared, but I haven't *come* yet." This woman and her sass. Let's see how my next move gets her going.

I fall to my knees and bring my lips to her center, and she immediately puts her hands in my hair and tugs hard. It only spurs me on to lick her sensitive center. She throws her head back on a moan, and I can tell she's going to come apart quickly.

I break away, and she protests, trying to bring my face back toward her.

"Move back and lay on the bed. Get comfortable. I'm starving for you, Lane."

She wastes no time moving her body toward the bed, and I pull her hips to the edge. I bring one of her legs over my shoulder, and my lips are back to her center, where she's ready for me to lavish her. I flick her clit, and she moans again, bringing her hands back to my hair. Feeling her lose herself in my touch does something to me, and I push forward, knowing that I can't do anything further before feeling her come on my tongue.

I slowly bring a finger, then two, into her, pumping at a rhythm with my tongue flicking her clit. She's riding my face, and it's the hottest thing I've seen. Fuck, I've missed her.

Her thighs start constricting my face, and she's moaning and panting, yelling out that she's coming while she moves her hands in my hair, trying to control the way my face moves against her pussy.

Her orgasm hits hard, and then she slows her movements while I lick her up. I'm so fucking hard for her now, and I feel my cock straining against my basketball shorts.

While she's catching her breath, I stand up and pull my shorts down. My cock is at attention for her, and I can't wait to feel her walls squeezing me.

I pull the shirt over my head and then begin to trail kisses up her body, pushing her sleep shirt over her head. The moment I expose her chest, I suck her left nipple into my mouth. She arches her back, and I'm happy to see the sensitivity to this spot hasn't diminished since I've been with her last. I'm kneading her opposite breast, loving the way she's writhing underneath my touch.

"You're so fucking perfect," I say as I lift my gaze toward hers. She's smiling at me, her eyes like slits, her cheeks pink from her arousal. "I need to be inside you, Laney. Are you sure it's okay?" I can't help but make sure we can go further. I don't want to put my needs ahead of what's best for her and the pregnancy.

"If you don't fuck me right now, Grant, I'm going to really lose it on you." She tries to sound all-powerful with her tone, but it's lost on me. It's hard to take her seriously while I'm pinching her nipples and nipping at them, and she's reacting to every one of my touches.

"Your wish is my command, love." I suck on her nipple again, this time pulling my lips off and slowly blowing some air onto them, causing her to moan again. While she's distracted, I line my cock up and begin to slowly push myself into her. The moment my crown is lost inside, I close my eyes and drop my forehead to her chest. She feels fucking fantastic.

I keep inching in while I feel her attempt to move things along a little faster by digging her heels into my ass in hopes it will spur me forward. Too bad I'm enjoying this a little too much, and moving fast is the last thing I want to do. I'm savoring this moment because I've been waiting too damn long to feel her strangle my dick.

I bring my lips to the crook of her neck and begin to kiss her there and up along her jaw. "Laney, I'm taking my sweet time with you. My cock has ached to be inside you, and I'm not going to rush this moment right now. Let me savor you. Let me love you."

"Mmmhmm." She succumbs to my slow rhythm and allows me to languidly pump in and out of her. I move her up on the bed so I can bring my legs onto the mattress. I sit up on my knees while she brings her knees toward her chest, her back flat on the bed. I grab a pillow and lift her hips for me to hit her at a different, deeper angle inside.

The moment the position change is made, I moan, and the feeling of my cock moving inside her feels like Heaven. With each stroke, I see myself bury further into her , and I just about come on the spot. I can't keep myself from moving just a touch faster now, loving the sounds she's making as I fuck her this way.

She brings her fingers to her clit, and it spurs me on to keep moving, my pace increasing each time I piston into her. Soon, I feel her walls strangle me, and she falls apart in front of me. The moment she falls off that cliff, I'm moving my hips in and out, my cock chasing its own release.

The moment I let go, I detonate and I feel my release empty into her. Her walls are spasming around my dick while I see stars, and my hips keep moving, slowing their pace as I come down from my climax.

I trail lazy kisses along her chest and up her neck. I start kissing her again, my lips feeling like they were made for hers.

We lie in bed, my fingers moving along her abdomen, already imagining her belly becoming larger as the weeks progress. The thought of our lives coming together with this little being causes my heart to soar.

"I love you beyond myself, Laney. You make me whole," I say to her, my hand continuing to move along her stomach.

She brings her hand to the top of mine and squeezes it.

"Grant, my love for you is the purest part of me fusing with you. I begin and end with you."

I come up onto my right elbow and lean over to kiss her. My left palm cups her cheek, and I continue to kiss her until I feel the tingling of my lips.

"Always and forever, Laney. You're it for me."

Laney

"Just one more push, Laney." Becca is way too close to my vagina right now, and fuck, this hurts. The epidural hasn't taken away this damn pressure I need to get rid of.

"You said that last time, Becca!" I moan and I'm beyond exhausted. This is too much. Grant is putting a fresh washcloth on my forehead and whispering words of encouragement into my ear. I thought I'd hate having him this close to my face while I was pushing, but it's become a source of comfort over the last ninety minutes since I started pushing.

"This baby is not coming out. Let's call it a day and try again later!" I declare to the entire room. The traitors laugh at me like I'm doing a stand-up routine at a comedy club. They think I'm kidding. Yeah. Fucking. Right.

"Babe, you're almost done. I see the head. The baby's got hair, dark like mine. I promise, you're so close."

Grant is being incredibly sweet, but all I can muster is a scowl, which he laughs at. If I were to punch him, would he laugh? I doubt it.

I feel the pressure build, and Becca is quick to notice

when she feels my belly harden. "Come on, Lane. You got this. The baby is almost here. Let's do this!"

She's way too enthusiastic right now, but my body has a mind of its own, and I begin to bring my legs back, mustering all the strength I can in hopes this truly is my last push to get the baby out.

Finally, I hear Becca give me new instructions, "Okay, easy does it, Laney. The baby has the cord around their neck, so stop pushing while I cut it. Hold on." I see her ask for something, and then it must be remedied because she's asking me to push again.

"Okay, now push and look down to see your baby enter this world." From the crinkling of her eyes, I can tell she's got the biggest smile on her face underneath that mask. How she's doing this knowing that her niece or nephew is about to be born is beyond me. Grant has been crying since the moment he said he could see hair.

Before I can even blink again, I hear the first cry from our baby. The sweet screams I've longed to hear are finally filling the delivery room, and the relief is immediate. I look down and see our baby screaming, red-faced with white goop all over their body. I'm so elated to finally learn if our new addition is a boy or girl. We decided to wait to find out until delivery. With this pregnancy being such a surprise, we wanted to have one bit of planned excitement.

Becca lays the baby directly on my chest, and the nurses begin to wipe vigorously, making my child scream even harder. I can barely see straight, because tears are streaming out of my eyes at this point.

I look up and see Grant in complete awe. Adoration is abundant in his features as he looks at the miracle we created.

His eyes look over at me, and then he's kissing me and whispers, "You're incredible. *You did it*. You've made me the happiest person alive." I feel his tears mix with mine on my cheek, and all I can do is smile.

I move my gaze to the baby and then toward Becca. She's giving orders to the nurse but also stealing glances at our newest family member. I know she wants to show some emotion, but she's in full doctor mode.

I got all hormonal weeks ago and felt bad to have pretty much forced her to be my doctor back when I first learned I was pregnant. So, I gave Becca the opportunity to sit this one out and simply be the proud aunt. But she wouldn't have it.

As long as I was okay with it, she wanted to have a part in the baby's arrival into this world. She sat by my side for the entirety of my forty-hour labor. It started at home, and she worked with me in the early stages to ensure Grant got enough rest, knowing this would likely take some time.

Now here we are, our family a little bigger and a little more fulfilled.

"I'm so proud of you, Laney. You were a champion pusher." She winks at me while delivering my placenta.

The room moves about while I stare at the baby, in awe of this creature I get to call mine. I'm speechless at the miracle in my arms and the fact that my life is coming into its own from the ashes of my past.

Once I'm cleaned up, and the largest ice pack and diaper arrangement is put on me in the ugliest hospital version of *Victoria's Secret* underwear known to man, I bask in this post-delivery glow. Grant can't stop talking to our baby, touching the fingers and toes, letting the little hand wrap around his one index finger.

Time passes too quickly, and it's time to let Grant have a turn with our Little Bean. He's quick to remove his shirt to start skin-to-skin. Becca has been in and out of the room, making sure we know the family has gotten updates about how I'm doing. She promised not to tell anyone if we had a boy or a girl, an announcement we wanted everyone to hear from us. Becca is doing us a favor and allowing everyone in the waiting room to come back quickly for us to do the big reveal.

The moment the baby's placed on his chest, I see his smile grow larger, which I didn't think was possible. "I never knew I could feel this complete in my life, Laney. You are perfection."

He kisses the top of the baby's head, and I notice him take a big whiff of that sweet baby smell. It's intoxicating, and I've only been a mother for the span of an hour.

But it's what Grant says to our baby that makes me fall in love with him all over again.

"I think all my steps in life have led to this moment. In reality, they've all led to you, my Little Bean."

Moving through the park, the warm breeze along my skin, I can't help the smile that overcomes my face. I look over to see my daughter's head resting comfortably on my husband's chest as he holds her in the baby carrier. Sleep has taken over her sweet little body after soaking in the sights and sounds of the city. This must be what bliss feels like, it's been far too long since I could experience this level of happiness without anxiety creeping in.

My fingers rub against the solid ring he wears on his left hand. I look down and remember that day as one of my absolute favorites.

A few months back, on the first day of spring, Grant took me to get ice cream. It was completely unplanned, and I kept complaining that the weather wasn't quite right for ice cream.

He insisted, and I let him drag me and my growing belly to the nearest shop to get some. Of course, it was empty, but he insisted. I was tasting multiple flavors, because I'm the most indecisive person when it comes to ice cream, and when I turned back to see what he wanted, he was down on one knee.

He told me that he could still remember us as kids ordering ice cream on hot summer days in Nebraska. He said despite all the years that have passed, watching me ponder over multiple flavors, just to choose vanilla bean, is still something he holds close to his heart. He told me that life started the moment we met, and he has never looked back.

Of course, not only was he romantic and saying all the things to make my heart melt, but I was a hormonal mess in my pregnancy at that time, and I screamed yes as fast as the words would spill out. A few short weeks later we were exchanging vows in my sister's backyard in an intimate ceremony with our families.

I kept it simple because everything leading up to that moment had been anything but. The love this man has always shown me has carried me during my hardest times, even if I didn't really give much notice to it at the time. He stabilizes me, keeps both my feet on the ground, and reminds me that even on our darkest days, we'll always find a way to see the light.

"What are you thinking about?" He pulls me out of my thoughts, and I look over to find that smile of his, dimples and all, beaming at me.

"Just thinking of the day you asked me to be yours." I return the smile, and everything around us fades, much like it always does when I'm surrounded by his love.

"Oh really, Mrs. Stanley? You thinking of when I asked or what I did to you after?" I feel the warmth of my cheeks deepen with the thoughts of the things he did to my body later that day when we celebrated.

I bite my lip and can't hide how just the notion of him touching me is setting everything on fire for me.

That reminds me. I pull out my phone and check my calendar app. I cannot believe I waited all this time to count out the weeks. Our girl is six weeks old today.

"Everything okay?" I can hear the concern etched in his tone.

"Everything is perfect. Let's get home and get a proper nap for our girl."

Right then, Cassandra stirs, her arms that were limp by her sides come up, her little fists balled up and rubbing her face. She slowly opens one eye, then the next, her bright, aqua gaze finding mine. They say babies take time to show their true eye color, but I find it hard to believe hers will change too much from this shade of blue-green she shares with her father.

She came out looking like a replica of Grant, and each day that passes, I see more of him in her. Her dark hair has a reddish hue in the light, so she's got a little of her mama mixed in there, too. The fact that we made this precious baby together, with love we didn't even know was possible between two people, is something that still captivates me each time I look at her.

When we get to our apartment, it's full-on baby care mode. Of course, on the ride up the elevator, Cassie had an explosive diaper. So, Grant is running her to the shower, now needing one himself, while I get myself ready to sit in her rocker to feed her before putting her back down. She didn't get a full nap while we were out, so I'm hoping I can get her back in the bassinet for a bit of a longer rest.

We'll be headed to my sister's house today after she and Wyatt get some weekend activities done with the kids.

School just started, so they're back to their hectic routine. Wyatt and Tessa moved in with them this past spring, shortly after Grant's proposal, and it seems the adjustment is going smoothly. It felt weird leaving the brownstone, but it was right for everyone.

Grant and I found a small space not too far away. He insisted we focus on a safe neighborhood, although housing prices are through the roof. After years of working but not settling, he had enough saved, and we were able to find a place that worked for both of us. Once I get clearance, I will return to the yoga studio and teach classes to help with the expenses.

This has been a constant argument between Grant and me. Although he supports my need to return to work, he is still having a hard time after everything with Tad. We just got word that Tad will spend the next year in prison for what he did to me. The fact that he held me against my will, physically assaulted me by grabbing my arm forcefully, and because I was pregnant, the judge decided that he should serve some time. Although, he may get out sooner for good behavior.,

It turns out Tad had fallen in love with a woman that he experienced the tragedy at his school with years ago. When those feelings weren't reciprocated, it pulled Tad further into a depression he was already fighting. Once Tad and I crossed paths, he believed fate had been at play and became obsessed with me and my past. His mental health kept deteriorating with time and he spiraled until it all came crashing down that day at the studio.

The issues that arose from this are the reason that I fought for him to get some mental healthcare. As much as what he did was disturbing and upsetting, on top of being potentially harmful for me and the baby, I can't help but feel like prison time is more of a Band-Aid than a solution.

So, I pushed for him to have less time behind bars and be transferred to a mental health facility that could help him deal with the trauma he suffered. If he's going to be released back into this world, he needs to know how to cope.

This was a point of contention for Grant and I. He was in favor of Tad rotting for as long as possible after what he did to me. But I had to explain how his trauma was so similar to mine and that if I hadn't had support from everyone around me the way I did, I could easily have suffered much like Tad did.

Luckily, Grant understood after many long chats, and he realized how important this was for me. Now here we are, understanding that we need to find a way to live our lives to the fullest. It's strange having this mindset while Grant struggles because, for so long, it was him trying to guide me to see the positives life could bring while I sat in fear of something catastrophic occurring around me. *I don't think I would've ended up kidnapping anyone, though.*

I hear Grant's voice carry over the small space, and it's hard not to smile. I make my way down the hall and into Cassie's room. The crib that's in here is one she rarely uses, only when I'm putting laundry away, or we're playing early in the morning, allowing Grant some extra hours of sleep.

Sitting in the rocker, I finally feel like my body is starting to mold back into what it once was. But I look in the mirror and see parts of me that will be forever altered, and I'm okay with that. So much of my past changed me in ways you couldn't see on the outside. To know that I grew this beautiful being and have altered myself physically to adapt to that growth is something quite amazing.

I hear Grant's footsteps and our daughter's sounds as they make their way toward me in the room. The moment he enters, his face lights up, our daughter in his arms, looking like the happiest man alive.

"The princess is ready, my queen." He winks as he hands her over to me. Cassie is quick to pick up on the fact that she's going to eat, already rooting to find her meal source. The moment she latches on, she calms, and I savor each second because I know from watching my sister and Becca raise their kids, that it all moves way too quickly.

Grant takes a seat on the floor, bringing his palms up my leg to massage my calves. I let my head fall back and I close my eyes. Something about these quiet moments together fills my cup in a way I never imagined before.

After she's fed, Cassie is completely out. Grant grabs her to place her in the bassinet. At least that's the plan, but he goes ahead and puts her in the crib. I'm buttoning my shirt when I notice where he's putting her.

"Grant, the bassinet," I whisper.

He's not answering me or making a move to take her into our room, where the bassinet is. Before I can understand what's happening, he's grabbing my hand and pulling me to stand, then moving us quickly out of the room and walking toward ours.

"What are you—" He cuts me off with a kiss. Not just any kiss, but a kiss that is bound to lead to us being naked in bed. Once we separate, I see a slow smile cross his features.

"You didn't really think I wouldn't know today is six weeks since Little Bean joined the world, right? I've been counting down until this moment, Laney." He's pulling my leggings down my body and throwing them haphazardly across the room. Next to come off are my panties.

"Do you want me, Lane?" he asks, hope lacing his tone.

"I always want you, Grant. It's not even a question." That spurs him on to remove my top, and my breasts fall, heavier and larger than I ever thought possible.

"Fuck, Laney. I love you so much. Look how perfect

you are." He buries his face in the crook of my neck and begins kissing me, biting my earlobe and whispering how much he wants to be inside me. I feel the wetness pooling in my center, and I'm pulling on his clothing, frustrated that he's still fully dressed.

"Get this off, Grant. I need to feel you on me." He pushes away from me and takes his clothes off. There's no finesse to this moment, because we're desperate for one another.

Once he's naked, he lunges for me, our movements frantic. He brings one of my tender breasts to his lips, and the moan that escapes my mouth is feral. My need for this man is something I depend on. I'm not complete without him. He's what makes me feel whole.

I feel his crown near my entrance, and I stop our movements.

"Grant, condom." I can't wait to have more children with him, but I want to enjoy what we have with Cassie before we add more.

"Shit, I forgot." He gets up and moves toward the nightstand.

"Someone was feeling lucky," I tell him, knowing he doesn't usually have condoms in the house for us to use.

"Let's just say my sister scared the shit out of me when I made the mistake of acting like breastfeeding was contraception enough." He chuckles, and I know what he means. Becca was very clear that just by breastfeeding alone, there was no guarantee I wouldn't be pregnant soon after starting to have sex again.

The moment he sheaths himself, he's quick to return, his warm body engulfing mine, his lips taking over, kissing me until my lips tingle.

I push him to lay his body on the bed, and I straddle him. I got used to this position when I was pregnant, and the way I feel him hit those sweet spots deep inside me, I long for that after so long.

I hover over his cock and slowly start to ease down, his crown disappearing and causing me to moan once again. I've missed this, and from the look of desire on his face, he is feeling the same way.

His hands are on my hips, helping to get his cock inside me. The moment I'm fully seated on him, we both take deep breaths, letting my body adjust to his size. I was nervous about how I would feel after delivery, but from how I'm feeling right now, I had nothing to worry about. *This is absolutely incredible.*

I slowly start to move, and my hands are on his pecs, finding my rhythm as he squeezes my ass.

"Laney, fuck, you feel so good. Baby, are you okay?" I nod at him, unable to form words, and I feel him hitting all the right spots inside me.

My movements get faster, unable to keep from chasing this high. I thought we'd take this slow, but I can't get enough of this feeling. I missed connecting with Grant on this level, and the moment I felt him inside me, I couldn't stop my body from moving.

"Grant, I'm gonna come." I feel his grip tighten on my hips, and I know I'll see marks of his on me later. Soon, I feel my orgasm take over my body, my hips moving of their own volition.

When I come off my high, I'm moved to lie on my back. Grant positions himself on top of me, bringing one leg over his shoulder, pounding into me, chasing his own climax. I watch his face, his reaction euphoric, and I feel like I could take that leap once more, feeling myself tighten around him yet again.

"Yes, fuck, you squeeze me so tight, Laney." His hips

continue to move erratically, and then I feel him explode, the condom catching his release.

He lies there, both of us trying to catch our breath. I can feel the sweat between our two bodies, and I know a shower is on the agenda right after this.

I use my hands to grab his face and bring our gazes back to one another.

"It just seems to get better." I smile, loving his post-orgasmic expression.

"I feel for you, Bean. Because I'm probably going to get you pregnant sooner than you expect. That was fucking amazing." He kisses me slowly and sensually.

I breathe him in and feel my love for not only him but this life, growing into something bigger. I know that there was a time in my life when I thought everything I was supposed to be died at that university. I believed that I would never see the world with beauty and always be ready for the next tough moment.

But Grant stood with me. He held me. He allowed me to build up the strength to live a better life on my own time. And that built trust, not only in my ability to embrace the next adventure, but to love beyond the hurt I carried in my heart.

I'm so glad Grant helped me find my way out of the darkness and brought me into this beautiful life.

Ten Years Later

Grant

"Cassie, where's Micah? Have you seen him? What about Wesley? Did he sneak in here?" Giggles come from the couch, and it's hard not to react with laughter of my own.

Before I can move about the room any further, both the boys jump up from behind the sectional couch.

I act scared. "Oh my gosh. Boys, you nearly had me peeing my pants." I bring my hand to my chest, and the fact that I said pee makes the boys really start laughing.

I hear my girls in the kitchen, making cookies for the Christmas dinner we're gearing up to host.

Walking into the kitchen, I grab a cookie that's on the edge of the cooling rack.

"Grant, don't keep eating the cookies. We won't have enough to serve for anyone else!" Laney scolds. I chuckle while inhaling yet another cookie. I can see her frustration wane once my dimples pop out. I know how to use my charm on my wife.

"Daddy, leave the cookies alone. We have to have enough for the guests and for Santa!" My daughter is my twin in looks, but she's all Laney when it comes to her mannerisms and behavior.

The fact I get to see pieces of the woman I love in all three of our kids is something I don't take for granted. I know how lucky I am, especially with the past that Laney has dealt with.

The last ten years have been straight out of one of Laney's romance novels. Of course, we have tough times just like anyone else, but, overall, we've been a great team. I think our love mixes well with the respect we have for one another. We may not see things from the same viewpoint, but we know that our communication needs to be first and foremost. Laney always tells our kids to lead with love. I used to laugh at that phrase when she started saying it a few years back, but I realize that it holds true when we're at a fork in the road, and we need to make a unified decision.

The boys come barreling in, already excited for the festivities and the fact that Santa is coming.

"Boys, careful. The oven will be opening and closing while your sister and I bake. Do you want to help in here?"

A unified "NO!" is yelled between the two of them, so they run off, hopeful that they won't be pulled back to clean something up.

The boys are seven and five, and they're each other's best friend. Cassie has taken on the role of second mother to the two of them, as she seems to always be putting them in order when Laney isn't around. It makes my life easier, because making Cassie mad seems to scare her brothers. She's usually pretty even-keeled, so if she's upset, something is gravely wrong.

"Can I go get ready, too, Mom?" Cassie looks up at her mother, and Laney nods. We haven't hit the teenage years yet, but I hope despite the evident hormones that will be taking over my daughter's behavior in the years to come, she never loses the respect she has for Laney. Once Cassie leaves, it's hard to ignore the quiet throughout this small part of our home.

"Can I help with anything around here? I got the table all set, and the kids' table is ready to go as well," I ask Laney, knowing the prep work can make nights like these more stressful than fun.

"I don't think so. Will you make sure the boys are ready with their matching pajamas?" I know they wanted to wear them tonight, and why put them in fancy clothes if they're just going to want to change right when I put my feet up?

I move through our kitchen and reach for Laney. I pull her into my arms, her back resting against my chest, and I breathe her in. I feel her melt into my grasp, and she lets her head fall back, resting on my clavicle.

"I can't wait until later when we have a minute alone together. I have a little gift of my own to share." I pull back, looking into her eyes.

"Not that kind of gift. That's not on the horizon." She tries to push me away a bit, but I just hold her tighter. Laney's referring to getting pregnant again. I won't lie; I wanted at least one more, but after Micah's delivery, she was done. He was our biggest baby, weighing a whopping nine and a half pounds. She had to have a cesarean section because he wouldn't come out any other way. Laney hated the recovery from that delivery, and it was too much for her body.

"Well, you know I'm always down for a little fun after everyone is in bed." Although the kids are always excited for Santa's arrival, they're quick to go to bed. They know that the sooner they go to bed, the quicker Santa will deliver their gifts.

"Good, because I have a few things, and depending if

you're naughty or nice, I'll let you have them." She giggles, and I nibble on her earlobe.

No matter how much time passes, there isn't a part of our lives that doesn't involve the other. From our earliest memory to this moment right now, we've been involved in every little aspect of one another's lives. There's something special to that, and it's something we're always talking about when we reflect on how life looks now that we have a house full of children.

We ended up finding a brownstone up for sale about three years after Cassie was born. It's a short walk down from my sister and Ellie's street, and it's the perfect size for us, as Laney was pregnant with Wesley when we found it. So far, the house has grown with us, and every year, we find something we want to redo and use that as our annual project. The last adjustment we made to the home was adding a garden for us to grow our own vegetables. Now that the kids are getting older, they're helping more around the house.

Laney has found a love for cooking and loves to come up with fun recipes that involve the help of the kids. It usually starts with all three, with Cassie outlasting her brothers and finishing the food with her mom. I tried to help once, but, apparently, I made the dish too salty. I was banned from doing much other than setting the table and grabbing items that were too high up for the children to reach after that.

I continue to work on my photography but try to take jobs that don't keep me far from the family for longer than a few days. If there's an opportunity abroad, I make sure it's booked at a time that would work for the kids and Laney to come with me instead of leaving them behind. I think I live with too many open wounds from when Tad hurt Laney.

Speaking of Tad, he hasn't been a problem since that

day, over ten years ago. Last I heard, he got out of prison and got some medical help. Due to the restraining order we had placed against him, I never saw him again.

It turns out, he was following Laney and I during that time his obsession with her became unhealthy. We only found this out for certain during the investigation. All those moments I felt like I was being watched were times he was following us. The moment I learned of his behavior leading up to that day in the yoga studio, my guard went up. I couldn't rest until I tried everything I could to keep him away from me and my family.

According to our lawyer, he ended up moving out of state. Sometimes, it pays to have an ex-brother-in-law who's a lawyer. Hudson was able to keep me informed of Tad's whereabouts until he left New York for good about six years ago. It allowed me to rest easy, and I saw Laney calm down some, knowing he wasn't close enough to run into if we were out, especially with the kids.

I slap Laney's butt and stroll out of the kitchen, stealing one last glance at her before I turn and head upstairs.

Before I walk up the stairs to our second floor, I look over at our tree, full of ornaments, all chosen with care by each member of this family. Laney had a vision that every year, each person would get to choose their ornament. She said she wanted us to fill our tree with memories, so that's exactly what we've done. On the mantel is every holiday photo we've taken as a family, framed with the year right below it. It's a tradition I cherish and one I look forward to each year.

My heart is full. My life has truly been a blessing. It's a reminder that we're not promised tomorrow, so living for today is a gift. After everything I've seen, from growing up without my father to watching Laney slowly come back to herself, I realize that life is a constant wheel of change. We have to move through it, not around it. It's not about avoiding the pain, but learning how to live with it. We can't avoid it, nor can we run from it. But I know that running toward the things that once brought us fear can sometimes lead to our biggest source of growth. In our case, that growth led to happiness.

Had I not taken a chance to make my friendship with Laney something more, I don't know what my life would look like right now. I can guarantee it wouldn't fill my heart with love in the way she has every second of each day we've been together.

Wyatt

"Ellie, baby, we've gotta go!" I know we're a short walk over to Grant and Laney's, but we're going to be late. And I know that Laney probably cooked one of the best meals tonight. I've been counting the hours all day, knowing I'd get her food as a reward.

"Wyatt, I swear. If you had a car horn, you'd be honking it right now!" She stomps her feet down the stairs, acting like she's pissed off after I just spent an hour in the shower eating her out.

"Sunshine, you didn't seem so agitated a bit ago when I was licking you until you saw stars in the shower." I wink at her as she smacks my chest.

I grab her hand and pull her close to me, giving her a kiss on the lips. I'll take any attitude she flings my way, because I love her beyond anything imaginable. My Sunshine. She is a ray of light on my mostly-cloudy persona.

"Let's go. I want to see everyone. Tessa texted me a reminder to grab the whipped cream for the pies."

"I thought that was for later!" I whine.

To say our sex life isn't dull is an understatement. Ellie is wild in bed, and I think I unleashed a beast when I met her ten years ago.

"Stop it, Wyatt." Her cheeks blush, and she acts all shy when I'm outwardly inappropriate.

"El, no one is here besides us. It's best I let it all out now instead of in front of everyone."

She doesn't even give me a comeback and marches over to the fridge and grabs the bowl of freshly-made whipped cream.

"I'm serious, Ellie. There better be more in that fridge for later. I love that stuff. Licking it off you is just a bonus." I may not be playing hockey anymore, but I've still got an appetite.

I retired from coaching a few years ago, knowing Tessa might need more of my help as she entered her teenage years. I'm glad I did, because being home and available for all the drama that has ensued since she started talking to boys has been a great way to keep her out of trouble. I swear, if she brings one more dickwad of a boy to this house, I may lose it. These kids look like they just tumbled out of bed to take her on a date. It's ridiculous.

"You thinking of our daughter's last date again, Wy?" Ellie chuckles as she passes me, grabbing her coat on the rack behind me. She smirks, and it's evident she knows me too well.

"Why does she have to date morons?" I stand there, grabbing yet another item to place in the bag for the dinner we're going to be late for.

"I doubt the dads you encountered as a teen thought highly of you either, sweetie." She taps my cheek like she's pretty much talking down to me, even though I'm towering over her.

"Excuse me, I'm a catch." I puff out my chest.

"Yes, a true ray of sunshine." Ellie rolls her eyes and opens the door. The moment the cold breeze hits both of us, we pull our coats closed a little tighter and make our way down the steps.

"You and I both know I'm the fun one between the two of us, right?" I love getting a rise out of her, and today is no different.

"Wyatt, don't you start. You're as pleasant as a colonoscopy for most." She laughs, loud, at her own fucking joke.

I stop in my tracks and stare at her. When did she become this sarcastic? Did I teach her this?

"Excuse me, you married me," I throw back.

"I did. You're amazing in the sack, and your daughter won my heart."

That's it. I put all the bags down. Fuck the cold weather and the snow that's threatening to fall. I pull her into my embrace, my gloved hands grabbing her cheeks, and kiss her hard. She's smiling at first, and then I deepen the kiss, and she melts into me.

I hear a soft moan escape from her, and a part of me feels awfully satisfied by my ability to make this woman melt in my arms, even after all these years.

I pull away, my eyes opening to see she still has hers closed, and her cheeks are rosy.

"You're more pleasant than a colonoscopy, Wyatt. I forgot how sensitive you are." She brings herself up on her tippy-toes and gives me another, albeit soft, kiss. I pull her up into my arms, her feet dangling off the ground.

"I love you, Wy. Merry Christmas Eve." She looks at me, her eyes full of love.

"I love you, Sunshine." Even all these years later, I don't know what I did right to deserve her, but I'm damn glad she has stuck by me as I have her.

Our years together have always been about adjustment. That first year married, I still found her taking in moments between us and probably feeling a pang of guilt for Beau. I always gave her that space. I never saw her love for Beau as a lack of love for me. I simply saw it as love for both of us but in completely different ways. We have complemented one another, and not a day passes that I'm not grateful we get to do life together. She's been my rock, especially as I've navigated raising Tessa throughout the years. She's been a mother to our kids, surpassing what I think even Tessa imagined possible in a maternal figure.

We've got two girls home now while Colton and Hannah are off living their lives. Colton ended up getting a scholarship for basketball and now lives in Connecticut, coaching a small college team out there, and seems to love it.

Hannah is studying fashion out in Los Angeles. To say Ellie took the distance harshly is an understatement. For an entire month, each time she passed Hannah's photo in our room, she would cry. It seems Hannah is feeling homesick as well and plans on moving back after graduation. I could bet money she'll be transferred to an East Coast school by next fall.

I'm trying not to focus on Mia and her impending departure to college next year. She's been my little sidekick, aside from Tessa. She and Tess pretty much grew up together once we all became a family, and to see a piece of my "duo-girls" move away will be hard for me. Maybe I'll be the one crying with her picture in my hands when she's off to college. I'm hoping one of the schools we toured in the city will entice her to choose them over leaving the state like her older sister.

"Where's your mind at, big guy?" Ellie smiles at me, her

blonde hair outside of her beanie flying around us with the breeze.

"Big guy, huh? Trying to butter me up for later?" I waggle my brows and give a slight thrust toward her. I swear I'm a teenage boy when I'm around my wife.

"Oh gosh. I've awakened the beast." She chuckles.

"Wow. Big guy and beast. Baby, you're making me want to turn around and take you to bed. Fuck that holiday meal. Let's go." I make like I'm taking us back to our house, and she starts laughing.

"Good things come to those who wait. Come on, they're waiting for us." She pulls on my hand.

This girl could take me anywhere, and I'd follow. The love she's shown, not only to me but Tessa, is something I never saw coming. Love, support, and partnership are all things she gave me from the moment we came together. She may have fought it, but I know deep down she felt that connection the instant we touched. The fact we're here all these years later, and I still feel like she hung the moon, only makes me more excited for what's to come.

Shane

My sweet Betty, even in her old age, favors me over her mama. Becs eyes me from the kitchen as she's moving around, putting leftovers away from dinner at Laney and Grant's tonight. Christmas Eve looks a little different now that all the kids are leading lives of their own.

I didn't get all the time with them as Becs and Hudson did, but from the brief time I lived with the twins, I got a little feel for what Christmas was like with a house full of children itching to open their gifts come morning.

Betty's snoring away on my lap when Becs finally finds her way back, a bowl of popcorn in her hands.

"How can you fit more in there after all that dessert?" I'm overflowing from all the food, but I know if there's an opportunity for popcorn, Becs is going to have some.

"You can't sit and watch *Christmas Vacation* without some popcorn handy. Plus, I only had some candy canes while at Grant and Laney's. I saved room for this Christmas Eve snack." She throws a piece of popcorn at me, and I catch it because I'm stealth like that.

She rolls her eyes, irritated that I still caught it. The

smell of the treat wakes Betty up, and she moves slowly to end up by my wife's side.

"Oh, so now we're friends?" She sounds annoyed, but nothing the dog does truly bothers Becs.

Betty is slower than she used to be, but she's still as sweet and opinionated as ever. The older she gets, the more she doesn't waste her time with people she doesn't want to get to know. She still comes to Laney and me first, over anyone else in a crowd. Most of the time, if I listen for it, I can hear Becs's muffled complaints, even from far away. It's hard not to laugh about it.

"Why do you have that sneaky smile on your face, Shane?" She's eyeing me, probably able to figure out where my thoughts went.

"No reason, love. Thinking about you, as always." I lean in to kiss her. As much as she knows I'm full of shit, she goes along with it, never missing an opportunity to kiss me.

"Will Olive get here in time to open gifts in the morning?" I ask, having a hard time that my daughter isn't under the same roof as us.

"Yeah. She's doing the Brazilian tradition of opening gifts with her kids tonight, giving her the opportunity to do the whole thing in the morning with us."

The fact we have an adult—a *completely independent* adult—child living her best life after the trainwreck that was her dating life before meeting her husband, is a miracle. Her kids are fantastic, and I love the man that she chose forever with. Luckily, she's back to living in the city; however, she didn't opt for a brownstone like the older family members she's surrounded by.

"Jack! Mal! The movie's about to start!" Becs yells. Betty looks up, annoyed by my wife's loud voice, and Becs just looks down, confused about how the dog could be that perturbed.

"Don't bother my dog. Why don't you just text them?"

She scoffs. "I'm not texting them, Shane. That's ridiculous." Without seeing her face, I know she's rolling her eyes.

I hear their footsteps coming down, it's such a comforting and welcome sound now that we have an empty nest. They always spend a week in the city during the holidays, before heading back to their realities. Mallory ended up liking what I did for work and began working at my company in Boston shortly after college graduation. Jackson was always into engineering. He took a job in Chicago after graduating college, and hasn't looked back. They're still only interested in dating, so they have no one keeping them in their homes instead of coming to spend the holidays with us.

Hudson usually joins us Christmas morning. He's also settled down with someone new, and he seems to be happy. The guy has grown on me with each year that has passed. Luckily, now that he has a new love, he doesn't have to keep looking like a lost puppy that fucked up with my wife.

"Mom, why didn't you just text? You didn't have to yell."

I whisper, "Told you." She elbows me in the ribs in return.

The moment the kids take their seats, Becs queues up the movie.

"Hold up, is Betty going to bark at the squirrel part again?" Jack whines, and Becs takes this opportunity to point at him and scold.

"Don't complain about my favorite child like that." It's a running joke in this house that Becs loves Betty over everyone else. I think the more she says it, the more I believe it to be true.

Jack puts his arms up to show he means no harm, and all our attention goes back to the television.

Within minutes, I can hear a faint snore from my wife as she's already sleeping, her full bowl of popcorn uneaten and nearly falling off the couch. I slowly remove the bowl from her, and she stirs, but continues to sleep. I don't know if I watched the movie or her more, because she still captures my heart with each breath she takes.

Once the movie ends, the kids are yawning and calling it a night.

"Merry Christmas Eve, Shane. Sleep well." Jack gives me a fist bump while Mallory kisses my cheek.

"Merry Christmas Eve, kiddos. See you in the morning. I think Olive will be here around eight-thirty or nine."

"I guess wake us when you're ready. I'm going to try to sleep a bit if my body allows it," Mallory says, followed by another yawn. She's a workaholic, and even though she's not mine by blood, she and I have a lot in common—specifically, our work ethic. Although, her mom has a similar work ethic; she takes after both of us in that regard.

Once the kids have gone up to their rooms, I slowly make my way off the couch, grab Betty, and take her to do her business outside. Snow is set to start soon, even though they've said that all day, and still no white flakes have fallen from the sky.

I know Wes and Micah were counting on some snow to blanket the streets tomorrow. We'll see everyone again tomorrow in the late afternoon for another gathering. This time we eat leftovers and enjoy our gifts. It's fun to see Ellie and Laney's parents, along with Grace and Rick. Wyatt's family comes along as well, and we all simply take in the time together. It's something I never get tired of.

Sadly, my relationship is still strained with my mother. For years, I couldn't even speak of her, let alone call her. I went a handful of years without any communication, although she called plenty, according to my colleagues at the office.

Surprisingly, it was Becs who pushed me to call her, because, as we all know, life is too short. I'm well aware my relationship and viewpoint of her is so incredibly different and shattered, but Becs made the point that I would regret not having some communication with her, especially as she's getting older.

Now we speak occasionally, but that's as far as I can go with her. I've never pushed Olive to speak to her, nor do I talk about her to my grandchildren. I let Olive make that choice. What my mother did is still unforgivable, and I'm not sure I'll ever see it as anything but the heartbreaking reality that it is.

Once Betty has done her business, she's quick to make her way upstairs to her little bed in the closet. She really loves her space, and routine is key for that pup. Betty has her place in this family, and she will be around people when she wants the love. But she has no problem putting herself to bed and seeing us in the morning.

I shut off the lights, start the dishwasher, and make my way back toward the family room. I find Becs in the same position as I left her. She's exhausted after all the prep work to ensure tomorrow is fun for everyone. I sit on the couch and begin to push strands of her hair off her face. I bring my lips to her cheek, then spread kisses along her face and forehead, ending with her lips. Soon, she's smiling, eyes still closed, moaning as I continue to trail kisses down her neck.

"It's time for bed, sweetheart. You ready?" I ask her, knowing she's going to fight me trying to get her off this couch.

"*No*. I want to lie here with you and soak up the holiday decorations before it's time to go to bed. I don't want the holidays to end," she whines, much like she did when we were teens. She's always loved having her decorations up early to enjoy them for as long as possible.

I motion for her to scoot over, and she does, giving me some space to lie down next to her; both of us on our sides, facing one another. I pull the blanket over both of our bodies and let Becs put her head in the crook of my arm. She nestles deeper into me, and I take in the fact that with all that time we spent apart, I'm a lucky man to have gotten a second chance. Even after more than ten years back together, not a moment passes where I don't thank the stars above for reconnecting us.

I see it's past midnight and officially Christmas Day. "I love you, Becs. Merry Christmas."

"Mmmm-hmmm." She still has her eyes closed, but she's moving her face toward me, hoping to find my lips. I give in because any moment we can connect, I jump on the opportunity.

The instant my lips find hers, it's like we're fourteen again. I feel like she transports me through time, reminding me that even in our fifties, we can still be young together. From what started as an innocent kiss, she moves on top of me and deepens our connection. Soon, she and I are in a full-on makeout session.

"Fuck, Becs, can we please go to bed?" I bring my hands to cup her cheeks and continue to devour her. She moves her pelvis into mine, and I'm reminded I have no problem in that department. I'm hard as a rock for her, and I need to get her upstairs. Usually, we don't have kids home, but tonight, we have to be careful. Getting caught by either Jack or Mallory isn't high on my list tonight.

"Take me to bed, Shane." A soft smile spreads across her face, and I see how content she is with the life we live in that simple gesture.

We turn everything off and I grab her by the hand and take her to our room. No matter how much time I'm granted on this earth with this woman, it will never be enough. My love for her goes beyond all the clusters of stars that surround us in the sky. She is my everything, and I'll live all my lifetimes trying to find her again and again.

Olive

He needs to be more approachable. Soften his edges is all. You're the one that can do that for him.

The words run on a loop in my head after my important meeting turned into a nightmare.

I run my hands down my face, still in shock that I'm in this situation.

For a person who thrives on honesty, this goes against all my usual instincts. But, somehow, my brain short-circuited and I agreed to help the famous football player. Well, to help his agent, really.

Crew Davidson could use some softening, although I don't think of that when I see him in the countless pictures that have come up on my internet sleuthing. Not only does he have muscles on top of muscles, he's got a different gorgeous woman standing next to him at all these fancy events.

The problem you ask? Well, turns out Mr. Wide Receiver has a perma-scowl and comes off as an unapproachable dick.

I mean, he is—I know this firsthand after my minimal

interaction with him—but he could at least *pretend* not to be. Even just a bit. Especially when the women he's been seen arm-in-arm with look to be on cloud nine.

I'm sitting at my kitchen table trying to figure out how to move forward after my meeting with his agent and the Los Angeles team's owner. I swear, I've got sucker written across my forehead, because I was the first to cave and agree to this stupid idea.

Now I didn't just agree right on the spot, mind you. The moment this ridiculous idea was thrown into the universe, I nearly turned around and walked out. Turns out, Crew was on the same wavelength and did that before I could, so I stayed rooted in place. I mean, there's only room for one asshole in this… relationship? Is that what we're calling this arrangement? It feels like the furthest thing from one.

But to the public, I'm Crew Davidson's new girlfriend. Of course, the word "girlfriend" is being used loosely. From the way I've seen him—less than enthused in all our brief interactions—this is going to require an Oscar-worthy performance, especially from him. Apparently, the broody star gives off cockwomble vibes.

I can't help the laugh that escapes. That term was used by one of the British papers that photographed him on some outing with an actress and I don't think I can let that go just yet. This search of mine has led me down a rabbit hole of sorts, because I've consumed countless articles on the man. Guess what I've discovered?

This man can't smile. I can't even say he has nasty teeth because I've caught a glimpse of those pearly whites and they're gorgeous, much like the rest of his dumb face. Even on draft day, he just held the damn jersey in front of his chest and his face lacked all emotion. The cameras flashed their lights in his face and not once did he crack. He stood there, unaffected.

Fucking hell, how am I going to pull this off? I'm a terrible liar, especially if my parents find out about this. They'll sniff this ridiculousness out all the way from New York.

Oh, have I not added that I can't tell anyone this is fucking fake? I can already see my best friend's face assessing me as I tell her the news. *I'm screwed*.

I have to meet with Crew tomorrow to go over all the details of our "relationship," and I'm staring back at a clean legal pad, unsure where to start on my terms for this arrangement. These things always need rules. Without them, it gets messy. Or so all the romcoms I've watched tell me.

Pen tapping on my bottom lip, I let out a frustrated breath. How do I go about starting this damn list? I mean, after the meeting, I was told to come up with the details of this agreement so that I'll feel comfortable with it. I nearly snorted when the word "comfortable" was used in the same sentence as PR stunt.

I'm still surprised Crew agreed to do this, because he came back into the conference room looking like he wanted to punch the owner of the team. But then he opened his mouth and said, "Let's do it."

Yeah, this wasn't on my bingo card, that's for sure. My little company has gained traction as one that helps people navigate dates. After I started posting my shitty dates, people started to inquire what to do if their dating life is going poorly.

After so many messages, I took a chance on myself and opened what is now a dating service of sorts. The odd part about it, my tag line is: "Getting through this life, one date with a nutcase at a time."

I never thought it would take off, but here we are. It got so big, I'm now fake-dating a football player. Not only that, but he also can't stand the sight of me if I'm to judge from the look he gives me each chance he gets.

This is going to be a long start to the football season, and I'll have to smile and swallow down the look of irritation each time I'm on Crew Davidson's arm.

Game on, Mr. Wide Receiver!

Acknowledgments

When I started writing these stories years ago, I truly didn't see it going anywhere. It was just an idea that wouldn't leave my head.When the opportunity presented itself to relaunch the series with my new editor, therefore bringing in a new cover designer, I was so excited to do so.

I truly loved this world I made with Shane, Becca, Wyatt, Elody, Grant and Laney. Their emotional turmoil, along with troubled pasts, really made for a heartbreaking story to tell for each one. I know many fell in love with Beau and I will say, I sobbed writing his story. The way his journey came to me broke my heart, but it was the only way I saw his journey when he spoke to me.

The love between Grant and Laney began to evolve into the emotional roller coaster it is right from the start of Becca and Shane's second-chance romance. I was eager, yet a little nervous, to tell the world all that had happened to her, as I know the trauma can be hard to read about.

I wanted this to be something more than a love story between the two main characters. I needed this to be a journey of discovery and healing; to show the push and pull of pain, and the way life can shift because of our own inner demons. Trauma is life changing and something that impacts all future movements. Laney's story is no different.

When writing a series that involves a group of people in each book, finding a way to depict each one differently from the other can be a challenge. Grant always came to me as someone that lived for Laney. His golden retriever personality was something that shined for me and it felt refreshing to have characters be depicted with so much love for another.

I will say, the story of Tad evolved very late in my writing journey of *If Only You Hurt*. It stems from a conversation I had with my best friend, telling her how annoyed I was with my orthodontic work. You see, I got my third round of braces while I was writing this series. I had a complex case and had to place "tads" in my jaw to allow for movement of the teeth to fix my bite. These tads were a nightmare, to the point that even the oral surgeon was starting to crack jokes with me each time I came in to fix an issue. In the span of five months, I had six tads placed. As a joke, in the midst of my frustration, my friend told me to write a character with that name to let out my frustrations. Hence the start of Tad, or as we liked to refer to him: *Fucking Tad*.

Much like all my previous work, there's one person that sits and listens to me constantly regarding my characters and how I want their story to be. Early on in the process, she simply takes my drafts and gives me the motivation I need to continue. Thank you Joanna, not only for simply being the person I lean on in the toughest of times in my everyday life, but for being the person that cheers me on throughout all phases. If it weren't for her, I'm not too sure I would have set off on this adventure, writing fictional characters that capture the hearts of many out there. I'm truly grateful to her for the time and effort she has put in to push me further into this world of writing. You mean everything to me ❤

To my Beta readers, thank you. We're all leading busy lives and you've taken the time to read my work. That means so much to me. I appreciate all the input, insight and moments we've shared along the way. From the bottom of my heart, thank you.

The *If Only series* launched my romance author career. I have learned a lot about the process of not only writing, but publishing. After putting this series out into the world, I had moved on to the *Boston Embers series*. It wasn't until I connected with Ashley Matthews that I felt confident a relaunch could happen for my beloved characters. I knew I wanted to add to and edit this story to make it stronger. What started off as a simple conversation is now a reality and I have Ashley to thank for it.

Ashley, you are someone I value in my life, not just as my editor, but as my friend. Thank you for being someone that doesn't hold back when bringing up changes that need to be made. Your honesty is refreshing and brings with it moments of laughter I will never take for granted.

My life is always chaotic. For a long time, I lived in that pattern, feeling like I had to juggle a lot of it on my own. Thanks to a chance encounter with Cynthia at a book event, she's been keeping me organized ever since. Thank you for all you do to ensure my author career is moving forward. I appreciate you so very much.

My husband and kids cannot go without a shoutout. It's become a thing in our home that if I'm not downstairs cooking something, it means I'm upstairs writing a book. Although it might be tough to manage at times as a full-time nurse, wife, and mother, the space all of you give me to dedicate to my writing each night is something I will never forget. Thank you for showing me love as I tap into this new side of my creativity.

I wanted to honor the journey Laney took. I didn't want to ignore the impact her college experience would have on her future. I made sure to do research and see ways in which someone would choose to cope. I also leaned on a therapist I value very much—Shira sat on a call with me as I explained the hardships Laney's character endured. She allowed me the space to express how her story was being told and she gave me the confidence that the way Laney was dealing with her trauma is in the realm of possibility. Thank you for taking that time with me, Shira, to make sure I told a story that held truth to how a person could deal with the difficulties of their life as they moved forward after such an impactful event.

I really love this trend of adding a playlist to accompany each story. Every book holds a different genre of music and this one is no different. I had to lean on my dear friend, Madeline. She took the time to listen to songs and add them to the playlist. Many of the songs you might scroll through on this playlist are ones she chose and I simply love the vibe that circulates as I listen to the music. Thank you for your time to ensure the playlist for this story fits the characters. ♡

Another shoutout goes to The Author Agency. They're quick to respond to my emails, always available to assist with questions regarding my release details and simply a pleasure to work with. They were insightful in how to approach this relaunch, which is always appreciated.

To my ARC readers: the biggest thank you to you for taking the time to read my book. If you've read my other books or if you're picking this one up as the first of my work, your time and dedication to review my novel really is something that doesn't go unnoticed. The time you dedicate, not only to read the book, but to review it, is something I'll never take for granted. Thank you so much for your time, your ability to be a cheerleader to authors all around, and for making this release special to me.

To all my readers that are here with me on this journey: each book you pick up, is an impact you don't get to see but is felt by me on this author journey. I appreciate everyone that takes the time to read something I wrote, because I know how valuable your time is.

If you haven't already, please take a moment to review my work. That review goes a long way.

Thank you to everyone who has made an impact on this little indie author. I thank you so very much for being on this journey with me. Here's to more stories that will likely pull at the heartstrings.

Love,

Stefanie xoxo

About the Author

Before she was writing swoony love stories, Stefanie Castro spent years sharing her words on blogging platforms and supporting families as a registered nurse. With extensive experience helping parents at the very beginning of their journey, writing became her way of connecting, comforting, and telling meaningful stories.

In May 2023, Stefanie released her first memoir—and shortly after, romance came knocking (loudly). A lifelong lover of the genre, she happily wears many hats: devoted reader and unapologetic cheerleader for fellow authors.

Stefanie debuted her contemporary romance career with the If Only series, highlighting love stories featuring characters in their forties, followed by the Boston Embers series—a firefighter romance featuring twenty-something heroes finding love under pressure. Whether writing seasoned second-chance romance or first-love sparks, Stefanie believes every stage of life deserves a great love story.

She lives in sunny Southern California with her husband, two kids, and their Cavalier King Charles dog, who fully believes he's the main character.

Also by Stefanie Castro

IF ONLY SERIES

If Only You Knew (Becca & Shane)

If Only You Fell (Elody & Wyatt)

THE BOSTON EMBERS SERIES

Embers in the Outfield

Embers in Our Past

Embers in the Dark

Embers in Our Souls

If Only You Hurt

Stefanie Castro

Visit the author's Instagram on @stefaniecastro.author and website authorstefaniecastro.com

ISBN: 979–8-9889847-4-0 (eBook)

ISBN: 979-8-9889847-5-7 (paperback)

Edited by Steph White (Kat's Literary Services) 2023

Edited by Ashley Matthews (Smashin' Edits) 2026

Proofread by Cynthia Pinto (Pinto Prose & Publicity) 2026

Interior Formatting & Design by Stefanie Castro

Cover design by Sophia Sidhu (Crimson Designs)

Formatted with Vellum